Joy Dettman was born in country Victoria and spent her early years in towns on either side of the Murray River. She is an award-winning writer of short stories, the complete collection of which, *Diamonds in the Mud*, was published in 2007, as well as the highly acclaimed novels *Mallawindy*, *Jacaranda Blue*, *Goose Girl*, *Yesterday's Dust*, *The Seventh Day*, *Henry's Daughter*, *One Sunday*, *Pearl in a Cage*, *Thorn on the Rose*, *Moth to the Flame*, *Wind in the Wires*, *Ripples on a Pond* and *The Tying of Threads*.

Also by Joy Dettman

Mallawindy
Jacaranda Blue
Goose Girl
Yesterday's Dust
The Seventh Day
Henry's Daughter
One Sunday
Diamonds in the Mud

Woody Creek series
Pearl in a Cage
Thorn on the Rose
Moth to the Flame
Wind in the Wires
Ripples on a Pond
The Tying of Threads

Joy Dettman

The Silent Inheritance

MACMILLAN
Pan Macmillan Australia

First published 2016 in Macmillan by Pan Macmillan Australia Pty Ltd
1 Market Street, Sydney, New South Wales, Australia, 2000

Cataloguing-in-Publication entry is available
from the National Library of Australia
http://catalogue.nla.gov.au

Typeset in 12.5/16 pt Adobe Garamond by Midland Typesetters, Australia
Printed by McPherson's Printing Group

MIX
Paper from
responsible sources
FSC® C001695

The paper in this book is FSC certified.
FSC promotes environmentally responsible,
socially beneficial and economically viable
management of the world's forests.

For those who allowed me to interrogate them,
Pete, Shani, Don, Rob, Donna and Karli . . .

LUPINE

Once upon a time there was a big bad wolf, quite charming
and disarming.
Born of a dog and a holy hog, he had appetites alarming.
A mutant seed, he feeds his greed.

*Christmas barely behind him with its tinsel and baubles, Easter seven
weeks away, but hot cross buns already on sale at the supermarket,
twelve for the price of six. They were not the hot cross buns of his
boyhood, fresh from the baker's oven, but an improved twenty-first-
century variety, vacuum sealed, guaranteed to remain mould free for a
month, or six, or maybe twelve.*

*He picked up a packaged dozen, seeking a use-by date. It was there,
or the best-before date was there, in print he needed to squint to see.
He smiled, tossed the buns back to the display table and continued on
to the checkout.*

*He'd queued at an ATM today, then queued at the post office to pay
a bill. Now he queued at the checkout, just another obedient sheep,
waiting to be counted.*

'Baaa,' he mouthed to big brother's hidden camera. They were every-where, watching every move. No man, woman or child would pass through this place today and not be trapped on security video. The assistant bagging, then waiting patiently for an elderly customer to swipe her card, to enter her PIN, knew big brother was watching — or her boss. A picture of patience — and what was the difference between one sheep and the next?

'Have a good day,' she said as she turned to the next sheep in the run.

The woman ahead shuffled forward to begin the unloading of her trolley; the woman queuing behind him, over-eager to get ahead, nudged him with hers. He didn't move, or not until there was space on the conveyer belt to place his supermarket-supplied basket down then take his time unloading it.

He hoped to annoy the sheep counter by offering two green environ-mentally friendly shopping bags. They preferred to use plastic, but she filled his bags, asked if he had a rewards card.

'My reward will come in heaven,' he said, and handed her a fifty.

There may come a day when cash was no longer acceptable, but perhaps not in his lifetime.

The sheep counter handed him both receipt and change, an annoy-ance to him each time they did that, so he held up the traffic until he'd sorted one from the other, until he'd put his change into his wallet.

'Have a good day,' she said.

'And you,' he said, then, taking up his purchases, he left the store.

The tinkling music of an infants' carousel drew him. He stood watching it turn in its slow circles, three infants riding on colourful fibreglass mounts.

And he saw her, his chubby-limbed Angie, a pink plastic bow in her pale white hair.

The carousel turned, but he stood on until she again came into view. Her features were not Angie's, only her hair and baby-fat limbs, her little white sandals. He smiled and wiggled his fingers in a wave, then stepped nearer, stepped close enough for her helpless circling to offer him the scent of her baby sweetness.

She didn't return his smile or his wave, but clenched her fat little thighs, her eyes searching for Mummy.

Mummy was leaning on the handles of an empty stroller, which would not be empty long. She was young, her belly fruitful.

Again the infant came into view, again he wiggled his fingers, and this time was rewarded with a full-bodied wail which moved fruitful Mummy to her offspring's side to seek the source of her fear.

The very young were on familiar terms with terror. Still so close to their time in that place before the light, they remembered old Lupine's hot breath on their naked skin, remembered the sound of his teeth snap-snapping at their pretty pink heels. Babies had no cause to fear him. He may be waiting out there somewhere in her future, but she was safe today.

He smiled when Mummy turned his way. Seeing no threat to her young, she returned his smile, but he'd dallied long enough for the shopping bags to grow heavy and, swapping them from his left hand to his right, he walked towards the escalator.

And he saw her, as she might be today, a long-legged gazelle of a girl, clad in her high school uniform, schoolbag over her shoulder. That sexless uniform failing to camouflage her perfection, she stole his breath.

He moved so she might pass close by, and when she did, a slight swing of his shopping bag nudged her, just enough to make her turn her face. He wanted to see her face.

'Sorry,' she said, and she was Angie, but gone fast, up the escalator, unaware that his eyes followed each swing of her skirt, each sway of her long clean hair. Watched her until she became lost in the morass of sweating humanity, until a piercing infant scream claimed his attention, and his was not the only head to turn.

Only chubby rider with her pink plastic bow, fighting fruitful Mummy's attempt to buckle her into the stroller, fighting so hard she lost her pink bow, which skidded across the polished tiled floor to his feet. Embarrassed Mummy didn't see where it fell. Eager to place distance between her screamer and the disapproving stares, she walked away from the bow. He retrieved it. A pretty thing with silver and gold sparkles trapped within the pink plastic. Made in China, no doubt. Everything else was.

The falderal in his hand, his grip on it strong enough for the points of its bow to punish his palm, he stood again to watch the carousel turn, its repetitive melody now urging on two male bronco-busting infants, obvious brothers, ugly little toads. He had no interest in infants of his own sex, so he went on his way, that plastic bow a promise in his hand.

Saint Valentine's Day

*F*ive days a week Sarah Carter boarded the 7.40 train at Blackburn Station, opened her current library book and read her way into the city. Not today. An oversized male boarded at Box Hill and sat beside her. She used up little space. He required a larger share of that seat, and his newspaper required more, so she closed her book and read his newspaper, a *Herald Sun*, its middle pages jammed this morning with messages of undying love from *Bub*, *Cutie* and *Sexi-boy*.

Only storybook love was undying. In life, it died, or the people you loved died. She read one message where Cupid shot an arrow from *Rob* to *Sarah*.

She worked with a Robert Webb but he was a Bob, not a Rob, and her office manager, who'd developed the recent habit of placing his hand on her shoulder when he wanted her attention – a light-fingered, timid touch, which reminded her of a huge hairy huntsman spider she'd brushed from her shoulder one day in the tent. Still cringed when she recalled that tent, and the creeping touch of the huntsman spider.

Some names slid easily from the tongue. *Bob Webb* did, *Sarah Carter* did. Other names twisted the tongue. *Jacqueline Jefferson* twisted it, *Jillian Jones* used to, though not any more. Never thought of her now. Never said her name.

And they were almost there. She pushed her library book into a too-large tapestry shoulder bag that needed a new zip – or she needed a new bag. Maybe she'd shout herself one if she got the job.

She deserved it. She'd worked for David Crow for twelve years and had barely missed a day. Five days a week she climbed those stairs at Museum Station, walked that same block to the same office building in Melbourne's sun and wind and rain, and she knew every crack in the pavement and knew it would be shimmering with heat when she walked it in reverse tonight to catch the train home. Channel Seven's weather girl had promised Melbourne a day in the mid-forties, and another total fire ban.

Sarah had been six years old the day she'd followed her mother's pointing finger to where the mists of distance had melded Melbourne's tall buildings into a singular mystical grey castle shimmering in the clouds, then Daddy had turned the old green wagon's back on that castle because Gran and Gramp's farm was the other way. They were going to live there. They were going to stay in Gramp and Gran's house forever, and live on honey.

Seven when she'd sighted that grey castle again, this time through the rear windscreen of a different car. A sad sighting, that one. It meant no more farm, no more honey and baby cows with their pretty white faces, no more Gran and Gramp and warm cardigans Gran made from the sheep's woolly coats.

Hadn't seen her grandparents or the farm again, or not until she was eighteen, when she'd bought herself a one-way bus ticket across the Nullarbor to that mystical castle in the sky, and got lost in its crowd. Not so mystical that day. Melbourne had been shimmering, but with heat.

Her office building was cool, and a lift was waiting. She ran to catch it, to squeeze in with ten more, and ride it up to the fourteenth floor, her fingers crossed, hoping that today would be the day she received her summons to David Crow's office.

The payroll officer's job had to be hers. She'd been acting payroll officer since Annette had to leave in a hurry. Wanted that title, *Mrs Carter, Payroll/Accounts Officer.* Wanted Annette's cubbyhole office, with its window and needed the extra money that went with the job.

*

David Crow's office had three windows. It was empty at nine o'clock that Thursday morning. He was battling the traffic on Monash Freeway with more on his mind than traffic. He'd got himself into a situation he had to get out of, and the only way out of it would raise greater problems than it fixed.

He wasn't alone. He glanced at the pale beauty at his side. She had the appearance of a vestal virgin. He knew otherwise. He'd spent the night in her bed. She had baggage too, and was older then he'd initially believed, old enough to expect commitment.

'I drove in this way yesterday,' she said. 'The traffic was worse at eight.'

'We call it the car park,' he said.

'I could get to work easier in Sydney.'

'The tram stop is a five-minute walk from the house, one of my reasons for buying it.'

'If you're wearing running shoes it might take five minutes – and it takes an hour or more to get into the city, and they set off before you're sitting down. I hate trams.'

'They can be slow,' he agreed.

'Are you driving me home tonight?'

'Sadly no. My appointment with Smyth is at four thirty. I could be tied up with him for over an hour.'

'About the divorce?'

That D word again. She'd shed her Yank. 'Yes,' he lied – or perhaps it was not a lie.

'When will I see you?'

'At work, my pet. All day.'

'You know what I mean.'

'I do,' he said, his words raising the memory of an earlier *I do*, in the holy Catholic church, Maureen at his side through an hour of smoke and bells. Catholics weren't into divorce. He'd never considered divorce.

Catholics were into separation. Maureen had found her own solicitor and they were threatening to split the company, the properties and bank accounts.

'You're so quiet this morning. What are you thinking about?'

He reached out a manicured hand to brush her flawless face. 'Your beauty leaves me speechless,' he said.

Like the Catholic marriage service, he was all smoke and bells – though not last night. She made him smoking hot. He'd burn out. He had before, and until he did, he had to . . . to appease the wife . . . and her parents. Nine twenty-five when he drove into the car park, and suggested she go up while he parked. Watched her walk behind the car, heard the click-click of her heels on concrete, saw the sway of her hair, and knew he had to find a way to keep this one, and keep the business intact.

*

Three streets south of Crow's office, Frederick Adam-Jones, of Ainsworth, Adam-Jones and Smyth, punched the down button then waited for the lift to trundle him to the ground floor.

A man of substance, Frederick; his voice had substance, his profession gave him substance, as did his most recent acquisition, a red Ferrari. He owned a significant property in Camberwell and was in the process of selling a less significant property in Vermont.

His handsome wife gave him substance – and might have given him more if she'd learn not to open her mouth at inappropriate times. He had a son, as handsome as his mother, and already being pursued by pretty girls.

Frederick had never been pursued. Pretty girls had been more likely to run from him. Physically, he had little substance, other than around his girth. At fourteen he'd measured five foot five and three-quarters, and had grown no taller. He blamed genetics for his weight. His wife blamed lack of exercise. She suffered from hyperactivity.

For twenty years, Ainsworth, Adam-Jones and Smyth had rented spacious rooms in an elderly building where an elderly lift made frequent appeals for retirement. It appeared too to be losing its memory. He'd hit the ground floor button but was delivered to the basement car park.

Frederick Adam-Jones didn't make mistakes – or perhaps he had. His Ferrari dominating his thoughts since parking it this morning, his subconscious may have overridden his conscious mind. A brief glance told him his prize was there, its red striking amid the silver, the blue, the white. He offered it a satisfied nod, then very positively thumbed G for ground, and waited.

A glance at his watch told him he was due in court twenty minutes from now. The courthouse was a five-minute walk away.

The doors hiccupped but remained open. Use the stairs, the stressmonger within urged, but no stair climber, he thumbed the button again and waited, tapping the heel of one pointy-toed shoe, ultra-pointy. They restricted his toes but offered small feet the illusion of size, and their higher than average heels gained him an extra centimetre of height.

Another hiccup, the doors closed and, arthritic joints creaking, the lift trundled on its way while Frederick turned his mind to the day ahead. He hadn't liked this case from the start and liked it less this morning. Losing it was not an option he cared to contemplate.

'They tell us you're the best, Freddy,' the father of the accused had said, words that meant more than they should have to one who'd spent his early years the least of the best.

The last born in a litter of seven, little Freddy had ever been the runt. His mother had loved him. His difficult birth had led to her hysterectomy. She'd told him once he had been sent by God to save her from his father's excesses.

She'd put her all into her last born; she'd had little Freddy reading from her Bible before he'd seen the inside of a schoolroom. By his eleventh birthday, she, her church and Freddy's headmaster had weaselled him into one of Melbourne's prestigious schools. All very exciting to an eleven year old – until he'd been buttoned into his scholarship-supplied uniform and dragged blubbering from his mother's apron strings.

John Swan may have been born wearing that same school uniform. Freddy had learnt to wear it. He'd learnt a lot during that first year, learnt that his mother who loved him hadn't looked or spoken like the other mothers who'd filled the auditorium on presentation night, and that John Swan's mother had. During Freddy's third year, he'd coveted John's mother, who hadn't been plain Mrs Swan but Lady Cynthia Swan.

And they'd come to him in their hour of need, John and the widowed Lady Cynthia. They'd ridden that antiquated lift up to his floor, sat on his clients' chairs.

'They tell us you're the best, Freddy.'

He needed to win this one, which, as far as he'd been able to ascertain, was unwinnable.

Swan's only son, heir to Lady Cynthia's fortune, raised to expect the best, had been on track to being the best at the age of nineteen. At twenty-three, Michael Swan was charged with the murder of his girlfriend's infant son, who according to the accused had received his fatal injuries in a fall from the kitchen table.

At a pinch, it was possible. Male infants were adventurous. Freddy's son had spent a few months of his life with a bruised head. He'd never broken his arm, been black and blue with bruises. The deceased infant, fourteen-month-old Cory Martin, had sustained a broken arm, multiple bruises and a crushed skull. The arm may have been the result of a desperate grasp, an attempt to break the infant's fall. The crushed skull?

The infant sleeping peacefully in his cot when the mother returned from work, the couple had gone to bed and slept late. Very late. Cory Martin had been dead for fifteen hours before an ambulance was called.

Freddy had lined up several of the upper echelon who were willing to swear to Michael's lack of violence. He'd found a paediatrician willing to state on oath that the infant's injuries could have been sustained in a fall from a table and a failed attempt to break the fall.

The prosecution had big Ross Hunter, the arresting officer. They had Cory's maternal grandparents' home videos, one in particular, taken at the infant's first birthday party, with a damn sight more on it than the chocolate cake – which Freddy had to keep out of court or he'd have a jury baying for Swan blood.

Out of the lift and walking, fat thighs rubbing, trousers bunching at the crotch, fat Freddy toddled towards the court-house. He had his suits hand-tailored, and his tailor did a stellar job of camouflage – when his customer wasn't moving. Freddy allowed his trousers to bunch until approaching the place of his greatest substance, where he slowed his pace, adjusted his trousers and forced his trio of chins to lift in a smile for the cameras.

His wig offered him an extra inch of height, which this morning wasn't enough. John Swan had hit the six-foot mark at sixteen and Michael topped his father by an inch.

He looked innocent. They'd decked him out in a dark suit, a white shirt and grey tie – eye candy for the female jurists. Freddy may have been eye candy for his mother; he'd been Freddo Frog to his siblings.

Hop to it, Freddo.

Jump to it, Froggie.

The year he'd started at the university, determined to disassociate himself from the brothers, Freddy had added the hyphen between his middle name and the too common Jones. He'd determined, too, to buy and sell the lot of them before he was done.

He could have done it today, but received better returns from other investments.

You can add a hyphen. You can shed your past. You can live in a 2.2 million dollar property in Camberwell. You can't escape your genetics. He'd seen himself at his mother's funeral, seen his gut, his round water-green frog's eyes looking back at him.

'All stand.'

The jury rose faster than Freddy, most of them wearing their serious first-day faces, a few looking pleased to have been chosen. If you had to do your lawful duty, the Swan trial was the one to do it on.

By eleven o'clock on Saint Valentine's Day the jurists were listening to the prosecutor's opening narrative, and Freddy was leaning on an elbow, watching their faces. He'd ended up with four women. No young mothers amongst them; two grannies, one in her late sixties, the other a few years younger who looked moneyed, who may relate to Lady Cynthia – though few could.

'. . . expert witnesses will describe to you the details of the infant's injuries. You'll be shown photographs that will disturb you. You will hear how fourteen-month-old Cory's tiny skull was fractured, how his arm was bruised and broken, how he lay dead in his cot for fifteen hours . . .'

As the litany of veiled accusations droned on, Freddy cleared his throat, and he set off a chain reaction. One juror first, then two more caught his tickle, relieved perhaps to know that they were allowed to cough in court. Always on their best behaviour on day one, always ultra-attentive. By the end of Freddy's last case, a long one, an elderly chap had spent his days nodding off in one of the rear chairs.

Bore 'em deaf, Freddy urged silently, turning his frog eyes on the judge, studying his face. He could be a fly in the ointment. Judge Blackwood, a long, lean coot of a man who would have looked at home in a Dickens novel, though relatively new to the bench, was gaining a tough reputation.

'. . . Cory Martin's death was no accident. We may never know the true circumstances. What we do know is that tiny Cory Andrew Martin died slowly, died painfully, and died alone . . .'

And Michael John Swan may well have been guilty of his murder, but the prosecution done, Frederick Adam-Jones rose to wash his client lily white. That's what he did, and he was the best at what he did, though maybe today he was pleased his old mother was dead.

THE SUMMONS

*T*he summons to Crow's office didn't come that Thursday, but at five minutes to two on the Friday, Sarah received an inter-office email. It set her pulse racing, sent her racing to the Ladies' to tuck in her blouse, to tidy her dark, wildly curling hair. She wore it short, the sides combed forward to cover her ears. She added a swipe of lipstick and at two o'clock on the dot she entered the lion's den, where she learned that her summons hadn't been a personal invitation. They were all there, a dozen of them, standing bunched together on the far side of Crow's desk.

Barbara Lane, a recent part-timer who'd transferred down from the Sydney office was there, but not standing with the crowd. She was seated, between David Crow and Bob Webb, where Annette, the previous payroll/accounts officer used to sit at office meetings, and without needing to hear Crow's words, Sarah knew. She knew too why Bob Webb had been dodging this morning.

Sand-dumped, the breath sucked out of her, her racing heart-beat pumping every litre of blood in her body to her face, she turned to Jackie – Jacqueline Jefferson, who liked to say, *She who expects nothing is never disappointed.*

Sarah had expected and Bob had allowed her to expect, and if preening, smiling Barbara Lane hadn't been looking at her, Sarah might have howled with disappointment. Instead, she looked over Barbara's head to that wall of windows and the white heat of the sky.

Forests were burning out there. There was a big fire out near Gramp's farm. People were losing their homes to it. That was worse than not getting a job.

Couldn't buy the Toyota she and Marni had been watching on eBay. Didn't have her licence anyway. If she'd stayed with Gramp for two more weeks she would have.

Jackie's middle finger drew her mind back to this place. She scratched Sarah's sleeve with it, and, having gained her attention, scratched her own chin. Jackie liked that middle finger. She loathed David Crow. Had names for him and Bob Webb. *Sleazebag and his briefcase.* Every week she'd said she was leaving. Like Sarah, she couldn't. She had four kids to feed, not one, and she had a huge bank loan to repay.

Some people didn't spend their lives worrying about money. Bob Webb didn't. He'd bought a brand new car before Christmas then flown to New Zealand for three weeks.

Dimples and his dwarf, Jackie called them. Bob wasn't a dwarf, just shorter than average. Crow had dimples, in his cheeks, in his chin. He had four kids and a wife who owned half of his business. Until ten years ago, she'd worked here. Twelve years ago, when Sarah had come in for her interview, Maureen Crow had been sitting in Barbara Lane's chair. She'd had a third daughter and a son since. He hid her now, with his kids on a ten-acre property at Pakenham. The staff only saw her at Christmas parties.

Shane, the IT boy, knew someone at the Sydney office who'd told him that Crow had been on with Barbara Lane in Sydney. She was older than his usual blonde. Eve, from HR, had been twenty-three. Barbara was thirty-six.

Sarah glanced at her, just briefly. Cool, beautiful, perfect nails and hair. She knew how to use a computer well enough to check her emails and Facebook. She'd need training.

And Crow was looking at Sarah, speaking at her. '. . . your supreme effort during these last disruptive months,' he said.

Her *supreme effort*? *These last disruptive months*? There were better words to describe what had gone on in this office since December. Sarah had worked back with Bob Webb until ten o'clock, three nights in a row, to get the payroll done – so he wouldn't have to cancel his New Zealand holiday. And while he was away she'd been acting payroll officer and general workhorse.

Knew every facet of Crow's office. Her computer gave her access to information she didn't want to have – like Jackie's loan, like how every month, half of her wage went to repay the bank, which didn't leave her enough to live on.

Sarah deducted only superannuation from her own wage. Most months her account at the Commonwealth Bank grew. Had it been larger, she would have walked out. It wasn't. She couldn't, or not until she found another job.

Glanced at Bob Webb, who must have known Crow's decision this morning, if not yesterday. He could have warned her.

He was looking at his shoes. Black lace-ups, rubber soles, well polished.

She couldn't see Crow's shoes. She could see Barbara Lane's. She wore gorgeous shoes, owned a pair to match every outfit.

Cut Bob Webb out of the frame of those windows and Crow and Barbara looked like actors in a daytime soap opera, too perfect to be real. Bob was a poor match, short, with reddish brown hair. And he must have felt her eyes on him. He looked up, caught her eye and swallowed hard – and he looked like a mullet who'd nibbled around the bait for so long he'd ended up with the barbed hook stuck in his throat.

'Get your application in,' he'd said before he'd left for his holiday. She'd told him it was no use and why it was no use. She'd told him how Annette had been promoted over her.

'I'll push it through for you,' he'd said.

She'd given up her own holidays for him – or maybe she'd given them up to prove to Crow that she was a team player, and could handle the job.

Could have handled it two years ago, which made today so much worse. She'd trained Annette, a temp brought in to take over her workstation while she'd had a month off. Before she'd returned, the old payroll officer had walked out and the job had been offered to Annette. Crow didn't have a lot of luck with his payroll officers.

And he was done. Dismissed, Sarah, last in, was the first out, Jackie beside her, Rena, fair, fat and fifty beside Jackie.

'What the hell is wrong with his head?' Rena said.

'It's in her pants,' Jackie replied.

Sarah was seated at her workstation, her hands on the keyboard, when she felt the hairy huntsman on her shoulder. She shrugged it off and turned to face Bob.

'You're getting a pay rise,' he said.

'Is he supplying her with a house too?' Jackie asked.

'The company agreed to provide a house before Mrs Lane moved down from the Sydney office,' Bob said. 'And like you, Mrs Jefferson, I'm paid to work, not to question my employer's decisions.'

'Confucius say, man who stand with foot on both side of barbed-wire fence end up singing soprano,' Jackie said, and she turned back to her screen.

'You'll be working with Mrs Lane from Monday,' Bob said to Sarah. 'She'll be coming in five days a week.'

Then gone, as silently as he'd arrived.

'Take a week of sickies,' Jackie advised. 'Let him train her.'

She could. She had weeks of accumulated sick days, or she could wait until April and get another job. She'd have four weeks in April. She'd find something, and today, cleaning public toilets looked better than this place.

Four thirty before she could get out – and Barbara Lane was waiting at the lifts, texting on her mobile. With no intention of riding down with her, Sarah stilled her feet while searching her bag for her sunglasses. She found them, then through their darkened lens studied Crow's new senior payroll/accounts officer, who would have looked more at home on a catwalk than behind a computer. Her white-blonde hair was chin length, cut in a straight bob. Always smooth, as was her complexion – botoxed smooth, Jackie said.

The lift doors opened. Still texting, Barbara Lane disappeared and Sarah continued on down the corridor.

She didn't own a mobile. She paid for a landline which, until two years ago, had provided her with dial-up internet connection for an extra fifteen dollars a month – until Telstra had slowed their dial-up service to such a degree it became unusable and she'd been forced to connect to broadband. She could live without texting but not without the internet.

Marni wanted a mobile. Last year when she'd been at primary school, half of her classmates had owned their own phones. Since starting high school, she claimed to be the second-last person in the world between the ages of eight and eighty who didn't own one, and that her mother was the last person.

Number two lift opened. Sarah rode it down, and was glad of her sunglasses when hit by the full force of the day; it was like walking from a refrigerator into a blast furnace, and that was mystical Melbourne, not shimmering in the clouds, but held to the earth by dazzling white cement and melting black bitumen.

She walked with the sweating swarm towards Museum Station, telling herself that there were worse things that could happen to people than being passed over for a job – twice. Breast cancer, for one. Annette had breast cancer. She'd had a breast removed and was now having chemo, and she had three little kids and a husband.

Sarah shook her left foot. Her sandal, irritating her instep since midday, was now hurting.

'It's not fair, Mum,' Marni would say when she told her about the job. Twelve year olds still believed in a world that was fair, then they turned thirteen.

The queue was long at the newsagency where each Friday Sarah bought a ticket in Saturday's TattsLotto. She queued for her turn to waste a little money in the hope of winning a million, and shouldn't have bothered. She'd been buying those same numbers from this same shop since her first payday, and knew that the first week she failed to buy them, her numbers would come tumbling out.

A middle-aged Indian man took her money. He'd been taking it for two or three years. Maybe he recognised her. She always handed him the correct money with her registration card. He always said, 'Good luck.' She always said, 'Thank you.'

Limped on then, to Museum Station, counted the steps down, her mind sifting the contents of her fridge for something for dinner. She and Marni shopped on Saturday mornings and by the end of the week their too-small fridge was bare.

A parking space wasn't a part of Barbara's package. She was at the station, now talking on her mobile.

The train stopped with its door conveniently placed for the new senior payroll/accounts officer, which of course it would. Old men of ninety would spring to their feet to give her a seat. Sarah limped down to the next carriage, where she clung to what she could until Richmond.

Train stopping at all stations, a slower train than the morning 7.40 express. She watched for Barbara to step down to a platform. Didn't see her. Wondered where Crow had bought that company house. Shane, who could ferret information out of a wooden chair, hadn't found out yet.

The train stopped at Box Hill. Still no sign of Barbara, nor at Laburnum. Then Blackburn, Sarah's station. She was stepping down to the platform when she saw that perfect blonde hair above the crowd.

Tailed it through the tunnel, at a good distance. Tailed it out to South Parade, where she watched that hair swing on its way towards the car park. There was free all-day parking near the station – if you got there early enough. Sarah had been planning to park there, had she bought that car.

Barbara drove by in a little red hatchback which must have been red hot. She'd wound down its windows and the wind was daring to disturb her perfect hair.

PEACH-PINK DRAPES

*B*arbara wasn't thinking about Sarah Carter. She was cursing Maureen Crow, who was being difficult about the divorce. Twelve months ago, David had told her he'd started divorce proceedings. It didn't take twelve months to get a divorce.

The splitting of marital assets could take years. She'd paid a solicitor for two before he'd got her not what she'd wanted but enough, and full custody of Danni.

If her mother had still been alive, she may not have moved to Melbourne, or at least not until she'd had a ring on her finger, but with her dead, there'd been no reason to stay, and she'd been fed up with getting herself out to the airport and flying south every second weekend, and fed up with her father's complaints about her flying south.

She hadn't expected to work five days a week, or to undergo training, which was all about appeasing Maureen. He was 'appeasing' her this weekend by taking her kids down to a beach house – and maybe taking her too, because Barbara had told him how Danni was bored to tears and how she loved the beach, and what a good opportunity it would be for her and Danni to meet his kids.

'It's too soon, my pet,' he'd said. 'Let's wait until everything is settled.'

He'd bought that townhouse for appearance's sake. He owned a gorgeous unit at Docklands, overlooking the water but right in the heart of Melbourne. They could have lived there. It had two bedrooms and there must have been a high school somewhere for Danni. Barbara had expected to be living with him but he'd stuck her out in the suburbs, in an enclave of identical townhouses, built wall to wall with their neighbour. They might have been a two-minute walk from the high school but they were over fifteen kilometres from the city.

The car's air conditioner finally blowing cold, Barbara wound up her window and braked at yet another traffic light. She'd had it with traffic lights, with Melbourne's weather – and Melbourne.

Made a right-hand turn into Mahoneys Road, a narrow road that fed traffic into a three-level shopping centre, a huge school, and a rehabilitation hospital. In Sydney, it would have been a one-way street. Not down here. It had speed humps, was a bus route, and she got stuck behind one at the roundabout.

She loved her garage door. A press of the remote opened it. She drove in, hit the remote again and it closed behind her, locking her in, locking her away from neighbours she had no desire to meet.

One of them had a dog. She'd heard it barking and when she'd looked out to identify its owners, she'd seen a male pushing a woman in a wheelchair. She hadn't gone out to complain but had taken note of which house was theirs, the last one on the opposite side, and she'd knock on its door one day soon if they didn't shut that yapping mongrel up. Hers was the first house on the right, only a fence between it and the street.

And its garage an airless sauna tonight, she opened the rear door and stepped fast into her laundry. The schoolbag on the dryer told her Danni was home. The heat in the laundry told her the air conditioning hadn't been turned on.

Everything in the house was new. They'd furnished it together, she and David, had spent a weekend driving around looking in furniture stores, and as soon as they'd seen the right piece, they'd known at the same time that it was the right one, as if their eyes were wired into the same mind.

'I've found my soulmate,' he'd said to her in Sydney. 'I've been waiting for you to show up for the longest time.'

She'd been waiting longer. She'd been waiting all of her life. The first day she'd had lunch with him, she'd known that she'd get him. He'd been everything she'd ever dreamed of in a man.

'Danni!'

No reply. She'd be upstairs, and without the air conditioner the rooms up there would be sweatboxes Barbara preferred not to enter. She reached for the small remote, hit two buttons, then stood waiting to feel that breath of cool.

The entire house was peach and off-white, the carpet a peachy beige, the drapes in her sitting room a darker shade of peach.

'It's you,' David had said the day he'd brought her out here. 'Peaches and cream.'

She touched a chair, upholstered in a peach and cream regency striped fabric. When they'd seen it down the bottom end of a furniture store, they'd both made a beeline for it, had both said, 'That's perfect.'

As was he, his looks, manners, the way he dressed, the places he liked to eat, and the bed. He turned her into someone she hadn't known she could be in bed.

When she'd told her father she was moving in with him, he'd told her that new love was ninety-five per cent sex and five per cent tolerance, that sex shrank and tolerance didn't grow. She'd told him that she could no longer tolerate living with a controlling, sweating old pig who needed to take a bath in deodorant.

There were two upstairs bedrooms. They'd furnished the larger one for Danni and the other as a study. She found Danni there, slouched over her laptop, smiling about something.

'Can't you answer me when I call?'

'I didn't hear you,' Danni said.

'Why didn't you turn the air conditioner on?'

'It was cool downstairs when I came in.'

'You were too eager to get onto Facebook to know if it was hot or not. That's the truth of it. And sit up straight. You'll ruin your spine sitting like that.'

'Yo, boss,' Danni said.

Barbara stood in the doorway, watching that kid's fingers racing over the keyboard. She was pretty when she smiled, which she hadn't done a lot of since they'd moved. She was halfway between twelve and thirteen and still showing no sign of maturing. At thirteen, Barbara had looked much as she did today. She'd won a modelling contest before she'd turned fourteen. Could have gone to America. Could have made the big time – if her parents had supported her. Her father hadn't. He'd told her that models were like butterflies, that they only lived for a day, that a good education would stay with her for life.

'David told them today he was making me his payroll/accounts officer,' she said.

'I thought you were his mistress,' Danni said.

'I could kill you sometimes—'

'They don't have manicurists in jail,' Danni said, and turned back to communicate with her computer.

'It's stinking hot up here.'

'It's hotter outside,' Danni said. 'Smoky too.'

'Did you get something for dinner?'

'I made a sandwich.'

'You can't live on bread. You need vegetables,' Barbara said.

'Lettuce and tomatoes are vegetables.'

'Stop putting on his accent.'

'Stop nagging me as soon as you get home.'

She'd get the last word. She always did. Barbara could give up now or in an hour's time, and it was too hot to stand up there arguing, so she gave up and walked down to the main bedroom, furnished around the print of a woman sitting before an oval gold-framed mirror, a vase of dusty pink and cream roses beside her. A perfect bedroom, it laughed at every other room she'd slept in. Her parents had never updated their furniture, and if she or her mother had dared to suggest tossing out one item, he'd tell them they'd do it over his dead body. Her mother had died of frustration at sixty.

Like the rest of the house the bathroom was peach and white. It had two walls of mirrors. She stripped before them, unclipped her bra and studied breasts that had never been large, except when she'd been pregnant. She stepped out of her skirt to look at the slight swell of her stomach. Hated what pregnancy had done to her. Her stomach muscles had never been the same and she'd been left with stretch marks.

*

Once seated on the bus, Sarah diagnosed her sandals problem and found and applied a bandaid – and caught a youth and his purple-haired girlfriend sniggering. The girl looked fifteen and she had more cutlery on her face and ears than Sarah had in her kitchen drawer.

They left the bus at the Forest Hill shopping centre, where new faces boarded before the bus moved on.

Hawthorn Road was Sarah's closest bus stop, which left her the long school block to walk. Twelve years ago, when she'd started walking that block, there'd been a large bush paddock opposite the school and every time she'd seen it, it had made her homesick for the farm. Not any more. That land was being swallowed up by McMansions, and tonight she wondered if Crow's company had bought one of them for Barbara. They looked like her, character-less, but posh.

Mrs Vaughn's house wasn't posh. It hid, pink faced and embar-rassed, behind a small forest of windblown and bird-sown trees.

A wattle tree and a spiky plum fought each other for space beside the letterbox; if you dared to carelessly steal a handful of junk mail a spike got you, and that plum tree didn't even pay for its space with edible fruit. It grew small red marbles, unfit even for jam. A fig tree, grown huge beside the western fence, grew incredible figs. Twice she and Marni had saved enough from the birds to make jam. Not last year. Every fig they'd reached for had been bird-pecked.

There were trees Sarah couldn't name in Mrs Vaughn's garden, a shiny-leafed thing, a white flowing thing, a eucalypt. She could name the camellias, which must have arrived in pots. Forced into wild company, they'd grown wild, grown tall, as had a huge magnolia tree planted in the centre of a once upon a time lawn. As a seven year old, Marni had named the magnolia *the Magic Faraway Tree*. It hid the front porch and was reaching out to block the drive, where it dropped a million leaves in autumn. The first winter Sarah had spent here, she'd thought that tree had gone mad when its dead grey branches had become a giant's bouquet of purple tulips.

And Mrs Vaughn's son, Raymond, was here, or his blue Commodore was parked where his mother's Hyundai spent its life. Sarah had attempted to start it this morning. She'd left her landlady waiting alone for an RACV man. The car needed a new battery. Perhaps Raymond had taken it to have one fitted, though a long drive usually charged it up.

She sidled between the chimney and the Commodore, parked too close to the twin wooden gates that locked off the backyard. Had to reach across its bonnet to a hand-sized cut-out beneath a *BEWARE OF THE DOG* sign, a perfectly positioned cut-out for a trespasser to lose their reaching hand, had there been a dog to beware of. During the years Sarah had been opening that gate, there'd been no dog.

She jiggled the rusty slide bolt from its keeper, released the left-side gate, stepped through, locked the gate behind her then walked diagonally across the brown lawn to the granny flat she rented.

No trees grew in the backyard. A small pink brick garage formed a part of the eastern fence but no car was ever parked in it. There was a large family-sized rotary clothes line in the space between garage and unit, a flat-roofed, two-room prefab, built thirty or forty years ago for Mrs Vaughn's mother-in-law – and as far away from the house as possible.

Sarah had her own garden, seven plants in seven plastic pots. They would have been happier in the earth, healthier too, but one day soon, Raymond would move his mother into a nursing home, Sarah and Marni would be forced to find somewhere else to live, and when they moved, their garden would move with them.

She'd done too much moving. Didn't want to do it again, ever. Comfortable or not, rooms become homes if you live in them long enough, and that granny flat was home – and close to Marni's school – and they paid next to nothing in rent.

She hung her bag over an arm of the clothes line and turned on the hose. The water in it hot enough to make tea, she sprayed her roof and walls until it cooled sufficiently to ease her garden's thirst.

Her lavender and two well-grown jade trees lived in pots and always looked healthy. She had a mean spiky cactus, which only bloomed for a day or two, but when it did, it made dodging its spikes all year worthwhile. She had a sickly daphne she'd been pleading with for two years not to die. She'd grown it from a flower brought home one day by Marni. For six months they'd kept it alive under a glass jar, daring to hope it was making roots. It had, but had been threatening to die since.

Marni caught her pleading with it again. 'Did he tell you about the job, Mum?'

'Yes,' Sarah said, and she turned the hose off. 'He tell everyone. Together. He gave to Barbara Lane.'

'Mum!' An elongated 'mum', it stretched into three syllables. 'He can't do that to you again.'

'He can,' Sarah said. She reached for her bag and went indoors to kick off her sandals.

'Did you say anything to him?'

Sarah shook her head, loving her girl for caring, but knowing that to care was useless.

'You should go to the anti-discrimination people. It's pure discrimination.'

'Nothing got worse,' Sarah said, and walked barefoot through the kitchen to their bedroom and their shoe box bathroom which should have been called a shower room. It had no space for a bath, had barely sufficient space for a small shower cubicle, a toilet, a tiny handbasin. She stripped in the bedroom, her hearing aids first. Always wore them. Had forever. They allowed her to hear fire sirens, big trucks and thunder, but no speech – and, as Marni knew, as Sarah knew, those aids were the reason she hadn't got the accounts officer job. She couldn't hear telephones. She could feel their ring. Couldn't hear who was calling, or reply to them.

She has a severe hearing loss, her mother used to say. Sometimes she'd say, *She has a profound hearing loss*. She'd never said, *She's deaf.* Her father had. *The kid's deaf and dumb*, he used to say.

Barbara Lane had said deaf and dumb today. She was easy to lip-read. Bob Webb had been explaining the importance of speaking directly to Sarah.

'I've never had anything to do with deaf and dumb people,' she'd said, and every word of it clear.

To Sarah, *dumb* meant *stupid* – and Barbara Lane was a *dumb* blonde.

*

Bob Webb may not say it out loud, but he agreed, and tonight he was seriously considering taking off to Peru with his backpack. He eased his new Mazda into an elderly garage beside his mother's older Mazda, locked it, closed the garage door and walked across to the house.

Like the bloke who sang 'I've Been Everywhere, Man', since his twenty-first-birthday gift, a seven-day trip to Bali, Bob had been everywhere, briefly.

Home was where it had always been, a street away from the East Burwood Kmart, in a vintage sixties red-brick house, well insulated commercially, insulated further by greenery and outdoor blinds, and being chilled today by a large split-system air conditioner. He required no key to enter, the back door was ever guarded by Footrot, their elderly Kelpie, who considered that doormat his place. He stood, woofed his welcome, received his pat, then stepped back and allowed the screen door to open, to close, before returning to his mat to snooze on.

Smell of dinner wafting into the rear passage, a greeting from the kitchen.

'You're late tonight.'

'I was late getting away then we got detoured off the freeway at Burke Road. There must have been another smash.'

'It will be on the news,' his mother said. 'What a day to be stuck on that freeway.'

'It's like a furnace out there. Did you hear what the temperature got to?'

'It was forty-four at two o'clock,' she said. 'There's fires ringing Melbourne and a bad one in some forest out near Kangaroo Ground, and they say tomorrow is going to be worse.'

'It can do what it likes tomorrow. It's Saturday.'

Four pots on the stove, four hotplates heating up the kitchen. He didn't need to lift a lid to know what he'd be eating. After thirty-five years of his mother's cooking, his nose could identify most meals.

'Corned beef.'

'So I'll have cold meat for the weekend,' she said. 'We've got the kids staying over tomorrow night.'

'Whose?'

'Joanne's. She called today. She's having another one,' his mother said.

'Hasn't she got enough?'

'They want a girl.'

'I'll give you five to one it's another boy.'

'Don't you dare say that to her, Bob!'

He had four sisters, was an uncle to eight boys and two girls. Had his father made old bones, Bob may have married and had a few kids of his own. He'd been fourteen and the eldest, and when his mother had told him he'd have to be the man of the house, he'd taken her literally.

Had she found herself another man, Bob would have moved on with his life. She'd got herself a job at Kmart, still worked there part-time, and had never looked at another man.

'Did you remember to tape *Hot Seat*?'

'I always tape it if I'm here. There's this huge woman on it tonight—'

'Don't tell me about it,' he said.

'I didn't watch it! I saw her when I was putting the tape in.' His mother still used the old video tapes. She'd be lost when her old recorder died.

He emptied his pockets into a bowl on the kitchen bench, car keys, wallet and small change; he poured a glass of chilled water then told her that Crow had given the job to his new blonde.

'He did not, Bob!'

'The smarmy bastard did, and I've had him, Mum. I'm chucking it in and going to Peru for six months.'

'Who'd want to spend six months in that place?'

'Me.'

'You were dead certain Sarah would get it.'

'She had it until yesterday. He had an appointment with his solicitor last night, and the bastard came in this morning and told me that Mrs Lane had transferred down from Sydney to fill the vacancy. She doesn't know her arse from her elbow.'

'I'll bet he does,' his mother said. 'I'll bet it's got something to do with his wife finding out about him buying that house, too.'

'It's got everything to do with it. Maureen is threatening to split the company and sell her half. She's a decent woman, and he's a cheating bastard, and I need to wash him and his bloody office off me. Have I got time for a shower?'

'Make it fast. I'm hungry.'

THE WOLF

*I*n the beginnings, he was an eager youth in pursuit of a new love. Love grew stale fast – or they grew stale. In their endings, in those slow, twisting fragments of time between their life and death, he was old, cold, clinical – and careful. The party over, he was left to clean up the mess and drop off the refuse before he brought his next guest home.

He'd started a trend with the dropping off of the second of them, had become newsworthy. Unable now to disappoint his readers, he couldn't deviate. The last delivery had its elements of danger, but this one had gone wrong. Forced to detour around an accident, he'd followed a loaded truck through unfamiliar backstreets because its driver appeared to know where he was going. He had, if he'd been on his way to Sydney or Geelong. They were now heading vaguely south on the Western Ring Road.

A relatively new freeway, or new to him, it circled the western outskirts of the city, feeding traffic out to the Hume Freeway, to Tullamarine Airport and Geelong, and was carrying too much traffic tonight for his comfort.

He'd done the other drop-offs on Sunday nights, during the dark hours before dawn, and rarely struck a lot of traffic. Truckies drove by night and they liked this freeway. There was one in front, one behind. He eased back on the accelerator, eased back a little more before the truck passed. A sedan took its place.

The hunters could have been out patrolling the freeways, and no doubt in unmarked vehicles. That sedan now tailgating him could have been one.

He glanced at the speedo needle then eased it back until it was brushing fifty-five miles an hour, which translated roughly to ninety k's. Not fast enough for the sedan. It left him for dead. On its way to Sydney?

The road had many lanes. He was relieved when he saw a sign directing him to the Hume Freeway exit. He was familiar with that freeway though not with this exit, and for a moment, his concentration and both hands were required on the wheel. The old wagon didn't have the same road-holding ability as a modern car.

And if this was the Hume Freeway it wasn't the one he'd known. They fancied them up these days with tall noise barriers. Not an ideal place for his purpose, but all things pass, as did the noise barriers to his left.

The speed limit was a hundred k's. He moved over to the left-hand lane, got his speedo needle sitting on sixty, then, the road clear ahead and behind, he reached across the garbage bag to his passenger-side door to release its catch. And more lights glinted in his rear-view mirror. And to hell with the traffic.

He was sweating, could feel it trickling. The protective clothing he wore allowed no perspiration to escape. Winter nights were better for the deliveries, wet winter nights better still. One hand on the wheel, he adjusted his corner window, directing air to his face. Back when this old vehicle had come off the assembly line, air conditioning in cars was unheard of. The makers had done what they could to make the HG Holden driver friendly.

They'd put good motors in them, and as a modern sedan zoomed by, he considered putting his foot down and burning it off. He had the power to do it, though maybe not tonight. Didn't need to be pulled over for speeding. There'd be a break. There was always a break in traffic for those patient enough to wait for it. He'd wait his chance, be Lupine, the wily one, his every sense alert for the hunters.

A heavily laden truck roared by and out of sight, and the road his, he braked, just a little, just enough, then reaching across the garbage bag he opened the passenger door, and as it swung wide, he pushed.

Memory in the release, the ache of that final letting go. It passed — and quickly tonight. There was another bastard coming up on his tail. He grasped a nylon rope he'd attached to driver and passenger-side armrests and yanked hard on it, needing to close that door and put distance between him and that truck's many lights. Too eager, the gloved hand gripping the wheel slipped, and the old wagon swerved hard to the right.

Forgot the rope and the door and, two hands gripping, his foot asking for power, the old girl corrected, then replied to his foot's urging with a surge of power. She'd been built to fly, and with her door still swinging wide, she left that truck for dead.

Finding Monica

*S*leep was something Ross Hunter had learnt to take as required. He could take it while watching television and frequently did. Six hours of solid sleep in bed was party time. On rare occasions he doubled that, but woke with a head, neck or backache.

He'd clocked up four hours when his mobile disturbed his dream, and he was awake and grabbing for the oblong of light on the bedside table.

'Who?'

'We've got her, Sarge. A truckie just called it in. Hume Freeway, nine kilometres west of the Ring Road exit.'

'Christ,' Ross said, hitting the light switch then closing his eyes fast against its too-sudden white glare.

'It gets better, Sarge. He got a look at the vehicle that dropped her, a late sixties or early seventies Kingswood, he says.'

'Rego?' Ross asked, juggling both phone and trousers. He hadn't worked out yet how to put his new phone on speaker.

'Not that close. We might get lucky with a speed camera. He's dead certain it was a Kingswood and probably white.'

Ross was pulling on socks. He needed new socks. He got his feet into his shoes, zipped his fly, buckled his belt while Roy continued.

'He swears that he recognised the tail-lights. He restored one three years ago and spent months chasing around swap meets looking for those same tail-lights.'

'Who is he?'

'Chap by the name of Collin Wallace. He's got a wife and three kids in Albury. Brings a load down from Sydney twice a week and takes one back.'

'Clean?'

'Lily white – and shocked to buggery.'

'I'm out the door,' Ross said.

'Do you need a car?'

'Got my own. Hold the truckie.'

'He's not going anywhere. The poor bugger is walking in circles. He thought he'd run over the bag.'

'Didn't?'

'He managed to straddle it – in an eighteen-wheeler.'

Ross's unit was in Southbank, a one-bedroom unit on the seventh floor, high above the world he liked to escape when he could. It was convenient, a bare five-minute walk from his St Kilda Road headquarters. The lift was conveniently situated diagonally opposite his door, and at this time of morning empty. It delivered him to the underground car park where he had a designated space – all very modern and convenient, but not home. The old house in Hawthorn had been home.

He lived alone, was free to take a phone call at four in the morning and not disturb a wife, free to eat what he felt like eating, smoke when he felt like smoking – as long as he did it beneath his kitchen exhaust fan or on his handkerchief-sized balcony.

He'd almost had a wife – twice; one had got sick of waiting, the other he'd cut and run from. Some managed to balance a wife and kids with the job.

We've got her, Sarge. Roy Bull had been on Ross's team since Wall Johnson put it together. A good reliable bloke, Roy. He balanced marriage and a couple of kids. Johnson had been married for thirty years.

They'd got her – or found her dead, twelve-year-old Monica Rowan, missing since mid-December.

Thrown everything they had at finding that girl. They'd studied hours of videos confiscated from security-conscious residents, had checked out sightings of blonde twelve year olds from Hobart to Cairns, and come up with nothing because that child-murdering bastard gave them nothing. And he was getting better at what he did, and keeping those girls alive longer.

The media had named him the Freeway Killer. They liked labels, and had come up with that one after little Penny Matthews, his second victim, had been found like his first, double-bagged in heavy-duty green garbage bags then tossed out to the side of the Monash Freeway. Monica was his fourth.

Back when the first of them, ten-year-old Nancy Yang, had been reported missing, Ross had been living with his mother in Hawthorn and stationed at Parham. He hadn't been involved in the Yang case. He'd transferred to St Kilda shortly after Penny's body was found. Johnson had asked for him.

Soon after, Heidi Jasper, an eleven year old, had gone missing from Chadstone Shopping Centre in mid-January, in the middle of the school holidays, kids and shoppers everywhere.

They'd locked that centre down. They'd had more police out there than shoppers but found no trace of Heidi. To this day they didn't know how the child-murdering bastard had spirited her away from a crowded shopping centre.

Found her emaciated little body six weeks later, bagged and dumped like so much rubbish beside the Eastern Freeway, near Ringwood.

That bastard always double-bagged them, always used identical heavy-duty dark green bags with orange ties, always knotted the bags in the same way.

Monica had disappeared from a residential street at around eight o'clock on a December evening, somewhere between her friend's home and her own, a bare block and a half between the two houses. The sun had been in the sky. Folk would have been out watering their gardens, walking their dogs, jogging for their health, and not one had seen Monica, her abductor, or his car.

He gave them no specific area to work in, no fingerprint, not a hair from his head. He'd taken those girls from Footscray, Caulfield, Glen Waverley and Doncaster. To date they'd found no motive, nor any connection between the families of the girls. His killing spree seemed random, and random was ... random.

Maybe they'd got lucky tonight. There weren't a lot of seventies Kingswoods left on the roads. A classy set of wheels in their day, weighty enough to pull a van, solid enough to become a tradie's workhorse, now collector's items – and they'd been lucky enough for one of those collectors to find that girl.

The Commodore had replaced the Kingswood. Ross drove one, a 2002 model he'd bought new. It kept going so he'd kept it. It hadn't done a lot of kilometres. He worked and when he wasn't working, he slept.

He checked the time on his dashboard and hoped he wasn't called in today to testify in the Swan case. Had expected to get it over and done with last week. It had been going for over a week and fat Freddy had been delaying. Ross knew his tactics well.

He'd come up against him when he'd arrested the ice-crazed little bastard, had him locked up on a Wednesday and fat Freddy'd had him out on bail by Thursday, and he'd been out since. Frederick Adam-Jones might resemble an inflated balloon with legs, but he was a tough little bastard who'd do what he had to do to get his client off.

Ross hadn't known who Swan was the day he'd searched his hovel. He knew his life story now. Michael Swan was the only grandson of Lady Cynthia Swan. His father was a neurologist, his mother a practising GP. At nineteen young Michael had been living at home, studying medicine at Melbourne University and dating the daughter of one of his university professors.

She'd smashed up Daddy's car one night and walked away from it. Swan, not so lucky, had cracked a couple of vertebrae in his neck and had got to spend the next few months with a metal cage screwed to his brow.

His mother blamed the professor's daughter for Michael's addiction. She'd ended the relationship. She'd blamed his friends' derision. They'd called her boy Frankenstein. His father, who charged a couple of hundred bucks for fifteen minutes of his diamond-studded time, blamed neurological damage. Lady Cynthia blamed an addiction to the painkilling medication pre-scribed for dear Michael during his months of treatment. She was no doctor but she may have got the diagnosis right.

He'd healed. The cage had been removed, the painkillers with-drawn, but young Michael, accustomed to getting what he wanted when he wanted it, had stolen one of his mother's prescription pads and self-prescribed for twelve months.

Twice they'd booked him into rehab. Twice he'd walked out. Two years after the accident, Michael Swan had drifted down to the bottom of the dung heap – a sad story to those of the bleeding hearts. Ross's heart bled buckets, but not for poor little rich boys. It bled for the tiny bodies he saw lying in mortuaries. Kids, hard to come by to some, were expendable items to others.

Ross was dogged, and he knew it. He had a one-track mind too, and a psychic nose that could sniff out guilt at twenty paces. Five minutes after meeting the bereaved mother's boyfriend, Ross had been sneezing his brains out.

He'd harassed Swan and his parents and Lady Cynthia, who had trouble closing her watermelon mouth, but hadn't opened it to him.

Then he'd started on Cory's grandparents, a pair of congenital pensioners who may not have had ten years of education between them. They'd known how to work a video camera.

They'd shown him their home videos that afternoon, and when he'd seen enough, he'd arrested Lady Cynthia's grandson.

THAT MONDAY

Sarah, her bag over her shoulder, was reaching to turn off the television when it showed a bank-up of traffic on one of the freeways. Her hand stilled while she read the subtitles.

. . . exit to the Hume Freeway closed . . .

The cameraman must have been in a helicopter. They were showing a curved, never-ending line of cars and trucks.

The body of a young female, found this morning . . .

Monica, Sarah thought, and she placed her bag on the table, catching that bus now a secondary concern. She'd followed Monica Rowan's story since her abduction, a too-personal story because of Monica's age and her date of birth. She would have celebrated her thirteenth birthday on the eleventh of July, the same day as Marni, who walked home alone from her friends' homes, walked to school alone, shopped alone at Forest Hill if they ran out of bread or milk.

She watched that screen until the news broke for a commercial, when she crept into the bedroom where Marni lay flat out on her stomach, sound asleep. Five mornings a week Sarah left her sleeping, and today she didn't want to leave her.

The Freeway Killer didn't steal into bedrooms, or he hadn't yet, which didn't mean he wouldn't. He'd taken Nancy Yang from out the front of her parents' corner milk bar.

Don't talk to anyone you don't know, Sarah warned often. If a strange man tells you he's lost his dog, his wife or himself, don't talk to him.

Marni liked to talk. As a tiny kid she'd become Sarah's voice and ears. As a four year old, Sarah had lifted her high enough to speak to a dental receptionist.

'Mummy broke some of her tooth,' she'd said.

Typewriter telephone and the relay service for the deaf had been around back then. She could have bought one; instead she'd continued to relay her problems through Marni until she'd bought her laptop. Emails had freed Sarah, but once that phone had been connected, it had became Marni's new toy. She'd been seven and had learnt to handle phone calls like an old woman.

She looked very young this morning, her arms spread, legs spread, no blanket, no sheet, childlike and vulnerable in her singlet top and pants. She could have been born deaf. Deaf would have been normal. A baby with perfect hearing had made Sarah afraid, afraid her perfect baby would grow up embarrassed about her deaf mother's speech, afraid too that her baby wouldn't learn to speak like others.

She'd been the reason Sarah had applied for the job at Crows, so she could make enough money to pay for a crèche where her Marni would hear other voices. She'd learnt. She'd learnt early that her mummy was different, that she couldn't hear her when she cried. She'd never sat crying where she'd fallen. Always crawled to Mummy's feet first.

As a two year old, her little mouth had worked hard so Mummy's eyes would understand. At six she'd said she was going to be a doctor when she got big so she could fix Mummy's broken ears, and since she'd been old enough to know about cochlear implants, she'd been nagging about them.

Loved her. Lived for her. Worked for her. Would have put up with ten Barbara Lanes for the next twenty years so her beautiful girl could have the best, the safest life she could give her. Would have cleaned Crow's toilets—

Marni must have sensed her nearness. She rolled onto her back, moving in an instant from deep sleep to wakefulness. 'What's wrong, Mummy?'

'Be careful,' Sarah said, brushing long sleep-tossed hair back from Marni's face, kissing the cheek she exposed. 'I think the police finding Monica.'

'Alive?' She was up, her feet on the floor.

'No.'

Marni nodded, then pointed to the clock on the narrow chest of drawers between their beds. 'You'll miss your bus.'

'You be careful,' Sarah said.

'You know I always am. Go, Mum.'

Kissed her again, then left her, left her locked into a granny flat behind tall gates, Mrs Vaughn playing watchdog at her lounge room window, and she ran up to the pipeline, through it to the school grounds and diagonally across, a shorter route to the bus. Out of breath when she got there, but she caught the bus and took a seat opposite two women who rode with her five days a week to the station. They didn't speak.

Barbara Lane didn't speak. All of last week she'd sat, bored, at Sarah's elbow, and was untrained because she didn't want to be trained. She wasn't waiting at the station. Had been last Friday. They'd sat in the same carriage, but at different ends.

Two deaf girls boarded at Box Hill. Sarah had seen them before, but this morning they sat directly opposite. Her book was open, but watching them was more interesting. They spoke with their hands, spoke fast.

She could sign but rarely did it. She didn't mix with the deaf, not in Melbourne. It would have been easier. Every word she spoke she fought hard for.

Easy isn't always best, baby, her mother used to say. *The world is full of people who can't sign, and if you're going to find your own place in it, you need to talk.*

She'd never found her place, not in Melbourne. She may have in the deaf world. There were clubs, activities. She'd looked them up on the internet but hadn't joined. The deaf asked too many questions.

Watched those hands asking questions. *Brisbane?* Watched the reply. *Next weekend. Cheap flight.*

Sarah had gone to a school for the deaf in Brisbane, for almost eight months. Wondered if that girl had gone to the same school. She looked younger, late twenties maybe.

Uncle Bill used to have a caravan in his backyard. For those almost eight months Sarah had called it home. Then they'd moved on again.

Always moving. One of her earliest memories was of being picked up from a bed and waking in a moving car. She could remember being carried from cars into a cold tent then, come morning, watching that tent packed up and off they'd go again. Spent most of her early years between one place and the next, between town and city, between states, because Daddy had only been happy when he was chasing rainbows and it had been very important to keep him happy.

She'd turned nine in Brisbane, had been big enough, old enough, to work out for herself that when Daddy had stopped chasing rainbows he'd started bringing home bottles.

A shudder, starting in her neck, passed through her to the train floor. She moved her feet to release it down to the wheels, down to the rails and away. Always felt that shudder when she thought about those bottles.

Turned ten in Adelaide. She'd gone to a school for the deaf there. Her mother had taken her to school on a bus, taken her home on the bus, until the day they'd picked her up in the car and kept on driving. He'd driven that old car all day, all night, until it died.

Nullarbor, baby. Null-ar-bor. It means no trees.

No trees, and no shade, other than beside the car, until a truck driver stopped.

The kid's deaf and dumb. We need to get her into school.

The truck driver had unloaded them and their tent and cases at a Perth caravan park, and for weeks her father had caught a bus to work to get money for another car. Sarah had caught a special minibus to and from a school for the deaf and her mother had ridden another to the Clarks' suburb where she'd looked after twin girls. They'd paid her well, but instead of giving her money to him for a car, she'd rented a cabin.

We've had enough, Joey. We want to stop.

Stopping wasn't good.

Some images jam in the mind. Close her eyes now and she wasn't on that train but in a hospital room, standing beside a high white bed, machine lights flashing. Like watching a movie with no subtitles, the actors' mouths making words that forged no connection to her brain—

Like those deaf girls' hands. *Very old . . . Ugly.* Other hands asking, *What for?* And Sarah, aware she'd been staring while her mind wandered, drew her eyes down to her book, or to the hand holding the book, to the small gold watch, her mother's, to the wedding ring, also her mother's. She'd worn both since the undertaker had taken them from her mother's hand. Too big for a twelve year old, she'd worn the ring on her middle finger and the watch halfway to her elbow.

Not his fault, baby.

Whose fault then? Sarah's? Maybe it was. He'd needed his wife but not his deaf and dumb daughter. Maybe his bottles had contained escape juice.

He'd been drinking the day he'd smashed his car.

Uncle Bill offered Sarah a home in Brisbane. Her grandparents had wanted her to go to them in Victoria. No school near their farm. She hadn't wanted to go to any school. Hadn't wanted to live anywhere.

Hadn't wanted to wake up each morning. Had been like an empty plastic bag, blowing in the wind, hoping each day that the wind would blow her onto a barbed-wire fence and rip her to shreds before another night came.

Made of non-biodegradable plastic, it floated one day to the battered old case Peter and Lynette Clark had brought from that rented cabin, all they'd brought from it, all Sarah and her mother had managed to hold on to. An old cake tin, an old camera, their old books.

Little girls liked her old books. Miriam and Mandy, two identical mouths making words, four identical hands, touching her. They'd stopped that plastic bag's floating – and Lynette Clark had known it.

'If I'm not back by three twenty, can you pick the girls up from school for me?' she'd said.

For an hour Sarah had watched the hands of her mother's watch, willing Lynette's car to come home, and when it hadn't, when the watch hands had got to three twenty, she'd had to open the front door and walk outside, walk to the primary school and wait at the gate for the twins to come out. They'd taken her hands to walk home.

As a mother, she knew she wouldn't have trusted a deaf twelve-year-old girl raised in a caravan park to walk Marni home from school. Perhaps Lynette had been hiding behind trees watching her girls all the way. That twelve year old had believed she'd been trusted.

She'd become Lynette's project that year. The Clarks hadn't made her go to Brisbane or Victoria. They hadn't made her go back to the school for the deaf. Lynette had found a private school with a deaf unit, then she'd turned Sarah into a person fit to go to that school. Bought her a new school uniform, new shoes and books, then enrolled her there as Sarah Clark because everyone had known her other name, and her father's and the names of the three teenagers who had died in the other car.

For six years Sarah Clark had worn that uniform. For six years she'd walked little sisters to school and home again to that beautiful house she'd been allowed to call home. Learnt about cooking there, about cleaning, about sitting down to eat at a dining room table. Learnt about a different life with the Clarks.

The train was pulling into Museum Station. Sarah closed her book, dropped it unread into her bag, slung the strap over her shoulder and stood to follow the workers out to the platform and up the stairs.

Like a swarm of Gramp's bees leaving the dark of their hive, they split into smaller groups as they hit the sunlight. Sarah walked not with the two deaf girls but close behind them. They were dressed like the other office workers; they looked like the other office workers, carried no cane, no crutch. Their disability was disguised until they spoke.

The morning she'd found her way to Mrs Vaughn's house, the old lady hadn't given her time to speak. She'd unlocked her front door, taken one look at her visitor, then slammed the door hard enough for Sarah to hear.

She'd advertised her granny flat in exchange for *housework, some cooking. Suit single woman, no children.* Sarah had applied for the job with Marni in a sling at her breast, an angry Marni, overdue for her ten o'clock feed and not pleased about it.

Back then, Mrs Vaughn's overgrown forest had offered privacy, so Sarah had sat on the porch steps and fed Marni, unaware she was being observed until she'd felt the prod of a slipper-clad foot in her backside and turned fast to an angry elderly face.

'I'll have no truck with unwed mothers. Get off my porch.'

That was the moment Mrs Sarah Carter was born, on Mrs Vaughn's porch steps, Marni suckling at her breast. She'd shown her mother's wedding ring.

'My husband die,' she said.

'You're deaf,' the old lady accused. 'What are you called?'

To this day Sarah didn't know why she'd chosen to be Mrs Carter, other than that it was easy to say and that name had belonged to a kind man, a plumber who had driven a white kombi van.

'I can clean very well, and cook.'

'There's nothing of you if you put that brat down,' the old lady had said, and clearly. Some people knew how to do it. Many didn't.

'I am very strong. Before, I cleaning very big house, and work on farm – before my baby coming.'

'How did your husband die?'

'He getting brain tumour.'

'You're on a disabled pension?'

'Not disable. I get for my baby.'

Mrs Vaughn had gone inside. Marni, disinterested in the outcome, had sucked on, so Sarah had sat on. And the old lady returned, with a cup of tea, two biscuits and more questions.

'How old is it?'

'One month. Her name, Marni Olivia.'

'Bring her in when she's done, and show me how you can work,' Mrs Vaughn said.

An hour could make the Clarks' house shine. Three hours of hard labour couldn't make Mrs Vaughn's rooms shine, but while Marni slept on a spare bed, Sarah had done her best, and made a mutton stew. It, or her cleaning, had been judged good enough, and two days later she'd moved into the granny flat with her case, an inflatable mattress, one pair of sheets, a pillow and quilt. The kitchen table and two wooden chairs had come by night. One man's trash is another man's treasure. She'd found many treasures since amid the piles of indestructible rubbish left out on nature strips for the council's hard waste collection. She'd found a near new baby stroller, an electric fan, the pots for her garden, the original jade tree, its roots bursting out of a too-small plastic pot.

Marni was seven months old the day she'd left her in the care of strangers at a crèche and walked into David and Maureen Crow's office. She'd worn her best frock to the interview, had bought a pair of new shoes with heels. She'd looked good enough to work in that office but had seen pity in Maureen's eyes when she'd spoken. Had seen worse than pity in Crow's – until their manager had sat her down at a computer.

In her element there, her fingers fast and accurate, her knowledge of computers vast. She'd had the best teacher in the world. Her skill had got her the job, or perhaps her hearing aids. At that time, large companies were being urged to employ the disabled.

She'd signed *Sarah J. Carter* on her application form. By then it had been no lie. It had taken months to do it – or months to find out how to change her name by deed poll. Her original birth certificate would always tell the truth, as would Marni's, but they were sealed into an envelope and buried deep beneath her mother's treasures in the old cake tin.

The day she told Mrs Vaughn she'd got a job and would only be able to clean at weekends, she'd been certain the old lady would tell her to pack her bags. She hadn't.

'How much are they paying you?' she'd asked.

'They talk not much to me.'

'I worked for fifty years. My first pay was two pound seven and sixpence – and I had to pay board out of that.'

'I will. And cook dinner. Every night. Weekend I will clean.'

'Too right you will,' Mrs Vaughn said.

Her bark had always been worse than her bite. For months she hadn't asked for rent, and when she had, she'd only asked for fifty dollars a week. Through the years it had been raised to a hundred dollars, but since her old car had died and she'd bought the Hyundai she couldn't back down her drive, since finding out that Sarah could drive, she hadn't increased the rent.

THE GIRL WITH THE
FANCY MOBILE

*M*arni ate her breakfast with the television news, where the kilometres of traffic banked up on the Hume Freeway seemed more important to the newsreader than the finding of Monica Rowan. Since she'd sat down to her cornflakes, every minute or two the newsreader said that the Ring Road exit to the Hume Freeway was closed to all traffic, but only three times had they interrupted their traffic report to show a cluster of police and police cars.

They hadn't mentioned Monica by name, and didn't need to. As soon as they said *freeway*, *body*, *garbage bag*, everyone in Melbourne would have known who they'd found.

Monica Rowan would have started high school this year. She would have had a thirteenth birthday party in July. Marni was having a small party this year, at McDonalds because they couldn't have it at the flat. Even if they'd had enough space and chairs for more than two people, Mrs Vaughn wouldn't have allowed it. She didn't like strangers in her backyard. She didn't like strangers setting one foot on her land.

There wasn't much she did like. She'd stuck a sign on her letter-box, *POST NO JUNK MAIL*, and her sign was the easiest part of it to see. The junk mail man deserved a medal for dodging the spiky plum to get his junk into her letterbox.

She had a sign on her front door, *SALESMEN DO NOT KNOCK*, and her *BEWARE OF THE DOG* sign on the gate, and if she'd ever had a dog to beware of, it had been dead for longer than Marni had been alive – and God help it if there'd ever been one because Mrs Vaughn hated dogs.

She liked pills and smoking and funerals and probably her doctor who gave her the scripts for her pills. She visited him every month. Never missed a funeral – if it was close to home. She didn't like the Chinese milk bar man but she bought cigarettes from him in an emergency.

She was hypo-allergic to mops, brooms and cooking. As far as Marni could tell, all she did all day was smoke and hammer on her window if anyone dared to use her driveway, even to turn their car around.

Marni and her mother cleaned her house on Sundays, did her washing and cooked her boring soups and stews, big ones they froze in empty margarine containers in her freezer. She had a big modern freezer. They didn't. They had a microwave and she didn't, so they had to thaw what they'd frozen, then serve it to her with their own vegetables.

She never thanked them – except with cheap rent and free electricity and water. Their phone bill wasn't free. It came addressed to her, but they paid it, because of their broadband.

Marni lived three separate lives. In one, she was Mrs Vaughn's servant and she never talked back. At school she was just another kid. At home she felt about eighteen. She was allowed to drink coffee and watch adult television, and if she had to go to the shops or milk bar she took her mother's purse that had everything in it, and her mother trusted her to turn the power board off before she left for school, because the television, laptop and fan were all plugged into it.

There was a second power board on the bench, for their jug, toaster, microwave and fridge, which they couldn't turn off because of the fridge. It had individual switches you could turn off. She turned off the toaster and the jug.

The fridge was antique. It had been in here when her mother moved in, as had the old stove. The fridge still worked. The stove's oven hadn't turned on for at least a year and a while ago another one of its hotplates died and Mrs Vaughn refused to pay anyone to fix them.

Marni took an apple from the fridge and the sandwich her mother always made for her when she made her own. She put them into her schoolbag, slung the bag over her shoulder, removed a packet of cigarettes from a carton that lived on top of the fridge and let herself out. The door locked itself if you slammed it.

Their granny flat had two windows. The one in their bedroom looked east at the clothes line, the kitchen's faced north. It had a good view of the back fence. Their door spent its days staring at Mrs Vaughn's laundry and toilet windows.

They'd worn a diagonal track across the back lawn, a track which branched into two near Mrs Vaughn's back door. Every school morning, Marni hammered on that door until the old lady came, and how fast she came depended on how desperate she was for a cigarette. Not very desperate this morning, so Marni hammered again, then listened.

A year ago when that door hadn't opened, she'd heard her yelling from inside. She phoned Raymond, and when he hadn't picked up, she'd had to climb in through the bathroom window. Mrs Vaughn had been on her bedroom floor, all bloody from a hole in her head – and as mad as hell when Marni phoned for an ambulance.

Another thing their landlady didn't like was hospitals. She'd signed herself out after two days, and came home in a taxi with about ten stitches in her head, which you could see because they'd cut her hair off around the gash and she hadn't had much to start with.

That fall achieved something. That night, she'd shown them where she kept an emergency key to her front door, which Marni wasn't going to need this morning. She could hear movement, old lady slow movement. She was about five years away from turning a hundred.

The door eventually opened wide enough for a scrawny old hand to reach through for its daily ration, which she pocketed, then from the same pocket took a handful of change which she took her time counting coin by coin into Marni's hand, her mouth slapping, raising saliva enough for her morning accusation.

'I could hear your television blaring again last night.'

'Sorry,' Marni said, knowing their landlady hadn't heard their television because it had been turned off and they'd been in bed reading by ten o'clock. 'Are you all right for milk?'

'I'll tell you when I'm not. Bolt that gate behind you.'

'I always do,' Marni said, and went on her way, counting the dollars and smaller coins, knowing she'd made almost sixty cents on the cigarette deal. Mrs Vaughn didn't know they bought them by the carton at the supermarket, which made them heaps cheaper than the milk bar man's. They didn't overcharge her to cheat her, just to stop her calling the milk bar man a thief the next time she went there to buy an emergency packet. With crotchety old people, you always had to think two steps ahead. Like not giving her the whole carton of cigarettes because she'd just smoke twice as many.

She could afford to. She'd written a cheque for twenty-two thousand dollars to pay for her Hyundai, then the first time she'd tried to back it out, she'd run into the fence and knocked down two metres of it as well as raking paint off the driver-side doors of a brand new car, which she hadn't even bothered to get fixed. The neighbours got the fence fixed and had to threaten her with a lawyer's letter before she'd write a cheque for her half of what it had cost, and she'd been the one who'd broken it.

Her son had fights with her about moving into a nursing home, which she would have been expelled from on her first day.

He'd booked her into one once and sent Marni and her mother an email telling them they had thirty days to find alternative accommodation. Told them before he'd told his mother. The entire street heard her the day he told her.

She looked like an Egyptian mummy, preserved in nicotine – and smelled like one because she'd only allow the district nurse to come once a week to shower her.

Marni sighed, dropped the coins into her schoolbag and walked on towards the pipeline, her short cut to school. Until she'd turned twelve, her mother who had made her go to the before-school care ladies, used to walk her there early before she caught her bus. Other kids with working mothers had grandparents or aunties or neighbours to look after them. Marni only had her mother.

Mrs Vaughn used to have two sisters. She had five grandchildren in Ireland who she'd never seen, and Raymond had sons she hadn't seen in years. He had a wife too. She never visited. If she had, Mrs Vaughn might not have been so crotchety. If she'd been less crotchety her daughter-in-law might have visited her, which was a case of what came first, the chicken or the egg?

No one in Marni's family had lived long enough to grow old. Her mum's parents had died in a car accident and her mother had to live with a foster family in Perth. She'd got married there when she was eighteen, then he'd died, before Marni was born, so her mother had gone to live with her grandparents, Marni's great-grandparents, then they'd died too.

They had a framed photograph of Gramp and her mother when she'd been about six. They had one of her mother's mother as a bride. Marni would have preferred one of her father, but they didn't have one single photograph of him, which was crazy.

She used to ask why. She used to ask heaps of stuff about him. He was a plumber, had driven a white kombi van and died of a brain tumour, and that's all she knew. Maybe when you loved someone enough to marry them at eighteen, and then they died a horrible death when you were pregnant, it hurt too much to talk about them – anyway, having a father who'd died before you were born was probably better than having one who'd run off with a girlfriend when you were old enough to remember, like Samantha Smith's father, who was alive somewhere but she hadn't seen him since her seventh birthday party.

'I was born posthumously,' Marni said if anyone asked where her father was. That's what newsreaders said when a baby was born to the wife of a soldier killed in Afghanistan.

Maria from school had brothers, sisters, cousins, a grandmother, and dozens of uncles and aunties. At weekends, her house was like a Greek party, everyone talking Greek. They had to because of Maria's grandmother, who'd been in Australia for almost forty years but could barely speak English. Marni used to think it was because Nona wished she'd never left Greece, but Maria said it was because she'd been too old to learn when she'd immigrated, which sort of explained a bit why deaf people who had cochlear implants as adults never learned to understand spoken English, but implanted deaf babies learned to speak like everyone else. It had something to do with brains needing to learn how to process speech before they got filled up with all the junk of living, like the difference between having a new sheet of paper to write on and one already covered with print.

That pipeline had something to do with water or sewerage pipes. For kilometres it cut across the land on an angle, just this stretch of vacant land with houses on either side. Parts of it had been turned into kids' parks, with slides and swings and stuff. The part Marni walked through had trees, not large enough trees for a man to hide behind, though some of the bushy clumps would hide one.

And she saw something, saw movement near the fence, and for an instant her legs wanted to run, or they did until she saw the edge of a school uniform and heard Samantha's laugh. Some people had a signature laugh.

Marni left the track to see what she was doing, then wished she hadn't. There were four of them, crouched low, their backs to the paling fence, sharing one cigarette, two boys Marni had known forever and a girl she didn't know who had a bunch of blonde hair half a metre long and a fancy mobile.

Obsessed by them, and in particular by iPhones, which did everything a camera or a computer could do, she joined the group.

'Can you take a photo of us?' the new girl asked. She had an American accent.

'Probably,' Marni said, eyeing her as the girl offered her phone. Marni put her schoolbag down to hold it, to feel the weight of it, the shape of it, while listening to instructions on how to make it work.

She got their cigarette in one of the boy's hands in the first shot, so had to take a second photograph because the new girl wanted to send it to her father.

'Her parents are divorced,' Samantha said. 'He's an American.'

Marni was more interested in the iPhone, now back in its owner's hands. She stood close, watching how she sent that photograph flying over the ocean to America.

'How long have you been in Australia?' she asked.

'I was born in Sydney but we lived in Kentucky until I was ten, when my folks split and Mom brought me back to Sydney – then down here.'

'She's not allowed to contact her father,' Samantha said.

'Why not?'

'I'm a hostage in Mom's war game,' the girl said. 'What's your name?'

'Marni Carter. Who are you?'

'Danni Lane.'

Marni turned away and picked up her bag, knowing who'd bought that iPhone. Lane wasn't a common name, not like Smith. She knew that Barbara Lane had divorced her American husband, that she'd transferred down from Sydney to steal Marni's mother's promotion.

Walked on then, thinking, *I'm a hostage in Mom's war game*, thinking how much better it was to have been born posthumously, better too to have your father run off with a girlfriend than having parents fight over who got custody of you.

HOME VIDEOS

*T*he finding of Monica Rowan's body had pushed the Swan trial from the headlines and Ross Hunter's mind, but not from the courts. He'd been sworn in at one thirty, had cleared the courtroom by one thirty-five and had since been sitting, cooling his heels while fat Freddy played his games behind closed doors.

After Ross's last run-in with Freddy, he'd watched a wife murderer walk, and if that clever little bastard got Cory's grandparents' home videos chucked out, Michael Swan would walk.

His girlfriend, pregnant with a possible baby Swan, had retracted her statement, and without it, all they had were those home videos. The grandparents had captured little Cory Martin's brief life story and Ross had seen them play it out on a modern television in their lounge room.

They'd raised him for the first eight months of his life, videoed a newborn not doing much, trapped a gurgling three month old wearing a Hawthorn football sweater, beanie and socks that Grandma had knitted. They'd caught a chubby two-toothed eight month old, crowing about how well he could crawl. Then the mother had taken Cory from his grandparents' care, and there'd been no further record of that brief life until his first birthday.

They'd videoed a rocking horse, a chocolate cake with one candle, and a wide-eyed matchstick boy who hadn't smiled for Grandpa's camera. They'd caught a bruised leg and backside before the screaming started. Not Cory's. Grandma's and the boyfriend's. There was a bare two seconds of it before someone turned off the camera.

'Did you report this?' Ross had asked the couple.

'We rang up a woman and I told her we had to get Cory away from those two or they'd kill him,' Grandma said.

'She did nothing,' Grandpa said.

'So we went around to where they were living to get him ourselves, and Mick went stark raving crazy. He attacked us.'

'We reported what he'd done to the police,' Grandma said. 'But they don't do anything when it's a family matter.'

Ross had done something that night. He'd arrested Swan and charged him with murder, on the strength of those home videos. They'd found a spot of Cory's blood on one of that bastard's shoes, but later. They'd found a dent in the hovel wall in the shape of an infant head – or a rounded bowl – or a bowling ball.

Without the home videos Freddy would make mincemeat of Grandma and Grandpa, and pretty boy Swan would walk, and if that bastard walked, Ross was running, taking off around Australia in his Commodore and leaving this shit behind him.

He checked his watch. Ten after two. Time moved more slowly within the great halls of justice. Closed his eyes and considered a tent, or a little fold-down van. A van maybe. He could damn near see himself heading out on the Hume Freeway—

Which switched his mind back to Monica.

They'd found his note. He always sent them a note. They knew the brand of shampoo he'd used on Monica's hair, where he'd bought the outfit she'd been found in. Hadn't found much else.

A careful, evil bastard, he drugged those girls, drowned then bathed them, shampooed their hair, brushed and tied it in pigtails with big pink bows and dressed them in brand new near-identical outfits, white socks, white briefs, pink t-shirts and short denim skirts. All the same. Then he tied them into identical garbage bags and tossed them from a moving vehicle to the side of a freeway.

The timing of the abductions suggested he was employed. All four had been taken on a Friday. Three of the four were found in the early hours of Monday mornings. Not Penny. A council worker had found her body out the back of Dandenong in the shrubbery growing beside the Monash Freeway, where it might have lain for two weeks.

Ross sighed and thought of the first of the victims, little Nancy Yang, a tiny dot of a girl, brought by her parents to Australia so she might have a better life. The investigation into her death had concentrated on the Asian community. Not until Penny Matthews was found had they known they'd had a child killer roaming the streets of Melbourne.

Then Heidi, taken from a busy shopping centre. She'd been caught on security video in the centre, and not one of them had shown her leaving it, either alone or with her killer. That bastard had got her out of there somehow. They'd found her dead six weeks later.

He shopped at Target. The outfits found on three of those girls had come from that store. All four had been drowned in tank water. In the last three, forensic had found high concentrations of diazepam.

But not in little Nancy. They'd found traces of penicillin in her, found inflammation in her lungs too. That murdering bastard had fed her the penicillin, wanting her alive longer to torment longer. He'd kept Monica alive for two months and two days.

Until the American case, that crazy Latino who'd kidnapped and kept three teenage girls as sex slaves, Ross had seen the killer holed up in a weekend shack. The Latino had changed his thinking.

He'd lived within the community and managed to keep his victims silent for ten years while going about his own life.

The bathing of those girls, the shampoo, suggested a house, and since the drought, half of the houses in Melbourne had rainwater tanks. Ross's sister had one. She'd kept her garden greener than her neighbour's. Ross shook his head, and got his mind back to Monica, back to the note, addressed to *The Hunters*.

How much less shall I answer him, and choose my words to reason with him. Though I were righteous yet would I not answer, but I would make supplication to my judge.

Taken alone, it suggested a God freak. They had four notes. The one he'd sent with Heidi had mentioned display boards, which had suggested to some that he might have been a collector of something.

Old cars maybe – old Holdens. To date they'd had no luck in locating his HG Holden on camera. Early days yet.

The wide pink satin ribbon he used on all four of his victims' hair flagged him, or his wife, mother, grandmother, as a hoarder. Johnson's team had done the rounds of haberdashers looking for that ribbon. A Lincraft employee identified it as discontinued stock. The killer had access to a roll of that discontinued stock, to a pair of sharp scissors, a measuring tape. Each of those hair ribbons had been cut to sixty centimetres in length, and cut on an angle, to minimise fraying.

A woman was more likely to cut ribbon in that way than was a male – unless he'd been in the haberdashery trade. The outfits, not too big, not too small, and the fact that he hadn't raped those girls, suggested to some that the killer was female.

A female behind the wheel of a forty-year-old Kingswood Holden? Possible, but Ross saw the killer as a male, a high achiever who may not have reached the heights he believed he'd deserved.

'A bloody lawyer,' he muttered. He didn't like lawyers. A cop worked his guts out to get a murderer into court, and along came some clever little bastard to put him back on the street. There had to be a better way than the jury system.

He glanced again at the courtroom door, knowing that fat Freddy couldn't allow those home videos to be viewed by the jury, that no one could view them and not come back with a guilty verdict.

The truckie who'd found Monica refused to be shaken on what he'd seen that night on the Hume Freeway. A light-coloured, probably white, early seventies Kingswood Holden.

'It braked, swerved to the right across two lanes, then took off like a bat out of buggery, its passenger-side door hanging open,' he'd said. 'For some reason, I thought wagon.'

The truckie could have seen some old codger with a faulty door, who lost control of the wheel while reaching to close it, or had seen that bag on the road and swerved to miss it. Ross had put those theories to the truckie, who'd come back at him with his own questions.

'Then why take off? Why not pull into the emergency lane, close his bloody door and walk back to see what was in that bag? I knew who was in it when I saw it disappearing beneath the truck. Anyone who watches the six o'clock news would have known young Monica was in that bag.'

He was right about that. Her abduction had been well reported, and her father had done what he could to keep her name in the news. A strong man, Monica's father. He'd broken when they'd asked him to identify his daughter. Back in the old days, women had been considered the weaker sex. Not these days. His wife had identified their girl.

A cop learned to handle death or he got out of the game fast. Ross had never learnt to handle the death of a child. Each one became personal. At one time he'd wanted kids, six of them. The job had killed that idea.

And he needed a smoke and glanced towards the exit, considering a quick puff. He wanted Swan off the street more – and he didn't want to front up here again tomorrow.

Weather conditions seemed to have played a role in how long those girls had survived. That was a definite. Nancy, the killer's only winter child, had lived for ten days; Penny, taken in autumn, might have lived for fifteen. Heidi, taken in midsummer, had survived for six weeks, and Monica, taken in mid-December, had made it through to February.

Given a motive and a fresh crime scene, good police work usually did the rest. The killer gave them no crime scene, no motive, no pattern to his method of taking those girls and no area to concentrate on.

He'd taken all four on Friday afternoons or evenings. Nancy had run out of her father's Footscray corner shop to get a library book she'd left in the car, some time between seven and eight. Penny had left her Doncaster school at three thirty to walk two blocks home. Heidi disappeared from a shopping centre at around four o'clock and Monica from a quiet residential street in Glen Waverley at eight on a summer evening. Other than abrasions around Nancy's ankle, any injuries to the bodies had been post mortem. He hadn't marked the others – he or she. Again Ross pondered the *she*. Nancy could have been picked up and carried by a midget. Not Monica. She would have been capable of fighting off the average woman.

Hours had been spent perusing porn sites on the internet. If the killer was into photography, his artwork hadn't turned up on the web. He had access to a computer. His notes were computer generated, laser printed on A4 paper he folded small before placing them into his victims' mouths. An evil, malevolent ghost, he haunted Ross's days.

And fat Freddy was wasting this one.

Not waste to him. Life's blood to him.

Ross glanced at his watch. Freddy had now been arguing for near on an hour. If it continued much longer, the judge would send the jury home. Like Ross, they were locked out of the courtroom.

Twelve strangers, each toting his or her own bias, thrown together for as long as it took, a ridiculous system in an era when information on any subject could be found on a mobile. The daily newspapers were available online, or their headlines were. Most readers only had time to read the headlines. Newspaper sales were down – and so they ought to be. Newspaper editors were fickle bastards. They'd been in love with Cory Martin for a week, after he was dead. They were in love with his murderer now, who came up well on camera.

Looks were important. Women starved themselves to look good, paid surgeons a fortune to chop off a bit here, suck out a bit there, inject a bit. Ross's brow could use a few shots of botox. He was getting a headache. A smoke would fix it.

A lot of years ago, a girl he'd almost loved, Janice, had told him he'd looked like Robert De Niro. Could have married her.

He'd had his mum back then. Lost her two years ago. She hadn't gone slowly, as the elderly were supposed to. She'd been full of beans when he'd left for work that morning and missing when he'd come home. He'd found her by torchlight, dead beneath her clothes line, her laundry basket beside her.

Lost his mother's Hawthorn house five months later. His sisters, eight and ten years his junior, had needed cash more than the memories. They cleared 1.2 million on that house, a bulk of money, even when split three ways. Could have bought a unit with it. Hadn't wanted to own anything, had wanted to be free to cut and run – and the longer they left him sitting out here, the more he felt like doing it, and the more frequently his hand moved to his pocket to fondle his packet of smokes.

Not so long ago there'd been ashtrays here. Not any more. Smokers congregated where they could these days. He'd had a few interesting conversations with companion lepers. Six months ago he'd begged a light from the mother of that wife killer when they'd shared a sheltering courthouse wall one windy day. She was a nice woman too, though he'd wanted to put a boot in her backside when she'd walked away celebrating with her murdering son, all thanks to fat Freddy.

Before presenting himself here today, Ross had snatched a smoke in the shade of that same wall and been joined there by a newshound he'd known all his life, Les, born with ulterior motives.

'Is he gunna walk, Ross?' he'd greeted him.

'Ask fat Freddy,' Ross said.

'Anything new on the Kingswood wagon?'

'Thanks to you lot, we've had callers from Mildura to Moe dobbing in their neighbours,' Ross said, knowing those words would turn up in tomorrow's headlines – but from an unnamed source.

And thank Christ, they were calling his name.

THAT TUESDAY

*S*arah blamed Barbara Lane for her sore throat. She blamed David Crow, and the stress of attempting to get his payroll done with his sulking mistress stuck to her left elbow and making it obvious that she was there under sufferance.

The Crows owned whitegoods stores in five states. They had small offices in Perth and Sydney, but ran their entire company out of their Melbourne office. The payroll was huge, as were the figures Sarah played with each day. She didn't make mistakes, but it took her full concentration not to add an extra zero or lose one. The computer's accounting system was brilliant. It did most of the work, but her attempt to teach it to Barbara was wasted effort.

If there was anything behind her perfect façade, Sarah hadn't seen it. She was smooth hair, perfect makeup, gorgeous fingernails attached to useless hands – like a mannequin in a boutique window, dressed each day to display another dazzling outfit, always cool, relaxed, beautiful, but lifeless.

Sarah wasn't cool. The office was chilled to a comfortable twenty-three degrees, and she was burning, and each time she used her voice, her throat felt as if someone had taken a rasp to her tonsils.

'I asked you to write it down!'

'Go,' Sarah said, and the senior payroll/accounts officer actually looked her in the eye, coolly.

'Go!'

Barbara understood her the second time, or perhaps understood the hand Sarah flung with the word. She went, not to her office but to Crow's. Ten minutes later, the huntsman spider crawled on Sarah's shoulder.

Bob Webb was paid well to manage Crow's office and Sarah knew to the last cent how much he was paid. Maybe he earned it.

'She needs to learn the job,' he said.

'Why bother when she's got three males to wipe her arse?' Jackie said, and Bob, one of the three males, forgot who he was, where he was.

'Stuff your comments up yours,' he said, then blushed to the roots of his receding hair, and Jackie laughed. She'd made a bet in the tearoom with Shane that she'd break through Bob's managerial façade before Crow sacked her, and she'd won. It was an unfair bet. She knew someone who knew someone who used to work nights with Bob Webb at Kmart, long before he'd been an office manager.

Shane turned his wheelchair to salute her. He was small enough to be a twelve year old, looked twenty but was Sarah's age, almost thirty-two, and he was in love with Jackie – because she refused to acknowledge his wheelchair. She'd accused him yesterday of sniffing around Barbie doll's arse like a mixed-breed mutt at a pedigree poodle. He'd accused her of being jealous.

'Crow needs her trained,' Bob said.

'She coming back, I will go home,' Sarah said.

*

At two forty, Detective Senior Sergeant Ross Hunter took his place in the witness box for the second time, and when he mentioned the grandparents' home videos for the second time, he didn't clear the courtroom.

At two forty-five, Sarah raised *Barbara Jean Lane* to her screen and saw the inflated figure she'd receive for a month of sitting on her backside looking decorative and it was too much for diseased tonsils to swallow.

She sat staring at the figure, which her hand refused to transfer. She told her hand to get on with it. It responded by closing that knowledgeable accounting program down then sending a fast email to HR, claiming a doctor's appointment.

A 75 tram from Flinders Street would deliver her to the Kmart Plaza where there was a medical centre, and if she wanted to pay herself for this afternoon and tomorrow, she'd need a doctor's certificate, which would cost her sixty dollars. She didn't have sixty dollars in her purse, so she walked the shorter distance to Museum Station and rode a train to Blackburn, the bus to Hawthorn Road, then walked, and was close to collapse when she got there.

School was out. Marni fed her two Panadols. She told her to go to bed.

'Mrs Vaughn dinner.'

'I'll feed her. You do as you're told, Mum.'

She went, and woke at dawn feeling worse.

Marni looked at her tonsils at eight and told her they looked like diseased minced steak and that they were getting a taxi to see a doctor.

No money, Sarah signed, her throat too sore to talk.

Two Aspros and hot porridge eased it, but not enough to argue when Marni picked up the phone to make an appointment. She got one for ten o'clock, then refused to go to school until her mother promised to keep it.

A walk south through the pipeline took her to Burwood Highway, only a short tram ride from the Kmart Plaza. At nine thirty she withdrew a hundred dollars at an ATM, then took a chair in the clinic's waiting room where she was still sitting at ten thirty, and when her name was finally called, the doctor was Asian.

Those who spoke with accents were near impossible to lip-read, so she showed him her hearing aids, took her notepad and pen from her bag, and wrote, *I have a very sore throat. I need a certificate for my work.*

'Where do you work?' he asked, and accent or not, his words were clear.

'Office. City,' she said.

He came from behind his desk to shine a light down her throat, and like Marni, he said, 'Yuck.' Then, 'Take your hearing aids out, Mrs Carter.'

She understood that too and took them out fast to prove it. He looked in her ears, felt her glands, then her forehead.

'You've got a temperature,' he said.

'Outside is very hot.'

'Are you allergic to any antibiotics?'

'I don't want, thank you. Only certificate.'

He took her temperature, took her blood pressure, and if it was high it was caused by Barbara Lane, not her throat.

'You need antibiotics and bed rest,' he said, and he started writing.

He gave her a prescription, and a certificate for work, not for today and yesterday but for the remainder of the week. And the payroll wasn't finished. Bob's fault, and he knew that accounting system, so let him worry about it.

*

The doctor watching, she replaced her hearing aids, and he asked how much she heard with them.

'Big noise. Fire truck. Banging things. Not much.'

'Your lip-reading skills are very good,' he said, and opened the door.

'Thank you.' She knew she said that well. She'd worked with a speech therapist in Perth to perfect the Y in *you*.

And he bulk-billed her. She had to give the receptionist her Medicare card but no money. There was a pharmacy at the other end of the centre. She considered the distance and the cost. Some scripts cost a fortune. Saltwater gargles and three days off plus the weekend would fix her throat. She had Panadol in her handbag and Aspros at home.

Couldn't read. She tried to. Couldn't find anything to watch on the television, so decided to turn a lump of frozen mince into bolognaise.

The microwave thawed it. The meat was frying in the pan when she heard, or felt, noise. Her hand traced it to the phone. It vibrated when it rang, and if she was at the bench where it lived, she usually felt its ring.

She felt it again while she was dicing an onion, and this time she hit the *talk* button and listened. Couldn't hear a voice, but the rhythm of the vibrations was different. Someone wanting to sell her something? She hit the *off* button and added the onions to her frying meat. And felt that noise again.

Indian call centres are tenacious – *ten-a-shuss*. Or was it Jackie, letting her know she'd sent an email? She'd done that once when Sarah had been at home on holiday. She stood over the phone, palms on the bench, feeling the rhythm of the sound. If she had an implant she'd hear a phone ringing, and maybe voices, if her auditory nerve woke up and learned to listen.

The noise stopped and she turned on the laptop. It was old and took its time warming up, but when it did, three emails came through, two from Bob.

Hi Sarah, will you be coming in today? Bob Webb. He'd sent that one at eight forty, then another at ten twenty. *Hi Sarah. If you feel up to it, grab a taxi. The company will pay. Bob.*

And Jackie's. *They're in the shit! Take a month off. J.J.*

Sarah wrote one reply she sent to Bob, Jackie and HR.

The doctor gave me the week off. I will be in on Monday.

Bare seconds after she clicked *send*, another message came through from Bob. It echoed Jackie's, minus the expletive.

Again Sarah replied. *I'm turning the computer off now and going to bed.*

She didn't go to her bed. She grated carrot, added it and a heaped teaspoon of minced garlic to her pan, then a flat spoon of curry powder. She was opening a can of crushed tomatoes when Mrs Vaughn smelt the garlic and invited herself in.

'What's that stink?'

'Dinner,' Sarah said.

'I'm telling you now, I won't be eating it, and what are you doing home at this hour of the day?'

'Doctor,' Sarah said. 'Very bad throat.'

'You young people don't know what sick is. I take twelve pills a day just to keep myself alive, and I need a new script for my heart pills.'

'I get the car out?'

'I'm not up to going out in this heat. If you'd told me you were going to the doctor I could have given you my script this morning.'

'Sorry,' Sarah said as her landlady came closer to sniff. There was little left of her. Sarah wasn't tall, but taller than her landlady.

'What the hell are you cooking?'

Bolognaise too hard to say, Sarah replied, 'Sauce.'

'What sort of sauce?'

'For pasta.'

'It stinks, and what am I going to do about my heart pills?'

'Marni will go. After school.'

'I'll probably be dead by then.'

The mess of meat transferred to a saucepan, the can of crushed tomatoes poured in plus a palm full of dried oregano, two bay leaves, salt then black pepper, and Sarah sneezed. Mrs Vaughn, who'd spent twelve years dodging her lodgers' germs, didn't trust that sneeze. She toddled back to her house.

*

Sarah was sleeping when Marni came in. Unaccustomed to having her mother at home before six, Marni went about her usual business of turning on the computer, making herself a milk coffee that she drank while checking the emails. One new email came through, an impersonal *Thank you* from HR. She read the previous messages, checked the bench then her mother's handbag for pills, and found a prescription. She checked the purse for money. There was plenty to pay for a prescription, and whether her mother wanted it filled or not, it was being filled. Marni had lived through Sarah's sore throats before.

The script folded and safe in the purse, she emptied her coffee mug, checked the level of milk left in the bottle, knew they needed bread. She was almost out the door when Mrs Vaughn came across the lawn wanting in – as if she owned the place, which she did, but she had no right to wander in and out of it, not when they paid her rent.

'Mum's sick,' Marni said, guarding the door against her.

'Your mother said you'd get my heart pills. I've been out of them all day.'

And the phone rang, and for once Marni picked it up willingly, pleased to listen to someone selling funeral insurance if it got rid of Mrs Vaughn. 'Marni Carter speaking,' she said.

'Bob Webb,' he said. 'I work with your mother. How is she?'

'Sick in bed. The doctor gave her a prescription I have to get filled.'

Mrs Vaughn was in and waving money and prescriptions under Marni's nose. She took them, waved a hand at her to go, then gave her attention back to the man on the phone, who was offering to pick up the script and have it filled.

'We need bread and other stuff at the supermarket,' she said.

'Make a list,' he said.

Couldn't give him Mrs Vaughn's scripts. If he forgot to get a receipt, she'd argue about her change.

'I have to get a few other things, but thanks,' she said.

'I'll drive you over,' Bob Webb said. 'I should be there in half an hour.'

Marni was thinking Freeway Killer before he came. He worked from Monday to Friday. She knew he lived at home with his mother. She was thinking of waiting for a bus too and walking in the stinking heat, so she waited to get a look at him.

He didn't look dangerous. He was small, had a boyish face and he drove a shiny blue-green car.

'I hope you're not the Freeway Killer,' she greeted him.

'Your mum will vouch for me,' he said and he smiled. He had a nice smile.

THE WANTING

*H*e saw her again, that leggy gazelle of a girl, in the supermarket
where the air was full of scents. A sniff of roasting chicken, of
cheese, of fresh-baked bread – but behind those scents today he could
smell her.

He edged closer in the meat aisle, close enough to watch the fall of
her hair as she looked at the bloody displays.

Wanted her. Knew he couldn't have her. Knew he shouldn't have
been tailing her, not in this place where big brother watched his every
move. He took a step back then looked up, seeking big brother's hidden
eye. Couldn't find it. Knew it was up there watching him, had been
watching since he'd sighted that pretty thing, and he swung around on
his heel and walked back to the coffee aisle. He'd come here for coffee,
not to window shop.

And there she was again, walking towards the self-service checkout.
Perfection in school uniform.

An Easter gift, his inner voice urged.

Too early, the voice of control replied.

When could you resist an early-bird special?

Wrong time. Wrong place. Wrong way. Go back.

Baked beans were on special. He picked up two cans, their weight in his hand a tangible promise: that though today's delay was necessary, it may be temporary. He was on his way to the checkout before he noticed the cans of beans didn't have ring-pull seals. He required ring-pulls. Annoyed, he returned them to the shelf and chose a more expensive can, with a ring-pull.

She was gone when he reached the checkouts. He knew where to find her, when he was ready. Twice now he'd seen her at this centre.

Playing Millionaire

Sarah was in the kitchen boiling a pot of pasta when they came in, loaded with supermarket bags. Caught barefoot, in short shorts, she was mortified, and more so when she saw what they'd spent her money on.

They'd bought a large bottle of orange juice, cans of tomato soup, Aspros, Nurofen, anti-bacterial lozenges, bananas, expensive bread, a huge bottle of milk Marni knew not to buy. There was nowhere to fit it in the fridge. And they'd found that script and paid for antibiotic capsules.

'You have to take two straight away, then one three times a day, half an hour before meals until they're all gone,' Marni said, popping two from their bubble pack and offering them, and with Bob watching, Sarah had to swallow them.

'He won't take any money for that, Mum,' Marni said, and left them in the kitchen while she delivered Mrs Vaughn's pills.

He stood, looking as uncomfortable as Sarah felt – and looking at the faded green curtains, at the two battered wooden chairs and Sarah, wanting him gone, did a fast totalling of what was in the supermarket bags, then pushed two twenties at him.

He wouldn't take them. He was on his way out when Marni returned.

'You're not leaving until we pay you,' she said, refusing him exit.

'Bossy boots,' he said, and took one of the twenties. 'I hope you're feeling better soon, Sarah. I live nearby – if you need anything. It's no trouble.'

'Thank you,' Sarah said, and Marni saw him out and closed the gate behind him.

'He's nice, Mum. I thought he'd be sort of . . . rotten,' Marni said.

'I don't say rotten.'

'You said he was a robot, that Crow pressed buttons on his remote control and Bob Webb moved. And you said he was little. He's taller than you. How tall was my father?'

'Taller than Bob.'

'It felt funny, shopping with a man,' Marni admitted, making space on the lower shelf of the fridge for the large bottles, squeezing them in on their sides. 'People probably thought he was my father. How come he isn't married, Mum?'

Sarah shrugged and read the instructions on the packet of Nurofen tablets, small tablets, white, and the packet said take two. She took one.

*

Be it the Nurofen, the doctor's capsules or the salt gargles, her throat improved in the night, and by midday on Thursday, after two more capsules and an overdose of Mrs Vaughn, Sarah sent Bob an email. It was the last day of February and she was well enough to work, if Crow provided a taxi to get her there.

His reply was immediate. *Taxi ordered for one o'clock.*

It picked her up in the driveway and delivered her to the kerb outside her building's door, where Bob was waiting with one of Crow's cabcharge cards. He rode up with her in the lift, walked in with her, and kept Barbara Lane busy in her own office.

Crow came to Sarah's workstation at four, effusive with his appreciation of her commitment to the 'team'. He didn't offer a cabcharge for a taxi home, but at four thirty, she felt the huntsman creep across her shoulder.

Bob drove her home. He picked her up on Friday morning and when she thanked him that night in Mrs Vaughn's driveway, he told her he'd see her on Monday at seven thirty.

'I can get train. Thank you.'

'It's no trouble for me to swing by here. Seven thirty,' he said.

Marni killed the discussion. 'The jury just came back and he's guilty, Mum.'

'Michael Swan?' Bob Webb asked while Mrs Vaughn hammered on her window.

'It only finished at lunchtime,' Marni said. 'A news man outside the court just said it took the jury less than four hours to reach their verdict – and you'd better go before she breaks that window.'

*

He went, but was back on Saturday morning. He and his mother were on their way to Forest Hill.

'Do you need anything at the shops?' he asked.

'We need a lift there,' Marni said, and Mrs Vaughn came out her back door to complain about cars in her driveway and the three cigarettes in her packet.

She followed them to the car, and when they were in, and the doors closed, when they'd met Bob's mother, she asked if Mrs Vaughn was their grandmother.

'Landlady,' Marni said.

A different Saturday morning, that one. Marni helped Bob and his mother choose a dark grey suit and two shirts, and she watched Bob hand over his card to pay three hundred and twenty dollars, then watched his mother hand over her own at the supermarket to pay for a leg of lamb and a pile of expensive items that Sarah never even looked at.

Then the best part of that morning, when she nicked into the Telstra shop to dream about mobiles, Bob followed her in and told her he had an old mobile she could use. For two minutes Marni thought she had her mobile, but phones needed a sim card and a plan and they cost money.

It was still a good morning. No walk home from the bus stop, loaded down like pack mules. Bob unloading their shopping in the driveway. They'd forgotten things. They'd meant to look for a dress for Marni to wear to Samantha's party, and to buy her a present. They'd forgotten curry, but they'd bought a huge bottle of tomato sauce and a whole pumpkin and a big bag of potatoes they wouldn't have been able to carry home from the bus stop.

Some days just get better and better. Marni's team won at basketball, and when she thought her perfect day was over, someone knocked on their door.

Bob again, with his old mobile and its charger, and a computer printout of Telstra's prices. He'd highlighted one which claimed that if they bundled their landline, broadband and mobile on the same plan, it wouldn't cost them much more each month than they paid now – and they'd get fifty free text messages every month.

He stayed for an hour, showing Marni how to use his new iPhone, a magical thing with a touch screen that could find their street and his, and show only Blackburn and Burwood Highway between them. He googled London and showed her a hotel where he'd spent two nights four years ago.

The television was on; it usually was. Only Sarah was watching it when the TattsLotto balls started tumbling out.

'I forgot!' she said, and rose from her chair because the first number out was one of theirs. Then out came sixteen, another one of theirs, and she ran outside.

Marni didn't. She slid from her seat on the table to stand before the screen, holding her breath, knowing that her mother's sore throat, caused by Barbara Lane, had just cost them a car, a house and two brand new iPhones.

It hadn't. The next number to roll out, a thirteen, wasn't one of theirs, nor were any of the others.

You can't call to a deaf person, and even if you hunt them down in the dark, they can't lip-read. There were ways around that problem. She flicked the outside light on and off until Sarah came in from the dark.

'How many?' she asked.

'Two, and that's all we ever get. Change our numbers, Mum.'

'We know them,' Sarah said.

'Mum knows hers too,' Bob said. 'She's been taking the same ones since the first TattsLotto draw and she's never won more than sixty dollars.'

'We got twelve dollars at Christmas time,' Marni said. 'And thirty once.'

Bob had a quick pick in Powerball, which had jackpotted to almost twenty million.

'What would you buy if you won it?' Marni asked.

'I'd spend six months in Peru,' he said. 'What would you buy?'

'We don't buy Powerball, but if we did and we won, I'd make Mum retire and get a cochlear implant,' Marni said.

They played millionaires in a room that was little more than a squat for the homeless, Marni, who'd given up her chair to Bob, perched on the table, beside their antique laptop. Their television was new, and currently showing a huge man having his stomach banded.

'How come invalid pensioners can afford to buy enough food to stay as fat as him?' Marni asked.

'Subsidised housing. Charity handouts,' Bob said.

'Turn it off,' Sarah said.

'It's interesting, Mum. Was anyone in our family fat?'

'No.'

'What about my father's family?'

'Operation make me feel sick, Marni.'

Maybe it made Bob feel sick. He said he supposed he ought to be getting home, and when the door closed behind him, Marni told her mother that she liked him, that he was like a normal person.

'You like his phone.'

'I love his iPhone. And I want a sim card, but I like the way he talks normal to you. Are you ever going to get married again?'

'No.'

'I wouldn't mind, or not if you married someone like him.'

'Go to bed.'

'It's Saturday and I'm almost thirteen. If you got married again, you might have more kids.'

Sarah switched channels, to a commercial. It was Murphy's Law that every time you switched channels you got a commercial.

'Can we get one, and bundle our phone?'

'We paying for the school camp this month.'

'I don't want the camp. It only lasts for ten days. I'd have that mobile forever.'

APPEASEMENT AND
AGGRAVATION

*D*avid left the office at midday to fly to Sydney. Barbara left at two twenty to have a light trim and her roots done. Like Danni, she'd been born a natural platinum blonde. Age had darkened her hair, but since returning to Australia she'd had it returned to its original shade, which meant having the roots done every six weeks. In Sydney, she'd had her hairdresser trained, but the fool down here had cut too much off her fringe, and she'd ended up screaming at him like a fishwife.

She'd had her nails done at the same place; they, at least, were worth the money. She'd chosen the colours to match her bedroom, peach pink with a gold flower on each nail, and she admired them again when she hit the remote to turn on the air conditioner.

'Danni.'

No reply. She never replied. Needing to show her nails to someone, she climbed those stairs. And she wasn't up there, not in her room, study or bathroom.

Downstairs again, and she was growing to hate those stairs, but she got her mobile and picked out a fast text.

I told you I'd be home early. Where the hell are you? A reply came back, a brief reply.

On my way.

Her own mirror agreed that the brainless swine had cut too much off her fringe. The colour was perfect. She combed her hair, checked the comb for fallout. No fallout.

David would notice her nails. He noticed everything – and he'd be out of town for two days – and she couldn't stand that bloody office without him – and she could have flown up to Sydney with him. She'd suggested it, suggested dropping Danni off to her grandfather up there.

'School,' he'd said.

He didn't like Danni, and she didn't like him. He hadn't known about her until two months into the relationship. Barbara had never advertised the fact to anyone that she had a half-grown kid. He'd told her that he had four kids before she'd come clean about Danni.

'I see them at weekends,' he'd said, which she'd understood to mean that he was divorced and had custody of his kids at weekends. She'd never met them when she'd flown down to spend weekends at his Docklands unit.

It was on the twenty-third floor and it had a view of the bay, and boats. She could have been happy living there. Five times she'd flown down before her mother died. She'd been in Melbourne the day her mother had the stroke that killed her.

And her father had blamed her for it, or blamed her divorce, and her involvement with David, the only light in her life. Being with him had been like walking out of a dark cave full of blood-sucking bats into sunlight. He was everything she'd ever hoped to find in a man – or he had been before she'd moved to Melbourne.

He was different now and Danni not only hated him, she hated Barbara, and her school, where she'd picked up with a slut of a girl who was allowed to run wild.

Nothing was as Barbara had imagined it would be. She'd never seen herself stuck out here in the suburbs, going to work every day – just to appease his bloody wife.

Danni said that he'd set her up as his mistress. She said he had plans for mother and daughter threesomes – and had got a slap across the mouth for that one.

She didn't need to work. She'd got money enough from her settlement to live on. It was David who needed her to work.

Knowing people too well ruined relationships. In Sydney, she hadn't known about his spider phobia. Barbara could squash one beneath her shoe without flinching. He wouldn't even stay in the same room to watch where it went while she got something to squash it with.

She had a phobia about turning forty and being alone. She had a phobia about having a stroke and dying paralysed with a twisted face. She had a phobia about working in a bloody circus, surrounded by David's freak show.

From day one she hadn't been able to look at Rena, the circus fat lady, or Shane. She couldn't stand Sarah Carter. She was educated, knew what she was doing, but sounded like a retard, and retards gave Barbara the creeps. When she had to communicate with her now she did it via email, and this morning she'd sent her three, asking for the code for the Geelong store, and that bitch hadn't replied to one of them. And when Barbara had complained to Bob Webb, who used to be helpful, he'd told her that her computer had access to the same information as Mrs Jesus Christ Carter's.

'I can't find them if she won't tell me where to find them, can I?'

'Try communicating directly with her,' he'd said.

And he wouldn't have had the guts to say that if David had been in his office, and if he wasn't going to be in his office for two days – she wouldn't be either.

Couldn't stand being there without him.

'It won't be forever,' he said when she complained, but every day was forever, and if he didn't stop appeasing his bitch of a wife soon, Barbara was packing up and going home.

Home to where? To her father? She couldn't stand living with him. She'd have to, unless she spent her divorce settlement on a unit and furniture, which, if she did, wouldn't leave her enough left to live on, or not enough to live the way she liked to live.

Appeasement: Appearances: Aggravation: Affair: Adulterer.

He'd probably taken his wife and kids up to Sydney, which was why he wouldn't take her and Danni. He'd probably sleep with his wife tonight, to appease her, so she wouldn't sell her half of the business. He liked being the sole ringmaster of his bloody circus.

And the front door slammed. 'Where have you been? Do you realise what time it is?' Barbara yelled, because she needed to yell at someone, because her fringe was too short and that kid had stuffed up her life. 'And if I've told you once, I've told you a dozen times not to hang around that shopping centre with that little slut.'

'You told me to buy something for dinner, too, and I had to buy Sam a present.'

'It doesn't take two hours to buy a present and something for dinner.'

'Try catching a bus sometime, Barb. Try walking. It burns up kilojoules.'

The cowboy she'd divorced had called her Barb – or barbed wire – and that kid could do his accent to a T.

'You put on his accent just to annoy me. You've been back here long enough to lose it, and my name is Barbara.'

She'd never called her Mum. Couldn't speak when he'd taken her home to America, and by the time Barbara had gone over there to get her, she'd forgotten she had a mother. She'd called the cowboy Daddy, called his parents Nan and Pop.

*

Danni ran upstairs to her bathroom. It had a lock on the door and she'd got a text just before she'd come inside, and knew what it would be about.

We've got a court date, Monday 22 April, Dano.

I can't stand it until April.

You can stand it. You're as tough as old boots.

If you get me, will we be able to go home?

Wherever we are, you and me are home, Dano. Hang strong.

Love you.

Ditto Daddy. xox

FRIDAY 15 MARCH

'He's got the hots for you,' Jackie said. Bob Webb and Sarah's altered relationship hadn't gone unnoticed in the office.

'He living near me. I pay for petrol,' Sarah defended.

He picked her up at the kerb each workday morning, dropped her off in Mrs Vaughn's driveway each night, beeped his horn in reply when the old lady hammered on her window – and refused to take money for petrol. Last Friday she'd put a twenty-dollar note in his glove box, and would put another one in it tonight – which didn't alter the fact that Jackie was right, that Bob wanted more from her than a business relationship.

Marni called him her boyfriend – and Sarah felt like one of Gramp's cows being herded towards a place where it didn't want to go.

It would be an easier place, for Marni. It would be a place where Sarah could spend money on both school camp and a mobile phone and not worry about her bank balance, but after the easier always came the harder, which no one showed in romance movies, which always ended when brides in beautiful dresses and handsome grooms drove off into the sunset. It was what came after the sunset that you had to live with.

And Jackie knew all about it, too. She'd been married twice, the first time for twelve years to the father of her four kids, who'd almost finished paying off their house when he'd died of pancreatic cancer. She'd been working at Crows when she'd met her second husband, online, a rich businessman who, like Crow, had businesses in every state, or so he'd said.

He'd lived with Jackie and her kids between his business trips, then when she'd married him, he'd wanted her to mortgage her house and put the money into his business.

She'd been in love, but was no fool. She'd found out that there were no businesses and that he'd owed a fortune to everyone so she'd divorced him, then the courts made her borrow a hundred thousand dollars on her house to give to him. And she dared play matchmaker?

She started it again at lunchtime, in the tearoom, so Sarah picked up her lunch and took the lift down to the street where she ate while walking up to buy her TattsLotto ticket. Being picked up and delivered home by Bob had changed more than one of her routines.

Five dreamers queued there to hand over their money, hope on some faces, annoyance on others. She was annoyed at herself for not being brave enough to stop buying her Saturday system seven. One man, full up with hope, handed over a fifty-dollar note to pay for his dream, and how could anyone afford to waste fifty dollars on gambling? That's what buying those tickets was, just wasting a few dollars in the hope of finding that pot of gold at the end of the rainbow.

She handed the Indian man the right money in coins, and her numbers and registration card, then watched his narrow brown hands count her coins before he wiped her card. His hands went still and he said something. She looked at his face. Maybe the price had gone up again.

'Pardon?' she said, and he said words that looked like, *You have a win*. His hand wasn't out for more money. She smiled, knowing that if she'd had a win it hadn't been in last Saturday's draw. She and Marni had watched it, and not one of their numbers had come out. She could have won something the week Crow gave Barbara Lane the job. Anything could have happened that week.

He spoke again, and his mouth may have said *Powerball*. She never bought Powerball. It cost more than Saturday Lotto, and even if all of her numbers came out, she'd need to have picked the right Powerball.

'No ticket,' she said. The queue behind her growing, the Indian man processed her numbers.

'Good luck,' he said.

'Thank you,' she said, and walked back the way she'd come, eating grapes and looking at the sky. Mystical Melbourne was in for a storm. It would wash the heat away – or make it humid and hot. You never could tell with Melbourne's weather.

They were still in the tearoom, Jackie, Rena, Shane and two part-timers. Sarah was making a coffee when Bob came in, so she made two – and she caught Jackie's wink to Rena. Bob took his coffee back to his office. Sarah sat opposite Rena.

'She's eighty-two and still thinks she's running the show,' Rena said.

She spent a lot of time talking about her mother-in-law. Jackie spent a lot of time running down the conman she'd shed – and judges. Sarah never offered personal information. She'd told them she'd lost her parents in a car accident, that she'd lived in Perth with a foster family until she'd married at eighteen. They knew that Marni's father had died of a brain tumour, but that was all they knew.

Everyone knew that Barbara Lane and David Crow had had a lovers' tiff. She'd taken another day off this week.

'He's got her pregnant,' Rena guessed, and Jackie laughed. In the smaller space of the tearoom, when sitting at her side, Sarah could hear Jackie's laugh.

'She came in late,' Shane said. 'He took her to lunch.' Some mouths were easy to read. Shane's wasn't, but he had an expressive face, which made reading him easier. 'His wife knows about her,' he said.

'She knew about Eve,' Jackie said.

Eve was the blonde before Barbara. She'd worked in HR and had made a lot of noise the morning Crow's previous manager had walked her out of the office.

Shane knew that Eve now worked for the estate agent who'd sold Crow the house Barbara Lane lived in. He knew that Eve had sent Maureen Crow an email about that house. He knew that the day Eve had been walked from the office like a thief, she'd vowed to get back at Crow.

And Sarah knew more than Shane. Bob was a gossip in the car. 'Just between you and me,' he'd say. Or, 'This goes no further.' Once he'd said, 'This is for your ears only,' then realised what he'd said, blushed and added, 'I forget that you can't hear a word I say.'

Marni said that. 'I forget that you're deaf, Mum.'

Lynette Clark used to say the same thing.

Bob returned to the tearoom to wash and dry his mug, and place it on the shelf.

'He's house trained too,' Rena said to Sarah. 'A house-trained man is a rarity, love.'

*

At four thirty that Friday afternoon, a taxi delivered Barbara home. She paid with a company cabcharge. She'd used a cabcharge this morning and it hadn't taken that driver as long to process it.

Snatched the ticket when he was done and ran. Unlocked her front door and gave it an almighty slam behind her, flung her handbag at the couch, then howled.

Fridays were her days. They went out to dinner on Fridays, then David drove her home and stayed with her until Saturday afternoon.

'Lying bastard,' she howled.

And the air conditioner wasn't on, and that bloody house he'd bought was a sweatbox without it, and she couldn't find the remote.

'Danni. Where did you put that bloody remote?'

She found it with the television remotes. Pointed, pressed, then pitched it at the couch and walked upstairs, yelling Danni's name.

She wasn't at her computer, wasn't in her room. Barbara slammed both doors and almost lost her footing on the way down, and who needed a bloody house with stairs you spent your life climbing, looking for a twelve-year-old bitch of a girl?

She was stripping to shower when she remembered David's pills. He left a packet in her bathroom cabinet, Xanax, his sleeping pills. That's what she needed, to sleep and forget about him and his bloody wife and everything else. She popped one from its bubble wrap, washed it down with a handful of water then stripped to her briefs and crawled into bed, unshowered and smelling of him.

She'd thought he'd had something big to tell her, thought he'd taken her out for an early lunch and ordered champagne so he could drop an engagement ring into her glass, like she'd seen once in a movie. She wanted a ring, had expected something more than an afternoon in his bed.

That's all she'd got, and when the bastard rolled off her, he'd said what he'd taken her out to lunch to say.

'My in-laws are celebrating fifty years of marriage tomorrow night. I've been given an ultimatum, my pet. They're meeting me here at four thirty.'

'Your in-laws?'

'Maureen and the children. I'm driving them up to Echuca.'

She was his life, not his bitch of a wife and her kids. She meant more to him than his stuffed-up life which she'd allowed to become her own stuffed-up life.

'Fridays are mine,' she'd said, and felt like his mistress, like his Friday night mistress.

'Her father isn't a well man. It may be the last time we see him.'

Then the bastard had looked at his watch.

'If you go up there with her, it's over, David,' she'd said.

'We have time for a shower, but insufficient time to argue, my pet,' he'd said.

She wasn't his bloody pet or his Friday night fling. She hadn't showered with him. She'd dressed, called a taxi, slammed the hell out of his doors then left.

Beautiful little pill. She could feel it dissolving her anger, feel it untangling the coil of stress in her lungs. She loved his pill but hated him. She was going home. She was packing up tonight and leaving before the traffic got bad in the morning, and stuff him and his cow of a wife.

*

There was a queue of traffic waiting to make a right-hand turn onto Burwood Highway, a dozen cars, trucks and vans in front of them when Bob invited Sarah to his mother's birthday party on Saturday night. She shook her head.

'She'd like you to come,' he said.

'Marni,' she said.

'I mean both of you. It's just family, and a couple of Mum's mates. There'll be kids everywhere.'

Marni would want to go so she could wear the new dress they'd bought for Samantha's party, a cute girly dress that showed her legs and her emerging shape. The tram stop was a minute away from Bob's mother's front door. They could go for an hour or two and come home before dark – if it wasn't raining.

'What time?' Sarah asked.

'We're walking in on her at seven thirty,' he said. 'She doesn't know anything about it.'

They made the turn onto Burwood Highway, then took a roundabout route to Mrs Vaughn's driveway, and Raymond's Commodore was parked again in the Hyundai's space.

'Whose car?' Bob asked.

'Her son. We can't make her car start. She don't driving far enough to charge her battery, so he take sometime to drive . . . a long way.'

'You drive?'

'I can. No licence.'

She'd taken a twenty from her purse while he'd been concentrating on the road, and held it scrunched in her hand until they were in the driveway, when she opened his glove box, tossed the note in, and was out the door, her back turned to his argument.

Thought he'd left until she attempted to close the gate. Marni was outside, watering the daphne, and probably pleading with it not to drop its last half-dozen yellowing leaves.

'It needs shade,' Bob said.

They moved the pot into the shade between the unit and the western fence, and he spoke again about his mother's party, and of course Marni wanted to go.

'We will come for little while,' Sarah sighed.

'I'll pick you up at a quarter past seven,' he said, and was gone, when Marni took the hose around to the daphne's new home and found the two twenties in its pot.

'What's this?'

'Bugger! I give him for petrol!'

'Forty dollars!'

'For last week and today.' Sarah took the notes, put them into her purse and removed the TattsLotto ticket. 'The TattsLotto man say we winning something.'

'When?'

'Maybe the week when I don't get the job.'

'How much?'

Sarah shook her head and they went inside. 'Have a look, Marni. Maybe from February.'

'What did he say, Mum?'

Sarah shrugged. 'He is Indian man. Talk funny. It look like, *You have a win.*'

'He didn't say Powerball or anything like Powerball?'

'Why?' Sarah opened a carton of eggs and found four. There was plenty of lettuce. A sharp knife got rid of the browning outer leaves while Marni turned on the laptop. It took time to warm up and decide to go, and lately, each time it showed a flickering light, they were pleasantly surprised. Had to take its battery out last week and give it a shake and a blow.

Marni left it to get its act into gear and went into the bedroom. Sarah watched a second light flicker on. In April, when she got her holiday pay, they'd buy a new laptop and a sim card for Bob's old mobile.

They'd bought their flat-screen television at Christmas time, with Crow's bonus. It took up less space than the bulbous old model it had replaced, which would have had to be replaced anyway when the television channels stopped broadcasting analogue signals.

Years ago, when she'd lived with the Clark family, she'd watched sitcoms, watched their action. She knew now why the Clarks used to laugh at *Everybody Loves Raymond*. They showed replays of that show now, with subtitles. They played old movies with subtitles. They were all new to Sarah.

And Marni was back at the computer, watching it with one eye and watching the contestant on *Deal or No Deal* with the other. He had six cases to open; one contained the two hundred thousand dollars and another one the seventy-five. The bank's offer was forty thousand.

'*No deal*,' the contestant said.

'He will lose a green,' Sarah said.

'He might have one of them in his case,' Marni, the incurable optimist, said. They watched him choose fourteen, and it was the seventy-five thousand.

The bank offer still went up to forty-two. 'Deal,' Sarah urged.

'*No deal*,' the contestant said.

'He's brave,' Marni said.

'He is gambler,' Sarah said. 'Boiled egg with tuna salad?'

'Boiled eggs in cups. We haven't had them for ages.'

Boiled eggs were easy. Sarah turned on the rear hotplate, always relieved when she felt it begin to heat. She placed four eggs into a small saucepan and allowed the tap to run over them until the water ran hot.

'You're wearing a dress to that party, Mum?'

'Jeans,' Sarah said.

'Dress, and your good shoes,' her little dictator instructed. 'Because I want to wear mine.' She clicked the mouse. 'Danni Lane wore a gorgeous dress to Samantha's party and she left her hair hanging. She's got yards of it. She said it used to be short when she lived in America and she never used to wear dresses. They lived on a ranch and rode horses.'

'Her mother? Ride horses?'

'She didn't say her mother did. She said she took her to Disneyland, and Graceland – Elvis Presley's house.' She clicked again. 'She's been everywhere –the Grand Canyon even, and New York, with both parents, and now she's not even allowed to see her father unless it's at a police station.'

'Why?'

'Because her mother told a judge that he tried to kidnap her. She said she's a hostage in her mother's war game.'

The eggs were boiling. Sarah adjusted the temperature, set her timer for five minutes, then placed two slices of bread into the toaster.

'It would be awful having a father you weren't allowed to see, or if you found out that your mother had found a sperm donor father for you on the internet and that he had kids splattered all around the world—'

'What!'

'Internet sperm,' Marni said. 'They order it online and it gets posted to you in a bottle – or something.'

'That what you learn at school!'

'Samantha said it. She said there was this gay woman in a magazine who ordered some, and she found out later that he'd posted his sperm off everywhere . . . like her baby had twenty or thirty brothers and sisters—' She stopped talking then, stopped clicking the mouse and stood, knocked her chair over in her haste to get away from the laptop, which she was eyeing as if it were about to explode.

'Turn it off. At plug!' Sarah said, afraid of fire, and when Marni didn't move, Sarah moved towards the solo power point, provider of power to an overloaded power board.

It wasn't smoking. She couldn't smell burning, and Marni was crying and pointing to the laptop's screen with a lotto ticket. Sarah took it from her, glanced at it. It wasn't one of theirs. She bought a system seven in the Saturday night draw. The ticket she held had four rows of numbers.

'I found two dollars near the escalator,' Marni howled. 'I was going to tell you.'

'Tell me what?'

'I had your purse . . . to buy Samantha's present, and we only paid ten dollars for two pair . . . of earrings . . . me and Maria.' And Marni's howling mouth became unreadable. Her finger wasn't, and it was pointing at the laptop's screen.

They weren't Sarah's numbers. They were the Powerball numbers.

'We got the third row, Mummy.'

Sarah worked with numbers. She could retain rows of numbers in her mind, but couldn't retain these. Looked at the third row on the ticket she held in her hand. The Powerball was an eight.

You have a win, the Indian man had said, and Sarah's stomach rolled over and her heartbeat pounded in her throat.

'Why you would doing this!'

'Bob said he had a ticket. And Samantha was saying worse things than internet sperm. And there were boys listening, and Maria wanted to go, and I found the two dollars. And it was up to twenty-eight million and I had your lotto registration card . . .' And she flung herself at her mother and clung.

Sarah held her. Marni's tears always got her own flowing, but not tonight. She stood at the table, eggs and toast forgotten, *Deal or No Deal* forgotten, brushing her girl's long wild hair back from her face with her left hand. Her right hand held that ticket.

She didn't look at it. She didn't look at Marni's hair, but beyond it, beyond the grey paling fence, beyond the sky, now black with the promised storm Melbourne had been waiting for all day. She wasn't thinking storms. She was thinking Perth, and Jillian Jones, and newspapers – and attempting to divide six into twenty-eight.

Bob had mentioned that there had been six winners and that neither he nor his mother had picked one number.

Six wouldn't divide into twenty-eight, not cleanly.

Through that northern window she saw the first flash of lightning. Perhaps she heard the clap of thunder. She felt it through her girl. Lived through her girl, existed because of her girl, who'd stopped crying to watch the approaching storm.

They were still standing, arms around each other, close, just the two of them, only ever two, watching the window when the rain came and came hard, slanting down, attempting to get through the glass.

Three sixes are eighteen, Sarah thought. Four sixes are twenty-four. Five sixes are thirty. Five was too much, but not much too much.

Six into twenty-eight equals four and four over. Borrow a zero from the black clouds, but six won't go into forty either, not cleanly. Six sixes are thirty-six, and still four over. Borrow another zero. Borrow as many zeros as you liked from those clouds and you still couldn't get rid of the remaining four.

Four million – and a row of never-ending sixes.

The devil's number, 666.

And outside their granny flat, the devil ripped Sarah's little world apart with lightning, shook her safe little world with thunder while on the old stove four eggs boiled dry in their saucepan.

They'd never know if the contestant on *Deal or No Deal* had taken the bank's last offer or if he'd opened the wrong case and lost the lot. *Deal* was over and the news was on.

Sarah's name might be on it tomorrow, or had she ticked the anonymous box when she'd registered? Too long ago. Couldn't remember.

Marni smelled the roasting eggshell. She turned off the hotplate and ran cold water into the saucepan. It filled the room with steam. She closed down the computer, turned the television off, then the power board. Lightning storms could damage electrical appliances.

Get Yourself Home

*S*heltered from the sound of rain by the floor above, from the lighting by heavy, black-out drapes, perhaps the final clap of thunder woke Barbara. Still heavy with the residue of drugged sleep, for an instant she was unaware in which bed she lay. Felt for him beside her. Felt only emptiness.

And could smell him. She didn't know if it was midnight or dawn, only that she had to wash his smell off, then pack her bags and go before he returned from his country jaunt.

Her mobile told her the time. She'd slept for almost four hours. Plenty of time. She'd be out of this place at daybreak and home in Sydney before nightfall.

'Danni!'

No reply.

That kid lived in headphones. She looked at the stairs and sighed. 'Damn you, Danni,' she yelled. 'If you make me go up there looking for you, you'll be sorry.'

She went up, and the study door was open. Danni wasn't at her computer. It wasn't turned on. Her bedroom door was open. She expected to see her on her bed, texting. Not there, not in her bathroom either. That little bitch hadn't come home.

She wouldn't have been expecting Barbara before ten, not on a Friday night. She'd be with Samantha and the boys who hung around that overdeveloped little slut of a girl, and downstairs she went to her mobile.

Get yourself home, we're packing up, she texted, then waited, expecting a fast reply. Danni wanted to move back to Sydney. No reply, so she sent another.

What the hell do you think you're doing staying out so late? I need you to pack up your room. We're going home in the morning.

She plugged her mobile into the charger on her way out to the garage to get the cases. Danni's schoolbag wasn't on the washing machine, which meant she hadn't been home to change out of her uniform.

Dog barking outside. The sitting room window offered a view of the paved communal drive, where that mongrel was yapping his brains out. Its owners were out there, the male and the cripple in the wheelchair, and cripple or not, on a block like this where too many houses were crammed up against each other, residents shouldn't have been allowed to have dogs.

She closed the drapes, loving the way they slid together at the pull of a cord, the way they met without leaving a gap. Whoever had owned this house before David must have spent a fortune on drapes. She loved the furniture they'd bought, but she'd show him that he couldn't buy her as his Friday night fool.

She took two cases into her bedroom, left one near the stairs for Danni, then sent a third text.

Answer me now!

Waited for a reply, and when it didn't come, she picked up her landline phone. Samantha's home number was in its memory. She found it, hit *talk*, then stood, foot tapping, until a voice came on the line.

Barbara didn't identify herself. 'Is Danni there?' she demanded.

'I haven't seen her today, Barb.'

Bloody Barb. She loathed the abbreviation of her name. 'Is Samantha home?'

'She usually comes home to eat.' Mrs Deadbeat Smith laughed. Barbara had never met her and didn't want to. She cut the connection, cursed that girl and her mother, and David Crow, and dialled Danni's mobile number.

In all, Barbara sent five texts and left two voicemail messages, which meant Danni's battery was flat, or she'd turned her mobile off, and, knowing her attitude lately, it was probably the latter. She'd come home to sleep, so Barbara went to her room and started packing.

*

Sarah and Marni fed Mrs Vaughn late that night, and only after she'd belted on her laundry window to let them know she hadn't been fed. Cooked her potato and frozen beans in the microwave. Reheated a container of frozen stew, then Marni ran through the rain to deliver the meal.

They didn't eat until eight thirty, when they sat down to ultra-hard-boiled egg and lettuce sandwiches.

From time to time they looked at each other, or at Marni's numbers, written now on scribble paper with the 4,666,666. They didn't believe in them, not yet, so they ate their sandwiches, drank their tea and struggled to find a word worth speaking.

The winning ticket, beneath the clock on their bedside chest of drawers since Sunday, was now zipped safe into Sarah's purse, and the purse zipped safe in an inner pocket of the tapestry bag, and the bag not in its usual place, on the floor, in the corner. It hung tonight within Marni's reach, over the back of her chair, so she could touch it, convince herself that it was there, that tonight was real.

'Do we need to phone them, Mum?'

'They know,' Sarah said.

'I could go on that school camp if it's not too late to pay,' Marni said. 'You can buy your car.'

'Licence first,' Sarah said.

'I thought that winners got phone calls from TattsLotto.'

'I got no phone when I register, no computer.'

'They might have sent someone around to tell us, and Mrs Vaughn hunted them away – or they gave her our money. Can I ask her if someone came?'

'No.'

'We can get two iPhones, like Bob's. We can fly to Disneyland when you get your holidays.'

'No passport,' Sarah said.

'How long does it take to get one?'

'More than April. Stop, Marni. It . . . making me feel sick.'

'Because you can have everything you ever wanted?'

'Because . . .'

'Imagine David Crow's face when you tell him you're leaving.'

'We tell no one,' Sarah said.

'The lotto people might.'

'I know when I write Sarah Carter I will tick anonymous.'

'I can tell Maria. She was with me when I bought it, Mum.'

'No one, Marni.'

'You're scared someone will kidnap me?'

'Many bad people are out there.'

*

At eight fifty Barbara again dialled the Smiths' number. Samantha took the call.

'Who was Danni with when you left her?'

'No one. She got mad about something and walked off by herself.'

'What time?'

'About an hour after we got there.'

'What time, Samantha!'

'Half past fourish.'

'It's almost nine o'clock and she hasn't been home. Do you know if she's been in contact with her father?'

'I dunno.'

'I need to know, Samantha! She's missing.'

There was muttering at the other end of the line, then Mrs Smith took the phone.

'Sam said that Danni texts her father all the time, that he sent her a text from his boat today at lunchtime.'

'He's not allowed to have contact with her!'

'Hang on a minute, Barb. Sam's checking around their friends.'

Barbara hung on. She heard the mobile beeps as replies came back fast to Samantha's mobile.

'No one has seen her,' Mrs Smith reported. 'She hasn't replied to Sam.'

'Her father's got her,' Barbara said. She cut the connection and dialled triple zero.

It took time to be put through to the police, and when she got through, the male voice on the line wasn't interested.

'He's taken her before. She was in contact with him at lunchtime,' Barbara said.

The constable followed procedure. He asked for Martin Lane's details. Barbara gave him the only address she knew, a nine-month-old Sydney address and phone number. She gave him Danni's mobile number, and told him she wasn't answering her phone.

Non-custodial parents who don't agree with the court's ruling too often made their own rules. The constable didn't say this, not in so many words.

'In most cases there is a reason why the partner is late in returning the child,' he said. 'In most cases there's no cause for concern, Mrs Lane.'

'You haven't heard a word I've said, have you? Her father has supervised visitation rights only. He tried to smuggle her out of the country on his brother's yacht eighteen months ago.'

'Have you contacted the father—?'

Barbara hung up and dialled David's mobile, no longer caring if she hated him or not. She needed him, or needed someone who'd listen. Danni was missing.

His voicemail replied. She left a message, then considered phoning her father.

If this had happened in Sydney, her father would have taken control and had that constable saluting him. Let him take control, she thought. Something had to be done. If Martin had picked Danni up at four thirty, they had a four-hour start. If his brother was down here with his boat, they could already be miles out to sea.

She phoned the exchange. 'Connect me to the Nunawading police station,' she said. It was her nearest police station.

A female answered. Barbara told her story again, told of Danni's father's supervised visitation. She spoke of his brother's yacht, and how Martin and his brother had almost smuggled Danni out of the country.

Men always won. In the end, it was the man who got what he wanted. She used to think she was using them, but each time, it was she who ended up the one being used.

The constable asked about Danni's contacts. Barbara told her she'd checked them last week, that Martin's name wasn't amongst them.

'Do you have your phone account handy, Mrs Lane?'

'In my computer.'

'It will show the numbers your daughter has been in contact with.'

And why hadn't she thought to check that? Should have. Too much David on her mind. Too much of his circus, his wife, his Mrs Know-it-all Carter on her mind.

The constable remained on the line while Barbara ran upstairs, turned on her computer and printed off her last Telstra account.

'You said that Danni is twelve, Mrs Lane?'

'Yes.'

'Can you give me a general description?'

'She's finely built, undeveloped, waist-length platinum-blonde hair, and would be wearing a Burwood Heights High School uniform.'

*

While Barbara clung to the lifeline of that calm female voice, Ross Hunter's mobile rang.

'Who?' he said.

'We've got a blonde-headed twelve-year-old girl who didn't come home from school, Sarge. Nunawading just called it through. A Danielle Lane, last seen at Forest Hill Chase at around four thirty this afternoon.'

'Him?'

'Her mother is dead certain the ex-husband has got her, but it's Friday, and you said he wouldn't wait long.'

'Half past four?' Ross said. 'That's four and a half hours ago!'

'Her mother works in the city. She believed her daughter was with a girlfriend. Five minutes ago she found out she wasn't . . .'

*

The police were on their way. Barbara phoned her father, briefly, too briefly for him to complete his sentence. 'You take my grand-daughter down . . .'

Down there and lose her . . .

He'd make it Barbara's fault. He loved Danni, loved her more than he loved his own daughter. He'd paid Barbara's airfare to America so she could bring his granddaughter home the first time Martin ran off with her, but when she'd finally brought her home eight years later and filed for a divorce, he'd taken Martin's side.

'You're not sixteen, my girl,' he'd said. 'You're a married woman and a mother, so start behaving like one.'

She picked up the computer printout to stare at the phone numbers she'd circled. There were five numbers Danni had contacted regularly. One would be Martin's so she picked out a text and sent it to all five.

Danni missing. Have you seen her? Please reply. Barbara Lane

Replies woke up her phone. One sounded like him.

Not since you took her to Melbourne

Almost heard his accent in text, his accusation. He'd accused her outside the court that day. 'You rip those who get too close to you to shreds. You keep your barbs out of Danni or I'll make you sorry you were born.'

Is that you Martin?

It's Emma, Danni's friend. We live down the road from your father's place. What do you mean missing?

She didn't come home from school. I think she's with her father. Do you know where he is?

He lives on a boat somewhere in Queensland.

He could have flown Danni up there by now. Once they got out to sea, no one would find them. And where were the police? The woman had said someone would be with her shortly. What did shortly mean?

Still stuffy inside, she walked out into the night, and that dog ran at her, and if it came one step nearer, she'd use it as a football.

'Snow! Here, boy.' A voice came from the dark. 'Nice to feel a breath of cool air,' he said.

Barbara had opened her mouth to complain about his yapping dog when her landline phone rang. She opened the screen door, but before she could step inside, the dog darted between her feet and got to the phone before her, and the yapping fool attacked it, knocked it down on the floor, and whether it was the police or not, she wasn't fighting a dog for it.

'Get him out!' she demanded.

'I'm so sorry,' the male said. 'Snow. Here, boy.' Having killed the phone, or silenced its ring, the dog ran out to jump up to the crippled woman's lap and lick her face.

'He's been housebound for days,' the male explained, then offered his hand. 'Jake, Jake Murray, and my wife, Joan.'

'Barbara,' she said, and she had to touch the hand his wife flung at her.

They didn't leave. A second couple walked up from the bottom end of that enclave of townhouses to join them, and Barbara had to be introduced to Annie and Luke.

She asked them if they'd seen her daughter today. They saw little, Jake said. 'We knew someone had moved in up here, but from where we are, we don't see a lot of the front neighbours,' Annie said. The two couples lived side by side and appeared to know each other well.

Barbara's mobile, on the charger inside, saved her. It beeped, and she got away from her neighbours. *Tried to call. Will call in the morning.*

From David. In Echuca, or on his way there, with his wife and kids, and where was Echuca? Barbara didn't know. She didn't know if David had lied about his in-laws' anniversary either. As men had always eyed her, women eyed him, and when they did he preened.

The police came, two officers, a male and a female. The dog barked at them, the neighbours stared until she got the police inside and closed the door.

She was sifting through her mobile photographs for a recent shot of Danni when her landline rang. The caller identified himself as Detective Senior Sergeant Ross Hunter.

'Two constables are here,' she said, then pushed that dog spit-defiled phone at the female, and searched on until she found a photograph taken in Sydney a few weeks before they'd left. She hadn't taken one since they'd been down here. That kid had been so rotten to her, she hadn't felt like taking one.

THE DEVIL FRIDAY

*F*rederick Adam-Jones owned three televisions sets, the largest of them fixed to his sitting room wall. He paid a fortune each month for Foxtel, could have watched horse, dog, car racing, football, baseball or ping-pong, but since childhood, Freddy had avoided all sports.

He had access to movie channels, to documentary channels, or with a flick of the remote could switch to umpteen free-to-air channels where a few of the commercials were more interesting than the replays of cooking shows, celebrity shows, hilariously un-funny comedy shows on the ABC, or movies he'd seen so many times if they'd played them backward he'd recognise them.

He paid a fortune for multi-gigabyte broadband, had access to computers, an iPad, and three mobiles that doubled as computers. No one was downloading gigabytes tonight. Freddy was home alone, downloading a bottle of ten-year-old malt whisky.

He wasn't a big drinker, not during the week. He could polish off a bottle of red with a meal but hadn't eaten yet tonight. No wife here to make and serve his dinner, he'd opened his last bottle of liquid gold and had been serving himself since, and gone through the last of the ice.

He was not fond of his own company, nor lately was his wife. She'd gone to Bali – or Thailand – with her girlfriends, who were no longer girls. She'd known them since they were. A keeper, Cheryl Adam-Jones, she kept her friends, had kept her looks and figure, and, to date, him.

He'd had a good day until three o'clock. He'd had the jury eating out of his hand, had walked away from the courthouse smiling for the cameras. His voicemail wiped that smile away, or the message from Rolland's principal had, and that message sent at one o'clock, stating that it was imperative that Mr and Mrs Adam-Jones present themselves at the principal's office at their earliest convenience.

Freddy had presented himself at four and wished he hadn't bothered. His almost seventeen-year-old son, his pride and joy, had been caught red-handed, selling marijuana to three year nine students. The evidence was on the principal's desk, in Rolland Adam-Jones's computer bag, in seven small snap-seal bags that Freddy recognised. Cheryl had a box full of them in her kitchen drawer.

The police hadn't been called, and thank Christ for that much. The three year nine students had been suspended for a week. Rolland had been suspended more permanently.

'Year eleven is an important year,' Freddy had said. 'A youthful mistake . . .'

For half an hour he'd argued his case for the accused, then the principal had dismissed him.

His only son and heir, kicked out of Freddy's old school, mid-term. Expelled. It was a dirty word. Freddy hadn't been expelled. Freddy had excelled – academically. His son hadn't. His son had gone into the drug-dealing business – and gone missing too, so Freddy poured another splash of liquid gold and picked up his mobile, then put it down. That shit of a kid who hadn't replied to Freddy's six messages was unlikely to reply to a seventh.

Flicked the remote again, allowing the screen to settle on Kirk Douglas wearing a Roman skirt. He didn't have the legs for skirts. Flicked, caught a prepaid funeral advertisement. Gave it the flick and wondered what time it was in Bali – or Thailand.

Cheryl needed to be told what her son had got up to while she was gadding about with her girlfriends. If she'd been at home, she would have taken the principal's call, would have sat in his office and taken the punishment, and maybe done a better job of defending Rolland.

She loved that boy, had wanted to replicate him half a dozen times. One had been enough for Freddy, who'd thanked Christ his first had taken after his mother and not after him. Should have given her more kids. She might have been at home cooking dinner for them instead of running around with her girlfriends.

And his gut rolled. It needed feeding. He'd intended to eat with Rolland when he came in. He hadn't come in.

Freddy did another circuit with the remote, stilling his hand a moment on the daily news. Nothing on it he hadn't seen or heard fifty times before. After a while viewers became desensitised to rape, murder and terrorism. Maybe that was what had gone wrong with the kids of today. They got desensitised early, saw the death and roadkill as one more video game where people died violently but not permanently.

He flicked to a deadbeat mother, mouthing off about her son. He could relate to her. Might have watched that had he been able to stand her voice. Couldn't. It reminded him of his mother's voice. Hit her mid-sentence with the *off* button, picked up his glass and walked out to the kitchen, to the freezer, well stocked with frozen meals and meat pies. Rolland liked meat pies and tomato sauce.

They used to heat up pies for Saturday's lunch when Rolland had spent his Saturdays at home, at home in Vermont. He hadn't wanted to move. He'd grown up there with his rat-pack mates. Cheryl hadn't wanted to move. He'd moved them. He'd needed that better address, the bigger house, its large dining room. He'd seen his wife playing the toff at his side in that dining room. She wasn't into toffs. He wasn't into frozen meals.

Rejected beef in red wine. He'd tried one of those yesterday, and the representation on the packet hadn't mirrored the contents. His rolling gut wanted chicken, stuffed and roasted with baked potatoes and gravy. It settled for a packet of curried chicken with rice.

It took time for chubby, inept hands to break into that packet, but he slid the plastic container free, pitched the box towards the garbage bag he'd placed in the corner. It held more than the under-sink kitchen tidy – wasn't as tidy. He slid his dinner into the microwave, typed in 7.30, then stood watching the countdown until the microwave beeped.

Everything beeped these days. Ovens, microwaves, mobiles, washing machines, dryers, cars too. They beeped until you plugged in your seatbelt. His Ferrari beeped when he backed past shrubs. Maybe it would beep if a neighbour's kid ran out from behind a shrub. Maybe he'd stop. Maybe he'd think it was beeping at a shrub and he'd run that kid down. After a time a man learned to ignore life's beeps.

He didn't ignore the microwave's. The instruction on the pack told him to let the meal sit for thirty seconds. He nuked it for those thirty seconds, the microwave a more reliable counter of seconds than he.

Cheryl had warned him to keep a close eye on Rolland. What had she known that he hadn't? She'd suggested he take him out to dinner, take him for a drive in the Ferrari.

He'd hit him where it hurt, that's what he'd do. He'd cancel his bank card, get him a job at McDonald's, or pack him off to one of those bush camps that specialise in sorting out teenage kids.

Expelled.

He removed the clear film sealing his pre-packaged dinner, then poked around in it with a fork, looking for the chicken. There were three slim slices of something in it, which didn't look like chicken.

As a kid he'd eaten roasted free-range chicken, not much of it. One chook had to stretch a long way, but he'd eaten his portion often enough to become a chicken connoisseur, and if those slices had been cut from a chook, he'd eat his hat.

He ate his meal while mentally adding its manufacturer's name to the long list of companies he planned to sue when he retired, most of which were food manufacturers. Five more days before he got a decent meal. Five since he'd had one.

The kitchen was a dog's breakfast. Freddy knew how to use the dishwasher, or maybe he knew. Their cleaner would know. She'd be here on Wednesday. And his gut didn't like that curry. It wanted roast chicken, and he was out of ice, and Cheryl was not here to make him more.

He knew where he could buy ice and a chook, and where he might find Rolland. He and his rat pack had spent a lot of the last two years hanging around the Forest Hill centre, a short bus ride from Vermont.

His Ferrari was unaccustomed to the hurly-burly of the centre's car park, but Cheryl's car wasn't. He picked up her keys, and five minutes later he hit the road in the old white Commodore she refused to part with.

That centre never failed him. He got a space close to the entrance. Shops changed hands regularly, but the escalators never changed. He rode one down to Coles, not too crowded at this time of night, and that supermarket didn't fail him. Half a dozen steps inside the store and there was his chicken, pre-bagged, hot – and reduced for a quick sale.

The bags of ice were at the other end of the store. He helped himself from the freezer cabinet then walked down to queue for service, the chicken becoming hotter, the ice growing colder. Minutes later, swinging two plastic bags, just for old times' sake he decided to have a look in their grog shop – and was pleased he had. He picked up three bottles of his particular poison for not a lot more than the price of two – or for what he'd paid for the last two in Camberwell. He added a packet of salted peanuts and two of salt and vinegar chips to his order then paid for the lot with his card.

Back at the escalators, bottles clinking in one bag, chips and peanuts rustling in another, the scent of chicken wafting from the third, the ice weighing heavy in the fourth, he remembered the other reason he'd come out here. Timezone. Rolland and his rat pack used to love that place.

It was on the top level and Rolland wasn't in it. Freddy glanced towards Vegas, the centre's hotel, the petty gamblers' happy place. The rat pack, having graduated to marijuana, might have graduated from video games to the pokies. Freddy was no gambler, but he walked in, ordered a whisky on ice then looked around. No sign of that kid or any kid in there. Plenty of older players at those singing machines.

And his shopping bags cutting off the circulation to his fingers, he placed the bags down in front of a machine displaying green frogs, placed his glass down on a conveniently positioned shelf, took out his wallet and dug for a coin to feed the frogs.

'Jump, Freddo,' he said, and hit a button. The frogs disappeared into a lily patch, so he hit it again, again, whittling that dollar down five cents at a time.

And they started jumping. They doubled his initial investment. Sipped his drink, made himself comfortable on the stool provided and hit that button again. And the machine started singing and spinning, running his investment up to triple figures – no doubt in cents. He was playing a five-cent machine, which had stopped, but two more prods at that button and off it went again to play alone.

'You've got a goer there,' the woman at his side said.

'It requires little help from me,' Freddy said, knowing why that woman came here. Old or young, male or female, rich or poor, folk didn't feel lonely when sitting beside another player.

He had a goer all right. It ran his dollar investment up to forty-two dollars – so his new friend informed him.

'Should I . . . hit *collect?*'

'I wouldn't,' she said. 'The way it's going, you might get the jackpot.'

He emptied his glass, considered a refill, but the machine had stopped playing alone, so he hit its button, expecting it to take off. It didn't. His frogs had stopped jumping and started gulping down his dollars. He played it down to thirty dollars before it gave back two, but the frogs had been kicking their last. He played his total down to twenty dollars, then claimed his winnings, and would have forgotten his melting ice and cooling chicken if not for his new friend.

He wasn't drunk. He'd poured his first whisky before six o'clock and it took more than five whiskies over a five-hour period to get Freddy drunk. He felt like a winner – until he reached the now near-deserted car park, a perfect place for a couple of druggies to bowl him over. He looked behind, around, then quickened his pace to the car, pleased to lock himself into it.

He hadn't found Rolland. Had Cheryl been at home, she would have. She knew the names of his mates, knew their mothers, knew their mothers' phone numbers. He knew Steve and Mick, knew that Steve had lived over their back fence at Vermont, that Mick had lived over the road from Steve, so instead of turning left into Canterbury Road, he turned right.

The Commodore may have made that trip a thousand times. It found its own way home to Freddy's old street, and to his old house. They'd watched it being built, he and Cheryl. It had cost them a hundred thousand. An Asian had paid close to eight hundred thousand dollars for it at the auction two weeks ago. There was profit to be made in property.

He pulled into his old driveway, his headlights illuminating weeds taller than the azaleas Cheryl had planted beside the fence. It looked deserted, lonely – which was not Freddy's problem. He'd got thirty thousand over his reserve price.

He sat a while, the motor running while he walked the rooms in his mind. She'd loved him when they'd moved into those rooms, when they'd had nothing but each other and a mortgage that would choke a horse. For five years they'd delayed starting a family, both of them working to get that mortgage down to a manageable size.

Then Rolland came, the joy of their lives.

Memory of the principal's office moved Freddy. There appeared to be light showing over the back fence. He might find Rolland there. He backed out to the road and headed down the street he knew would take him through.

Well treed, this area. Trees shed leaves, mountains of them in autumn. He was thinking autumn, thinking of his trees at Camberwell, when he flicked on his left blinker, and made the turn—

Movement.

Yellow.

THUMP!

And blind.

Braking, a reflex action, the Commodore's ABS brakes stopped him dead, and Freddy sat, foot jamming that brake pedal to the floor, jaw hanging, frozen in his seat, his round frog's eyes staring blind at the shattered windscreen, aware that any movement on his part and he'd shatter.

Yellow. That's all he'd seen. A runner.

He sat gripping the steering wheel, willing that running man to attack his car, smash the rest of his windows, drag him out to the road and kick his head in.

Seconds, minutes, eons . . .

He had to . . . render assistance. He had to . . . call for assistance.

And one, then the other, he drew his hands from the wheel, put the shift into *Park*, pulled on the handbrake, released his seatbelt, opened the door and got his feet onto that road – and his legs refused to support him. He clung to the open door, not wanting to see what was out there, and seeing nothing, not on the road behind nor in front of the car.

He'd seen yellow. He'd seen movement before the impact. His windscreen was shattered. One headlight was dead. He'd hit something.

Someone.

Assist the victim. Phone for assistance.

Looked to where the intact headlight was highlighting the trunk of a tree, the kerb.

And saw. White. A bare white leg.

'Oh my God!' he wailed, and he ran to the leg and to the female it was attached to. 'Oh my God, my God.'

She didn't move. He didn't touch her. He reached into his jacket pocket for the mobile he never moved without. Not there. He checked every pocket, found his wallet, found that nest of dollar coins in his trouser pocket. Found no phone.

Knew where it was. Beside his bottle where he'd left it, after six texts to Rolland.

Time to face the music. Call me. I'll pick you up.

If that shit of a kid had called him . . .

'Oh my God,' he moaned and stepped back, and trod on something unstable. The tree trunk saved him landing on top of that girl. He picked up a silly high-heeled platform shoe, and how the hell could anyone run in that?

Not his current problem. She was injured. He had to . . . to render assistance. Had to knock on a door.

Late. Who'd answer their door in the middle of the night?

Had to.

Knew what he had to do, just couldn't make himself do it. He'd had four drinks at home and one more at Vegas, bigger drinks at home than that poured at Vegas. The first thing the police did at an accident scene was breathalyse the driver. He might not be over the limit – or not far over it – but if any alcohol was found in his system, he'd be at fault.

And he had those three bottles in the car.

BARRISTER ARRESTED. DRIVING WHILE INTOXICATED.

Freddy looked at a house three doors down on the far side. It was showing a light. He had to walk across that road and knock on the door.

He knew what the law required him to do, but his legs didn't want to walk him over the road. Instead, they took him back to the girl's side, where this time he got down to a knee, got close enough to listen for her breathing.

She wasn't.

'Oh Jesus Christ, help me.'

He found her arm, her wrist, willing her pulse to throb, and when it didn't, he felt for the artery at her throat.

Blood there. Warm sticky blood and no pulse.

He'd killed.

And couldn't get back to his feet to get away. Wiped his hand on the grass, on the leg of his trousers, then pushed himself to his feet on the tree trunk and turned to the house showing a light.

And saw neon-lit headlines.

DRUNKEN BARRISTER KILLS VERMONT TEENAGER

She's dead, Freddo. An ambulance won't save her, the devil whispered in his ear. *You're dead too if you walk over there. Everything you've worked your guts out for is gone.*

Freddy's heart wasn't dead. It hammered in his throat, ears, lungs. He wasn't going to live long enough to knock on any door.

At least whoever finds you will recognise you, Freddo. If you dropped dead in Camberwell, your nearest neighbour wouldn't recognise you.

FREDERICK ADAM-JONES DROPS DEAD A STREET AWAY FROM WHERE HE SPENT THE BEST YEARS OF HIS LIFE WORKING HIS GUTS OUT FOR LOVE

All gone. His love gone to Bali. His son, his pride and joy, gone to the dogs, and Frederick Adam-Jones was going to jail to join a few of his disgruntled clients.

The car motor was still running, urging him to get in and run. He looked at it, aware that it wouldn't get him far, not with a shattered windscreen and one headlight. He turned off the motor, the headlight, and then in a darkened street walked back to the girl.

He hadn't been travelling fast enough to kill anyone. He'd made a left-hand turn out of his street, one he'd made a thousand times before. She'd come running out of nowhere and it hadn't been his fault.

It would become his fault. His eldest brother had done time for manslaughter. Freddy might have got him off with less time but had kept his distance. Hadn't set eyes on a few of them since the day they'd taken a little kid who couldn't kill a cockroach pig shooting and he'd spent the day howling.

He'd killed, and his frog's eyes leaking, his nose dripping, as he stood over his first kill.

And the lights at the house across the street were turned off.

Reporting what you've done won't bring her back, Freddy. Cheryl's in Bali. Rolland will crash wherever he ends up tonight. He won't come home. Your mobile is at home, Freddy.

*

Frederick Adam-Jones was nothing if not methodical. He'd never knocked out a windscreen, and when his useless little hands failed him, he kicked it free of its frame. He had no conscious plan, but watched the road like a thief, like the murderer he was when he carried the jacket-wrapped windscreen glass around to the boot and dropped it in.

He emptied peanuts and chips onto his passenger seat then, the plastic bag in hand, he walked the road picking up pieces of smashed headlight, feeling for pieces with his shoes. He moved the car up level with the dead girl, checked the road where it had been, swept the gutter with his shoe and when he could find no more fragments, he tied the handles of that bag and tossed it into the boot.

Only desperation gave him the strength to load the dead weight of that girl, and while he was struggling, a flash of white lightning lit the macabre scene – but showed him where he'd dropped her shoe. Thunder shook the dark cave of that tree-lined street, before he got her in and closed that boot as hard rain came pounding down.

He drove wet, and became wetter with no windscreen to keep the storm out. He drove back roads through that storm, knowing that he was now one of the bastards he defended, but knowing too that he was one who knew how the law worked, and that if he was going to do this, he'd do it right.

WINNERS AND LOSERS

*T*he photograph of smiling Danielle Lane could have been Heidi Jasper, grown a year or two older. Ross had been thinking 'Heidi' since he'd heard 'shopping centre'.

The missing girl's mother was convinced her daughter was on her uncle's boat, with her father, heading for American shores. Parents always cling to the safer options. They hope when there is no hope.

Ross hoped Danni was with her father, but by Monday he knew that Martin Lane had an April date in a Sydney court, and that no father was going to kidnap his child and jeopardise his chance of gaining legal custody of her.

Her mother was a beauty. The old photograph he had of Martin Lane was of a tall, good-looking blond. Between them they'd produced something out of the box. Perfection, that kid.

He'd spoken at length to Barbara Lane. She'd told him what she'd wanted him to know, that she'd been modelling in America when she'd met and married Martin Lane, that she'd wanted their daughter to be born and raised in Australia, that when Danni had been in her second year, she'd allowed her husband to take the child to America to meet his parents, and how he'd refused to bring her back, how she'd had to move back there, where she'd remained until Danni's tenth year. She hadn't been specific on dates, but from what he'd gathered, her daughter had been around three years old before Barbara had joined her husband in America.

Ross had spoken to Samantha Smith and the youths Danni had been with at Forest Hill. All three kids told the same story, that she'd done her block about something and walked off in a huff, that they'd last seen her heading towards the escalator.

There were three levels to that centre, shops by the score, access to the car park on all levels and security cameras everywhere – as there had been at Chadstone. He'd spun through a thousand hours of tape when Heidi had gone missing, and was doing it again, searching for a blonde-headed girl, searching blind for a needle in a haystack, uncertain whether her father had taken her or if the killer had taken his fifth. Martin Lane wasn't answering his mobile.

Ross knew what he looked like. He had no description of the killer, so he trawled on through that mire of moving bodies, sifting an ocean of mud for one grain of gold and willing that grain to jump out and hit him in the eye.

A male wearing a white t-shirt and Nike cap jumped out as he strutted by Danni and her school friends in that upstairs shot, before they'd separated. Ross marked the spot, then searched on.

Half an hour later, he picked up Nike again, on the bus stop tape. He knew that cocky strut. Couldn't bring to mind why he knew him, kept thinking Han Solo, from *Star Wars*.

He spun the tape backward, played Nike forward, slowed that strut to a stroll then stilled the tape and zoomed in on a grainy face.

And Roy Bull dropped a file onto his desk.

'Take a squiz at him,' Ross said. 'We know him.'

Roy studied the screen for a moment then shook his head. 'He rings no bells with me, Sarge.'

'My bells are ringing but no jackpot,' Ross said.

They'd found two positives of Danni, one at the Woolworths checkout, and if she'd been preparing to abscond with her father, why bother loading her schoolbag with supermarket shopping? She would have packed her favourite outfit, her laptop.

They'd gone over her room, her mother watching their every move and telling Ross every two minutes that she'd already told him a dozen times that nothing was missing, that Martin Lane had money enough to buy Danni anything she wanted.

A strange woman, who might have been a top model before she'd given up her career to bear her daughter – and maybe resented giving it up. She'd divorced her husband eighteen months ago. At that time, they'd agreed to joint custody – until, according to Mrs Lane, Martin and his brother had attempted to kidnap Danni.

Ross had quizzed her about the kidnap. She'd admitted that she'd dropped the charge but had been awarded full custody, and if 'that cowboy' had wanted to see his daughter he'd had to do it at a police station, and only twice a month.

'After every visit, she was impossible to live with, which is why we moved to Melbourne,' Barbara said.

She had difficulty speaking her ex's name. On several occasions she'd called him 'the cowboy'. She'd been unaware that Danni was in contact with him.

Samantha Smith had been more informative. 'Her father and her Uncle Alan take tourists fishing in Queensland,' she'd said. 'He used to send her photos from everywhere up there.'

Samantha knew about the court date on 22 April. She knew that Danni wanted to go home to America. She knew that Barbara Lane had moved down to Melbourne because her boyfriend lived down here, and that her boyfriend was married with four kids and that Danni's mother worked for him.

Ross had spoken to David Crow and his office manager this morning. The manager claimed to know nothing about his employer's or Mrs Lane's private life. Crow denied any relationship with Mrs Lane, other than that of employer and valued employee.

He'd been out of town from Friday to Sunday night, and claimed to have known nothing about the abduction until his wife had turned on the television on Sunday night and they'd seen Mrs Lane's appeal to her ex-husband.

Ross had recorded it. He'd watched, expecting tears. Barbara Lane hadn't cried for the camera.

*

By eleven o'clock that Monday morning, Sarah knew that she was a millionaire. For years she'd scrimped to save five thousand dollars, enough to buy a second- or third-hand car. Now she could afford a brand new BMW, buy a house, fill it with beautiful furniture, buy anything they wanted.

She'd come into work late, had opened the file she'd closed on Friday, before becoming a millionaire. Couldn't concentrate on the figures. Kept visualising that 4,666,666, kept wondering if anyone at the Commonwealth Bank would notice the transaction, or if it would be achieved anonymously, between computers. Kept telling herself that the figure would look better when the bank added her five thousand three hundred dollars to it – or the second 666 would.

She'd had to jump through hoops to open Mrs Sarah J. Carter's account. Had to open it so her pay could be transferred electronically and she'd had no licence or passport. She'd had to get letters. Had to show her original birth certificate and her old bank card and go to the bank with Maureen Crow.

And when she'd finally got her first pay, it had been swallowed up by Marni's crèche and business clothes and train fares. The next month she'd had a bit left over. Every month since there'd been a balance remaining in her account. It had grown slowly, but it had grown – except for the month Marni had started at the high school when she'd had to pay a fortune for books and uniforms and fees.

Could have bought her secondhand uniforms, a secondhand bag, secondhand books. Couldn't. She'd never forget her first day at high school, the day she'd been Sarah Clark and brand new. Sarah shook that thought away and attempted to force her mind to the computer screen.

What would happen to Mrs Vaughn if they weren't there to look after her? She couldn't look after herself.

She was Raymond's responsibility, not Sarah's, or Marni's.

Marni wanted to buy one of the new houses opposite her school. She didn't want to change schools.

An exhausting day, Monday, Sarah watching the hands of her watch for most of it and was pleased when it was over, pleased to ride the lift down with Bob, walk at his side to his car, buckle in and sit back, her eyes closed.

He liked to talk. 'We had a visit from the police while you were at the dentist,' he said.

'Dentist?' For a second she'd forgotten her phantom dental appointment. 'Oh, yes, Jackie said.'

Jackie saw all. She'd told Sarah about the two officers who had been waiting when Crow came in this morning, how they'd holed up with Crow and Bob, in separate offices, for almost an hour.

They wouldn't have learnt much from Bob. He kept his working life and his other life well separated, except with Sarah. She'd become a part of both.

He'd kissed her on Saturday night when he'd driven her and Marni home from his mother's party. Her fault. She'd encouraged him by clinging to his side for the hours she was there, too many hours because Marni hadn't wanted to leave.

Near midnight Bob had walked them to their gate, and when Marni had gone ahead to unlock the door, in the dark cave behind that gate, he'd put both of his hands on Sarah's shoulders and kissed her. She'd escaped him fast, his kiss disturbing her, but not in the way it was supposed to; she'd been embarrassed by it. She didn't want to kiss him or have his hands on her.

It would be easy to become lost in his family. His mother was nice, his sisters friendly, and there were enough of them to absorb her and Marni, and it would be good for Marni to have those people in her life – life-changing.

Their lives would change anyway. The man from TattsLotto had said so.

'A life-changing amount,' he'd said.

You can't change lives. You can move away, change your name, hide in a granny flat with a landlady playing watchdog at her front window, but inside you're still stuck with who you were born to be, because every memory of who you were is still jammed inside with every image of where you've been.

She'd dreamt of Perth last night, a convoluted nightmare about the TattsLotto people delivering garbage bags full of money, that she'd had to get back to Victoria because the Freeway Killer had Marni and she had to give him that money as a ransom.

Afraid to sleep again, she'd looked up Peter and Lynette Clark on the internet. They were still in Perth. She'd googled their house, seen their backyard, their swimming pool. She'd googled Uncle Bill's street in Brisbane. He was probably still there. He'd had an electrical business in Mount Gravatt. She'd looked for Gramp's farm. She used to know the roads out there. In the months before Marni had been born, she'd driven into Eltham, and further than that, Gramp at her side. He'd been near blind, but a careful teacher. He'd made her drive around and around his front paddock, made her reverse down his drive, parallel park between a big rock and a tree before he'd allowed her to drive him to a farmers' market where he'd sold his honey. Near the end, unable to see much more than night from day, he'd walked with his hand on her shoulder. Loved him, truly loved him. He'd loved her too and he would have loved Marni but from December until June, she'd hidden the bulge of Marni beneath big sweaters, because along with driving him and cooking for him and keeping Gran clean, she'd read newspapers and letters to him.

The last letter from Perth had made her know that it was time to go. It had started everything. Gran had ended up in a nursing home; John, Gramp's son from Dubbo, wrote to say that he'd be arriving on the Saturday.

She'd walked away with twenty dollars in her purse but over a thousand in her old bank account, Centrelink money. They'd paid her a carer's pension, because of Gran.

They'd given her more money once Marni came, and had continued paying that allowance until she was almost eight months old, when Sarah had withdrawn all but fifteen dollars from that account then told Centrelink that she had a job and didn't need a pension.

She'd opened her current account with ten dollars of that pension money – and today she was a millionaire.

Ridiculous, she thought. *Re-_dick_-you-luss.*

Could see that word written in blue biro on her mother's notepad, could remember watching the biro writing, her mother's mouth teaching her how to say it.

It means silly, funny, baby.

I've had a ridiculous life, she thought.

An-_on_-a-muss: It means no one knows you, baby.

Sarah Carter was anonymous.

Her mother had taught her to read words before she could say them. Printed them on cardboard she'd cut from cereal packets. *Chair. Table. Car. Shoe. Tree. Tent.* Should have been a teacher of the deaf, not a house cleaner, not a child minder.

A dreamer, her mother, an incurable optimist.

One day the doctors will be able to fix your ears, baby.

And a fool.

He loves us, baby. We are all he's got.

Marni was an incurable optimist but no fool. She wanted Sarah to retire, get a cochlear implant and pay a personal speech therapist to live with them in their McMansion. She'd said last night that if they made Sarah wear a blindfold, she'd be forced to listen to speech, and that if she listened for long enough, her brain would become so frustrated it would start processing the sounds of spoken English.

It wouldn't. A study done recently claimed that babies implanted at twelve months had better results than those implanted at two years. At fifteen, it would have been too late for Sarah. She was thirty-two. The part of her brain meant to process spoken language would have atrophied.

At-row-fied: Turned into rock, baby.

Her cochlear had probably turned into rock and the doctors wouldn't be able to push their electrodes in, and even if they got enough in, even if she got the optimum result, the noise of the world would probably drive her crazy. Barking dogs drove Mrs Vaughn and Marni crazy. Not Sarah.

She could afford to retire. Even earning interest at three per cent, those millions would make three times more than she could in a year. She wouldn't have to pay tax on what she'd won, but would on the interest that money earned.

And thinking about it was giving her a headache.

'Traffic very bad?' she said.

'This freeway wasn't built to carry the amount of traffic it carries today.'

'I will buy a car when I get my licence.'

'You're having driving lessons?'

'Soon. I will get my learner first.'

Get a chequebook too. She used to write cheques for Gramp, then place the pen where he had to sign. He'd paid everything with cheques. She'd write one for Jackie to pay off her house, and one for Rena so she could fly home to Greece.

That money could change a lot of lives.

THE COVER-UP

Washing a car inside and out with a sixty-five-dollar shirt and three bottles of top-shelf whisky had been life-changing for Freddy. As had driving through a rainstorm with one headlight and no windscreen, crossing over intersections where every car was a police car, turning corners where at every turn he'd seen that runner in yellow.

By the time he'd got to where he was going, he'd been as sober as a judge, sober enough to know what he'd done, but too far away from where he'd done it to turn that car around and undo it.

The old place was deserted, as it had been the last time he'd had a poke about out here, but he'd got that car off the road and under cover, got out of it and collapsed in a heap on the dirt floor, got his back against the shed's paling wall and slept like one of the dead until the birds had got going at daylight.

He'd seen the dried blood between his fingers, around his nails, before he'd seen his shirt. Its cuff, its gut, its sleeve was stained, as were his light grey trousers, where he'd wiped a bloody hand.

Stripped that shirt from his back, looked down at his bloated toad-white belly and stood bawling like a baby.

There were two ex-army jerry cans of petrol on the bench. If he'd had a match in his pocket, he might have ended it there, burnt the shed, car, girl and himself. No match. He'd tried washing the blood from his shirt with petrol. He'd tried whisky before giving up and using his shirt and whisky to wash Cheryl and Rolland's fingerprints from the car's interior.

A methodical man, Freddy, he'd been washing the glove box door when he'd found the small bottle of water. He'd found nail scissors, a packet of Panadol, two of which might have saved his mind. They'd stopped his bawling, had got him thinking.

He had that ice, most of it turned to water. He had chicken, chips, peanuts. What he had to do was stay where he was until nightfall – then do what he had to do, and what better place to do it?

Old tools in the corner, woven together by dusty cobwebs: axe and crowbar, pick, shovel – and a wheelbarrow.

The car's interior was still wet from its soaking when he'd backed it out of the shed and taken to the back roads again. No rain had fallen on Saturday night.

Somewhere between Seymour and Heathcote, he'd eased the Commodore down a goat track into heavily timbered country, where he'd emptied the glove box and his pockets into a supermarket bag. He removed his trousers last, tossed them onto the driver's seat and poured the contents of a jerry can over them, the upholstery, over the motor, and in the boot. He'd used his sixty-five-dollar shirt as a wick in the petrol tank, lit it and run.

Feet unaccustomed to being walked on, clad in shoes not made for walking, hadn't done it well. He didn't know how far they'd walked him during the hours before dawn, or how often he'd sat down to rest his feet and allow his hands to labour on.

They and Cheryl's nail scissors had shredded his bank cards, licence, wallet, then dug holes where he'd buried the shreds. His hands were buggered before the scissors fell apart and before they'd shredded his banknotes. He'd tossed them to the morning breeze, had used his poker machine dollars to mark each hundred of his final steps, his final coin pitched at a farm fence before he'd stumbled down to the house.

Two tied dogs raised the alarm. A middle-aged farmer found him, boxer-short clad, eaten alive by mosquitoes, on his knees, praying to a garden tap.

The farmer's wife phoned the police while the farmer led Freddy into a bathroom where he offered him a towel, a blue polo shirt that stretched and a pair of navy blue tracksuit pants, his wife's. She was a big woman.

Freddy had no identification on him. The farmer and his wife didn't recognise his name or his mozzie-bitten face, but they fed him fried eggs on toast and two mugs of tea and looked kind, so he tried out his story on them, and when the country constable came, he tried it out on him.

Frederick Adam-Jones had spent most of his adult life washing the guilty innocent. He did a whitewash job on himself that Sunday morning. He'd come up with a carjacking, of the five Islander types, one big chap covered in tattoos. The gang had made their attack as he was driving out of his Camberwell property. They'd tossed him into the boot and hadn't opened it until they'd stripped him a few hundred yards from that farm gate – and by the time he was back in the city and relating his tale to city police, he damn near believed it himself.

Carjacking was becoming a common occurrence around Melbourne. Freddy was uninjured. He refused to go to a hospital, and any evidence he might have had on him had been washed off in the farmer's bathroom. He had no family member to call, no money on him to pay for a taxi, so a young female constable drove him home to Camberwell and waited with him until he found Cheryl's emergency key to the back door. She told him to take it easy, that they'd be in touch.

He reported his stolen bank cards online, an inconvenience, certainly, but what man who'd been carjacked and robbed wouldn't have cancelled his cards? He swallowed two more Panadols then hit his pillow and died until Monday morning.

The first reverberation hit him when he picked up the *Herald Sun*, delivered to his letterbox seven days a week. They'd given him the front page, had dug up an old photograph of a frog-eyed fat old bastard.

TOP BARRISTER CARJACKED

On Saturday night at ten o'clock, well-known barrister Frederick Adam-Jones was backing out of his Camberwell property when a group of youths he described as being large men of Islander appearance forced their way into his vehicle. 'One had a knife with a blade about a foot long,' Mr Adam-Jones said. 'I didn't argue with it.'

The carjackers threw him into the boot, where he remained until dawn when a battered and bruised Mr Adam-Jones was thrown naked onto the roadside fifteen kilometres west of Heathcote . . .

There was more. They'd spoken to the farmer and his wife. They'd printed a description of the tattooed Islander and his big knife, had suggested that the carjacking may not have been a random attack. They'd rehashed Freddy's recent loss of the Swan case, had mentioned Swan's known addiction to ice – which could also have repercussions. Freddy was currently appealing Swan's conviction.

Wanted to hide from Monday morning. His burying of that girl's body haunted him, as did the knowledge that bodies were usually found – most of them were – sooner or later.

He knew the burnt-out shell of Cheryl's Commodore would be found. He was an arsonist now as well as a murderer. He'd set fire to the forest out behind Heathcote. It hadn't burnt much, may not have burnt enough – the front seats had been soaked – and whether it had or not, the engine block wouldn't have burnt, and each one was numbered. Given time, that Commodore would be traced to Cheryl Anne Adam-Jones. However, given the minimum of luck, that car wouldn't be connected to the body of the girl.

Had to keep going, keep doing what he had to do. He had to keep playing the injured party. His appearance helped, his limp, swollen face, his aching muscles and protesting sinews.

*

He'd caught a taxi to the office. Smyth paid the fare then gave him a handful of notes from petty cash. Freddy's refusal to discuss the trauma of his weekend earned him a smidgen of respect from the newshounds and maybe the judge, who asked him twice if he wished to continue, and Freddy nodded, aware he was getting the jury's sympathy vote. Then the judge went and dismissed them early.

Rolland had been in touch. He preferred the less personal text to voicemail, and neither text expressed remorse or concern for his father's health. Rolland's concern was for the health of his malfunctioning bank card.

On his sixteenth birthday, Freddy had given him access to the family everyday account – limited access. He'd been allowed to withdraw up to four hundred dollars per month, Freddy's means of teaching that boy the art of money management. Apparently, he'd used his allowance to set himself up in the marijuana business.

Freddy replied to him via text.

Will be home by five. Will speak then.

Lack of funds or the need to charge his mobile drove Rolland home at seven thirty. No greeting, a grunted reply to Freddy, but he plugged his mobile into the charger, opened the freezer, ripped his way into a packet of frozen meat pies and placed two, unwrapped, into the microwave before setting it humming. A search of the refrigerator revealed no can of Coke, nor would it until his mother returned.

'Where have you been?'

'What's it to you?'

Not a lot, Freddy thought, then shuddered and thought of the parents of that girl who hadn't come home on Friday night.

'Where have you been sleeping?'

'As if you care.'

He hadn't slept at home. Rolland left behind mute evidence of his every passing.

Children are born into love, Freddy thought, but as with a fine pair of shoes, love pinches, then wears out. Freddy's pinching shoes were in the green bin. He was barefoot tonight. Born with faulty feet, or feet made faulty by hand-me-down shoes, for the greater part of his adult life he'd suffered the agony of ingrown toenails. Since his walk through the bush, both big toes were preparing to explode. He needed an appointment with his podiatrist and Cheryl wasn't at home to make it.

The microwave beeped – too soon to have heated those pies through. Freddy considered advising that boy, but a poorly heated meat pie wouldn't be the worst he'd put into his gut.

He had the sort of looks that might take him a long way, and was already three inches taller than his father. He might have had a brain had he sat still long enough to find it.

Watched him search the pantry for the tomato sauce dispenser. Watched him find it, squeeze, and when nothing came out, pitch it towards the garbage bag in the corner, then return to the pantry for a two-litre bottle of sauce. Plenty in it. It came out fast to drown his pies. He picked up the plate, relieved it of one pie, bit, spilling pie and sauce as he left the kitchen.

Like blood on the floor.

And the phone rang. It jarred Freddy's mind back to the moment. He was reaching for it when Rolland materialised behind him and snatched it.

'A customer?' Freddy asked.

Not a customer. The snarling youth's demeanour altered as he began his mother manipulation. Freddy had witnessed it before.

'Mine isn't either,' Rolland, his son, said. 'He won't tell me.' He listened a moment, then slid the phone along the granite bench. Freddy caught it before it fell overboard.

'What's happening with our cards, Freddy?' Cheryl asked. Banks, known thieves, were apparently efficient thieves. The repercussions of the cancelled cards had reached Bali – or Thailand.

'I had to cancel the lot,' Freddy said.

'Why would you do a thing like that with me stuck over here?'

He had to lie to her. It didn't come as easily as it had to the police and farmers. 'I was carjacked,' he said. 'They took everything.'

'I told you when you bought that car that flaunting your money around was asking for trouble,' she said. 'Are you all right?'

'I was in your Commodore,' he said. 'Five wouldn't have fit into the Ferrari.'

'Five?'

'Islanders.'

'Where were you going on a Saturday night?'

'I was looking for your son,' he said.

'Were you harmed?'

'I was in the boot for hours, trying to kick my way out. My feet need an appointment with the podiatrist.'

'I wrote his number down on that pad I left beside the phone,' she said, then got down to business. 'I've got around twenty Australian dollars on me, Freddy.'

'I thought your tour was all inclusive?'

'All inclusive doesn't cover everything. Did you give them our PIN?'

'I told them my wife knew it, but was currently in Thailand.'

'Bali,' she said. 'I left you a copy of my itinerary beside the phone.'

'When are you coming home?'

'We fly out late on Thursday night – and I can't manage for a day on twenty dollars.'

'The locals manage on less,' he said.

'I'm not a local. I'll have to borrow from one of the girls, I suppose. What's the matter with Rolly? He sounded upset when he answered the phone.'

'He missed school today,' Freddy said, and offered the phone to her Rolly, who had his hands full, helping himself to ice-cream from the container. 'Your mother wants to know why you missed school, Rolland.'

MISSING

On Tuesday, in their own individual styles, two of Melbourne's newspapers featured an identical school photograph of Lisa Simms, missing from her home since Friday night. Their headlines were similar.

FAMILY FEAR FOR FIFTEEN-YEAR-OLD LISA

The second headline made no mention of her age.

FAMILY FEAR LISA FREEWAY KILLER'S FIFTH
Lisa Simms was last seen leaving her friend's house on Friday evening . . .

Her colouring was similar to that of Monica Rowan, who too had left her friend's house on a Friday evening. There were similarities enough for many readers to relate Lisa's disappearance to the abduction of Monica. To those who looked deeper, there were none.

Lisa Simms wasn't fifteen. She was seventeen, and her employer's description didn't match the schoolgirl image in the papers.

He described Lisa as a well-developed, independent sort of girl. The killer took immature girls.

It was Lisa's employer who'd raised the alarm when his previously reliable employee, after failing to arrive for her Saturday shift, left him in the lurch again on Monday. He'd called her mobile half a dozen times before her boyfriend picked it up and told him that he didn't give a fuck where Lisa was, that she'd pissed off with someone called Liam on Friday night and forgotten to take her phone.

Her parents had been located, one in Frankston, one in Canberra. Neither had been in contact with Lisa in weeks. Her housemates hadn't seen her since she'd left for work on Friday morning.

Seventeen-year-old girls may take off with a new love, but they don't forget to take their mobiles. Seventeen-year-old girls can't live an hour without their mobiles. Ross smelled foul play, though not the child killer. He was waiting now for the boyfriend to be brought in. To date he'd been uncooperative. Running the gauntlet of a bunch of newspaper and television reporters could loosen the tongues of the innocent.

Danni Lane's disappearance had been given no space in either newspaper. Casualties of matrimonial warfare didn't sell papers. Until Captain William Daws, ex-army, Danni's grandfather, contacted Inspector Johnson on Monday afternoon, Danni had been considered such a casualty.

'Take no notice of my daughter's nonsense about a previous kidnap attempt. She used the uncle's boating mishap as a weapon in a prolonged and acrimonious custody dispute,' he'd said.

He'd told Johnson that Martin Lane was on a boat due to dock at Townsville sometime on Tuesday afternoon. He said he'd been in touch with the agent who handled the Lane brothers' fishing tour bookings. Ross had contacted them since, and according to the agent's records, the Lane brothers had sailed on Friday afternoon with half a dozen American tourists on board, three of whom had planes to catch at six thirty this evening.

William Daws was en route from Sydney, estimated time of arrival thirteen hundred hours – one o'clock.

Too much, and nothing happening right now. Ross was waiting to talk to Lisa's boyfriend, waiting for Captain William Daws to arrive, and filling time spinning through security videos, sifting that ocean of mud for a grain of gold, his eyes and mind disconnected.

Or maybe not. A neuron sparked on something. The tape had moved on before he got his sight and brain connected. He spun it back, seeking the place where that neuron had sparked. He was playing it forward on slow speed when he caught the edge of a schoolgirl who could have been Danni, in a car park, carrying a shopping bag.

He stilled the shot, demanding it say more than it did. He moved it forward, and he lost her, moved it back and she disappeared, but not before he glimpsed the swish of that overly long white-blonde ponytail.

He was about to call someone over to verify what he was seeing when a kid constable with a baby face and an unpronounceable name approached.

'The boyfriend's here, sir, with his parents and a lawyer.'

'Take a squiz at the girl,' Ross said. 'Danni?'

'Could be. Got any more of her?'

'That's it,' Ross said.

It wasn't much, an edge of uniform, a bunch of hair, slim neck, slim leg and an environmentally friendly shopping bag. That bag wasn't right. Danni had been carrying a schoolbag in the upstairs shots.

'Meeting her father down there maybe?' the kid said.

It was possible. The brother could have sailed alone with his tourists. Martin Lane could have flown down and flown her back before her mother reported her missing. Captain William Daws could have been wrong, but, according to Johnson, he wouldn't like being told so.

They spun the video forward and back, looking for Martin Lane but seeing little more than an elderly couple walking hand in hand towards the entrance and an elderly female toddling away from the entrance, not far behind the schoolgirl.

'Has Martin Lane got a mother?' the kid asked.

'Dead,' Ross said. 'That woman's carrying a similar shopping bag.'

'They're two a penny, sir. Mum's got dozens of them – forgets to take them with her and buys another one.'

The security camera had picked up a good shot of the elderly woman and her walking stick; she wasn't dressed for Friday's weather, was wearing a pleated plaid skirt and a long dark cardigan.

'Friday was as hot as hell,' Ross said.

'That storm was forecast. If she'd taken her cardi off she'd have had to carry it, sir, and she looks as if she's having trouble enough carrying herself,' the kid said, then stared at Ross who'd grabbed a bunch of tissues to sneeze into. He followed it with two more explosions before blowing the irritation from his sinuses and looking back to the screen, where that girl was beginning to look more like Danni.

If it was her, she'd got that bag from someone. They had a clear shot of her at the supermarket checkout loading items into her schoolbag. In the upstairs shot, she had that bag over her shoulder. Could have been carrying it over the shoulder that was out of frame. The time on the tape told them that shot was taken nine minutes after the upstairs shot, and in the western under-ground car park, which was at the opposite end of that centre. A man could walk a long way in nine minutes. A kid in a hurry would do it faster.

'Her mother will know if it's her or not. Get her in here,' Ross said.

'She doesn't like our decor, sir.'

Ross didn't like Barbara Lane's decor. It had got up his sinuses, or her air freshener had – or she had. She'd told him he stank of cigarettes, that she was allergic to the smell of stale nicotine and would prefer to speak to a non-smoking officer.

Ross's youngest sister didn't like his smell.

'Johnson's waiting, sir – and the boyfriend,' the kid reminded.

Ross killed the video and got to his feet, staring for a moment at the controlled chaos of desks, computers, whiteboard, filing cabinets and bodies, sitting, leaning, walking, talking. A dog's breakfast, his sister would have named it. She kept a tidy, sweet-scented house. He had dinner there once a month – usually – was supposed to have eaten there last Sunday – hadn't.

He sneezed Barbara Lane out of his system before entering the interview room where the boyfriend, an eighteen-year-old kid looking scared, sat beside his lawyer.

He talked. They couldn't shut him up.

'She's been cheating on me for weeks. I found out who she was cheating with on Friday night. Liam someone. She got a message from him. I snatched her phone to read it and she hauled off, belted me in the eye, then took off. I pitched her phone and went to bed, and Mum knows I was in bed and knows where that phone was. She found it when she came in to get my washing. It was flat, so I put it on my charger, then her boss rang.'

Before that Tuesday ended, Daws had arrived in Melbourne, the Lane brother's boat had been accompanied into port and the Townsville police had been over it with a fine-toothed comb. Martin Lane was currently flying south, or would be shortly. Ross had spoken to him. He claimed that his ex-wife had pulled this stunt because he was going after full custody of their daughter.

It was looking bad for pretty Danni Lane, though her mother refused to admit it. She'd confirmed that the schoolgirl in the car park shot was Danni, but was convinced that her ex had sent someone there to pick her up. She'd had an explanation for the shopping bag too.

'Her father would have got money to her to buy what she needed. That's why she didn't take anything from home.'

No use trying to tell her that nine minutes wouldn't have given Danni enough time to go shopping, and if she had she would have shown up in the shops' security videos. No use telling her that nine minutes wouldn't have been enough for her to buy the shopping bag, though wasted breath or not, he told her.

'Then whoever she was meeting bought it – and he was carrying her schoolbag,' Barbara said.

She'd glanced at a shot they'd found of full-faced Granny Plaid Skirt standing behind Danni in the supermarket queue, and had waved a manicured hand at the image she didn't recognise and had no desire to.

Granny Plaid Skirt had been pushing a shopping trolley at the checkout. If she'd had a walking stick, it had been in the trolley.

Why ditch that trolley? The car park was on the same level as the supermarket. There was something not quite right about Granny Plaid Skirt, something very not right about her winter skirt and cardigan on a day like last Friday. There was something wrong about Danni's environmentally friendly shopping bag too – and something more wrong about her mother.

She'd come in here today wearing an ice-blue frock and looking fragile enough for a breeze to sweep her off her feet. A gale wouldn't move that woman. To date Ross hadn't seen her shed a tear, or look capable of shedding one.

He'd watched her Sunday night interview. She'd looked as if she'd been interrupted on her way to a modelling assignment. He'd become obsessed by her hair, by the way it moved as she'd moved, as if each hair had been trained to know its place. He'd thought wig. Today he'd taken particular note of her parting. Her colour may not have been natural but her hair was her own.

She had the complexion, the delicacy, of a porcelain doll, a collector's item, to be handled only by those wearing white gloves. The Sunday night interviewer, one tough lady, had taken her gloves off. She'd chipped away at Barbara Lane for fifteen minutes, determined to squeeze out a tear. They were good for ratings. She'd failed. Delicate Mrs Lane was more vitreous enamel than porcelain.

He'd learnt a lot about her in the days since Danni had disappeared. He'd spoken to her boyfriend, who'd denied any personal relationship with Mrs Lane – which was not so according to a couple of his undervalued employees and young Samantha Smith had seen Danni's mother's boyfriend come out of the downstairs bedroom wearing only a short dressing-gown.

'She used to live with him at Docklands, in his penthouse, until she brought Danni down from her grandfather's place and he moved them into the Barbie's doll house. That's what Danni used to call their house,' Samantha had said.

Crow didn't own a penthouse at Docklands. He rented a classy two-bedroom unit there. He owned, or he and his wife owned, a ten-acre property at Pakenham and a beach house at Mount Martha – a beach house Johnson's team had searched. Crow was the right age to fit the killer's profile, was a lying, cheating bastard of a man, and Danni would have got into his car willingly.

Ross hated admitting it, but Crow was innocent of abduction. At the time Danni had gone missing, he'd been with his wife and kids, preparing to leave for a weekend in Echuca, which he'd spent at his in-laws' place. His wife and their seventeen-year-old daughter backed up that part of his story. His wife, who owned half of the business, had refused to discuss their payroll/accounts officer.

Ross looked at his watch. A direct flight from Townsville to Melbourne took around three hours, so he went outside to pollute Melbourne's evening air.

He knew who had Danni. He'd known on Friday night. She was the killer's type. A pretty immature kid, as fair as her mother, blue eyed like her mother but very different. Danni's eyes had warmth behind them, laughter, the hint of a rebel.

March now, mid-March. Given a warm autumn, unless they found that murdering bastard, they'd find Danni's body in May, beside a freeway, double-bagged, her long pale hair shampooed and tied high with pink satin bows.

'Fight him, Danni. Stay strong and give me time.'

BLIND

*P*itch dark. Airless. Everything hot, metal bars and floor beneath straw which stank of wee and vomit, and because she couldn't see where she'd vomited, she smelled the same as the straw. Couldn't see anything. Like a blind mole locked in a cage.

Didn't know who had put her in it, or how. She'd woken up in it, had screamed until she'd had no more voice to scream. Didn't know how long. Seemed like weeks, except it couldn't have been weeks or she would have died of thirst before she'd found the water. Two big Coke bottles full of water, on the floor outside the bars, on normal floorboards. She'd felt the grooves between those boards.

They were the only things that were normal. The wall behind the bottles wasn't a wall but spongy, like the walls of padded cells in old movies about insane asylums. The mad people they'd put in them could stand up. She couldn't even sit up, not straight up, or her head hit the top bars.

She'd thought she'd been blind when she'd woken up. She wasn't blind, because opposite to where she'd found the water she could see a slit of grey, like light seeping through the gap between two floorboards. And there was something else that came and went, near where she'd found the water bottles. It looked like a smudged circle with a tail like a comet.

Nothing to see now, only a dead blackness like there'd been a storm and they'd all had to go down to Nan and Pop Lane's basement, then the powerlines had blown down and they'd waited in that solid black for hours. There'd been air and space down there. She'd heard things, heard the wind roaring, things banging against the outside of the house. Couldn't hear anything in here, except her own noises. It was as if even the sound of her breathing was trapped in that cage, her swallowing sounds, her growling belly.

She'd drunk too much water too fast when she'd found those bottles and it had come up just as fast and gone everywhere, in her hair, the straw, on the bars. She sipped water now, had sipped all of one bottle and started on the other one.

And thoughts were coming back, and they made her panic, and when she panicked, she couldn't breathe. Better to pretend she was in Nan and Pop's basement and when the storm was over she could get out.

They'd sold it. Sold the house, the land and the horses—

Didn't want to think about that either, but if she didn't fill her head with something, then the words from the television came at her.

Psychopath.

Paedophile.

Monica Rowan.

Emaciated.

She knew, knew, knew.

Body found beside the Hume Freeway . . . identified as that of Monica Rowan . . .

'Don't scream. Don't scream. Don't scream.'

Heard that, like a husky whisper.

If Samantha had agreed to go home when she'd wanted to go home—

'Stop!'

Apples spilling everywhere, big pink lady apples. Grapes, falling out of their plastic bag—

Monica Rowan had been found dead in a garbage bag beside the Hume Freeway, and there'd been three more before her. Penny. She remembered Penny because of Grandpa's pennies. In Sydney. He had an album full of the old money from before her mother had been born and he'd shown her a penny and a half penny and a tiny silver threepenny bit, and old paper money.

Good times in Sydney. Her father had been there . . . then they'd gone to court and he'd gone to Townsville and Grandma had died and everything changed.

Like in America after Nan and Pop Lane's funerals. It was as if funerals were some sort of catalyst.

Her back was aching and her stomach was starving.

Emaciated.

Psychopath.

Paedophile.

If people had water they could stay alive in the Australian desert for days. She had water. If people who were lost had water, if they kept their heads, they stayed alive until someone found them. Panic made people do stupid things, and it was doing the stupid things that killed them. She had water. She had to pretend she was lost in the desert, and if she kept her head, her father and Grandpa would find her. She had to stop herself from screaming so her vocal cords could recover, then wait until she heard someone out there.

Out where? Didn't know where she was. Didn't know for how long people could stay alive on only water.

Refugees who went on hunger strikes didn't die fast. Their bodies ate up their fat, then ate up their muscle.

Emaciate: To reduce to flesh and bones.

She'd been running down the escalator to catch the four-thirty bus. Escalators throw people off at the bottom and that stupid old lady had stopped—

She could hear something out there, or beneath her. A refrigerator motor maybe. Something. Then it stopped. Like a car when someone has turned off the motor.

Did what she'd told herself not to do. She screamed. Had no voice in her lower register but could still make a high shrill scream. She made it long. Then listened.

Nothing.

Her mother would have come home late on Friday night, with him. They wouldn't have noticed that she wasn't in her room. They would have gone to bed. They would have noticed on Saturday, would have phoned the police.

If you gave a police dog a piece of clothing the missing person had worn, the dog could track that person's scent.

They'd had two months to track Monica. They hadn't found her, not until she was dead.

And there was someone out there. She could hear scratching, scraping now, and close.

'Help,' she tried. Just a husky whisper, so she did the high-pitched scream again.

And a door slammed, like Grandpa's screen door used to slam, and there was a light, proper white light where she saw that grey slit, flashing light, like it was signalling. She grabbed for the empty water bottle and ran it backward and forward against the bars. Only plastic. Not noisy enough. Reached between the bars to hammer on the wooden floor with the side of her fist. Someone was out there and they had to be able to hear that.

A wolf heard it. It howled. Then a door opened and she was hit in the face by a blast of light, and whatever was holding the light was howling, and she screamed and huddled in the corner, hiding her face from the light and that inhuman thing that had put her in this cage.

'I have gags for squealers,' it said, and she screamed again because the voice sounded like Mr Watts, her maths teacher, and because knowing who he was made her know something she'd been refusing to let herself know. She'd done something stupid.

Saw a white hand inside the cage. It was emptying something from a can into a bowl and she screamed at it because she knew she was going to be dead before 22 April and that Daddy would go home to America without her.

'You won't like my gags,' he said. Then he was out that door and gone with his light, and the black was back and it was everywhere.

Not everywhere. Her eyes had photographed his light and his hand. Now her eyes played that image back, played it green, played it orange, and she sat quieting her breathing by watching it, clinging to it until it grew small and dissolved. She cried for its absence and because he was probably Mr Watts who had given her and Samantha a ride home from the shops two weeks ago and he hadn't been like a teacher. He must have offered to drive her home on Friday. She must have got into his car alone – and she'd called her mother a fool for being tricked by David Crow?

She was sitting on her hair and it was hurting, and that real hurting stopped her tears. She'd had an elastic band around her ponytail at school. Lost it, and her hair was everywhere. Her hands reached up to gather and plait it. Useless fingers in the dark – until she closed her eyes against the dark, which didn't change what she could see, except maybe her brain knew why it couldn't see so it sent different messages to her fingers. She got her hair plaited, got it tucked down the neck of her uniform. There was little enough space in his cage without tangling herself up in hair.

Tried then to think of getting into Mr Watts car, but all she could remember was almost knocking that old lady down, then chasing her spilled shopping, chasing an apple beneath a food court table and knowing that she was going to miss the four-thirty bus.

She could remember the couple sitting at the table an apple had rolled beneath. They'd been eating a huge plate full of fish and chips, at half past four in the afternoon – and if she could remember what they were eating, why couldn't she remember getting into Mr Watts's car?

Because she was starving hungry, that's why, because her stomach was aching so bad for food, she'd have eaten a raw fish if she had one.

He'd put something from a can into a bowl. Probably dog food. There were too many stinks in here to smell anything. How long would a starving person starve before she ate dog food?

Dogs ate meat and meat rotted in your stomach and the bacteria from its rot gave you cancer of the bowel, so her mother said. Sugar was poison too. It gave you diabetes. Grapes were full of sugar, so eating too many was bad for you. Broccoli tasted like poison but was full of iron, stopped bowel cancer and had no kilojoules in it, so was good. If you sat slouched over your computer, your spine grew twisted.

Her mother might have been right about spines. Danni's felt as if it was going to snap. She had to straighten it, and there was only one way she could, by putting her head against the top end bars and her legs between the bottom bars, which was how she'd found those bottles of water.

And one shoe found more. Pulled her foot back and swivelled around to reach for what she'd kicked. One, two, big cool bottles.

Whoever he was he didn't want her to die of thirst, or not yet, and he'd put something else on the floor, a can of something with a ring-pull top. She picked it up and shook it. It didn't feel solid like the jellied dog food Samantha's dog ate, which had to be gouged from the tin with a knife. She brought it into the cage to shake close to her ear, and it sounded squishy, like it could have been baked beans. Her mother ate baked beans because they were full of fibre and protein and low in kilojoules.

She placed it in the corner with the bottles, then, leaning low, sniffed where she'd seen that bowl. Maybe she could smell dog food, but it didn't smell bad. Anyway, dog food was probably mostly cereal and vegetables with a bit of whale or horse meat in it. She hadn't eaten meat since she was ten. Grandpa did though, great slabs of it he fried in butter.

She sniffed again, her nose almost in the bowl, and it smelled almost like baked beans. She stirred it with her fingers, and it felt like baked beans so she licked her finger, and it tasted of baked beans juice. Like an animal then, she crouched low over that bowl, not lapping beans with her tongue but scooping them up with the spoon of her fingers, scooping and swallowing, not caring if they hurt her throat or not.

She'd care if they came straight back up so she stopped herself and sat back, licking her fingers clean before reaching for one of the new bottles of water, cool water.

She'd hardly peed since she'd woken up, and when she had, she'd done it on the straw, like her pet hamsters used to pee on their straw.

Her cat had been fastidious about its personal habits. It used to dig holes then cover up what it had done. Samantha's dog didn't. He wet and pooped anywhere, then walked away from it, laughing about who was going to step into it. Thank God she hadn't needed to do more than pee. It was like her intestines had sense enough to hang on to what they had in them.

She ate two more scoops of beans, then left the rest to eat when the smudgy grey comet came back, which must have shown her that morning had come. Cats and dogs and hamsters couldn't think ahead to being hungry in the future. She could, and she wasn't hungry now, so she did what she'd started to do, got her spine straight, her legs between the bottom bars, head against the top bars and shoes against the padded wall. Almost comfortable, she allowed her mind to wander to a game she used to play on her father's old computer, where a cartoon man was locked into a castle and she'd had to make the right choices for him to find his way out. The game had rules, and a *Help* box she could click on.

What were the rules of Mr Watts's game? Maybe he'd told her one. *I have gags for squealers,* he'd said.

If he gagged her, she'd die of thirst.

It was like she was locked into a horror video game, where the cartoon man's one object was staying alive until the crusaders came to save him.

Screaming did no good. She couldn't fight, so it was a brain game, and as she lay on her back, staring into black, she began to build her own help box.

Rule one. No more screaming.

Rule two. Eat whatever he gives you, even dog food.

Rule three. Stay alive until Daddy comes. The police might give up but he and Grandpa won't ever give up.

THE PHONE CALL

'Just because they searched his brother's boat and didn't find her doesn't mean that he hasn't got her hidden somewhere,' Barbara told the telephone. 'He's got her, David, or he's paid someone to hide her until the police get sick of looking.'

'Have you had any sleep?' David asked.

'I wake up, and he's stuck here . . . my father . . . and he backed up everything Martin told the police, and about you and everything.' No reply from his end. Nothing. She waited. 'I can't breathe, David. Get me away from him.'

'Not a good idea at the moment. We need to take particular . . .'

'I'm sick of appeasing the whole fucking world,' she said and pitched the phone at the three-seater couch where her father had set up his bed.

She'd told him to sleep in Danni's room. He didn't do stairs, and when she'd told him he wasn't sleeping on her couch he'd all but accused her of renting a house with stairs just so he couldn't visit his granddaughter. She'd booked him a room at a motel. He'd cancelled it, and when she told him straight out that his sweat stank, he'd showered, in her bathroom, and she'd had to clean and spray it, and it still stank of him when she went in there to get one of David's Xanax, and she only had two left.

Have to go to a doctor and get more, swallow pills all day, tune out. She'd done it before, done it for months after she'd had that kid. She washed down the small pill that matched her bathroom then she slid into bed to count down to that place where her brain switched off.

Sleep was beautiful. It was the waking that hurt, and being woken by voices from the sitting room, her father was loud.

'Look on the bright side,' he said. 'You can't pay for this sort of advertising.'

Then David's voice, and Barbara rose and dressed, and went out to the men, and to a newspaper on the dining room table advertising Crows in large black headlines . . .

CROW DENIES RELATIONSHIP WITH MOTHER OF MISSING DANNI

So much for Appearances and Appeasement. The whole of Melbourne now knew that David Crow was an Adulterer.

Her father had called him an adulterer in Sydney, had called him a fake bastard too, and the fake bastard didn't greet her with a kiss. He sat, his back to the window. Her father was seated on Barbara's recliner. Two males, on two well-separated chairs.

Her father liked that recliner, placed conveniently for watching the television. He had the remote in his hand. A commercial was playing, but muted. He didn't like commercials.

No place left for her to sit other than on the three-seater couch that stank of her father's folded bedding.

Needed David beside her. Needed him to hold her. He had at her mother's funeral – and made love to her after it.

He hadn't come out here to hold her but to offer his valued employee any assistance she may require.

'Then convince the police that Martin paid someone to take Danni. She wouldn't get into a stranger's car!'

'You're in denial like you've been in denial your whole life,' her father bellowed. That room was too small for his bellow – and the television was now bellowing, or the police inspector on it was.

'Turn it down!'

'*Danni Lane's mobile was tracked to an address in Box Hill,*' the newsreader said.

Knew that already. Knew a ten-year-old boy claimed to have found her phone on the nature strip out the front of his house.

Martin knew that the police could track mobiles. He would have told whoever he'd paid to pick Danni up, to get rid of her phone, which Barbara had told the police last night.

She looked at David, then her father. Like bookends to those peach drapes, the Roman emperor, his perfect profile cast in bronze, and the giant lizard man with his spiky white army haircut.

In Sydney, David had said that he loved her, that he was in the process of divorcing his wife, but because the business was in both their names, it could take a little time.

In Melbourne she'd found out that he was scared witless his wife would divorce him. In Melbourne she'd worked out that he needed his wife and kids to keep him safe while he played with fire, unafraid of burning his fingers, because Mummy and the kids would haul him back from the flames in the nick of time.

Just a pretty boy who'd grown so well protected from the heat of life, he'd bypassed maturity.

Martin had bought himself a pretty model with his parents' plush New York unit, then he'd tossed her into the flames and expected her to come out a wife and mother.

She'd never wanted to be a mother. She'd wanted her photograph on the cover of a *Vogue* magazine.

It was on the cover of today's newspaper. They hadn't got hold of a photograph of her standing with David. They'd boxed them separately, but side by side. It was a good one of her.

Shouldn't have dropped the kidnap charges that time Martin and his brother had taken Danni on that boat. Should have let him rot in jail. Hated him.

Hated that bronzed Roman emperor too. Give him ten more years of good restaurants – and his wife's cooking – and his dimpled chin would become many.

She'd grown an extra chin when she'd been carrying Danni. Had stirred sugar into her coffee, eaten chocolates, biscuits, eaten anything to satisfy the alien eating her from within.

'A big baby,' the doctor had said, then he'd let her scream it out, let her spend twenty-four hours screaming it out, and when it was out, when they'd tried to put that bloody thing on her, she'd damn near pitched it at them.

Hated the way it had left her, the bloated flabby belly, stretch marks all over it, her bulging breasts. To this day, every time she looked in a mirror she saw that bloated self standing behind her.

Phone ringing. The old controller couldn't get out of his chair fast enough to control it.

'Barbara Lane,' she said.

'Barb? It's Martin.'

'Where is she?' she screamed.

'I know you're frantic,' he said. 'I believe your father is with you. Can I speak to him, please.'

'Stay away from him and me.'

'I lost my phone in transit—'

'I don't give a shit what you've lost. Where's Danni?'

The lizard man wrestled the phone from her hand, and she ran from him to her room, to her bathroom, slammed the door and snatched that last Xanax, washed it down with water from her tooth-brushing glass. And the water tasted of toothpaste, so she threw the glass at the basin. The glass shattered.

He came, David. He stood behind her in the doorway. Saw their reflections in the mirror standing side by side. Saw his non-smiling mouth, the sag of his throat. Saw her own face washed clean of makeup, her staring eyes. Ran from herself.

David gave way. Her father tried to hold her, but she got out the front door and out of that house.

It was too close to the street, and news vans, cameras were out there. Turned the other way. Yapping dog down the bottom end of that enclave of townhouses – and Jake, and she knew Jake and she ran his and the dog's way.

'I can't,' she said. 'I can't take it. I can't.'

'You poor lady,' Jake said. 'Has there been news?'

'They're doing nothing,' she said. 'They're listening to lies.'

'Come inside for a moment,' he said.

She looked back at the house David had bought for them, and he was getting into his car. Saw her father's back. He liked newsmen. He was walking out to the street to talk to them. Safe from them down here. There was a long paved drive and many houses between Jake's and the one she called her own, and she turned to her neighbour, and followed him and his dog into a house which was a mirror image of her own.

It made her dizzy, or the pill she'd taken was making her dizzy, or her blood sugar was low. She swayed on her feet, and he steadied her with an arm, and his arm around her, he guided her towards his kitchen.

'Joan believes that a cup of tea will cure all,' he said.

She wasn't there. He made the tea, and Barbara sat at his kitchen table, in a kitchen more worn than her own. She drank his tea there, ate his dry biscuits with cheese.

He spoke of his Joan later, of her stroke, of their need to live close to the rehabilitation hospital.

'She was Professor Murray. She lectured at the Melbourne University,' he said proudly.

'My father wanted me to go to university,' Barbara said.

'It is a lucky parent who has his expectations realised.'

'He told the police to take no notice of anything I said about Danni's father kidnapping her, and now he's down here too and telling them more lies.'

She spoke of her mother's stroke later. She told him how they'd kept her alive with machines for a week, and how her father had told the doctors to turn the machines off.

'He's a control freak,' she said. 'He's spent his life ordering everyone around. I came down here to get away from him but I don't know anyone.'

'You know me and Joan – and Snow,' he smiled, and he patted her hand, and why couldn't she have met someone like him instead of selfish bastards.

She sat with her new best friends for two hours, and when they had to leave, they walked her to her door.

The Howl

*T*he traffic was not heavy at eight on a Saturday morning. He enjoyed driving and was feeling the kinks of the week smoothing out, or he was until he flicked on his left-hand-turn blinker and saw a truck and its spilled load of building material blocking his road. Slowly but surely the city was moving out to claim its share of his hill. During recent years, arty houses had been erected out this way.

From his hill, he'd watched a mud-brick creation rise on an acreage to the east of his land, not close, but too close for his comfort. He glanced at it as he braked well back from the trucks shemozzle. From this distance, the new house appeared habitable – and by the look of what had spilled on the road, it appeared that he was to have a second neighbour.

Two burly males were out of their truck, one smoking, one mouthing off into a mobile. It may have been possible to drive around them. The sides of the road were relatively flat but may not be dry. He didn't chance it – or chance being seen too close to his lair, so he made a U-turn and drove back the way he'd come, annoyed by the delay but more annoyed by the city's invasion of his privacy.

He'd visited his prize briefly on Tuesday night. She'd been noisy, which was to be expected. Given time, she'd settle. The take had gone like clockwork. What he'd believed would be his most difficult had been his easiest. Put that down to planning. He'd put himself to sleep at night in the planning of this one. He'd chosen his space in the lower car park weeks ago, aware that the positioning of his vehicle was integral to a successful take, then, when he'd cruised by on Friday afternoon and seen the tail-lights of a sedan backing out of that space, he'd known he'd have her.

He'd found her at the supermarket, not alone, but he'd kept an eye on her until she was alone.

Anonymous places, car parks, drivers only intent on putting their cars down, buckling in offspring, lifting offspring out. He'd done it swiftly as she'd reached in to place his shopping bag down. A swift tap behind the ear, sufficient to stun, unlikely to cause serious damage, and as she'd begun to crumple, he'd tumbled her in on top of the shopping.

Several cars had cruised by while he'd taped and bagged her. If a driver had glanced his way, he would have seen little of the action between the vehicle and the wall, and it had been over in less than a minute. It had taken longer to get out of the car park.

During the planning stage, the time of day, the after-school crowd looking for a space to put their cars down had been his greatest concern. In the doing, it had offered privacy.

A rank amateur the night he'd taken his first, he'd had no plan. She'd fallen into his hands. He'd had no bag, no duct tape, no pills, and she'd put up a good fight for her size. Mistakes are only mistakes when we don't learn from them. With the second, he'd been well prepared. Another small one. He'd slid her into a floral quilt cover.

His third had been his most difficult. He'd had limited space in which to work, and limited time. Had to hit her twice, and, afraid she'd come around before he'd got her out to his car, he'd placed two pills into her mouth before gagging her with duct tape, folding her into a travelling case – then travelling.

A busy shopping centre with its multiple security cameras was not the optimum taking place. He may well have been trapped on a few of those tapes, but at no stage had he walked at his pretty gazelle's side, and when you have no choice there is no choice to be made. Since the day he'd seen her near the carousel, that pink plastic bow day, he'd known she was his, and at each sighting since, the wanting had grown stronger. Done now, and he had today and tomorrow morning to spend with her.

He made a second U-turn and drove back. The truck was still there, and what the hell were they waiting for? A forklift? Loading timber not in their job description? Probably. A month or two back, he'd watched eleven men stand around for an hour while a twelfth, up a cherry picker, cut limbs from a tree.

How many men does it take to change a light globe, Daddy?

He swung the car around again and drove back to a supermarket where he picked up a packet of latex gloves, a freshly roasted chicken, a tub of coleslaw and a bag of frozen chips. He'd serve himself a hot meal tonight and have chicken left over for tomorrow.

Third time lucky! The truck was gone and the road cleared. He made his left-hand turn onto a narrow road capped with bitumen. It meandered for some distance through forest land, uphill and down dale. Land aplenty along its route, and he was wondering how far that truck had meandered along it when he saw a dog guarding a new gate.

His neighbours had moved into their arty creation, which to his less than arty eye appeared more sprawling shed than conventional dwelling. He saw a car but not its driver.

His own gate, well distanced from its neighbour, wasn't new. He left the car running while he opened it and drove through.

His lair, set well back from the road, midway up a timbered hill, was barely visible from the road. Scraggy grey wattles, gums and native scrub surrounded it. A tin garage was highly visible. Prior to its construction, the ground to the east of the house had been cleared and gouged level, leaving rock and greasy grey clay behind, a discouragement to windblown seed. That garage sat on its clay-pan like a solar-powered lighthouse on a rock, flashing its warning to those passing by. If the sun was in the sky, it found the galvanised roof, wall, or door, and as he drove on up that slope, its door flashed a warning. Once upon a time he'd promised it a coat of camouflage paint, but had found better things to do with his time.

He didn't stop before that flashing door but swung the car to the right and drove across to a crumbling timber shed which required no camouflage. The native scrub of this land leaned on its wall, branches of gums brushed its rusting roof and did what they could to hide the fact that the shed had no door. It contained nothing worth stealing, or hadn't since February, when he'd decided the shed may not be the best place to park his Kingswood.

Until February he'd driven that old wagon about at weekends, had filled its tank at service stations, checked the air in its tyres, had long discussions with other Holden enthusiasts who'd patted its panels, commented on its condition as they may have commented on the condition of a retired Clydesdale workhorse.

Not any more. It was locked behind that flashing door, and for the first time since he'd sighted that eyesore garage he'd been pleased it was there.

He'd made a mistake with his last delivery. From the start, it had gone wrong. He had to get rid of the Kingswood, give it a quick coat of paint, then take it for a long drive – though not today. Today was spoken for, and hot.

He parked the car, then walked outside to look towards his new neighbour's dwelling, barely visible from this angle. He turned to the west to look beyond the eyesore to one man's dream of a fine family home, back at the turn of the old century. Its walls, which hadn't seen paint in fifty years, blended in well with the dirty browns and greys of this land. It had a metre box, a power wire connected to it, but no power. He managed without it. He paid no city water bills, not for this place. A big old tank supplied water to the house. He didn't drink it. He brought his drinking water from home.

The Hyundai's hatchback lifted, and he began his weekend unloading supplies into an ancient wheelbarrow. He'd bought two plastic-wrapped packets of firewood from a service station, at a premium price. There was fallen timber enough on his land, but the weather was not conducive to axe work, and the noise it made advertised his occupancy. He preferred not to.

He tossed a bag of ice into his barrow, also service station supplied. He stacked six large bottles of drinking water around the load, then peered into a plastic Target bag before adding it. He'd shopped yesterday for his pretty gazelle, bought her a pair of pretty pink pyjamas.

The barrow was necessary. The shed had been built at a distance from the house. A narrow path led between low-hanging trees to his back door, and he and his loaded barrow trundled off towards it.

No lock on the flyscreen door. A snib. He opened it, positioned the barrow to hold it open while finding the right keys for the two locks on the main door, one old, one new. He'd fitted the new twelve months ago, a deadlock. He was inserting the second key when he heard that dog barking and it sounded close.

He didn't use the second key, but walked back down the path to look for the dog. No sign of it.

Noise carried out here. It hit the hill and bounced back. He glanced at the hill. From its peak he had an overview of the area, and might be able to see where that truck and its load had ended their journey. The keys dropped into his pocket, he started up the bush-covered slope.

From a distance it looked like a hill. From his back door it was little more than a pleasant stroll to its peak, where a convenient rock offered him a seat, or today an extra half-metre of height from which to look down on his neighbour's elongated, flat-roofed barn which an architect had no doubt charged a fortune to blend into the natural surrounds. Given a year or two, it might blend, though its paved driveway wouldn't. He'd sat on this rock the day they'd come in force to level and pave it and had wondered at the mentality of the owners, who'd done what they could to hide their house then advertised its presence with that driveway.

And he sighted a female on it, her colours raw against the land. Saw that dog too, and it looked as big as its handler. It was some yellow-brown breed. He watched them to their gate, out their gate, willing them to walk east. They turned west, and he'd left his gate open. Had she seen him drive by? Had she seen where he'd driven and decided to do the neighbourly thing and introduce herself?

Barely breathing, he watched their progress, her dog, unleashed, watering trees and fenceposts along the way and the woman not waiting while it watered — until she reached his gate, where she stopped to shade her eyes and peer up at the glare of the garage door. She didn't walk up, and he heard his release of breath. Should have closed that gate, though a closed gate won't stop some. He needed a lock. A chain and padlock would stop most.

The house and trees now blocking his view of the walkers, he stepped down from his rock and walked to his right until sighting her patch of colour again. Her clothing suggested youth. Her slow pace belied her clothing. He couldn't see her dog.

Apparently she could. 'Herod! Get back here!'

A humorist? he thought. Herod the great was barking like a pup. Had he caught a whiff of human habitation? Watched the animal, watched the arty woman leave the road and walk to where the fence crossed over a gutter.

'Get out of there! Bad boy! Heel, Herod!'

Her bark the louder of the two, the beast emerged, then they both disappeared where the road curved into overhanging trees.

Was there a male half? Where there was a colourful female there was usually a male. He gave her a minute more before beginning his descent, slowly. Once he'd run like the wind down that hill, and if he'd tumbled, he'd rolled to his feet and kept running. Once, he'd run headlong at that gutter and jumped, determined to reach the other side — landed in it many times before his legs had grown long enough to make the leap across.

It had grown no deeper since his youth, wider perhaps. If enough rain fell on that hill that gutter became a muddy stream down to the fenceline, where it disappeared into a concrete culvert, or it did when the culvert wasn't blocked by debris and topsoil.

He closed the gate, then considered the shed as a potential supplier of lock and chain. You name it, and it had been in that shed since Christ had been a carpenter. A few of Christ's own tools may still have been in there. He'd found a large handcrafted padlock, its singular key attached by a length of twine – and found a use for it. He owned a small relatively modern padlock, last sighted on the kitchen mantelpiece, though too small perhaps to use on the gate. Bunnings would provide. He'd go shopping tomorrow.

Watchful then for his new neighbour, he followed his fenceline to the gutter, where he stood a moment, listening. He could hear her dog's staccato bark, but at a distance. She too may have gone in search of that truck's final destination, which hadn't been visible from the hill.

A pile of brambles, washed down by the storm, had formed a beaver dam against the fencing wire. A convenient woodpile. Tomorrow morning, before the heat became intense, he'd bring the barrow down here and get himself enough firewood for next weekend. About to return to the house he caught a whiff of what that dog must have smelt. Something dead had washed down with that bracken.

Kangaroos liked this land, rabbits, possums, foxes. One hand on a fencepost for support he leaned over, sniffed, then stepped down, finding safe footing on clay and a branch. He was still thinking firewood when he saw yellow, bright yellow.

Windblown detritus? he thought. An item from the arty one's clothes line blown in by the wind?

And buried. Her house had been unoccupied on the night of the storm.

The smell was intense in the enclosed area of the gutter. He reached for a length of bark and tossed it, followed it with half of a small dead shrub, and it stabbed him. He cursed it, glanced at blood welling in the web between his thumb and index finger, and instinctively sucked and spat.

And saw where his spit landed. Saw matted, soil-covered blonde hair.

Some bastard had been here! Some bastard had done the unthinkable.

Forgot the arty one and her dog. Unmindful of his hands, he tossed bracken and bark, scraped earth away with a sheet of bark, uncovered . . . uncovered not his pretty gazelle. A female, yes, but clothed in a yellow vest and unquestionably not his prize.

The dog bark sounded close, and like a rat peeking out of its hole, he peered out from the gutter. The walkers had not yet reached the curve in the road. Tossed back what he'd removed, covered what he'd exposed, then ran at a crouch along the gutter to a tree, its roots clinging to rock and clay, where he got down to his haunches, his back to the exposed roots, his heart pounding, certain the dog would come through the fence and uncover that thing, and find him cowering there.

She had it on a lead. They walked fast by his fence, by his closed gate. He watched them. He watched them move out of sight before scuttling up the gutter to where the sides were low enough. And out. Hidden then amid the trees surrounding the house, he approached his back door via the western side.

Clay on the hand that reached into his pocket for the key, blood on it, and the hand inserting the key not steady.

The door scraped as it opened, the arc of its many openings worn into the floorboards. Stood for a moment, doorknob in his hand, thinking not of his prize but of what was in the gutter, aware that it was the stroke of luck his hunters prayed for.

Clay on his shoes, on his slacks, rage in his heart and head, directed at the one who'd dared to choose this land as a burial site. Rage was not good. It gave birth to rash decisions. Rash decisions led to mistakes. What was required of him was calm, cool-headed thinking.

He closed the door, and closing it stole his light. He pulled on the blind cord until it got the message to roll up, then by the window's light, he looked at his hand, at a triangular rip in the web, a position constantly in use. It wouldn't heal fast, and he had no medical supplies out here, no disinfectant, no bandaid.

Release the gazelle. She'd be unlikely to identify him.

That dog would be back. The neighbour would find that body and police would swarm this place and find the Kingswood.

They wouldn't trace it to him.

Go, he thought. Drop the gazelle off on the way and keep on going.

'Feed her,' he said. 'Think the problem through.'

He'd fed her on Tuesday night, left her a can of beans. She'd be hungry enough to eat whatever he gave her.

Such plans he'd had for his weekend.

'Dispose of the problem,' he suggested.

With disposal on his mind, he turned on his sink tap and washed his hands well with soap. It stung his wound, but he washed it clean, sucked it cleaner, spat what he'd sucked into the sink, then with one hand and his teeth, ripped his way into a four-pack of paper towels he bought in bulk. He went through a lot of them out here. He ripped off a length to wrap his wound.

He'd bought a bundle of newspapers with him on Tuesday night. They were on the hearth, his fire starters. Half a dozen pages crumpled and placed into the firebox of an elderly combustion stove, a handful of dry sticks tossed in, and he reached for the box of matches always on the mantelpiece.

Old mantelpiece, older than the stove, which had been sending up smoke signals for fifty years. It had a boiler tank beside the firebox with water pipes feeding in and out. Given time and fuel, that stove heated water in a ceiling reservoir where more pipes fed it down to sink and bathroom.

Lighting fires calmed him, the crackling of twigs, the creeping of flame to larger pieces of wood. He stood watching the flames until their heat suggested he close the firebox.

The iron kettle, older than the stove, he filled at the sink. Required two hands to carry its weight, and he lost his paper towel bandage, his blood on it. Paper burned. He ripped two more towels from the roll and this time fixed his bandage in place with rubber bands, then went out to unload his barrow. A familiar routine, it got his mind back on track. Ice in the esky, bottles of water on the table, small bottle of water on ice. The packets of firewood he dumped one at a time onto the hearth then slit each of them open with a kitchen knife.

Other than an elderly wooden table, an ancient wicker chair and his folding camp stretcher, the house was unfurnished. He tossed his overnight bag to the stretcher then stood staring at it.

One night. That's all he had. If he was going to dispose of the gutter's refuse, it would have to be tonight — and he couldn't use the Kingswood.

He opened the door to his passage, a long and narrow passage, and he walked it, up to the eastern bedroom, turned on his heel and walked back. A hollow house, it echoed with its emptiness as backward and forward he went, walking the stress from his neck and shoulders to his feet, and away.

She must have heard him. He hadn't heard her.

Knew he should release her. Didn't want to. 'Get rid of the problem and we're back to square one,' he said.

Burying it deeper was not an option — as the fool who'd made the poor decision of choosing this piece of land had learnt. Put a shovel into these acres and an inch down it struck rock and root.

Back in the kitchen, he stood listening at the pantry door. Not a sound. Was she on the other side, listening to him?

He had to feed and water her, then do what he'd come out here to do, and put the new problem aside for an hour or two. Whatever his resolution, he could do nothing before nightfall.

He'd built a pyramid with six ring-pull tins, beans in tomato sauce, spaghetti in cheese sauce. Her last meal had been beans. He chose spaghetti, peeled off the lid, took a sheet of bubble-wrapped tablets from his wallet, popped two to the table, then one more. The third he placed into his mouth. It would calm his mind. It needed calming. He opened a bottle of water, washed the pill down, then, between two spoons, crushed the others to powder which he added to the tin of spaghetti. He gave it a stir then allowed it to rest while he eased the screw-top lids on two bottles of water. Experience had taught him that his guests lost strength in their hands quite quickly.

His penlight torch beam tested, he locked the back door with the old key he never removed from the latch, pulled the blind then unlocked the pantry door, and stood a moment, listening.

No scream, not a whimper, which didn't mean she wasn't whimpering. After the first of them, he'd spent two weeks setting up that pantry, stripping it of shelves then soundproofing it. A mammoth task, it had required multiple tubes of glue, multiple metres of foam rubber or plastic. He'd run out of time — or patience — before he'd got around to lining the floor and ceiling, but the pantry was landlocked, the wash-house behind it, the bathroom beside it, the passage and the front rooms to its north and the kitchen to the east. Before installing his second guest, he'd turned his transistor radio up to full volume and locked it in there. Little music had escaped, and four metres from the house, he'd heard not a sound. A scream carried further, as did the pounding of fists on floorboards.

He turned on the torch, positioned it between his teeth and bit down on the cushioning tape and rubber he'd added to its non-functioning end. Having spent a veritable fortune on the preservation of his teeth, he took no chances with them. Two water bottles cradled against his chest, the tin of spaghetti in his hand, he opened the door, sidled in fast and closed it behind him.

She scrabbled back to the far corner, but remained silent. Take light and sound away from them and most tamed fast. He placed the bottles down, emptied the spaghetti into her bowl, then, his hands free, he removed the torch from his mouth and played its beam in her eyes.

'You're Mr Watts from my school,' she said.

'I'm Mr Wolf,' he replied. It was a mistake to engage with them.

'Why?' she asked.

The stench was bad in here, and no place to linger. He picked up her empty water bottles, reached for the baked beans can.

It was not empty. Its contents splashed his injured hand.

'Shit!' he said, dropping the bottles but not the can.

He'd caught himself a rare one. He let himself out, let himself out the back door, where he pitched the baked beans tin and its contents, washed his hands again, with soap again, and it stung again and he needed disinfectant and a bandaid, and that bloody dog was barking, the scent of death tormenting it. And would continue its torment.

The gutter's refuse had to be got rid of, and tonight – and Saturday night not the optimum night for touring freeways.

'But it will confuse the hunters. Confuse the opponent and retain control of the game.'

All he required for a delivery was on the table. He'd bought a new packet of latex gloves, though perhaps they would not be adequate for the task. That bracken was sharp. He'd need solid gloves.

His morning was gone, all thanks to that truck and its lost load – and his neighbour. He made coffee, took a ham and salad roll from the esky and sat down to his lunch.

Twenty minutes was usually time enough for those pills to take effect. Twenty minutes later, he was dead to the world, his feet propped on the table, the coffee mug in his hand, and if not for a screeching bird he might have slept longer.

And she hadn't eaten the entire meal. One pill wasn't enough – or perhaps it was. He'd slept for two hours. She lay on her side, her back to the door, one foot between the bars and the other in graceful bend. She didn't turn to his light.

'Sleeping beauty,' he whispered, directed the narrow beam down through the top bars to her long plaited hair, to her face. She moved, but barely.

She was longer than the others, but a featherweight; he'd handle her should she wake. He returned to the kitchen where he lit an old hurricane lantern. Its light was minimal, but would be enough. He couldn't work with a torch in his hand or mouth.

He ran a couple of inches of water into a red plastic bucket, added a dash from the kettle to warm it, dropped a new bar of perfumed soap in, placed a roll of paper towels beneath an arm then, lantern in one hand, bucket in the other, he returned to his sleeping beauty, this time pushing the pantry door wide.

The house designed in an era when man had been more reliant on what he could store, the size of that old pantry put today's to shame. The cage, built to transport large dogs, used up less than a third of the floor space.

He fitted the key into a padlock as old as the house; its lock opened more smoothly than today's versions. Its clasp looped over the top bar, he eased the side of the cage down to the floor then carefully slid her out.

She flung a hand at him when he unbuttoned her school uniform. She was wearing a small white bra beneath it. Had nothing to fill that bra, but he didn't remove it. He didn't remove the black stretch shorts she wore beneath her uniform. Washed her face with a wetted paper towel, and when she moaned and raised a hand in protest, he caught it and washed it. Later he unbuckled her shoes and removed them, stripped the socks from her feet, then washed her long lean legs, feet and pretty toes. Toes came in all shapes and sizes. Many were not attractive.

She made no protest when he dressed her in her pink pyjamas, sweet smelling and new, didn't move when he left her sleeping on the floor while he stuffed the defiled straw into the now empty Target bag and fetched an armful of fresh from the bedroom at the end of the passage. He'd hired a trailer before his second take, had bought half a dozen bales of hay and two loads of firewood. Not enough firewood, but plenty of straw. He gave her plenty.

She fought him ineffectually when he eased her back onto fresh straw, but he got her in, got the padlock on, then left her to sleep while he went shopping for gardening gloves – and something other than a baked beans can for her to pee and poop in. Until today his guests hadn't found a use for their empty cans.

He bought her a bucket and paid dearly for its well-fitting lid and for the three yellow ducks on its shiny white surface. He bought bandaids, Savlon cream, Dettol, and in the centre's washroom, he used all three on his wound before driving on to Bunnings to buy a padlock for his gate. The shed would supply a chain. He searched for a NO TRESPASSERS *sign and found shelves of signs with warnings of high voltage, and you name it – but they reminded him of another sign, and he saw it again, red.* WRONG WAY. GO BACK.

And a sign on his gate was more likely to draw attention to it than it was to deter visitors. A chain and padlock would make the same statement, but silently.

She didn't stir when he unlocked the cage again to position her bucket. It used too much of her space, but he wanted no more surprises.

At six she was still sleeping. One Valium had relaxed him to the point of stupidity.

A night slow in coming, and not the night he'd foreseen when he'd left home this morning, nor when he'd purchased his chicken and chips. The chips had thawed in his esky, the chicken had cooled. He'd heat them when he was done. He ate a biscuit for his dinner, drank two mugs of coffee, watched the sun disappear behind the trees, and heard that dog howl to the loss of day.

Ten o'clock when he began his preparations. He'd need his wheelbarrow, still parked at his back door. He'd need two garbage bags. He looked at the roll of pink ribbon, his signature, the hunters said, as were his computer-generated notes. His laptop and printer were at home. He'd play no games with the hunters tonight.

There were four minute plastic bags on the table, each of them containing a tightly packed plastic raincoat. He opened one and shook its contents free, amazed anew at what the Chinese could produce for such a minimal cost. Two years ago he'd found those coats at a two-dollar shop and bought their entire stock, eight, and was pleased he had. He'd seen no more of them about.

He slid his arms into plastic, clipped the studs, pulled on a pair of latex gloves – also made in China – twenty-four of them in a packet he'd paid three dollars for. The sleeves of the coat pleated and tucked into the gloves, he secured them at his wrists with rubber bands, then slid his hands into the gardening gloves. They stole his fingers' dexterity, but were necessary.

The night was not as dark as he'd hoped. No moon about, but the sky was alive with stars – a pleasant night for an unpleasant task, and

too warm to be sealed into plastic and latex. He was sweating before
he took up the handles of the barrow and rattled off downhill towards
the gutter. He hadn't noticed that rattle by day.

The dog noticed it; it started barking and kept it up until the
barrow's rattle silenced beside the gutter where he stepped carefully
down. Garbage bags in hand he walked along to that pile of bracken,
and, by a narrow beam of light, he got it done.

*

The weight was not minimal. He heaved the load over his shoulder,
like Santa with his bag of presents for all good children. With the light
guiding his feet he made it back to where he'd left the barrow, and,
after a breath or two and an almighty shove, he got his load out onto
the grass then climbed out after it to rest a while.

The barrow's return trip uphill was slower, but its rattle was
somewhat diminished by its load. The dog remained silent.

The garage door advertised its opening with a metallic thump, and
by the time he got the refuse loaded into the Kingswood, sweat was
running down his back.

Using the Kingswood was a risk, but if the hunters had come to the
conclusion that Danni Lane was his guest, they wouldn't be expecting
her to take her final ride for weeks, and the Hyundai's bucket seats
were designed to hold, not to release. The Kingswood's vinyl bench seat
offered the required slide.

It had come off the assembly line in seventy-one, back when
all that was required of a vehicle was four wheels and a powerful
petrol-guzzling motor to drive them. No bluetooth, no stereo, no air
conditioner. The front doors offered armrests for driver and passenger,
and to these he fixed a nylon rope.

One o'clock when he locked up and from the assortment of keys on
his key ring, found the right key. He inserted it into the ignition but
didn't start the motor or take his seat. He stood at the open driver's-
side door and pushed. A heavy, all-metal vehicle, it took considerable
rocking before its wheels moved forward, but not until the old girl

smelled freedom and felt the incline beneath her wheels did he jump in to guide her merry descent, his foot hovering over the brake, a smile twitching his lips as he visualised tomorrow's headlines.

FREEWAY KILLER STRIKES AGAIN

Thought perhaps tonight he'd stay away from the freeways. Since February he'd developed an aversion to them. Get onto one and you couldn't get off, and they had speed cameras everywhere. He'd disappoint his fans but this delivery was about cleaning up the mess of another.

The slope of his driveway offered sufficient momentum to roll the vehicle out to the road, where, like a feral thing exiting its lair, like a minor moving shape seen darkly, the Kingswood freewheeled by the arty one's retreat, with only the crunch of tyres on bitumen to mark its passing. Not until he made a right-hand turn at the T-junction did he start the motor and notice the fuel gauge.

How ridiculous if he ran out of fuel and along came a friendly hunter.

'I didn't do it, Officer,' he said, and he chuckled as he drove on.

He got rid of his load in the driveway of a fine tall house in a dead-end court, and when it was done and the door closed, he was uncertain of how he'd got there.

FREEWAY KILLER DRIVES IN CIRCLES AFTER DROP-OFF FREEWAY KILLER ABANDONS ELDERLY HOLDEN. PETROL TANK EMPTY.

He'd filled two cans weeks ago, aware that the Kingswood's tank was low. Had forgotten to pour it in. Had meant to do it this morning but lost his morning. Nothing had gone to plan today, and nor did his right-hand turn. He'd lost all sense of direction, was swimming now in sweat, his hands squelching inside those latex gloves and his wound stinging. He was considering opening that door, shedding his protective clothing and continuing on foot when he found Church Street, and relief opened his throat in a wolf howl sufficient to wake the sleeping flock and to give their lambs nightmares.

He'd become one of God's sheep for a time, had obeyed the warped rule of society where the wolf must learn to sit on command.

Not any more. The wolf walked alone now, and alone he drove back to his lair.

His oven felt hot enough to heat his chicken and chips, but he added a lump of wood then removed the large hotplate so he might feed the flames. Gloves first, raincoat, her school uniform, paper towels, and like a cleansing deity that fire took each offering and processed it. He fed it the defiled straw and the plastic Target bag, fed it her socks, one at a time, then her shoes — and the stink of burning leather and rubber sole too strong, he replaced the hotplate and went to the bathroom where he bathed, shaved, then walked, towel-clad, to the kitchen to check his supper then replace his wet bandaid while listening at the pantry door.

Nothing.

He opening it, just a crack. Enough.

'You're not Mr Watts,' she said. 'He would have worked out the maths.'

'Cryptic puzzles were never my thing,' he said.

'It's too big,' she said. 'But thank you.'

Thank you? What had he caught himself? He closed the door fast, castigating himself for his stupidity in replying to her.

Mr Watts would have worked out the maths, he thought, then thought of another, also fond of cryptic puzzles.

'What do you call a deer with no eyes? What do you call a deer with no eyes and no legs?'

She'd been addicted to hot chips, and greasy fish in batter.

He used his towel to protect his hand when he lifted the tray from the oven. The chicken was sizzling, the chips were brown and crisp.

A chicken has two legs. There were enough chips on that tray to feed an army. He served two meals. He shared his tub of coleslaw, kept cool all day in his esky, then, barefoot and clad again in his towel, he returned to that room with a piled-high party plate he had to bend to fit between the bars.

She took it from his hands. 'Thank you,' she said.

'Curse me, don't thank me, my pretty Yank,' he said, and ran from her, locked the door, cursing himself for a fool but recalling a

blue-tinged butterfly he'd chased one sunny Sunday, also a rare and beautiful thing.

He didn't go to bed. He ate his meal, dressed, fetched his axe from the shed and returned to the beaver dam in the gutter to fetch a few loads of firewood – and to cover up all evidence of his night's work – then later to stand and stare in awe at the pink and lilac dawn.

He was home by seven thirty and eating breakfast with the morning news.

SUNDAY MORNING

*T*hree bike-riding Templestowe kids found the garbage bag. Half a dozen adults stood guard beside it until the first police car arrived. The television news vans and their cameramen arrived before Ross, but not before the street was ribboned off, the site screened and both kids and adults hunted back to their fencelines. With little to aim at with their cameras, they aimed them at Ross, and caught him with a smoke in his mouth and a frown between his eyes.

'Is it Danni?' they asked. 'Is it Danni?'

A murder of crows, cawing around roadkill, Ross thought – and considered passing on his thought. He turned his back and went under the ribbon as a female voice asked him if smoking in a street full of children was really setting them a good example.

Here? Now? Pretty little Danni Lane dead behind that screen? Ross turned to look for the owner of that question, and recognised her. He opened his mouth to suggest she get her priorities straight, then closed it, aware that the comment wouldn't go across well on morning television, or with Wall Johnson. It didn't pay to say what you were thinking, not these days.

Australia gave lip-service to freedom of speech, but call a man a bastard these days and he'd have you in court for insulting his mother, call him an ugly great ape, and if his skin wasn't white, he'd sue you for racial abuse. Let a cop defend himself in a melee and the rabble screamed police brutality, and this morning, Ross wanted out, wanted a tent beside a creek where he could scream his abuse at cawing crows who didn't own cameras.

He'd been promising himself that tent since his mother's death. He hadn't done it. He hadn't murdered the Sloan swine who'd bought her house and cut down her avocado tree.

She'd planted that seed. He'd watched that tree send up its first baby leaves, then waited fifteen years to taste its first fruit, and that bastard had cut it down. He'd driven by the house a week ago and noticed it gone.

Its falling leaves had made a mess. The tree had never produced enough avocados to warrant the space it claimed, but had grown the best-tasting avocados in the world.

He wouldn't be driving by his old address again.

He didn't want to be here, either. Didn't want to see behind that screen. Didn't want to find pretty little Danni Lane come out of that garbage bag.

*

Her two phones at her side, Barbara Lane sat on her peach leather couch, watching the massed police on her television screen.

Martin was here, had been here since her father had opened the door to him on Friday. He was pacing, pacing close to her telephones. His own was two thousand kilometres away, as was his bed. Her father had offered him Danni's bed.

'This is bigger than your private war, my girl,' he'd said when she'd protested. He was in control now. She sat.

They filled her house. They ruled it. Her kitchen stank of their frying meat. Her sitting room stank of men.

Lost. Lost everything.

She'd lost her remote control. Captain William Daws had commandeered it for the duration, along with her recliner chair, all the better to chase news reports on every channel. He sat there like a giant gecko flicking his two-metre-long tongue at flies – until he caught the tail end of an interview with Lisa Simms's mother.

'They know it's not Danni,' he said, rising from the chair. 'They're replaying that thing because they know it's that other missing girl.'

'They'd contact us if they knew,' Martin said.

'*Me and Steve always done our best for*—' Mrs Simms said, and the gecko's tongue flicked her away mid-sentence, flicked to a channel showing the massed police.

Barbara hadn't done her best for Danni. She hadn't wanted her. Had been given no choice in the matter. She couldn't take the pill. Every time she'd gone on it she'd put on weight, and in her business, she couldn't afford to put on an ounce. Had been modelling lingerie at the time.

Watched that cowboy pace. Wondered what she'd ever seen in him, if she'd ever seen anything in him, other than his parents' unit – and their money.

Should have flown home and had an abortion the first time he'd got her pregnant, but she'd been so sick and he'd told their parents they were getting married. And her mother had flown over and taken her shopping to buy a fairytale gown.

Lost her reason for marrying him on the honeymoon – and celebrated.

He hadn't.

Hated him for what he'd done to her life – and for what her father had done – or hadn't done. She could have made it big in Australia when she'd won that beauty contest. If she'd had his support, she could have got into modelling back then. He'd made her finish school, had wanted her to teach. She couldn't stand kids. Dropped out of college that first year when she'd got the chance to go to America. Too old by then. Gorgeous fourteen year olds had been strutting the catwalks.

Martin had pursued her. She hadn't pursued him – and knew he'd done it on purpose when he'd got her pregnant the second time. She'd had access to his money by then, and booked a ticket home to have an abortion. He'd found out about her flight and got himself a seat in first class, on the same flight. She hadn't known he was on that plane until she'd gone through customs. He'd gone through faster. She'd seen him kissing her mother, shaking her father's hand.

And telling them about the baby.

They'd given up hope of grandchildren. If she'd mentioned abortion to them, they would have had her certified.

Wouldn't let him near her after that kid came. Told him he wasn't touching her until she'd had her tubes tied. He'd wanted them to fly that kid home to meet his parents.

She'd told him to go, and to take his shitting kid with him. He had, that kid in his arms. A week later she'd had her tubes tied. Keyhole surgery barely left a scar. She'd had a good time for twelve months, had got a bit of catalogue work. Hadn't missed him or his kid.

Her parents had. They would have paid for a solicitor to get her back. She'd been born in Sydney. She was an Australian citizen, and Martin had no legal right to keep her in America.

She followed them to the US, had every intention of bringing Danni home but the old Lanes had bred racehorses and they'd owned their own small plane. She'd got to fly to race meetings all over the country. Hadn't returned home to Australia until after her father-in-law crashed that plane into a mountain on his way back from a horse sale and Martin and his brother inherited everything.

Danni was ten years old when Barbara brought her back to Sydney. She'd found a divorce solicitor. Her father wouldn't pay for him. She'd been too old to return to her line of work so had taken the receptionist job at Crows.

For two years she'd paid that solicitor before he'd got her what she'd wanted, a pile of money and full custody of Danni.

Then her mother had to go and die.

'Stop combing your hair, Barb,' Martin said.

She looked at the comb, at the mat of white-blonde hair woven around and between its teeth, then threw it at his head, and when it missed, she threw the landline phone. He needed that phone. He caught it. He didn't catch her coffee mug. He dodged it, let it spray its dregs all over her peach drapes.

His fault. Everything. And that old gecko's. The whole mess of her life was their fault, and her ruined drapes. She stood and cursed them to hell for ruining her life, and when the cowboy tried to hold her, she raked his face with her fingernails, and when Captain William Daws came to control her, she spat in his face, and screamed.

*

The neighbours, involved in the drama by proximity, had been watching the morning news broadcasts. When they heard that scream, they knew who had been found in those garbage bags, believed they knew, and they came to their doors, a few stepped out of doors.

They saw the ambulance arrive, watched Barbara Lane carried out to it on a stretcher, watched her menfolk get into the big khaki-green four-wheel drive, parked there since Tuesday, its tow bar overhanging the paved communal driveway, a hazard for drivers reversing out of their own garages.

MONDAY 25 MARCH

*T*wo weeks ago, Bob Webb, the car driver, had asked what Sarah planned to do with her month of holidays, and had told her he'd bring in a temp to take over her workstation.

This morning, Bob Webb, Crow's yes-man, stood at her workstation and told her that all holidays prior to the end of June would be delayed.

'No,' Sarah said.

'No one could foresee this happening,' he said.

This terrible thing that had every mother who had a daughter living in fear. Mrs Simms's seventeen-year-old daughter was dead and had been dead since she'd gone missing, and the police were no closer to finding Danni Lane than they'd been to finding Monica Rowan. Barbara Lane was in hospital – but whether she was or not, it would make no difference in this place.

'School holiday in April. I will be home with Marni.' And have driving lessons and go for her licence test on Wednesday, 24 April, and Bob knew about her lessons and her test.

It wasn't his fault. He did what Crow told him to do, as had the last manager, and the manager before. Sarah had been afraid of them. She wasn't afraid of Bob, but at lunchtime, when she saw him walking towards the tearoom, she went down to the street to window-shop.

When she bought a house, they'd need everything new. She'd told Marni they'd look for a house in April.

Her entire life revolved around her month of holidays in April and she wasn't giving them up. She'd given up Christmas for the promise of April, and if Crow tried to take her holidays away, she'd leave.

Marni wanted her to retire. She had very specific plans for Sarah's future: retirement and a cochlear implant.

A part of Sarah still wanted the senior payroll/accounts officer title – but not enough to give up April.

Back at her workstation early, she was about to turn on her computer when she felt the huntsman spider on her shoulder. Had to stop flinching when he did that. He was a gentle person with gentle hands. He only touched her to let her know he was there.

She turned to him, reading what he was about to say by his expression. 'April, Bob, or I leaving,' she said.

'You don't mean that.'

'Yes.'

'We're a team—'

'Team is for games, netball, football. I work here, not playing game.'

'He's in a crap mood and won't give an inch,' Bob said.

Crow hadn't been his dimpled self since the day he'd had his face on the front page of the *Herald Sun*, with Barbara Lane's face. The reporters had stolen a photograph of his wife and printed that the next day.

'If I can get him to agree to you taking the school holidays, will you consider it?'

'No. He agree before to April.'

'All holidays have been delayed, not only yours.'

And Sarah turned her back and started emptying her drawers, stuffing what she removed into her tapestry bag.

And his hand was on her again. This time she shook it off.

'I am very sick. This place making me very sick. I will get him a certificate – for all of April, or maybe six week like he is owing me – before I leave.'

'You can't leave,' Bob said.

'Very easy.'

'You'll be sorry five minutes after you walk out the door.'

'No, you will be. You have to do his payroll.'

And Jackie was back. 'Having a lovers' tiff, folks?'

'Stay out of it!' Bob said and he gripped Sarah's arm, not so gently. 'Sit down for a minute. Give me a minute.'

'What's going on?' Jackie asked.

'I can't have holiday,' Sarah said and continued stuffing her bag, which didn't want to hold what was already in it, and maybe didn't want to leave. It toppled from her chair and spilt its load.

Jackie helped pick up the scattered items. 'How are you going to live?'

'I can.'

'If I could, you wouldn't see my heels for dust.'

She'd miss Jackie, and Shane, and Rena. She picked up the mobile she didn't need, that Marni had demanded she buy. Marni was in love with her own. She collected new contacts daily. Sarah had six. She checked her phone after its bounce. Its glass hadn't cracked. It was working. She checked her contacts. *Bob, Ben, Jackie, Marni, Rena, Shane.* Ben was her driving instructor. He didn't text. His wife did but Sarah didn't know her name. His wife sent emails she signed *Ben.*

They'd spent almost three thousand of their winnings on mobiles and a new laptop that had six hours of battery power and a touch screen. They'd bought a non-stick electric frying pan and half a leg of lamb to roast in it, and it had roasted it perfectly, and roasted potatoes and pumpkin, carrots and onions, then made a delicious gravy.

Marni had baked scones in it, inspired by the recipe book that came with the pan.

They hadn't bought plane tickets to Dreamworld.

And Bob was back. 'Crow wants to talk to you,' he said.

'So he can sack a very sick person and save him some money for long service leave?'

'When you're ready,' Crow's yes-man said.

She was ready. Twelve years ago, when she'd come in for her first interview wanting that job so badly, she'd vomited in the Ladies' before entering Crow's office, and her breath had smelt of vomit. She'd sat across from Crow, his wife and the manager and shown them her hearing aid, knowing that as soon as they saw it, they'd know she wasn't good enough, that as soon as they heard the way she spoke, they'd want to get her out of their sight.

Didn't even tidy her hair today. Didn't tuck her shirt in, just settled her bulging bag on her shoulder and followed Bob.

'Take a seat, Mrs Carter,' Crow said. She took a seat, Bob's translation not necessary. She didn't look at him when he sat beside Crow, on his side of that flashy desk. She sat on the other side, where she'd sat that first day. Crow's hair had been less grey then, his wife had been younger, slimmer, a mousy blonde, but no mouse.

She settled the tapestry bag on her lap, one arm wrapped around it to hold its load in, and she looked Crow in the face.

'A large office is like a machine, Mrs Carter. Each cog is inter-connected, each one driving the next. One cog falls off its mount and the interdependent cogs still . . .'

Sarah waited until he was done with his monologue then replied. 'I am owe holiday from before Christmas, Mr Crow.' Should have said *owed* but that *mister* had always been a tongue twister, as had *Christmas*, and she'd been thinking ahead of how to say them and said *owe*. Perhaps he didn't care what she said. Probably hadn't understood her anyway.

'You are aware that Mrs Lane had a nervous collapse and was taken by ambulance to hospital yesterday morning?'

'I am very sorry for her,' Sarah said.

'I believe you have a daughter of a similar age to Danielle.'

Sarah nodded, but his cold blue eyes were on her face, expecting more than a nod. 'She is have . . . having school holiday. We will go to Sydney.' She said *Sydney* because it was easier to say than *Queensland*, and tonight Marni might decide on Darwin. With the whole of Australia suddenly accessible, she couldn't make up her mind which bit of it to see first.

He offered a nod before continuing. 'Given the best possible outcome, it is unlikely that Mrs Lane will be returning to her position.'

'I am very sorry, but . . . but what position?' she said, and felt the blush rising and was pleased when Crow looked away from her to Bob.

His full face was difficult to lip-read, his partial impossible. She sat a moment, hugging her overflowing bag, but with four and three-quarter million dollars in the Commonwealth Bank she was no longer desperate for his job, for her holiday pay or her long service leave, so she stood.

That got their attention. 'Sit down, please, Mrs Carter.'

'You decide. You send me email.'

'Please,' he said.

She didn't sit, but waited, the bag's strap over her shoulder, an arm holding the bag's contents in.

'Bob assures me that you are more than capable of filling the vacancy we again find ourselves with,' Crow said. 'If given the responsibility, would you—'

He was offering her the job she might have sold her soul for in February, and she turned her back before he was done, and walked out. He wasn't offering it because he knew she deserved it. He was offering it as a bribe, the title, the office with its window, the extra money in exchange for her holidays.

His offer had come too late. Her soul was no longer for sale at his bargain basement price, but because Bob believed it should have been, the floor and the walls blurred. She didn't howl, wouldn't, not in this place. Walked out, her chin as high as a millionaire's.

No lift waiting with its doors open. Bob came, and he dared to put his hand on her.

'Go!' she said. She wasn't being walked from this building like a thief, as Eve had been walked out like a thief. She moved to the second lift and hit its button, and when he followed her to it, she walked back to the first.

'Go away from me, Two face,' she said, knowing he'd suggested that bribe and hating him for it. Unable to look at him, she searched her bag for her sunglasses. Couldn't find them amongst the clutter, and didn't dare disturb it.

The lift doors opened. He stepped in beside her. She closed her eyes until it stopped, then stepped out fast, walked fast towards Museum Station.

'Talk to me,' he said at the traffic lights.

'Go, Two face,' she said.

'I was proud of you—'

'Bullshit!' she said.

'He offered you his prize and you turned your back and walked. I was proud of you.'

She spoke faster, louder, and not clearly when she was angry. 'You tell him offer me bullshit prize. You think he will buy dumb Sarah's holiday very cheap. You get stuff, Bob.'

'He tells me what to do. I don't tell him.'

'You crawl for him. Yes, Mitter Crow. No, Mitter Crow.'

'He pays me well to crawl,' he said.

'And talk bullshit,' she said, this time stressing *bullshit* with an old sign once popular at Perth's school for the deaf where she'd been old enough, had stayed long enough to learn many satisfying signs. This one required both hands and the left elbow, and with a little imagination was self-explanatory. Even her father had understood it.

She crossed over with the green, with the crowd, then offered that sign twice more before he caught the strap of her shoulder bag. Her hands busy, grabbed too late. Her bag slid.

It spilled her sunglasses. She snatched them, put them on, picked up her library book and bag and ran for the station. He followed her down the stairs with her blue lunchbox.

'You don't want to do this.'

'Very much I want this. Tell him he can get new dumb blonde for my job. Tell him get one for you too.'

No train. She'd wanted that train to be there, waiting.

He removed his jacket, loosened his tie, undid his collar, shedding the office with its fake atmosphere and stepping down into the cavern world of the workers who kept the wheels of this city turning. Or was this face the fake and his office face real? Sarah didn't know any more and didn't want to know.

He'd seen where she lived, how she lived. He didn't know she could afford to pay cash for a McMansion, that she could fill it with million-dollar furniture, that she could buy a better car then his – and she knew that she too wore two faces, and more than two.

The train came, and as she walked away from him to board, the huntsman landed.

'Let me drive you home.'

'Train more honest,' she said.

'I love you,' he said. 'This is killing me!'

His words slowed her boarding. For an instant she looked at his face, searching for a reply to his declaration, but unable to find a word, she turned her back on him and boarded before the doors closed.

Saw him standing there, small and alone, frowning, looking for her on that not so crowded train. Wished he'd never come to Crows, that she'd never met him so she wouldn't have to leave him standing there alone, so she wouldn't have another image to add to the thousand images of loss and leaving that huddled in her head. There'd been too many leavings.

MAUREEN CROW

A long wait for a bus. A long walk home that afternoon, and the weight of her bag heavier with every step. The hardcover library book made it heavy. Train travellers who could afford an ereader downloaded books to read on trains. Less weight to carry.

More cars than usual parked on Mahoneys Road. More visitors than usual at the rehabilitation hospital?

That hospital owned a huge acreage which should have offered space enough to park workers and visitors' cars. Had until a few years ago, when some bean counter in a distant office had decided there was money to be made from car parking. Employees and visitors alike now used nearby residential streets. Mrs Vaughn's street was nearby. Until three years ago it'd had a solid white line painted down its centre. Someone had come along in the night with a can of black paint and broken up that solid white line.

Sarah knew all of the road rules now, knew why that line had been broken, knew that drivers could be fined for straddling an unbroken line, but with cars parked nose to tail on either side of the street, straddling it had been the only way to go.

A dangerous winding street, Mrs Vaughn's. An old street full of old houses, pink, red, brown or cream. They'd been built on large blocks, built in the sixties, long before the rehabilitation hospital, before the school, before the Forest Hill shopping centre had become so large.

A few houses had a second level. A few had modern drive-ways. Not Mrs Vaughn. Her driveway was old, uneven, not badly cracked, but worn old by fifty years of use – as was her house.

She had money. She could have paid a man to fix her down-pipes, paint her windows, put in a new driveway so her house wouldn't looked so embarrassed beside its neighbours. She could have bought a new stove for the granny flat.

'You pay your rent,' Bob had said when she'd explained why she'd bought the electric frying pan. 'Demand she replace your stove. Stand up for yourself.'

She'd stood up for herself today – and felt desolate. Having money offered choices. Had she made the right choice? Didn't know, and sighed for not knowing as she sidled by the Hyundai to the wooden gates.

And Mrs Vaughn must have seen her. She greeted her from her back door. 'What are you doing at home at this time of day?'

In no mood to talk, Sarah told a lie. 'Sick,' she said.

The old lady was sicker and needed someone to care about her ills. She followed Sarah into the granny flat and sat.

Was still sitting when Marni came in from school, and came in smiling.

'You left,' she said.

'Sick,' Sarah said, then signed *silence*, a finger to her lips.

'Mum.' That three-syllable *Mum*. 'Truly?'

They fed their landlady early, to get rid of her, and at seven they sat down to cheese and tomato sandwiches, fried in their magical pan, and Sarah spoke of her day, and of that Asian doctor she'd seen before, and how she might go to him and tell him she'd hurt her back because Crow owed her too much money to walk away from.

Marni spoke about Danni's father and grandfather, who, according to Samantha was two metres tall and one wide.

'What was my father like, Mum?'

'Like you, a bit.'

'What about my grandfather?'

'White beard, skinny . . .'

'You're describing your grandfather.' They had a photograph of Gramp. 'I meant your father.'

'Oh. Black hair. More taller than Bob.'

'Everyone is taller than Bob. How much taller?'

'I was twelve, Marni. I don't measure.'

'My father was your first boyfriend, wasn't he?'

'I tell you that many times,' Sarah said, then searched the channels for something to watch.

'Was it love at first sight?'

'Stop now.'

'Why?'

'Because . . . because I am thirteen when I see him the first time. You know that too.'

'Juliet was thirteen when she fell in love with Romeo.'

'What?'

'*Romeo and Juliet*, the famous love story,' Marni said. 'Samantha asked me today how old you were, and if you were pregnant when you got married?'

'Say mind you business.'

'Did my father have the brain tumour when you married him?'

'Yes.'

'Then why did you? Marry him?'

'When I get sick, you will run away, ah?'

'How long was he sick for before he died?'

'Long time.'

'I know where I want to go for our holiday, Mum.'

'Where?'

'Perth, to see his grave.'

'No.'

'Why not.'

'Not Perth.'

'You said anywhere I want, and I want Perth and a photograph of his grave.'

'We going to Queensland.'

'I don't want to any more, and it wouldn't just be to see his grave. We could visit the Clarks and find some of the kids you went to school with.'

'I can see Uncle Bill in Brisbane.'

'Then do both. Fly to Perth, visit the grave and the Clarks, then fly right across the middle of Australia and visit your uncle.'

'We stop in Sydney when we coming back, eh, visit . . . someone. Then we get on ferry to Tasmania?'

'Can we?'

'No.'

'Why not? It would get rid of some of our money. How much extra would you have got as the payroll—' Marni looked towards the door. 'Someone just opened the gate.'

'Lock the door.'

Marni locked it and turned on the outside light. Sarah went to the bedroom to peer out the window, thinking maybe Raymond, maybe prowler, or the Freeway Killer. She saw Bob. He was with a woman who didn't look like his mother. Then she turned her face, and it was Maureen Crow.

*

Marni had to borrow two chairs from Mrs Vaughn. Bob helped move the table away from the faded green curtains, and four chairs around that table was a crowd, and when everyone was sitting with their mugs of coffee, Maureen Crow dropped her bomb.

'From tomorrow, David will be working out of the Sydney office. I will be taking over the Melbourne office.'

Marni looked at Bob, and his face said he already knew, and hooray! Maureen Crow must have kicked her husband out, which she should have done years ago.

A strange meeting in a squat for the homeless, Sarah's back to the curtains, Bob on her left, Marni on her right and Maureen Crow facing her, and just talking to Sarah as she'd talk to anyone. Some people gabbled, some thought if they spoke loudly she'd hear them. A few tried Pidgin English, when all they had to do was face her and talk.

'I haven't been involved in the day-to-day running of the business for some time. I will be a little rusty. I've talked Bob into remaining with us for at least six months. Can I rely on you, Sarah?'

'What about her holidays?' Marni asked.

'The new arrangements won't interfere with your mum's plans, Marni.'

She sounded very businesslike and confident, not posh though, and she didn't look much more than forty. She wasn't fat or skinny, wasn't wearing a suit and high heels either. She was dressed like a normal mother dressed, in trousers and sandals and a light black sweater top.

'Our previous payroll officer received fifty-six thousand per annum. If you decide to stay with me, Sarah, you'll receive the same, starting from this week.'

Fifty-six thousand was huge money. In February, her mother had thought she might get fifty-two. To Marni that promotion had been all about the extra money. It had never been only about the money to her mother. She'd wanted the title, and now she could have it – and not have David Crow.

And Marni left her to discuss it while she filled the jug and counted biscuits. Mrs Vaughn hadn't left many. She could make a batch of scones in a hurry, and she turned on the frying pan to do it, which allowed her to hear what they were talking about while not obviously listening.

A life-changing amount, the TattsLotto man had said. He hadn't been wrong. It was like their win had changed the entire world around them. It would change where they lived soon.

And who'd feed Mrs Vaughn and clean her house. She couldn't. She'd have to give in and move into a nursing home where not being allowed to smoke would probably kill her.

Bob came to help make coffee when he smelt hot scones. 'You decided on Sydney, I hear,' he said.

'Perth,' Marni said, washing, drying plates and knives. 'My father is buried in Perth and I want to see his grave.'

'How old were you when he died?'

'Not even born. He had the tumour when Mum married him. I don't know why anyone would – if they knew their new husband was going to die,' she said, then shrugged. 'I suppose if you love someone, you take what you can get of their lives.'

'She got you,' he said.

'Yeah, I'm pretty glad about that.'

'I reckon the world might be glad too one day, Marni,' he said. 'Have you got relatives in Perth?'

'Only Mum's foster family. She lived with them after her parents got killed.'

'How did they die?'

'Car crash, when she was my age.'

*

Bob learned more from Marni in two minutes than he'd learnt from Sarah in as many months. He looked at her when he placed her coffee down. She was nodding, but saying little. She hadn't met his eyes yet.

He hadn't gone back to work today, or only long enough to type out his resignation and hand it to Crow. He'd been reporting to Maureen monthly since taking the job, so he'd done the decent thing and phoned her.

She'd called back at five. He'd been with her since six.

His trip to Peru was off, or delayed, and when he handed Sarah her mug of coffee, she met his eyes.

'Thank you,' she said.

Maybe Marni was on the right track when she'd said that if you loved somebody, you took what you could get.

A CLUMSY DISPOSAL

*F*REEWAY KILLER'S DNA FOUND ON FIFTH VICTIM
It was headline news – as was Michael Swan.
GRANDSON OF LADY CYNTHIA SWAN UNDERGOES
CRANIAL SURGERY AFTER BRUTAL PRISON ATTACK

Someone had taken offence to his pretty face. He had screws in his eye socket to beep along with the metal in his neck if there came a day when he attempted to pass through airport security.

Traces of blood not belonging to Lisa Simms had been found on her body. A minute trace was sufficient these days to give up DNA. It wouldn't help in the search for the serial killer, but with luck, might be enough to convict the callous bastard who'd run her down, buried her, then returned to the site and attempted to mimic the Freeway Killer's method of disposal.

The two heavy-duty garbage bags she'd been found in had been evidence enough for the media. Forensic were more particular. They'd found glass fragments in her hair, consistent with glass from a shattered windscreen. Her skull injury, severed spinal cord and broken leg marked her as a road casualty – a hit-and-run victim, but the perpetrator had taken her and run, and more likely than not, on the Friday night she'd gone missing. According to forensic she'd been buried for a week.

She'd given them more than that smear of blood. They'd found soil from the burial site, grass seeds, traces of kangaroo faeces, leaves, one identified as that of a Japanese maple, which, by its position on the body, forensic believed may have been carried from the scene of the accident.

A lot of footwork had been, and was being, done. There was a kilometre of streets between the boyfriend's house and the house Lisa had shared. If she'd been on her way home, they may find the site. An impact capable of doing the damage done to that girl would have broken more than the vehicle's windscreen. A head-light maybe. Something.

The removal of her body from the scene of the accident suggested to Ross that the driver may live, or be known, in the general area. His initial thought, a car full of drunken hoons, didn't compute — unless they were local hoons, unless she'd landed in one of their driveways — and even that didn't compute. Hoons, having got away with it on the night, wouldn't return to the burial site.

To date the car hadn't turned up at a body shop. They'd find it locked in a garage somewhere, or torched.

Ross had eaten a solo meal tonight. He sat alone now, with his coffee, playing scenarios in his head while keeping an eye on the box, awaiting an update on Swan's cranial surgery, not overly interested in his health or in Lady Cynthia's protestations of her grandson's innocence, but in her ankles. He'd seen them on the six o'clock news and set up his box ready to record when the channel played that interview again. They would. Give them a new piece of news and they wore it out, played it until it bored the viewer blind, until any pity initially felt for the victim had died stone dead.

Mrs Simms had been boring the viewers blind for two days. When they replayed her, Ross hit the mute button.

A week ago, that woman had stated on national television that her daughter had been out of control since her twelfth birthday. Since her body had been found, Lisa had made the swift transition to precious angel. That woman would find someone to sue for the loss of her angel.

That box, propped in the corner of most sitting rooms, had too much power. Be it politics or disaster, it manipulated the emotions of the masses, breaking down, then remoulding community attitudes.

The media could make or break a Prime Minister, create a hero then turn him into a villain. In the week following Lisa and Danni's disappearance, they'd fed the public fear in heavy doses, had made mothers afraid to take their kids to school, had played and replayed an interview with a retired FBI profiler, played snatches of an interview with two American cops, instrumental in the capture of one of the Yankee serial killers. Inspector Johnson had been given fifteen minutes of prime time – and for the next two days, even Ross had started turning off his cop-speak.

Where they had a fresh crime scene, where they found a readily identifiable motive, a bit of footwork and surveillance did the rest. Given no crime scene, no motive, attempting to track Melbourne's serial killer was like tracking a black ghost through a dark tunnel while blindfolded.

They'd spoken again and again to the parents of the dead girls, seeking a connection. They'd traced the owners of Kingswood Holdens and come up with nothing. They'd questioned paedophiles, set up Granny Plaid Skirt and Danni models at Forest Hill Chase, each one holding an environmentally friendly shopping bag, had made appeals on the box for Granny Plaid Skirt to come forward, and for the public's assistance in identifying the woman. She'd had her face and outfit on the cover of the *Herald Sun* – and not one useful call had come in.

Ross had worn out his eyesight studying that underground car park security video, and kept returning not to that brief edge of Danni but to the full-length shot of Granny Plaid Skirt. He'd worn out the Woolworths supermarket checkout tape, or the section that had trapped Granny Plaid Skirt behind her shopping trolley.

She haunted him, and the more he watched her, the more she haunted him. He knew he'd seen her somewhere, seen that outfit, her short grey hair . . . somewhere, sometime, someplace. Like Nike cap and his cocky walk, Granny Plaid Skirt hung around the outer perimeter of his clashing neurons. She had a good head of hair for an elderly woman, too good maybe. Something was not quite right about her. She irritated his sinuses. As did her shopping trolley in the supermarket and lack of trolley in the car park – and her cardigan on a day of excessive heat. It was more than that. He'd seen her before.

She could have reminded him of one of his mother's friends. A few had worn similar skirts and cardigans – though not on days of muggy forty-two-degree heat.

All gone now, his mum, dad and gran. Not dead, just gone away to someplace.

He had his sisters, had his nephew. Liked that kid. Would have liked one of his own if he'd turned out like that kid. Didn't have a kid and wasn't likely to, and in a world like this one was turning into, who'd want to inflict it on a kid? He picked up his smokes and walked out to his balcony to look down on what the owl saw when he flew Melbourne skies – if there were any owls left in Melbourne. With the lights blazing, it was a beautiful sight, and growing taller every year. There were people living in the sky down at Docklands. David Crow's fancy unit was on the twenty-third floor. He was probably watching boats go by, not cars. 'How high can man live before he needs to carry an oxygen pack?' Ross asked the night. He yawned ashing his smoke into a slim tin, which had contained peppermints before making the transition to portable ashtray, when he heard the late news playing, and Lady Cynthia's voice.

He ran for the remote and hit record, then turned on the kitchen exhaust fan and stood beneath its sucking whisper while he sucked the last from his butt. He'd set off his smoke alarm one night with his smokes, shortly after he'd moved in, and had security up here wanting to bust down his door. His lease would be up in July. He'd do something about getting himself a garden – and planting an avocado seed – and smoking where he felt like smoking.

Watching an angled Lady Cynthia made her mouth appear wider. Wondered if she'd been born with that watermelon mouth, or if it had been stretched wide by overuse – or one too many face lifts. It wasn't her mouth that he was recording. He wanted her ankles, and before the channel cut to another batch of commercials, he got them, trapped them on his flash drive.

The thunderbolt didn't hit him until he was playing it through, and when it hit, it exploded out in a sneeze that may have shaken the building. But he knew, knew that his two ghosts were one, that he'd wasted two weeks of Danni's life in searching blind for the killer when he'd had the bastard on the western underground car park on day three. He was her, Granny Plaid Skirt. That bastard dressed in women clothing to get those girls.

Her hair hadn't looked right the first time he'd seen her, because it wasn't right, because he was wearing a wig. Her shoes were right, as was her walking stick, her walk. Her legs weren't. They weren't elderly and they were a male's legs, with thick bony ankles.

He checked the time on his microwave. Five after eleven. He turned off the exhaust fan, the television, removed the flash drive, dropped it into his pocket and was out the door.

*

Midnight found him at his desk, attempting to fiddle two pairs of unrelated ankles to sit side by side on his screen. The kid constable interrupted his concentration.

'I wouldn't have picked you for a foot man, sir.'

Ross turned to the flyweight, who looked sixteen but may have been born knowing more about computers and mobile phones than Ross would ever know.

'The pair on the right belong to a male,' Ross said, daring the kid to disagree.

'Or she's on steroids,' the kid replied. 'Knowing some of the old girls today, it could be possible, sir.'

'She's a bloke in drag, and she's got Danni Lane.' Ross got rid of the ankles and clicked on the photograph of Granny Plaid Skirt at the Woolworths checkout, the cleaned-up, cropped shot of her head and shoulders they'd released to the media. 'Do you know how to get rid of her wig?'

The kid knew. From a standing position, he gave Granny Plaid Skirt a bald head. With no flash of recognition, Ross asked for hair, and was confronted by Granny with a red Mohawk.

'Get serious, kid,' Ross growled, and the kid sat down and got serious, Ross's breath on his neck, his eyes frozen to the screen as Granny became funeral serious, dark hair, dark suit, black tie.

He gave him grey hair later, then dark-rimmed glasses and a sweater, and he looked like a professor – and like no one. The kid gave him a goatee beard, a moustache, a partially bald head. He removed the goatee and moustache and gave him a full head of blond hair. Still failing to put a name to any of his faces, they printed six of their better enhancements, Ross promising each as it came hot from the printer that it would be a television star by nightfall.

With nothing more he could do before running his theory by Johnson, he considered his bed, but instead went in search of the security tapes collected from Chadstone the day Heidi was abducted. They were there, burned to disc and archived, and in the darkest hours before dawn, he found that bastard again, found him clad in that same plaid skirt and navy cardigan, pushing a loaded shopping trolley away from the Ladies' toilets.

How many times had he played that tape, praying for one glimpse of Heidi? How many times had he fast-forwarded past that old dame and her loaded trolley? Enough for his neurons to remember seeing her.

The shot was grainy, and more so when he zoomed in on the trolley, but he hunted down his whiz-kid mate again who cleaned it up then printed it.

Too late to go to bed, and too early to wake Wall Johnson, Ross walked outside to Melbourne's early light, and to its silence – or to as near as that city ever came to silent. Pigeons cooed, a lone tram trundled by, empty. A truck came then to pollute the pure morning air with its stink of diesel, so Ross lit his own pollution stick and leaned against a tree to watch his city come to life, feeling hopeful for the first time in years. They had him. Now all they had to do was find him.

They'd never worked out how Heidi had been spirited away from that shopping centre. That murdering bastard had wheeled her out in a supermarket trolley, zipped into a suitcase, and he would have been long gone before Heidi's mother noticed her girl was missing and raised the alarm.

*

Inspector Walter Johnson wasn't a fast mover and never had been. In his fifties now, he looked more kindly grandpa than cop. He'd had no family when he'd worked with Ross's father thirty-odd years ago. He'd had six kids since, eleven grandkids and still counting.

He got things done, and by eleven that morning, Ross at his side, they faced a barrage of reporters. Johnson started proceedings with his classic cop-speak, then stepped to the side, and Ross, who'd never mastered cop-speak or microphones, wished he hadn't been born with foot-in-mouth disease.

Done now, all said and done. Midday when he escaped, yawning. Bed not an option, he did the next best thing, made a beeline for his smoking place, where Les tracked him down.

Ross had given up attempting to dodge little Les years ago. Their life-time relationship had led to an unspoken understanding that what was said off the record didn't end up on page one.

'You'd remember Shane Lourie, Rosko,' Les greeted him.

'Lourie?' Ross had known a few Louries, a few Shanes too.

'A year or two our junior, thought he looked like that bloke from *Star Wars*.'

Ross shook his head. His neurons had stopped firing since they'd turned the cameras on him. He'd come out here to suck smoke and forget those bloody cameras, and what he might see played back to him umpteen dozen times.

Les hadn't become a newshound by giving up easy. 'You remember the cocky little bastard. He lived in one of those hovels down near Willy Wilson's place and got done for raping Willy's twelve-year-old sister,' Les said.

And a neuron fired. 'The bantam rooster?'

'That's him. They gave him ten years but let him out after six. Willy and the rest of them have been stalking him since.'

'Including you,' Ross asked.

'I keep track of him,' Les admitted. 'What I started out to say was, your photo could be him.'

'He doesn't fit the profile – unless they gave him a brain transplant while he was inside. As I recall, he was too smart to go to school.'

'Get that suit off him and stick a dirty Nike cap on his bald head and it's him, I tell you.'

'Nike,' Ross said. 'Where?'

'Living with a woman and her tribe of kids in a house we subsidise, within bloody walking distance of Forest Hill Chase.'

'You're having me on, mate.'

'I'm bloody not, Rosko.'

'Address?'

'Dunno, but I know someone who will,' Les said, reaching for his mobile. His contact not answering, he left a message and dropped the phone back into his pocket.

They stood side by side then, puffing smoke and watching the now unbroken stream of traffic crawl by, a big man, his dark hair beginning to grey at the temples, and a smaller, slimmer, sandy-headed man, both heavy smokers, a dying breed – literally dying, if you believed the hype. They'd been born during the same month, forty-two years ago, raised in the same Hawthorn street, attended the same schools, had troublesome sisters in common, one for Les, a Down syndrome girl who may have been easier to live with than Ross's two. Les's parents were still alive, and still caring for their girl, in her mid-forties now, but eternally a girl.

'A man reaches a point in his life when he stops growing,' Les said. 'Cities don't know when it's time to stop. We'll outgrow Sydney in a year or two.'

'Could do,' Ross said.

'We had the best of it, Rosko.'

'You're right there, mate. She's degenerating fast.'

'Still planning on pitching your tent beside that creek?'

'Is the Pope a Catholic?'

'They were good times,' Les said. 'I remember your father . . .' And his phone rang.

*

Ross was back at his desk, watching Nike walk towards the bus stop. He couldn't see enough of his face to say if it resembled the killer or the bloke from *Star Wars* but that bus stop tape gave him an alibi, or the time on that tape did. An Olympic sprinter couldn't have run back into the centre, decked himself out in his wig, plaid skirt and cardigan then got down to the bottom car park, not in three and a half minutes.

For a time Ross had believed. Outside, a smoke in his hand, he'd wanted to believe. He'd almost built an image of that Nike cap behind the wheel of an unregistered Kingswood. Gone now, like the smoke from some forgotten fag.

A lot of resources had been wasted on tracing the owners of that model vehicle, or those still registered. Most belonged to car enthusiasts. The killer had been flagged as a collector by that retired FBI profiler. Maybe he'd got it right.

They'd get him. His face would be on national television tonight. Someone knew him, lived next door to him, worked with him, slept with him – or not. The Yankee profiler had also suggested he was impotent – because he didn't rape those girls. The bastard starved them, drugged and drowned them, but other than Nancy, he hadn't marked them.

He'd kept little Nancy tied up, by her ankle. Forensic had suggested he'd used some type of collar. The skin above and below it had been rubbed raw. He hadn't used that collar on the other girls.

Little Asian Nancy was the odd piece in the puzzle. Serial killers usually kill within their own ethnic group. Penny, Heidi, Monica and Danni were blonde, blue or brown eyed. Not Nancy. She'd had the dark hair and eyes of her race. Had she been his practice run, her abduction opportunistic?

Maybe.

There'd been early theories of paedophile rings. The fact that no photographs of those girls had turned up on the internet didn't mean that there wasn't a coven of sick bastards out there with brains enough not to put their photographs online. A paedophile ring didn't fit Ross's personal profile of the killer. He saw him as a loner, as white, thirty-five to fifty, and intelligent enough not to give them a hair from his head.

He sent them notes he signed *The Wolf.* He was computer literate, which didn't mean much these days. You couldn't survive in this world if you weren't computer literate.

Ross had memorised the note he'd sent with Heidi.

How she flapped her tattered wings on my display board. The tenacity of a child for life never fails to amaze me . . .

If he didn't rape them, if he didn't photograph them, what was his motivation? There was always a motive, which at times may have only been clear to the perpetrator, but there was a motive. If he was into photography, why starve them until they lost their allure? Or was that a part of his game, his proof of power, that he could reduce perfection to skin and bone . . . to tattered wings, pinned to his display board?

A power game, played out by a little man who had little power, who got his kicks by instilling fear into a city of millions. He was of average height and weight according to estimated measurements of Granny Plaid Skirt and her shopping trolley. The experts had placed him somewhere between five foot eight and nine and his weight around seventy kilograms.

They'd get him. They'd get Lisa Simms's killer too.

Once the press meeting had been thrown open to questions, Ross had been hit with a barrage, most relating to Lisa – the media not yet prepared to give up on the fifth victim theory – and a resident of the street where she'd been found hadn't helped. He claimed to have heard a hotted-up car roar by at around two that Sunday morning. An old Kingswood with a buggered exhaust pipe could roar.

Lisa wasn't one of his. She'd done her block with her boyfriend, socked him in the eye and run – had run across a road and been hit by a vehicle that had been moving fast enough to kill her.

She hadn't fought him. Her death would have been instantaneous, so how had she managed to bring back a sample of his blood?

Bumped his head? Cut his finger on broken glass?

On one of the FBI shows, they would have had DNA in twenty-four hours and the perp in twenty-five. Not the way it worked where Ross worked. They'd get DNA but it might take weeks, or months if they had to send it overseas, but they'd get it. With luck they'd find the accident site too, and the car.

Ross's mind flitted to America, to the Latino and the three teenage girls. When that news had broken, it had sounded like a Stephen King scenario. But how many out in the suburbs knew what their neighbours got up to behind closed doors?

As a kid he'd known every kid on the block. As a kid he couldn't recall his parents' back door ever being locked. His dad was an overgrown copper. They hadn't needed locked doors.

He could remember Gran taking him and little Les to a movie theatre once and in came a group of rowdy pre-teen boys to sit on the seats in front and block Les's view. Twice Gran asked those louts to be quiet and to sit still. She hadn't asked a third time. She'd taken the ear of the main offender and twisted it. Do that today and she'd be in court for child abuse – or the kid would turn around and knife her.

Commuters sat, eyes down when they rode on public transport, ignoring the gangs of drunken, drug-crazed youth. It wasn't safe for a woman to walk the streets of Melbourne alone, not by night or by day. Humanity had advanced as far as it could go. It was regressing now, back to the animals' random mating, back to the kill or be killed, to the hunting in packs. And a cop was expected to psychoanalyse them, to stand arms folded when an ice-crazed feral came at him swinging a machete.

Blame the system, the nanny-state, the bleeding-hearts and the taxpayer who provided. If Ross had his way, no man or woman would have been allowed to vote unless he'd paid his taxes for twenty years.

THE CAKE TIN

'*B*reak-through in the Danni Lane abduction.'

If there was an interview, documentary or news item about serial killers on the television, Marni found it and watched it. It wasn't good for her, nor was her recent obsession with her dead father.

Two policemen on the screen at the moment, one of them the image of Robert De Niro, the other an older man.

Sarah sat down to watch when the one who looked like Robert De Niro took his place at the microphone. The subtitles couldn't keep up with his mouth.

Psychopath, she read.

We like to believe our psychopaths all look like Hannibal Lecter. Most look like our neighbours. Most are our neighbours. Many have been described as charmers, as charismatic high achievers.

A successful abduction requires intelligence and patience. The abductor may stalk his victims for months before deeming it safe to strike, but when he does, it is with the finesse of a snake, swift and deadly.

Nancy Yang, the killer's first victim, was taken under cover of darkness. He has gained confidence since. Penny, Heidi, Monica and Danni Lane were taken during daylight hours, Heidi and Danni from busy shopping centres. In all five cases, the parents of the missing girls have assured us that their daughters had been well warned about stranger danger, that they would not have spoken to a strange man.

How many of our daughters would walk by an elderly woman if they saw her struggling with heavy shopping bags and a walking stick?

'You hear what he saying?' Sarah said.

'I'm trying to, Mum!'

'You listen then.'

Marni's reply was to turn the volume higher as the screen filled with a photograph of the grey-headed old woman with a shopping bag and walking stick. It was followed by another, of the same elderly woman, but in this one she was pushing a loaded shopping trolley and had no walking stick.

The first of these photographs is from a security tape collected from a Forest Hill car park the day Danni Lane disappeared. The second, also found on a security tape, was taken at the Chadstone shopping centre the day of Heidi's abduction.

'She look very old . . .' Sarah started, then fell silent as a slide show of photographs began, of five men – or one with five altered hairstyles – who no longer looked like Mrs Vaughn, but like—

'He's Harrison Ford,' Marni said. 'From that movie we saw about—' But the detective was back and looking directly at her.

We don't know the killer's age. We don't know if his hair is black or grey, short or long. We believe he is around 170 to 175 centimetres in height, and his weight is between seventy and seventy-five kilograms.

All five abductions took place on Friday afternoons or evenings. Three of his victims were thrown from moving vehicles in the early hours of Monday.

If you think you may know this man, call Crime Stoppers. If you believe you may have seen him or his vehicle at a car club, or a shopping centre, we need you to call. If he resembles someone you knew twenty years ago, call the number you now see on your screen. If you were in the western underground car park at the Forest Hill centre at around four thirty on Friday the fifteenth of March, call Crime Stoppers. We are few. You are many. We need your help in identifying this man.

And the channel cut to commercials.

'So, are we going to Perth?' Marni asked.

'No,' Sarah said. She knew why Marni wanted to go there. Samantha Smith had put some rubbish on her Facebook page about Marni's father, which Marni wouldn't have known about if another friend hadn't shown it to her.

They watched the weather girl promise two days of heat then more thunder storms, then Sarah changed the channel.

'Put it on the ABC news, Mum. They might play more of what the police said.'

'They say the same thing. I like *Raymond*.' She'd found a replay of *Everybody Loves Raymond*.

Marni couldn't stand Raymond Vaughn, so didn't love *Raymond*. She woke the hibernating computer and asked Google for bus tours around Perth, Australia. She looked up airfares, looked up Perth hotels, and when *Raymond* ended, she offered Sarah four printouts. Their new printer lived in the corner, on the floor.

Sarah glanced at the pages. 'Brisbane,' she said.

'Perth first, then Brisbane.'

'Not Perth.'

'I do everything for you. Why can't you do one thing for me?'

'Because . . . because people can find me there.'

'What people?'

'Crazy people. No Perth, Marni.'

'If we went on that six-day tour it's not even in Perth. It tours around it and even takes us on a ferry to Rottnest Island.'

'No.'

'We wouldn't need to book motels and stuff. You pay for the tour and it pays for motels and meals and everything. Have you been to Rottnest Island?'

'No,' Sarah said, and she went outside to water her garden, the daphne looked happier for its holiday in the shade. She gave it a spray and thought about the perfume of the Clarks' giant daphne. She'd borrowed it for six years, borrowed little sisters and a beautiful house. Then she'd caught a bus and left them.

Should have let Marni grow up knowing the truth. She'd never lied to her, or only about her father's name. Carter had come fast to her tongue that day with Mrs Vaughn, and once she'd moved in, she'd been stuck with it.

Hadn't expected to stay here. It had been a safe place to stay and work only until she'd saved enough pension money to buy a ticket on the ferry to Tasmania. Over there, she'd have water between her and Perth. Had become too comfortable here, where everything had been provided, where all she'd had to do was cook and clean and look after her baby. She'd got to love Mrs Vaughn's heavy wooden gates, her *BEWARE OF THE DOG* sign.

She'd lied about having no photograph of Marni's father. She had one, but justified that lie by telling herself he hadn't been her father when the photograph was taken.

Should have told her the truth.

For an hour she stood outside, wasting Mrs Vaughn's water, but the old lady wasn't watching, and that dead lawn was growing green again, and Sarah wanted it to stay green.

Marni came to the door. 'There's a movie starting. We haven't seen it.'

It wasn't worth seeing. Marni went to bed. Sarah sat staring at the screen while her mind roamed to Maureen Crow, who was no Barbara Lane. Show her something once and she had it. She'd known that office well ten years ago. She was rusty but her rust brushed off easily.

David Crow hadn't been back.

The show ended at ten forty when Sarah crept into the bedroom to stand beside Marni's bed, looking down at the length of her. She'd grown fast this year. Thirteen was the year of change. She'd mature soon. Sarah could remember the day she'd bled, could remember Lynette Clark telling her that it was her new beginning, that she'd become a woman, and would one day be a mother.

Had become a mother by accident, and too soon.

Should have told Marni the first time she'd asked if she had a daddy, but she'd been so tiny, and there had been so much time, and she'd thought she'd forget about him and they could truly become Sarah and Marni Carter, just one more mother and daughter lost in a city of millions – as they had for such a long time.

She opened the built-in robe, or the left-side door of the robe, did it slowly, one eye on Marni, who didn't move. Quickly then, from the top shelf, from amongst her old books, her old sweaters, she removed her mother's cake tin.

It was a battered round tin that had never stored cake. It stored war medals, important papers, photographs of the many roads it had travelled and of the places it had called home for a little while.

For six years it had lived in a drawer at the Clarks' house. For two days it had travelled east across the Nullarbor in a brand new case. It spent six months zipped into that case beneath Gramp's spare bed, then seven lonely days in a cheap hotel before it went to live beneath a narrow bed in a women's refuge. It had gone to hospital when Marni came, then returned to the refuge, until Sarah brought it out here.

She hadn't opened it in five or six years. Remembered it well, remembered the battered, dented blonde on the lid she'd lifted too often before Marni.

It had been all she had, a cake tin, full up with helpless, hopeless memories.

Her birth certificate was in it, Marni's too, and Sarah's parents' marriage certificate. Her mother had believed it important enough to keep, so Sarah had kept it. Kept the old war medals, the two bulky Kodak envelopes stuffed with photographs her mother had taken with an old camera she'd loaded with rolls of film, and when all of the film had been used, her mother would rewind it, remove it and take the roll to a Kmart to be turned into the miracle of trapped moments and people.

Remembered standing in one street looking at herself and Gramp her panda bear cardigan, remembered her mother buying a little frame for that one. Still had it.

Sarah carried the tin into the other room and sat at the table, sifting through old photographs, finding one of long wiry old Gramp in his working clothes, a laughing roly-poly Gran at his side. She found Uncle Bill, a chubby, soft little man. He'd had four children, her cousins. Somewhere out there, they'd grown, as she'd grown. Somewhere out there, they'd have children Marni's age. She would enjoy visiting them in Brisbane.

Her mother had only kept the best of her photographs. She'd ripped up the rest and tossed them out of the car window. Used to say she was leaving a trail behind them, like Hansel and Gretel, so they could find their way back. He'd never gone back, just forward, always forward, getting to no place—

Until Perth. Until her mother had got that job with the Clarks—
I can't just walk out. They depend on me, Joey.

Shook that memory away and opened the small brown cardboard box containing her maternal grandfather's war medals. She hadn't known her mother's parents.

My daddy was a war hero, baby.

Learnt about wars and men with guns that day—

Put them away. Opened an envelope and removed Marni's original birth certificate. She could give it to her in the morning then let her ask her questions.

Marni Olivia. Date of birth July eleven, 2000.

A new-millennium baby. A life-changing baby. She'd made Sarah become what she'd become. Everything she'd done, she'd done for Marni. And telling her about Perth would only make her want to go there more, so she slid the truth back into the envelope, back into the cake tin, and she buried it beneath the war medals.

Television still playing. She felt its noise. Harvey Norman's advertisement vibrated. If Marni had been out here, she would have hit the mute button. Muted or not, it made little difference to Sarah. Most of the ads had subtitles.

As did the newsflash. If not for the subtitles, Sarah wouldn't have recognised Barbara Lane being shepherded towards the passenger-side door of a dark green four-wheel drive, then assisted up to the seat by a giant of a man who'd need that four-wheel drive to hold him.

That woman didn't look like Barbara Lane. Her perfect hair hung limp, her face was clean of makeup. She looked broken – which was of no concern to the cameraman, who had to dodge the four-wheel drive when the giant man backed out.

Barbara Lane was released from hospital this afternoon. A spokesman for the family said today that they hold little hope that the police will find Danni alive, a female reporter said.

Have you got a daughter, Sarah asked that woman silently. If you had a daughter you couldn't speak like that.

Again they showed the policeman, or the part of the inter-view where he'd mentioned Hannibal Lecter, then the news cut to something about tattoo parlours and Sarah turned back to her photographs, sorting through them as she might through a pack of cards, selecting a few she placed on the table.

She was in most of them, from babyhood to twelve years old, twelve and a half. She found the last photograph her mother had taken: Sarah, standing with the Clark children, in her bathers, beside their swimming pool.

Her mother had been dead for two months before that film was rewound and taken to the Kmart. Sarah hadn't ripped up any of those last precious twelve. She'd needed to hold on to what little she'd had after the funeral.

Glanced up at that woman who had no daughter, back on the screen now and speaking about Michael Swan.

... *convicted of the manslaughter of toddler Cory Martin, was today granted an appeal.*

And Marni came out and caught her. 'They're going to try him again! What for?'

'Appeal,' Sarah said. 'Not trial. You can hear that when you sleeping?'

'It's loud enough for Mrs Vaughn to hear, Mum, and if you'd get an implant, you'd hear it,' Marni said. She turned the volume down as Sarah slid photographs back into their packet. Not fast enough. Marni swooped on the one of Sarah and the Clark children. 'I didn't know you had these.'

'You see them many time before.'

'Not since I can remember, I haven't. Who are they?'

'Clarks.'

'You're thinking about Perth!'

'You make me think about Perth – only think, Marni.'

'Show me the rest.'

Sarah passed her a packet and watched them spread, on the table, on the computer, on a Brisbane brochure and the printouts of Perth.

'Who's he?'

'My father,' Sarah said.

'And you, as a baby?'

'Yes.'

'Was he driving the car when it crashed?'

'My mother can't drive.'

'How come you don't want to visit their graves?'

'Grave don't have people. Grave is only stones with names. People who die stay in here,' she said, tapping her head.

'It must be awful to lose your parents when you're a kid. Is that why you won't go to Perth, because everyone you loved is in a cemetery?'

'Gramp and Gran get put on their farm.'

'You can't bury people on farms, can you?'

'They getting cremate. Gramp wrote . . . in his will.'

'*Cre-may-ted*,' Marni corrected.

'Cremated,' Sarah said. 'They will have both ashes put around a beautiful tree, pink bark. He show me his tree. Gum, with red flower that smell like honey. It is very beautiful.'

'What's this?' Marni asked.

It was an old bank card Sarah hadn't seen in twelve years and couldn't remember putting in with the photographs. She took it from Marni's hand, glanced at it, then tucked it into the cup of her bra.

'It's not even your name on it.'

'From before. Long time before. Go to bed.'

'You know we won't get tickets to fly anywhere soon.'

'Places all the same. Town, city, tree, road.'

'Yeah, but you've seen them and I haven't,' Marni said and she returned to bed.

Do You Know
This Man

*H*é'd underestimated his hunters' imagination. Their mock-up portraits hadn't overly concerned him. The shot of Nelly and her loaded trolley exiting the public toilets concerned him.

He was making mistakes, and get two of them side by side and like mice they bred. He'd bred up a plague with this one, and he'd known it. He'd intended buying Nelly a new outfit, just hadn't got around to it.

He had to finish this. He had to get rid of her and the Kingswood, then get out of this place and keep his head down.

He checked his watch as he unlocked the gate. Plenty of time. He drove through, got out, closed and locked it, and cursed the neighbour who'd caused him to lock it. That padlock was a mistake. It advertised ownership. The newness of it advertised recent occupation. He cursed the hunters for forcing his hand with this one. He'd made his own rules with the others, had decided when the time was right. The time wasn't right. It was necessary.

The Herald Sun *had printed a photograph of a Kingswood, cleaner, in better condition than his, but otherwise identical, and every man and his dog in Victoria would recognise it if they passed it on the road.*

He'd sprayed cars before. Yesterday he'd bought a dozen spray packs of black enamel from half a dozen two-dollar shops. That paint dried in fifteen or twenty minutes. It could be done. Given time every problem was surmountable.

He'd bought petrol, twenty litres of it in plastic containers. He'd be making no stops for fuel tonight.

Made a mistake in buying his little Yank a sweater at a small womenswear shop. It was pink and it had beading on the front, and he'd wanted it for this one. The woman who'd served him was probably phoning Crime Stoppers this morning. He'd gone through the self-service at Kmart when he'd bought the sneakers – and was probably on one of their cameras.

The note was done and folded ready in his wallet. He'd taken its wording near verbatim from the Bible, and as he pushed his loaded barrow across to the house, he mouthed the words silently.

'Heaven and Earth shall pass away, but my deeds shall not pass away. Watch ye therefore and pray always that ye may be accounted worthy to escape all these things that come to pass.'

It was a good note to end on.

About to drop the first bag of firewood onto the hearth, he noticed a pool of water there and looked up. The roof leaked over the sitting room, but to date the rest of the house had been dry. The kitchen ceiling looked dry.

He lifted a carton of kindling and newspapers away from the pool. The carton lifted. Its saturated base dropped its load, and he kicked it, cursed it, then noticed the trickle escaping from beneath the firebox. That treacherous bastard of a stove had sprung a leak in its boiler tank, or in the pipes feeding in and out.

The tank fed water via gravity to the house. There should be a stop tap on its pipes. If he could turn it off, he'd stop that leak, and with that thought in mind, he returned to the shed for a stepladder.

He found the stop tap, had to hit it with the heel of his hand to move it, bruised his hand before it moved, but it turned and he ran inside to watch that trickle slow, then stop.

Lack of water to that boiler wouldn't affect the stove's function. No hot water tonight could affect him.

'Phone a plumber,' he sneered. 'Or put a match to the bloody place and burn it to the ground. Plenty of petrol and those aerosol cans would go off like bombs.' And he could no more bring the fire department racing out here than he could a plumber.

He stood staring at the stove, knowing a plumber would find a way to repair it – or replace the boiler or pipes – or would have done fifty years ago, back when household items had been reparable. Nothing was repaired these days. A three-year-old video player was a throwaway item.

He lifted the large hotplate and peered in, opened the firebox, got his penlight torch and guided its beam around the internal surfaces. The sodden ash towards the front suggested the leak's likely position, suggested it may not be the pipes. They'd be on the far side. He swung the beam around that maw, which he'd never considered more than a wood-guzzling space, then, placing the torch down, he removed the two small hotplates and the twin metal plates supporting them. A noisy, filthy occupation, but with the wider area exposed, he could see the boiler tank and he fetched a knife to scrape off the build-up of carbon.

He found a leak, a bead of water at the front top corner where a joint must have given way, or rusted away from within.

There were products available these days guaranteed to repair metal. He'd seen them advertised in junk mail. You could buy anything if you knew the right place to go. A few days ago, he'd bought himself a computer power supply adapter from a place in Ringwood. It plugged into the cigarette lighter of his car and charged the computer battery – so they claimed. He hadn't tested it yet.

'Bunnings,' he said, and went to the sink to wash his hands, turned on a tap, and when it failed to give up its water, he cursed it and took his bar of soap out to the tank to wash.

Lost too much of that morning. Everything took time. The opening and closing of the gate, the finding of an epoxy adhesive at Bunnings, a two-phase product guaranteed resistant to alkalis, solvents, acids and heat – and not cheap – nor was the bottle of heavy-duty hand-cleaning liquid he found there. He bought a hose that was cheap. If his stove repair failed, he couldn't see himself bucketing water from tank to bathroom – and cold water wasn't an option anyway.

Wasted fifty minutes with his shopping. Lost another twenty in scraping fifty years of built-up carbon from the boiler's corner and wherever else he could reach with his kitchen knife. He lost ten more minutes in wiping the boiler tank clean, but the instructions on the epoxy packet demanded a clean surface, free of grease.

Remove caps. Pierce seals with rear of caps.

He pierced both.

Squeeze equal amounts of resin and hardener onto clean disposable surface and mix thoroughly.

He emptied both tubes onto a party plate, mixed them well with his kitchen knife, then, with the same knife, plastered that paste heavily around the front top corner of the boiler where he'd seen that bead of water, then anywhere else his knife would reach. By the time he was done, he'd lost most of his morning, but the epoxy left on the plate and knife was setting. It might work.

According to the manufacturer, it took an hour to cure and twelve more to reach full strength. He didn't have twelve hours, but could find something to do for an hour. Keys in his hand, newspapers under his arm, masking tape worn like a bracelet on his wrist, he went out to the garage and unlocked the side door to make a start on masking the Kingswood for its paint job.

He'd once loved the silence, the perfect peace of this land. No perfect peace today. The arty one's dog was barking, and he kept it up for the hour it took to cover the windows, to fiddle newspaper around the chromed bumper bars, around the van's grille.

His back killing him, he walked across to the house to stretch it and to check his repair.

It wasn't pretty, and a touch with his finger told him it was barely touch dry. He'd plastered it too heavily around that corner, and he cursed his plastering and the hands of his watch, and no boiling water for a coffee as he returned to the Kingswood.

He was easing a length of masking tape along the chrome door strips when the light entering in through the side door altered and he stopped what he was doing to turn.

That big yellow mongrel was filling the narrow doorway.

'Get!' he warned, standing, his eyes seeking a weapon. Spray cans close by, scissors, masking tape. He chose a spray can. 'Get, you ugly bastard,' he roared and belted with the can on the galvanised wall.

It backed off. He continued yelling and belting that wall until the mongrel turned tail and loped towards the house. He'd left the doors open for light, had left the screen door propped open.

He picked up a second can, got both lids off, then, his fingers on the triggers, he followed the dog.

And she was screaming and if the arty one had followed her dog, he was a dead man. He ran to his back door, and her scream was loud and the dog's bark louder. Unaware if it was inside or out, he stayed out, but hammered on the wall, on the window with a can, and it scrabbled out from beneath the house to face him, and the bastard was showing his teeth. It appeared to be a labrador-boxer crossbreed, with something larger in its genealogy.

'Get, you ugly bastard,' he bellowed, and shot a spray of black mist towards it.

It didn't like that. It shook its head, licked its nose, backed up, so he gave it a second dose, stepping back while that can sprayed, kicking the barrow out of his way. He got inside and closed the screen door, his eyes never leaving that mongrel, who was too big to tangle with. His guest now hammering on the floor, that bloody dog went back beneath the house.

He had to shut her up! The spray pack placed down on the sink, he reached for the tap, then remembered – and he wasn't going out there to wash his hands. He locked the door, pulled the blind, opened a can of beans, pitched its lid at the stove then popping three pills from their bubble wrap, he crushed then stirred them into the beans. Positioning the penlight between his teeth, he picked up the beans and a bottle of water and let himself into the pantry.

Once a place of shelves, of baking pans and oversized pots, of sugar, flour and the scent of all things good. The stink of his guest's latrine greeted him today. He placed the bottle of water down, shook the beans into her bowl, then, his hands free, he took the torch from between his teeth and played the beam into her eyes.

'If you're going to murder me like you did those other girls, what are you waiting for, you cowardly sicko?' she said. 'I wish that dog had eaten you alive.'

She wouldn't tame, not this one. He let himself out and closed the door.

'People can't live on fucking baked beans!' she yelled.

He heard her. Her appearance suggested that butter wouldn't melt in her mouth. Appearances lied. She was a rarity he wished he'd found sooner.

'Other things come in cans,' she yelled. 'Fruit comes in cans.'

He felt his epoxy repair again, and where he'd plastered less heavily, it had solidified. He ate a sandwich at the window, drank water from a bottle, his guest now silent.

He gave her twenty minutes before opening the door. She'd eaten half of her beans, and now lay with her face turned to the wall and something other than straw beneath her neck – a strip of his foam lining. He moved his light around the bars, found the place where she'd removed a fifty-centimetre strip of his soundproofing. With her fingernails? It wasn't easy to cut with a knife, and well he knew it. His torch beam returned to play a moment on his sleeping beauty.

She would have made his eighty-three days, all he'd asked of the first of them. She'd brought her own killer with her, had been coughing her lungs out on the second day. Now this one had to leave early.

DO YOU KNOW THIS MAN

It had to be done. He had to get the Kingswood well away from this land, park it within walking distance of a railway station—

His light in her face roused her. She flung an arm in its direction. The chill of cold water could have her flinging more than an arm.

Lack of options led to haste. Haste led to mistakes. Was he making his greatest mistake? Having shaken the undergrowth to flush him out, his hunters would be patrolling every freeway. Was he planning to do exactly what they expected him to do, to run blind, run scared?

He'd stay off the freeways, as he had when delivering the gutter's refuse—

His initial response that day had been flight.

DO YOU KNOW THIS MAN

Few looked twice at him, and those who did wouldn't relate him to the Freeway Killer. And he was running out of time to paint the Kingswood—

'Bloody dog.'

He allowed the torch beam to play on her foam pillow.

'You've just been given a reprieve, Miss Piggy,' he whispered. 'I believe we need to wait until the hunters stop shaking the undergrowth.'

He'd bought a bag of grapes to eat during his planned night drive. Beautiful grapes, large and seedless, their skins crisp. He popped one into his mouth, then began reconstructing the stove.

He gave her two more bottles of water before he left, and two more cans of baked beans, then, as an apology for those 'fucking beans', he broke off a bunch of grapes and placed them into the bowl with her leftovers.

THE BREAK

*A*t seven o'clock on Easter Sunday morning, Ross rapped on the front door of a Forest Hill commission house, rapped twice more before the door was opened by a chocolate-coated four year old, who, when asked to get Mummy, pointed a portion of chocolate egg towards the east, then returned to his/her chocolate-coated companions on the floor, within touching distance of a large flat-screen television.

A second member of the group, a definite male of six or seven, scuttled up a passage towards the east, then scuttled back, unwilling to miss the televised action.

He came then, Shane Lourie, not wearing his Nike cap, not wearing much.

'What the bloody hell do you think you're doing knocking on my door at this time of day?'

'I'm on my way home from a bit of a reunion, Shane, me and a few of the old Hawthorn boys. We got talking about you,' Ross said as the girlfriend came, clad in a purple towelling dressing-gown and half of her hanging out of it.

She knew who he was, or what he was. 'Are you got a warrant?'

'I can come back with one and frighten the children, Mrs Lourie, or we can call this a social visit. I knew your husband in primary school.'

'What do you want with him?'

'We believe Shane has information which may assist us in a current investigation,' Ross replied and stepped back as she pushed the screen door wide to look for the *we*.

'What's he supposed to know?' Shane's mouthpiece asked while he attempted to shoo kids back to their television. He'd got himself a herd of kids – or inherited them from his predecessors. Their televised show unable to compete with the live action at the door, three of them got by their mother. A crawler was currently pulling himself to his feet on one of Mummy's tree-stump legs. She swung him up to straddle the bulge where her hip should have been.

'What's he supposed to know, I asked you?'

'We can have him home before breakfast, Mrs Lourie. If I have to come back and do it the official way, it could take a while longer.'

'Have you done anything, Shane?'

'I don't bloody go anywhere to do anything, and I know nothing about nothing,' Shane said.

'Go with him then. The kids don't need to see you dragged out of here in handcuffs,' she said, still looking for the *we*.

It was obvious who wore the trousers in that house, but two minutes later, Shane came out wearing shapeless jeans, worn-out sneakers, and his Nike cap.

There wasn't a lot left of that once cocky kid who'd looked like Han Solo. He used to wear his hair like the movie star's and he'd spent more time combing it than he had at school. He didn't need a comb these days.

Ross led the way to his car, where he opened his passenger door.

'Talk here if you want to talk,' Shane said.

'I'm partial to a McDonald's breakfast. How about you, Shane?'

Shane leaned on the car. 'What do you want to talk about?'

'How long have you been married?'

'What's it to you?'

'I was wondering how many of those kids are yours.'

'What if they are?'

'You were seen eyeing off a couple of twelve-year-old girls, ten minutes before one of them disappeared,' Ross said.

'You copper bastard! You're talking about that Danni Lane chick! You're not pinning that shit on me. I never went near her,' Shane said, and he turned to the house, to his woman, now standing on the porch, listening to what she could. To annoy her, Ross stepped closer to Shane and lowered his voice.

'At four twenty-three on the fifteenth of March, we can put you on the upper level at the Forest Hill shopping centre, very near her, Shane, within a metre or two of her, Shane.'

His woman's hearing was acute. 'Who seen him there?' she yelled.

'Get in the car, Shane.'

'Who seen me there?'

'A couple of security cameras. You still like 'em young, eh?'

Shane got in the car and slammed the door. Ross walked around to his door and got in beside him.

'I been with her for five years and those last two kids are mine, and I was eighteen bloody years old, and Willy Wilson's bitch of a sister only yelled rape because her mother caught us going at it. And that's a bloody fact, and no bastard would ever believe me.'

'She was still twelve years old, Shane. I take it that your missus doesn't know about it?'

'No she bloody doesn't, and you keep your mouth shut about it—'

Ross bought him a McDonald's breakfast in Canterbury Road, and over coffee and bacon and egg McMuffins with hash browns, he told his guest what the security camera had witnessed.

'We've got you eyeing off Danni and her girlfriend as you walked by to the escalators, then she cuts away from her friend to follow you. It looks suspicious.'

'I wasn't eyeing anyone off. I was bloody walking on air, that's what I was doing. I'd put five bucks into one of those thieving machines while my missus did the shopping, and the bastard finally paid up.'

'Pokies?'

'There's no law against them yet, is there?'

'Should be – when you're playing with the taxpayer's five bucks.'

'Try looking for a job at our age.'

'I've got one. How much did you win?'

'What's it to you?'

'The bastards see me coming and start laughing before I drop in my first coin,' Ross said.

'I took two hundred and seventy-five bucks from it – and I never got closer to that girl than on the escalator. I got on it before her, but she was in a hell of a hurry to get somewhere. She goes running past me and gets stopped by that old bird you've been looking for. She stopped, the old bird, and when the escalator got down to the bottom, that chick bloody near knocked her over. The old bird's shopping went flying.'

'You helped pick it up, I dare say?'

'Yeah, right. I went out to the bus stop to tell my missus what I won, that's what I did, and all I bloody did too.'

Ross drove him into the station when their coffee mugs were empty. Constable Whiz-kid typed up Shane's statement.

I've been living with my girlfriend for five years. We go to Forest Hill on Fridays. She does the shopping and I chuck a few dollars in the pokies.

The missing chick was arguing with another chick as I walked past them to the escalators and one of them sounded like she'd come from Yankee land. If I looked at them, that's why I looked at them. They weren't arguing quiet either. I get on the escalator. They've got signs down the bottom telling you to keep moving but the old bird you've been showing on television got on before her and down near the bottom she dropped her walking stick and stopped to pick it up. The young chick (Danni Lane) went stumbling into her. The last I seen was (Danni Lane) picking up the old bird's shopping.

Me and my missus got the bus home with our shopping then phoned up a taxi and took the kids to the McDonald's in Canterbury Road, Blackburn South. We'll be on their security videos too.

I seen those models you had set up over at Forest Hill and I told my girlfriend what I seen that day. She told me I'd end up getting involved in something if I opened my mouth, so I kept it shut. It wasn't like I seen anything worth seeing anyway.

Shane Lourie. 31 March 2013

Crime Stoppers had taken a lot of calls, most in response to the enhanced shots of Granny Plaid Skirt. He was a doctor from Harvey Bay, an ex-prisoner from Perth, a preacher from Dubbo. He was a Benalla banker, a Doncaster schoolteacher, podiatrist, shoe salesman, you name it. They had a list of names, some familiar. Melvin Sloan was on it, and Indiana Jones.

Ross might have enjoyed interviewing Melvin Sloan, the bastard who'd cut down the avocado tree, but he had pigs' eyes and was as fat as a pig – and Ross was pretty certain who had made that call to Crime Stoppers. Les, his favourite newshound, had been fond of avocados. The bugger had nicked a few.

Crime Stoppers received a second rush of calls after Danni's grandfather's five minutes of fame. He commanded that every viewer do his or her duty. Born to command, at seventy-five, out of uniform, but he raised a battalion of callers, one of which was a Mrs Andria Hall. She'd been in the Forest Hill car park the day Danni was abducted and had given them the possible colour and make of the vehicle Granny Plaid Skirt had been driving.·

I believe that elderly woman got out of a metallic dusky blue Hyundai i30 hatchback. It was parked opposite to where I parked in the west-side lower car park at Forest Hill. I know the model because my sister-in-law drives a twin to it. Until the driver got out, I thought it might have been my sister-in-law's car.

The woman was alone and looked to be around my height (seventy-two centimetres). When she walked past me and my daughter, she smiled and waved her fingers at my daughter. She wasn't using a walking stick but she had grey hair, worn in that same style, and she was wearing a dark cardigan.

I know the approximate time because I'd just picked up my daughter from kindergarten, at three o'clock, and Forest Hill is about a ten-minute drive from the kindergarten. I noticed her cardigan, because we had to fly to Tasmania at six and I was thinking about what to pack. My mother lived over there and she was dying of cancer.

I spent the next week with her at the hospital then stayed in Tasmania for the funeral and to help pack up her unit, so I didn't see a lot of television or look at newspapers at the time Danni was abducted. It wasn't until I saw the big write-up in the newspapers and the photographs that I realised that I'd probably seen that elderly woman.

Andria Hall. 2 April 2013

A Janet Willmot, who'd never been to Forest Hill in her life but was a regular shopper at Chadstone, had given them a statement the same day.

I saw that woman at Chadstone, sometime in January last year. I'd taken my children shopping to buy school shoes. We were ready to go home and my youngest was dancing with wanting to use the toilet and when I got him to the toilets, I couldn't open the door.

There was no sign saying that they were locked for cleaning, so I gave it an almighty shove and it opened and that elderly woman you've been showing on television was behind the door with her loaded trolley.

She said something like, 'Thank goodness you got it open. I was ready to start screaming for help.'

She seemed very normal, very pleasant. I held the door open for her and never thought another thing about it, or not until I saw that photo and heard where and when it had been taken.

I've been trying to remember what I can since. I knew she was wearing a wig, because I remember wondering if she'd had chemo.

I remember telling my mother too that I'd seen an elderly woman wearing what could have been one of my grandmother's skirts. After my grandmother died, Mum donated all of her clothing to our local Salvation Army opportunity shop. I remember Mum saying that she was glad someone was getting a bit of use out of it because Gran had paid a fortune for that skirt at Fletcher Jones.

Janet Willmot. April 2013

Crime Stoppers had taken a call from a male who'd identified himself as Ian. He'd used his mobile, which was currently being tracked. They'd recorded the phone call.

'I don't know anything at all about Danni Lane. I'm calling about Nancy Yang. My wife's family live opposite what used to be little Nancy's father's milk bar. She used to serve in the milk bar and had better English than her parents.

'It's probably unrelated to anything, but for months before that little kid went missing, we used to see a white Kingswood drive up and park out the front of my in-laws' place, and every time we saw it pull in there, my father-in-law used to say,

229

"Not the Kingswood" – like in that TV show that used to be on. We thought the driver must have had a girlfriend in the area.

'Why I'm ringing in now is because my father-in-law said last night that he spoke to the driver one night about his Kingswood, and he said that he could have looked a bit like that dark-headed photograph you've been showing on the box; that the guy had dark hair that was going grey.

'We know he stopped parking there around the same time that Nancy went missing. We probably should have said something at the time, but until that truckie found young Monica Rowan, no one mentioned old Kingswoods. Cheers.'

Ross hadn't worked on the Yang case. Clair, the older of the two females on Johnson's team, had, and Ross picked her brains for information.

'Most of our enquiries were centred around the Asian community,' she said. 'After Nancy was found, and that note found in her mouth, we started looking further afield. It sounded like payback. *Blessed are they that keep judgement and he that doeth righteousness at all times.'*

Ross had read it. It rang of a sins of the father sermon. 'You looked into the father's history.'

'With a fine-toothed comb, for a connection to drugs, initially. Other than losing his licence for twelve months, he and his wife were clean.'

'Licence?'

'He entered Chadstone Freeway from the off ramp, caused half a dozen cars to run up each other's backsides. No serious injuries. After Nancy's body was released for burial, he and his wife took it home to China. I don't know if they came back.'

'Find out,' Ross said.

*

The schoolkids on holiday, there was a mass exodus from the city at Easter time, the weather still warm enough to go bush or beach. To Ross that exodus meant little more than accidents on country roads but less traffic in the city, and fewer people at shopping centres. He shopped when he had to, bought in bulk and stuffed most of what he bought into his freezer.

He looked at calendars, at long-term weather forecasts; he counted the days Danni had been missing and he told himself he had until around the end of May to find her.

On Wednesday evening, Mrs Cindy Thompson walked into her local police station and told the duty constable she was feeling guilty about not wanting to get involved, but she'd seen that elderly woman drive out of the Forest Hill car park at around four forty-five the Friday Danni Lane was abducted, and she was having nightmares about that girl.

I call into the Forest Hill shops to pick up what I need after work and I saw that woman in the underground car park and a schoolgirl who may have been Danni. I can't say for certain it was her, but I'm dead certain it was that elderly woman following her, and that the girl had a blonde ponytail and was wearing the local high school uniform. She kept looking over her shoulder as if she was as annoyed as I felt.

It was a stinking hot day. I always try to get a park underground when it's hot, and so does everyone else. The place was jam-packed. I was cruising, looking for someone to follow back to their car. I considered following that woman, but she was as slow as a wet week, and kept stopping and starting, and when I saw the tail-lights of another car backing out, I propped and got her space.

I didn't see either of them get into a car. I don't know a Hyundai from a Holden but I did see that same woman driving a metallic dusky blue hatchback towards the exit with her stereo belting out Arab music.

I was out of my car by then and walking up towards the entrance and the noise coming from that car turned my head. I expected to see a mob of Muslims in it so you could have blown me down with a feather when I saw that same woman behind the wheel – and not driving the way she'd been walking either.

If Danni Lane was in her car, if she'd been yelling for help, no one would have heard her above that Arab music.

Cindy A. Thompson. 3 April 2013

FRIDAY 5 APRIL

*S*he *was alone, alone with her dog. He caught them in his headlights as he made the turn into his drive. He considered backing up, driving back the way he'd come, but he'd had a long day, so he got the gate unlocked and drove on through. Contemplated driving straight up to the shed, but the last thing he needed tonight was that bloody dog following him, and her following the dog, so he parked a few metres in, where scrub grew close to the drive, turned the lights off and walked back to lock the gate.*

'Good evening,' she called from a distance. Her dog, off its lead and faster on its feet, came to the gate to bark.

Attack always the best means of defence, he attacked. 'Your dog is a wanderer and a pest, madam, and his barking at all hours is becoming intolerable.'

'I'm so sorry,' she said. 'Sit down, Herod, and behave yourself.' She clipped a lead to its collar then attempted to haul the brute back from the gate. 'He's been a city dog. He's not used to having so much space and wildlife around him. Sit, Herod. Sit!' she yelled.

Herod sat, and the woman laughed. 'I'm Sylvia,' she said. 'Sylvia Moon,' and she offered her hand across the gate.

She was the only moon out tonight. He hadn't shaved in a week, was wearing a tweed cap, and she was no chicken. With luck, her night sight was failing. He took a step forward and shook her hand.

'Jack,' he said. 'Jack James.'

The dog didn't like his name or his touching of its owner. It snarled.

'I wasn't aware he'd grow so big when my daughter gave him to me. He was such a cute puppy,' she said. 'Once he gets to know people, he's more likely to lick them to death than snarl.'

'It bailed me up at my back door the other day, and I would thank you to keep the thing in your yard.'

'That's easier said than done out here. You'd be very welcome to pop in for a coffee sometime. Once he becomes familiar with your scent—'

'I'm something of a hermit,' he said.

'I thought I was until I moved out here. Solitude can become rather lonely, I've found. I lost my husband three months after we started building that house. I blame the stress of selling up and building. He had a heart attack on the golf course.'

'I noted the delay in construction,' he said.

'We shouldn't have done it. That piece of land looked like our utopia when we bought it. We lived in St Kilda for most of our married life, and after years of fighting the crowd and traffic, we were so looking forward to the silence of this place. It can be deafening – the silence.'

'My occupation demands solitude,' he said.

'What do you do, Jack?'

'I write,' he said.

'Are you published?'

'Well published in recent years,' he said.

'Would I know any of your books?'

'You won't find my name on the bestseller list.'

'I taught art until last Christmas, at a girls' school. I like to call myself an artist now. I did a painting of your old house a few years ago and named it Solitude. It's all we wanted back then.'

The dog, bored with the conversation, wanted to go, and was weighty enough to get what it wanted. She laughed, again invited him to pop in for a coffee, then continued on her way.

He stood watching their shapes disappear, disturbed by her, and weary. He hadn't slept well for a week.

He parked in front of the garage, locked the car and walked across to the house.

She was awake. 'I dreamed that the police caught you, and were torturing you to make you tell them where I was,' she said.

He placed two cans, two bottles of water down, and was reaching between the bars, shaking the solidified contents of a can of spaghetti into her bowl, when like a striking snake, she grasped his wrist.

Her action shocked him. His jaw slackened and his teeth released their grip on the torch. For an instant more he had its light, then it hit the bars, bounced to the floor, and the light died.

Locked in with her in this noisome space, in a blacker dark than night, the black crawled up his back to his brain. He broke her grip on his wrist against the bars and turned to the door, his hands feeling, finding foam but not the doorknob. Higher, lower he felt, and no doorknob.

'Are you lost?' she asked, and the little bitch chuckled.

'Die soon,' he snarled, shaken by Sylvia Moon, by her bastard of a dog, by his week in hell and his disorientation.

And the doorknob was in his hand and he was out, and lost in the dark of his kitchen, but he got his hand against the wall. It guided him to the sink, which guided him to the door, and from the door he found the mantelpiece and his matches.

*

She'd snatched up that can he'd dropped, afraid its beans would spill. It was spaghetti. Most of it was still jammed into the can. She drank its sauce, more thirsty than hungry, then placed it in the bowl and reached for a bottle of water, and drank too much of it because she needed too much. For the last two days she'd been rationing her water, pretending she was lost beneath a desert sun in the middle of Australia, that her water had to last until she got back to civilisation.

He'd come. He always came. She didn't know why she'd grabbed his wrist. Hadn't even known she was going to do it until she'd done it. Maybe she'd wanted to prove to herself that he was only a man and not the monster of her dreams. She hadn't dreamt the police were torturing him. That was her favourite daydream. They ripped his fingernails out, stuck cattle prods on his private parts and he screamed more than she'd ever screamed.

His wrist had felt like a man's. She hadn't been able to get her fingers around it. If she had, he wouldn't have broken her grip as easily. It had given him a fright. She'd heard his breathing change, heard his fumbling for the door.

The dark didn't worry her, not now. Running out of water did. For two days she'd only been allowing herself tiny sips, and she'd only had about ten tiny sips left in the last bottle. It was water though, and, fresh or not, her body needed it. She put the lid on her new bottle and drained the old before shaking the spaghetti into the bowl.

She only ever ate half of what he gave her, then the other half in the morning. Nan Lane had never left food sitting out of the refrigerator overnight but there were bigger problems here than bacteria multiplying, and anyway, anything that multiplied in here was her own, and she was more worried about what he put in her food than her own germs.

He'd put something into the last lot of beans, some sort of sleeping medicine, and it wasn't the first time either. He'd put her to sleep with something the night he'd taken her school uniform and shoes, but the night of the dog, she'd been yelling at it between mouthfuls, then it just sort of became too much trouble to bother yelling, and the next thing she'd known the grey comet was back and birds were dancing and pecking on the roof and singing. They always sang at around the same time that she saw the first splodge of comet.

Then she'd proved that he was drugging her, because she'd found grapes in her bowl of leftover beans, and her mouth had been watering for one, but by the time she'd finished the beans and licked the bowl clean, she'd forgotten the grapes and gone to sleep again – which had made those grapes last longer.

They'd tasted like paradise, like pockets of sugar and water. She could have eaten the entire bunch, ten times over. He'd given her thirty-eight big fat grapes. She'd counted them, had allowed herself ten that first day, not to scoff but as treats, maybe one per hour, and done the same the next day, and the next, then pigged out on the rest because one of them had started to go rotten.

Grapes were stuffed with kilojoules: about ten big grapes had around three hundred kilojoules in them. Her mother knew how many kilojoules were in everything. She'd only ever allowed herself to eat six grapes in a day.

She used to say that the body only required a certain amount of kilojoules to keep its organs working and that eating more than it required made you fat. She hated fat people. A can of beans contained about sixteen hundred kilojoules. Including the drugged beans, she'd eaten three cans in a week, plus the grapes, which levelled out at around five hundred kilojoules a day, which wasn't enough, though her stomach had learnt to call it enough. She'd eaten too much the night he'd given her the chicken and chips – and the coleslaw, which had tasted better than paradise.

Her mother would have died if she'd seen her stuffing that chicken in, stuffing that pile of chips while they'd been hot then licking coleslaw from the party plate.

She ate anything he gave her. She'd promised herself she'd do that the first day she'd got her head together, had promised herself too that she wouldn't waste water crying.

Tears were an admission of defeat, her father said. 'We're not defeated, Dano,' he'd said the last day she'd spoken to him. His court date was 22 April. It must have been April by now. If he didn't find her soon, he'd have to cancel that court date.

He'd be looking for her. So would Grandpa, who had probably called up the whole Australian army to search. She could almost see him sitting in his Jeep, barking orders.

Die soon.

She wasn't going to. She had water, a full stomach of spaghetti, which was also stuffed with kilojoules, and more left for breakfast, and two unopened cans of something.

Wished one of them contained peach halves, or pineapple, apricots, even plums. One might. He'd given her grapes. Probably not. She was lucky he'd put the cans and water down before she'd grabbed his wrist or he mightn't have given her anything.

Shouldn't have done it. He had to be some sort of mad to do something like this – and he was still out there. She could see his light seeping beneath the door and hear his footsteps.

She heard every sound now, heard a dozen different sorts of birds at different times of day. She heard trucks too, and that dog. Heard a helicopter one day and convinced herself that it was the police or Grandpa in an army helicopter. It hadn't landed.

His slamming door sounded like Grandpa's screen door—

And she heard that door again, and he came in again, with a big torch. He didn't shine it on her, but on the floorboards, and she could see the shape of him, see his shoes, the bottoms of jeans.

Her eyes feasting on sight, she didn't immediately name what she saw where that greyish splodge of comet came to tell her that it was morning. She didn't name it until the torch lit that place again. It was a hole in one of the floorboards, near his foam wall, a longish splintery break.

His light moved to where he put her cans and water bottles, then his hand reached down, and she thought he was going to take her water.

'Don't,' she said. 'I'm sorry.'

But he'd picked up the narrow-beamed torch he'd dropped when she'd grabbed his wrist. It was just a tiny one, not much fatter than a biro. It had rolled between the end of the cage and the wall, and she could have reached it. Should have looked for it. Could have shined its light in his face the next time he came in and seen what he looked like.

A lot of good that would do. If she knew what he looked like, he'd never let her go.

He wouldn't anyway.

Die soon, he'd said.

When he picked up her empty bottles, she held her breath, scared stiff he'd take the full ones. Cowards fed on fear. He was a coward or he wouldn't pick on kids, so she did what she always did when she was scared stiff.

'If people can't get out in the sun they need vitamin D,' she said. 'It's in fish. Tuna and sardines come in cans with ring-pull tops – and fruit.'

He didn't reply. His light showed him the doorknob and he was gone, and really gone this time, because she heard the key turn in the lock, then that screen door slam, which meant that he was leaving.

Sat listening for his car to start. She always heard it. Always heard it coming before it got here too, and listened now for the motor to fade away into the distance.

The straw rustled when she moved, but she got to her knees, then stilled again, straining to hear what wasn't out there. Didn't know what was out there.

She heard the dog. Not close though. He'd been right beneath her the day of the grapes, so close she'd felt its bark coming up through the boards, and the more she'd yelled, the more it had barked. She'd learnt something from that day; she was in a house that had space beneath it.

Where there was one house, there were others. Where there was a dog, there was an owner – unless it was a wild dog. Australia had wild dogs. It didn't belong to him, which had been pretty obvious. He'd yelled and banged things like a crazy man.

That dog could have come from anywhere. They had acute hearing, and could smell things from a mile away. If he'd got his nose to that comet hole, he would have smelt her. She couldn't smell much now – except when she took the lid off her bucket, which he never emptied.

She'd secreted the lid of a baked beans can beneath the straw so she could cut her hair. It hadn't been any good for that, but was effective at cutting his foam rubber walls. She'd got a skinny bit of it off and was working on a decent-sized pillow now, which, if she ever got it cut, she should be able to drag between two of the bars. It was pliable.

Prisoners in the old days had survived in dark dungeons with rats chewing on their toes and nesting in their hair. People captured by terrorists survived, and she would too, unless he drugged her and drowned her. She had to distrust everything he gave her, test a bit before she ate the lot, and if she started feeling like she wanted to sleep, stop eating.

The first time he'd put his sleeping stuff in her food, she'd felt herself being pulled away and she hadn't even cared. She'd cared when she'd woken up and her shoes and dress were gone. She'd panicked, thought paedophile, and naked photographs on the internet. The second time, he hadn't taken her clothes off, or if he had, he hadn't changed them. Maybe he'd just wanted to stop her yelling.

Wished her father would find her before 22 April and get her out and take her home to America. Wished they'd never left, that Nan and Pop Lane were still alive over there. Wished . . .

Nan Lane used to say that wishing for the moon wouldn't make it fall into your lap. 'If you want the moon, get out there and lasso it, Dano,' she'd said.

She'd got herself a pillow with that baked beans lid, and now she wanted a bigger one so she was cutting a bigger one. It was something to do.

There were six bars on the short sides, strong bars, wider then her thumb with about twelve or fifteen centimetres between each. The long sides had nine bars. They were her calendar. She'd counted off the days on one short, one long side and was around the bottom corner now. Didn't know how many days she'd lost in screaming herself hoarse but should probably add three more bars which probably meant that she had about two more weeks before 22 April.

Prisoners did exercises to fill their days. She couldn't do much, but she conjured up Michelle from *The Biggest Loser* most days and did lift-ups on the top bars, and push-ups. She'd never been able to do proper push-ups, but could now.

She'd watched television the first Friday they'd spent at Forest Hill, only because her mother had gone to bed with The Crow, like, a wall away, and because she'd wanted to annoy them. She'd turned the volume up and sat until after one o'clock watching a film about a prisoner who'd spent his life escaping, being caught and being brought back to a worse cell. He'd been in one with bars for a roof once, and had been half-starved, too, but he'd exercised.

Fifteen push-ups was easy, so she pushed herself to do twenty, or Michelle did. *Man up, Danni. Are you here to win or to throw in the towel at the first hurdle?*

'I'm going to win,' Danni yelled.

How are you going to win, Danni? Michelle yelled.

'By being stronger than the opposition.'

THE COMMODORE

*R*oss was leaning against his favourite tree, sucking smoke and readying himself for another day at the office, when a red Ferrari glided into a parking space six or eight metres away. He did what he usually did, profiled the driver – high-flyer, thirty-odd, divorced – and the door opened and fat Freddy stepped out. He didn't fit the profile, though the woman he was with might have.

Client? Ross thought, or had fat Freddy caught himself a racing model? He knew Freddy had a wife who used to drive a six-year-old Commodore. They'd located it, out past Heathcote, not five kilometres from where the carjackers had tossed Freddy out to the side of the road in his boxer shorts. That woman didn't fit the old Commodore profile.

And Freddy turned and caught him staring. Ross raised a hand in a salute, the barrister returned with a sweep of swamp-green frog's eyes and a partial nod. An odd couple, definitely a couple. She took his hand as they walked towards the building Ross called the office, and when he judged them far enough away, he walked across the grass to the kerb to admire the lines of Freddy's thorough-bred, and to make an educated guess at its value – and another as to where the money had come from to pay for it. Lady Cynthia paid her grandson's bills. Since the night of his arrest, Frederick Adam-Jones had been in Lady Cynthia's pocket.

A beautiful-looking car, it screamed class from its wheels to its luxurious interior. A fair replacement for a six-year-old Commodore. Ross was thinking insurance, thinking that what an insurance company might pay out on the Commodore may just about pay for the Ferrari's wheel trims – which got him to wondering how much his own Commodore would be worth as a trade-in on a four-wheel drive. His was older, and it had a couple of cigarette burns in the upholstery but a bare seventy thousand kilometres on the speedo.

His smoke down to the butt, he dropped it into his peppermint tin. Until a few years ago, smokers dropped their butts anywhere. Do that today and you'd cop a fine. The lid of the tin secure, he shook it to cool the new ember with the ash of the old, then dropped the tin back into his pocket – and his phone, sharing that polluted pocket, protested.

'Who?' he said.

'Roy. We've struck paydirt, Sarge. The data bank's come back with a biological match—'

'Biological?'

'From degraded DNA, biological is good.'

'Whose?'

'Clarence Daniel Jones, a petty crim. We've got his details coming up now.'

'Hoon?'

'Fifty. Where are you?'

'Walking. What's his form?'

'Amphetamines. He served time in Fremantle in 2007 . . . Jesus H. Christ! You've got to see this, Sarge. He's got something of Baldy Plaid Skirt in him.'

'I'm with you,' Ross said, his mind doing triple jumps. Lisa had given them that DNA. She wasn't one of Plaid Skirt's.

He dropped his mobile back into his pocket, his mind pole-vaulting then to the ex-con, a Ron someone who'd called Crime Stoppers identifying the dark-headed Plaid Skirt mock-up as a crim he'd served time with in Western Australia; he'd known him as Indiana Jones. Johnson had likened that shot to Harrison Ford who had played the role of Indiana Jones – and Han Solo.

A crowd had gathered around the screen. Ross, taller than most, looked over Clair's topknot and Constable Whiz-kid's clipped scalp to view Clarence Daniel Jones's mug shot, and he did have something of Plaid Skirt about him. He had a record going back to '86.

'An ex-wife and four kids,' Ross said.

'Three sons and a daughter,' Clair said. 'A daughter he last saw wearing a pink t-shirt and denim skirt, sir?'

'Wrong eyes,' Ross said. 'Wrong build.'

Clarence Jones had rolled his double wheeler up north of Perth and had walked away from it with enough amphetamines in him to choke a horse, and enough in his cabin to supply a hundred truckies. He'd been locked up in December of 2007 and released in July of 2009.

'The timing's right,' Johnson said. Nancy Yang was abducted in July of 2010.

'He's taller and no lightweight.'

'Didn't appreciate prison food,' Constable Whiz-kid surmised. 'Came out thinner than he went in.'

The crowd segmented. Ross stood on, staring. They had a six-year-old address for Clarence Jones. Ex or not, his wife and kids could still have been living there.

Johnson wanted the name of the chap who'd made that call to Crime Stoppers about Indiana Jones but Ross stood on, staring at the mug shot's eyes, protruding eyes he knew well.

'Fat Freddy,' he said. A few turned. 'Frederick Adam-Jones. I saw him coming in here.'

'His kid was picked up last night doing wheelies in his mate's mother's car, blind drunk and carrying a fake ID,' Constable

Whiz-kid said. 'He came clean when they came at him with a needle to take his blood.'

Ross's sinuses itching, his neurons tripping over each other, he turned again to the screen. Clarence Daniel Jones: Frederick Adam Jones: Good biblical names, both. Similar ages; an ex-con and barrister, one short, one tall, but identical eyes.

A biological match . . .

Freddy's Commodore torched. His hoon son picked up doing wheelies in his mate's mother's car – his hoon son who didn't like needles.

Or didn't want to give up his DNA.

Ross's sneeze was an explosion. It shook the office.

'You need to give up the smokes,' Johnson said.

'Why do five carjackers drive a hundred kilometres—' He sneezed again '— drive a hundred kilometres out of Melbourne to torch a stolen car? How did they get home?'

Clair's expression suggested Detective Senior Sergeant Hunter may have finally blown his brains out of his nostrils. His next words didn't alter her opinion.

'Why drop Freddy off next door to where they torched his car?'

'It's his psycho sinuses,' Constable Whiz-kid said. 'They've got a bad habit of making quantum leaps.'

'Put them to work in tracking down that caller – and the ex-wife. They've got four kids. You don't move around when you've got kids,' Johnson said. He'd know. He'd bought a house when he'd married and was still living in it. 'Jones lost his licence. Find out if he got it back. By nightfall I want to know what Clarence Daniel Jones ate for breakfast and where he ate it.'

Ross wanted to get a look at the burnt-out husk of Freddy's wife's Commodore.

He wasn't able to contact Clarence's ex; he had found out where the Commodore was, though the day was done before he got a look at what was left of it.

It was a blackened hulk but most of its panels were intact, and the dents in its bonnet and hood were consistent with those he might expect to see on a car involved in a hit-and-run, and when added to fat Freddy's disinterest in identifying his attackers – they'd lined up a few for him to take a look at and had trouble getting him in there to point the finger – because the little bastard hadn't been carjacked.

Who does a sixteen-year-old hoon call when he's in trouble, other than dear old Dad – or a solicitor. Freddy's hoon had got the two for the price of one, and a devious little bastard into the bargain.

Ross could see it playing out, see fat Freddy taking that late night phone call, getting into his Ferrari and driving off to save his hatchling, and Ross wanted that car gone over by the experts. He wanted Freddy's phone records. He was about to use his phone when it rang.

'Who?'

It was Johnson. Clarence Jones's ex-wife had been located at the same address. She'd been evasive about the current whereabouts of her ex-husband.

BACKPACKS

*R*oss was the last to board that early morning plane and made it only by the skin of his teeth, and he heard his bellowing seatmate before sighting his aisle seat. There were two squawking ankle biters, his fate for the next four hours. He stowed his luggage, sat and buckled in. Neither infant appreciated being buckled down – and Ross didn't appreciate either infant, or their mother, probably flying on his tax dollars.

They were up, the plane levelling out, when a flight attendant took pity on him. Leaning low, she suggested Ross might like to move to a rear seat. Like? You've never seen a big man move as fast as he'd done it. Grabbed his luggage so damn fast he almost dropped his bag on the major bellower's head. Good reflexes saved him.

And he'd hit the jackpot. His new seatmates were slim, fresh-faced girls who had to be sisters. He stowed his bag for the second time, making space for it between matching black backpacks, then sat, sighed with relief and took a few notes from his breast pocket.

'Turn them off, Mum,' the younger of the two sisters – obviously not sisters – said, and she caught him staring. 'Not the engines,' she added for his benefit.

He nodded and turned back to his typewritten pages, thinking *Mum*, thinking a few more of his tax dollars were being squandered on a quick trip home for the holidays. We feed them hormone-laced chicken and they go clucky in the schoolroom, he thought.

Five minutes later when he glanced their way again, he caught them in deep conversation, their mouths going ten to the dozen but no sound issuing from their lips. Intrigued, he stared – until the younger girl caught him again.

'We were just saying that you're that policeman we saw on television, and that you look different when you're not wearing a suit and tie.'

'Most of us do,' he said.

'Does the Freeway Killer really look like those photos in the newspaper?'

'We believe so,' he said.

'Danni went to my school for a little while. It's horrible not seeing her there and knowing that he's got her.'

He nodded and turned his eyes back to his notes.

'Is she still alive?' the girl asked.

'I believe so,' he repeated.

'Are you having a holiday?'

'Work,' he said.

'We're going on a tour. Mum lived in Perth until she was eighteen but she never saw anything, except the city. We're going on a ferry to Rottnest Island, where the quokkas are.'

'How long since you've been home?' Ross asked Mum.

The girl replied for her. 'She's deaf. She wears hearing aids, but the pressure or something was hurting her ears.' She nudged Mum. 'The policeman spoke to you.'

And Mum looked at him with a pair of big brown worried eyes, no black paint marring them and no paint necessary, and Mum or not, she looked like a pretty clean-faced girl.

He'd dealt with the deaf on a couple of occasions; he'd interrogated a deaf chap once in a four-way conversation, through his solicitor and a hand-signing translator. He knew no signs but had seen her reading her girl's mouth, so he tried his question again, and this time she replied.

'Fourteen year,' she said.

'You fly home often?'

'First time,' she said.

'It's the first time both of us ever flew. Mum came over on a bus and it took two days. We'll be there in less than four hours, and we get like two hours back when we land. Do you fly very much?'

'Only when I have to. I plan to drive across the Nullarbor one of these days.'

'Mum's father drove an old car across it from Adelaide, or almost across. It broke down and they had to leave it on the side of the road, out in the middle of nowhere, and get a lift the rest of the way with a truck driver.'

He was on this plane because of another truck driver – or the truck driver's wife, who'd said on the phone that her husband was driving up at the mines and staying out of trouble and to leave him alone, that he wasn't a bad man, just a bit of a larrikin. She'd said too that he had umpteen brothers and that Frederick Adam-Jones was one of them, and an up himself little shit of a man. Ross agreed with her on that point.

It does the heart good to be proven right. He knew he was right about Freddy's hoon son too, and he would have preferred to stay at home and follow his nose than be up here and not too certain he'd get down again.

But the flight attendant was offering him breakfast, and he needed it.

'We have two already,' Mum said.

'I'll eat yours,' the girl said.

'You got hollow leg.'

Again the girl caught him eavesdropping. 'Have you got any kids?'

'No,' he said, and slid his notes back into his pocket and put his table down. The smell of coffee activated his smoking reflex. There'd been a time when you could smoke on planes.

'School holidays,' he said.

'For one more week.'

'What year are you in?'

'Seven.'

Which made her around twelve years old. Her face wasn't a kid's, her slim frame could have been. Mum had left Perth fourteen years ago. How old had she been when she'd left? She was as slim as her daughter. Their eyes were similarly shaped, but Mum's were more watchful, worried eyes, working hard to take in everything, to work out what was about to happen before it happened. The girl's eyes spoke a different language. Hers were taking in the world and loving every minute of it.

He drank his issue of coffee in two swallows and looked for more. He drank his juice, ate his omelette, and when the flight attendant returned to offer more coffee the girls passed their cups across for refills.

'You're too young to drink coffee,' he told the daughter.

'I saw a documentary on television that said it was good for asthma.'

'You're an asthmatic?' he asked.

'No, but maybe coffee is the reason why I'm not,' she said, and he smiled and looked at deaf Mum who'd raised a kid unlike any twelve year old he'd previously come across.

She offered him a mint when their tables were packed away. He accepted her offer, and she continued quizzing him and offering mints to keep him replying.

They talked their way to Perth and he did his own fair share of quizzing Mum, who only replied when he asked her a question. He asked if she'd travelled alone to Melbourne on the bus, asked where she worked, and raised his eyebrows when she told him. He'd been to Crow's office twice. He hadn't seen her there.

Watched her slip two hearing aids into her ears when they were back on the ground, then he quizzed her on how much she heard with them.

'Big noise. Not much.'

He lifted their matching backpacks down, shuffled behind them to the exit, then walked at their side to the taxi rank where he queued behind them.

'Where are you staying?' he asked.

'At a hotel in the middle of the city tonight,' the girl said. 'We get on our tour bus in the morning. How long are you staying?'

'I'll be flying home while you're touring,' he said. 'How would your mum feel about sharing a taxi?'

'She likes saving money,' the girl said. 'Mum. He wants to share our taxi.'

Mum wanted to pay her share of the fare when he unloaded their backpacks outside the hotel. He told her his boss was picking up the tab.

'Find Danni soon,' the girl said.

He had no reply to that, then with a wave of their hands they were gone, and he didn't know their names.

He knew that Mum was a senior payroll/accounts officer at Crows. He knew they lived in a granny flat behind an elderly tyrant's house, that they'd left her home alone for ten days and were worried about her already. He knew they were going to buy a car after their holiday, if Mum got her licence. He knew there was no father on the scene, that he was buried in Perth, that they were going to visit his grave before they flew home. He knew, too, that had he been less set in his ways, he would have asked their names, got their phone numbers. That's what people did these days, met on planes, in bars, online.

For much of his life, Ross had been making snap judgements about those he met in odd places. He liked or disliked, trusted or distrusted on sight. He liked that girl. He liked her Mum's worried eyes.

He didn't like the desk clerk when he fronted up at the reception desk to check in and was told his room wouldn't be ready for occupancy until one o'clock. He was, however, welcome to leave his luggage.

Ross's laptop was in his sports bag, and, having no intention of being separated from it, he walked out to the pavement where he lit a smoke and wondered if his seatmates were having the same difficulty at their hotel. It was only a block or two from his, so he walked back, telling himself he'd ask their names if he found them wandering the morning streets.

A small world, he thought. What was the likelihood of flying across the country to speak to the ex-wife of an ex-con who was probably driving up at the mines and keeping his nose clean, then being seated by default, or the fault of two out-of-control brats, beside a kid who'd gone to school with Danni?

He knew where she'd gone to school. He'd been there. He knew where she'd lived. Been there too. His seatmate's granny flat would have been in that general area.

*

He had a busy day. It was after five before he checked into his room, and the first thing he saw in it was the *No smoking* sign and the fine smokers would incur should they light up in that hallowed space. He tossed his bag on a bed, made certain his door was locked then walked around the corner where he bought Chinese for dinner.

Space and time are good teachers. He found a card game on his phone and flattened his battery playing it and when he checked in so he could charge it, he couldn't find his charger. No more card games – and his borrowed bed was as hard as the hobs of hell.

He turned on the television and flicked around until he found a movie – and was asleep before it ended.

A ratbag morning show woke him – and probably his neighbour, and when he failed to find the remote to turn it off, he dressed and got out, checked out, which took as long as it had to check in – and no, he had not attacked their minibar. Maybe they sent someone up to check, which could have been why it took so long to check him out.

Annoyed by the dictates of those at the top of the tree, he lit up a metre from the hotel door and hoped his smoke infiltrated their sterile space.

His flight home left at ten, and with hours to kill, he went sight-seeing, or mind travelling through yesterday.

He hadn't found Clarence Daniel Jones but had eaten a ham and pickle sandwich with Jones's ex-wife, who ran a childcare centre for five grandkids. Their conversation was interrupted half a dozen times while she broke up fights, but between the fights he'd learnt that Clarry had worked at Bridgestone Tyres after *they'd* let him out the last time, but that *they* must have given him back his truck licence because the last time she'd heard from him he'd been driving up at the mines.

She'd said she had no way of contacting him. She said again that he was never a bad husband, just unreliable. He still sent her money when he thought about it and he never forgot the kids' birthdays, or hers. She still loved him, she said. 'Just couldn't live with him.'

She gave him the names of Clarry's six brothers, told him all about fat Freddy's hyphen.

'He added it when he got his scholarship into university. He thought he was too good to be a common Jones. I only met him two or three times but he always came across as a smart-arsed little runt. His mother thought he was Jesus Christ himself.'

She'd given Ross the addresses of two of her brothers-in-law. 'We send Christmas cards,' she said.

He'd spoken to his Perth colleagues. If Clarence Daniel Jones was driving up at the mines, they'd find him. They'd had no luck to date in tracking down the 'Ron' who'd called Crime Stoppers about Indiana Jones.

Ross was standing with a group waiting to cross at a traffic light, a smoke in hand and a woman looking at him as if he were a terrorist carrying a load of explosives. He butted out in his peppermint tin and considered what he might do on these streets if he had a week of space and time.

And he saw them, the girls from the plane, waving at him from the far side of the street. He smiled and waved back, didn't cross over when the lights changed. Waited for them to cross to him.

'Are you tailing me?' he greeted them.

'We didn't pay for breakfast at the hotel,' the girl said. 'Mum thinks she can remember a McDonald's near where we catch our tour bus.'

'Would Mum mind if I joined you? I don't mind a bacon and egg McMuffin.'

'It will save us wearing ourselves out trying to keep you in sight,' the girl said, and he laughed, halfway in love with that middle-aged twelve year old.

THE HOUSE

*C*larence Daniel Jones was still missing. Bill Jones hadn't seen Clarry since their father's funeral but kept in touch with John, who'd lost his wife six months ago. Joe he'd last heard from a few months after their father's death. Bert was overseas somewhere, Gordon was a widower with a buggered back, and then there was Freddy. You only needed to look in a newspaper to find Freddy.

Ross had run his hoon theory by Johnson. It took a better imagination than his to visualise Frederick Adam-Jones and his son digging a grave and burying that girl then returning a week later to dig her up – and maybe a better imagination than Ross's. He put it aside, pushed it aside but it ate at him, so he gave in and paid Freddy one of his social calls.

He owned a nice-looking house but a common doorbell. The woman who opened the door wasn't common. She was taller than her husband and looked as if she kept in shape, dark hair, shoulder-length and tied back at the nape of her neck.

Ross introduced himself, flashed his ID, and told her he'd appreciate a word or two with her husband.

'Freddy,' she called.

He came, in his shirtsleeves.

'We're attempting to contact your brother, Clarence,' Ross said for openers.

'I'm unable to help you,' Freddy replied. He didn't invite his caller inside.

'When were you last in contact with your brother?'

'Why?'

'We believe he may have information . . .' Ross gave his spiel. Freddy, disinterested, wanted him to go, but in no hurry, Ross turned the conversation to the carjacking. 'I hear you've had no luck yet identifying the carjackers?'

'The night was dark. They were dark.'

'You saw the tats on the big bloke with the knife.'

'As I was being tossed into the boot, Sergeant. There is a light – was a light – in the boot of the Commodore.'

He was good – and he looked bored, so Ross stopped boring him and walked back to his car, thinking that should there come a day when he decided to murder Melvin Sloan for cutting down that avocado tree, fat Freddy would be the bloke he'd want defending him.

*

The elusive Ron was still missing, but the Perth cops found an ex-crim who'd served time with Indiana, not at Fremantle, but in Perth, back in '99.

'He was doing time for manslaughter, and a dead ringer for Indiana Jones. There was this big old blonde bird who used to come in once a week, a volunteer supposed to be learning us good English but who spent more time saving our souls and eyeing off Indiana. She called him Indie. I never heard anyone call him by another name. Don't know what his real name was.'

Clarence Daniel Jones hadn't served time for manslaughter. It was another piece of a puzzle where none of the pieces fitted.

Ross's trip to Perth had achieved little but much. He'd become proficient at the card games on his mobile and had some inkling of why every kid over three spent half of their life staring at a screen.

He'd heard his own laughter at McDonald's, and had damn near looked around to see who it was that was laughing. He'd heard Sarah's laugh. It hadn't sounded deaf. Her daughter would have made a cat laugh that morning.

They'd exchanged names over egg and bacon McMuffins and he'd felt himself shedding years with his skin cells. Could have sat with them all day, talking about everything and nothing, with a deaf woman and her daughter, but they'd had a bus to catch and he'd had a date with a plane.

He'd walked them down to their tour bus, where they were met by a guide and a dozen elderly citizens.

'Enjoy your trip,' he'd said.

'We're going to enjoy every second,' Marni said.

He hoped they had, but feared they'd spent their week tripping over walking sticks – and he wouldn't have minded spending that week with them, tripping over those walking sticks.

Loved their eyes, big, wide, chocolate-brown, honest, innocent eyes, and if he hadn't flattened his mobile battery playing cards, he might have asked for their phone number.

Back here in his own world, he'd regrown those lost years fast, had stopped laughing and told himself when he thought about those girls that he was eight years away from fifty and that cops died young, and that he should have been making a new will, not googling the streets adjacent to the Burwood Heights high school and searching backyards for a granny flat.

HEAT

Cheryl had replaced the Commodore with a grass-green Honda hard pushed to hold four, the perfect little city runabout, she'd claimed until yesterday, until her Vermont mate's seven-seater four-wheel drive was run over by a tram.

The 'girls' had been planning a trip to Canberra in it, a long weekend of hilarity, and now they'd have to split up and travel there in two cars. That had been the plan, until Cheryl hired a replacement seven-seater she was not accustomed to driving.

'Take it slow,' Freddy warned. 'Don't take your eye off the roads.'

'Don't worry about me. You worry about Rolly. Don't take your eyes off him this weekend,' she'd warned.

Blame teenage hormones, mixed with grog, weed and maybe worse, but that kid had gone to the dogs. Freddy watchdogged him. Cheryl phoned him. He hadn't got away on Saturday. He'd made a break for freedom on Sunday afternoon but Freddy cut him off at the pass, and with his mother on the phone for back-up, he'd got him back to the house where he'd deadlocked the doors and put the keys in his pocket.

Cheryl had enrolled him at the local high school, bought him the right uniform, and when school went back on the Monday, Freddy drove there, pleased with his son's appearance and his pleasant manner. He liked the Ferrari.

'Good luck,' Freddy said when he'd dropped him off at the school gate.

'You too,' Rolland said. Then that shit of a kid took off running in his new school uniform, and Freddy had to go. He had a client depending on him.

He phoned Cheryl. She phoned back during the lunch recess. She'd spoken to Rolly. He'd been nervous about fronting up at a new school and was currently out at Steve's place, at Vermont.

'He said he'll see you at dinnertime,' Cheryl said. 'Take him out somewhere nice, Freddy.'

Freddy ate a frozen dinner, lasagne, alone – or with his phone. Cheryl wasn't answering, and nor was Steve's mother, with whom he'd left three messages.

Eight o'clock before she called back. 'Steve said that they're meeting a couple of girls at Forest Hill then going to a movie,' Steve's mother said – and if she believed her son, she was a bigger fool than he'd previously believed her to be. It was all he had to go on though, and at eight thirty, Freddy left the Ferrari at risk in the top-level car park at Forest Hill. The theatres were on the top level.

He had a look around there. No sign of Rolland or his ratbag mate. He looked at the list of films playing. There were a couple that a bunch of sixteen-year-old kids might consider cool. He walked out and glanced at Vegas, and his heart started its palpitating dance. Every time he thought about that night it started dancing.

They had his DNA in their data bank. He'd sweated that night, he'd cried, puked, worn the skin off his hands in gouging a hole deep enough, long enough to bury that girl – and it hadn't been deep enough. He only had to see a woman wearing yellow and his pulse lost its rhythm. And it hadn't been his fault. He'd had a few drinks, but not enough to affect his driving. He hadn't been speeding. She'd run out of nowhere, had run into him, and now his DNA was with that of his deadbeat brother in the national data bank's computers – and he needed a drink so he bought one.

Vegas had balcony tables which offered a view of who went in and who came out of the theatres. Freddy chose a seat that also allowed him to look down on the escalators where he'd see Rolland and his rat pack, either coming or going.

He saw a group of Islander youths – and he had a flashback to his carjacking, or to the pair of carjackers he'd been called in to have a look at. He'd damn near identified the larger of the two. He'd had tattoos down one arm. Could have. Should have.

Freddy sipped, his eyes turned to a television screen on the far wall. No sound coming from it. Nothing was allowed to disturb the song of the pokies.

Couldn't believe he'd done what he'd done but knew why he'd done it. He'd seen everything he'd worked his guts out to achieve disappearing into a sinkhole. It was disappearing anyway. Cheryl spent her life disappearing, as did her son. He'd done it for them – and for himself. He'd been the best and it had taken him a bloody long time to climb to the top of the pile.

You can't make silk purses out of a sow's ear, his father used to say. *Leave the lads alone and let them be lads.*

One way or another, his mother hadn't done much of a job of raising sons. Bill had taken off at sixteen. Clarry might have taken off younger. John had hung around long enough to get an education. Joe had stuck it out for years. Bert hadn't. He'd gone overseas and never returned. Gordon was up in New South Wales with a buggered back. He'd phoned Freddy a while ago wanting to sue someone but couldn't afford to pay a solicitor.

You're my brother, for Christ's sake, Freddy.

His brother who hadn't gone near him. Frederick Adam-Jones was a self-serving bastard.

Should have identified that tattooed Islander and got him off the street. He'd threatened a young mother with a knife and would kill someone with it one day – and Frederick Adam-Jones would end up defending him – if the price was right.

Who'll defend you, Freddy?

A group of three approached with their drinks. Freddy watched them sit at the table to his right.

Had Ross Hunter put a tail on him? Did they know more than he thought they knew? He looked at his glass. They could get his DNA from that glass. They could get it off this table, from a hair fallen from his head, a skin cell.

He'd turned that corner, seen that flash of yellow movement. Then *THUMP*, and he'd been blind. He'd killed her. He'd buried her, but he hadn't gone back and dug her up, and that's what was giving him palpitations, the knowing that whoever had dug her up and tied her into those garbage bags had taken Danni Lane. He had to tell someone.

He knew who'd inherited that land, back in 2002. He could find out who she'd sold it to—

He could, but he couldn't. Chasing up property owners left a paper trail, or a computer trail and he couldn't take the risk of it leading back to him, which one way or another it would.

The voices of the trio to his right were loud. 'The family need closure,' one of them said.

Closure, the word of the moment, and Freddy wanted some of it. He sipped, and as the whisky settled soft and warm in the swamp of his gut, he lifted his bad foot up to a vacant chair.

He'd had trouble with his feet since his boyhood and his walk that night had done for the big toe on his left foot. It needed his podiatrist, but he couldn't shed his nail clippings there. He needed to see his GP about the palpitations, but the last time he'd seen him he'd demanded blood tests for cholesterol, diabetes and Christ knew what, and no phial of Frederick Adam-Jones's blood was getting out to the public arena.

'They've got an interview on with the family of that Rowan girl next Sunday night,' one of the trio said. 'We saw a commercial for it and the mother looked fifty. Back when it happened I remember her being a good-looking bird.'

'You'd age too if you went through something like that,' a second replied.

'How the fuck could a kid ever get over something like that? I mean, if they found young Danni alive now, she'd never be the same again.'

Freddy eyed them, wondering if they were cops attempting not to sound like cops. They were succeeding – and two of them looked like brothers.

Freddy looked like a couple of his brothers. At their mother's funeral, Cheryl had walked straight up to Bill. She hadn't picked John, who, like Freddy, had done what he could to disassociate himself from the family. John the Baptist, they'd called him. He'd done the funeral service. Freddy had paid for it.

The trio at the next table was discussing Lady Cynthia Swan's face, and if Cheryl had been at Freddy's side, she might have joined in that conversation. She'd had her own words about Lady Cynthia the last time they'd seen her on the box. 'Silly old bugger,' she'd said. 'She'd look better with wrinkles than with her mouth pinned up behind her ears.'

At thirteen, Freddy had wanted that silly old bugger to be his mother. He was eighteen and driving his own car the day he tried to turn his mother into Lady Cynthia. He'd bought her a fancy outfit for her birthday and taken her to one of those photographic studios where a makeup artist turned clients into something they were not. Paid dearly for that session, but when he'd picked up those photographs he hadn't resented the bill.

He'd bought her a second outfit and paid another artist to work her magic before introducing her to Cheryl and her parents, at a restaurant. He'd introduced her to his son at a restaurant. She might have shown more interest had Rolland been a granddaughter. She might have been in the early stages of Alzheimer's too.

The trio's conversation had turned to parolees, released early to murder or maim. 'It costs the taxpayer hundreds of dollars a day to keep a crim in jail. That's why they let them out,' one said.

'You can buy a couple of metres of rope for a few dollars. Bring back public hangings, I say. String the bastards up at the MCG and charge fifty bucks a head to watch the show. I can think of a few who'd draw a bigger crowd than the Boxing Day cricket.'

'Good for tourism,' one said, and they laughed, and their laughter was loud and Freddy flinched from it and sipped his whisky – and listed a few candidates likely to pull a crowd. Cheryl would pay a scalper's price for a front-row seat to watch Michael Swan swing. The bastard who'd killed Lisa Simms would pull a crowd—

His foot back on the floor, and Freddy stood staring at his empty glass, almost seeing his DNA crawling all over it.

He did it fast, his bulk guarding his action – dropped the glass into his pocket and walked, one hand disguising the bulge.

PADLOCKS

*H*er bath was filling, but slowly. He'd turned on only the hot water tap. It wasn't hot. The stove had been burning now for two hours and the water in the reservoir was barely lukewarm, but he could wait no longer. He'd fed her. Onto her habit of leaving half of her meals, he'd doubled the dose of Valium. His week had been too bloody hard. He needed easy tonight. He was waiting now, counting down the minutes, giving those pills time to work.

The refuse in the gully had been a warning he'd misread. The leaking stove, the artist and her dog moving in; all were warnings he hadn't heeded.

Too late now. He'd set the ball rolling and he had to roll with it.

'You.' That pointed finger. The disbelief. 'You.' She'd seen the photographs of the cars and the mock-up of him. 'You.'

He'd got rid of her. To date there'd been no repercussions and he wasn't expecting any. He had to get finished out here, deliver the gazelle tonight, get rid of the Kingswood and be home by one thirty tomorrow for the funeral.

The hurricane lantern shed little light to his kitchen, barely enough to allow him to see the hands of his watch. The kettle was boiling, and *when his watch told him he'd waited long enough, he took the kettle up the passage to the bathroom and emptied it into the less than half-full tub. That hot tap was too slow. Everything was too slow tonight. He wanted it done.*

The kettle refilled, he pushed a lump of wood into the stove's maw. His epoxy repair was the one thing that had gone right since he'd taken that little Yank; his repair and the rain. His water tank was full.

Opened the pantry door then, guided the narrow beam of torchlight to her bowl. Empty? She'd been hungry tonight. All to the good. He swung the beam up to her face, hidden by her mat of hair. She didn't move. He used the torch to prod her elbow, and not a flinch out of her – and with twenty milligrams of Valium in her, she wasn't likely to flinch.

Got the padlock off, looped its clasp over the top bar, eased the side down to the floor, then gently moved her out. A long lightweight, this one, and limp in his arms as he carried her into the bathroom, where he eased her slowly down to the water.

They usually responded to water. She didn't move. Nor did she slide deeper. Too much length in her and insufficient depth of water. He stood watching her long hair, floating like pale seaweed in an ocean current as the water crept up to her chin, up to her mouth, when he spoke the words he'd spoken to each of them.

'Time to pull the plug, angel. Sleep tight. Don't let the bed bugs bite.'

Turned on his heel then and left her. He never watched their final puny fights for life. An amazing thing, the human body, and its will to live. The third of them had fought for minutes.

In the kitchen her outfit lay ready on the table. Angie would have loved that pink sweater with its beading. She'd loved sparkly things. The denim skirt, left too long folded, had deep creases. He gave it a shake, a slap, then placed it down. White briefs, white socks, pink and white sneakers joined by an elastic thread. He snipped it, studied one of them. Made in China and sold at Kmart for twelve dollars.

Listened for her fight. He could hear water running but no sound of splashing.

His preparations were familiar: the plastic raincoat, the latex gloves, the rubber bands. Not the plastic shower cap. He pulled that on as an added precaution. He had more hair now to shed, longer hair, and the hunters had got his DNA from the gully's refuse. He knew he'd bled there, had sucked blood from his wound and spat it. The shock of what he'd uncovered had made him fling natural caution to the wind.

One mistake after another, after another. There'd be no more.

'You.'

He couldn't shake the expression in her eyes, the disgust and disbelief.

He'd get rid of the Kingswood tonight, get a train back to the city, hop on a tram and be home in plenty of time.

He'd walked here tonight, or walked the last kilometres across country and over the hill. His neighbour hadn't seen him. He'd burn this place tonight, spread that hay around and be long gone before anyone saw the flames – and he had to get on with it.

He picked up a roll of paper towels, the shampoo and was walking towards the passage when he noticed that no light was escaping from the bathroom. He'd left a candle burning in there, and he turned and picked up his lantern.

Looked for her. The tub was near full and she wasn't in it. He turned the tap off and lifted the lantern higher. She had to be in it. She had twenty milligrams of Valium in her system. Five milligrams was enough to knock him out. He dropped the shampoo and paper towels to reach into the water, feeling for her, creating waves that slopped to the floor, to his shoes, his trousers.

Feeling around in a tub of water wasn't going to alter the fact that she wasn't in that tub. The window was small, high, and sealed. He looked behind the free-standing bath, behind the door, then ran back to the kitchen to check his back door. He'd sealed the front door with screws, sealed every window. She hadn't got out.

Saw her trail of water then, and followed it to the eastern end of the house and into the room where he stored his bales of hay. Found her standing on one, attempting to open the top window.

She heard him, turned, then sprang down from that bale and ran at him. Had to drop the lantern to grab her, but he got her, held her until she hooked a foot behind his knee and threw him off balance. He went down hard. Hit the wall, hit the floor, hit the lantern, but took her down with him.

Lantern on its side, flame flaring high, eager to taste spilled hay, playing shadows on the ceiling as she ripped the shower cap from his head. He swiped at her with a wet glove, but the fighting bitch slammed her closed fist into his new glasses, driving their plastic bridge into the side of his nose and momentarily blinding him with pain.

He never marked those girls. He'd had cause to, but he'd kept his hands off them. He was fighting for his life in a house that would go up like matchwood, and that bloody lantern had a bowl full of kerosene and looked ready to blow. He hit her with a closed fist to her jaw.

It killed her fight long enough for him to get a grip on her hair, long enough for him to right that flaring lantern. Its glass shade had cracked, but there was no time to worry about it. Her scream was bloodcurdling, shrill and unending.

She screamed down the dark passage, screamed when he dragged her by the hair into the pantry, where he attempted to manhandle her into the cage. She got a grip on the bars and fought him with her feet, and one of them got him in the throat. Already breathless, he fought then for the air in that stinking hole, and that fighting bitch slammed the door, and screamed her victory.

Priorities alter when a door closes, when there is no light. His penlight torch was in his pocket, his pocket was beneath the raincoat. He was digging for it when she floored him with something harder, heavier than her puny fist or foot. It mashed into his ear, and he heard his own roar of pain, and while he roared, she hit him again and he was down, on his backside, ripping plastic to get at his torch.

Saw her in that first sweep of light. Saw what she'd hit him with. Saw it disappearing down the hole in that floorboard.

He'd known that hole was there. He'd broken the bloody board when he'd been ripping out the shelving, when one of the supports had come away with a section of rotting floorboard attached. On his knees, gripping that torch, he sucked stinking air in through his open mouth while staring in disbelief.

And she kicked the torch from his hand, and the light died and she was out that door.

He moved then. He got out before she could lock him in, disbelieving the strength of her. They'd all weakened in that cage. She'd been in it for weeks and there was nothing of her. He'd weakened, and if she got hold of his scissors or a knife, she'd kill him.

He was bleeding. He could feel it trickling wet to his collar. He'd bruised his hip when he'd landed, hurt his head. And he couldn't see a bloody thing without light.

He could see the stove. He burned his hand when he opened the firebox, but it gave him light. Gave her light too. The cans she'd loathed became her missiles. He took his gloves off, bailed her up between the table and the corner, where he felled her with a closed-fisted blow to her mouth.

Straddling her to keep her down, he ripped the plastic coat from his back and wrapped it around her face and head, held it bunched at her throat, prepared now to do this any way he could. She'd fooled him. He didn't fool easily, and didn't like being fooled.

She stopped fighting him to fight the plastic, and his position was killing his hip and his ear was killing him, and his blood was dripping, and she must have been sucking air from somewhere. He had to get her back into the pantry and lock her in until he could retrieve that padlock.

She'd scream down that hole in the floor and bring the dog and its owner running — or rip up the bloody floorboards with her fingernails. They were all rotten where they backed up against the washhouse.

Should have done something about that floor, a bit of masonite, foam rubber, something.

He had duct tape. That would silence her. He looked at the dog chain he'd fixed to the skirting board two years ago. Its padlock was on the mantelpiece. He had to do something before his hip seized and he never moved again.

He got to his feet, dragged her with him to the mantelpiece, dragged her back to the corner, then, requiring two hands to get the collar around her ankle, he released his grip on the plastic.

She ripped it from her face. 'Murderer,' she panted.

He backhanded her, knelt on her, working blind, his hands shaking while searching for the holes he'd punched into the collar. He got the padlock's clasp through them, heard the click of its closing, and that fighting bitch going nowhere, he fetched his lantern.

'I made . . . you bleed,' she panted.

'That is your misfortune,' he replied.

'How can you . . . hate someone . . . as much . . . as I hate you?'

He hated her more. At that moment he could have used his scissors to cut out her heart. He used them to cut duct tape.

'I know what you look like,' she said.

'That too is your misfortune,' he said. She had no fight left in her. He closed her mouth with duct tape, rolled her onto her face, immobilised her hands, and she was silent and still.

A bunch of tissues gathered from the box on his table, he pressed them to his throbbing ear, killed his light, then walked out into the night, locking the door behind him.

Stood a while listening. Noise carried at night. There would have been noise, and much of it. The dog wasn't barking. He walked across to the shed, then made his way down the rock-strewn slope, through long grass and scrubland to the fence he shared with the arty one.

More trees on her side. No light showing through them, no blather of television or music. Gone to bed with her dog? Gone out? Perhaps he'd had some luck tonight.

In no fit state to do more, in no fit state to walk, but with no other option, he'd have to.

He'd had it worked out down to the last detail. He'd ridden a taxi to the fish and chip shop Angie had loved, then cut across open land. They'd done that a few times together. It wasn't much of a walk. He looked up at his hill and his hip said no. It said no to following the fenceline down, but it accepted downhill.

He'd done a lot of walking in his time and a lot of it in circles. It wasn't raining, there was a partial moon up there, lighting his way, and at this time of night there'd be little traffic about.

Walked on down the centre of the road.

TOMBSTONES

*M*arni had fifty-three photographs on her mobile, of quokkas and pinnacles, boab trees and sunsets. Sarah's mobile was in Melbourne, but Bob had Marni's number. He messaged her and she replied. In this morning's text, he'd said that Barbara Lane had gone back to Sydney with her father and that her house was to be auctioned.

'What if the police find Danni? She'll have no home to go home to,' Marni said.

'Two month not long enough for places to be home,' Sarah said. 'Two month will be like when we staying at motels. Carry in, carry out, nothing left.'

Except a toothbrush at one motel and sunscreen at another.

They'd showered in palatial bathrooms, bathed in a spa bath, and laughed about going home to their own tiny bathroom. They'd worried about Mrs Vaughn, who had been told three times that they'd be away for ten days, then told again the night before they'd left, when they'd delivered two cartons of cigarettes and half a dozen packets of long-life milk. She had bread enough in her freezer, pills enough, and her son knew how long they'd be away.

They'd sent him two emails. He hadn't replied to either, but they'd be home tomorrow, or tomorrow night.

'Perth reminds me a bit of Melbourne,' Marni said.

'Not so big,' Sarah said. She remembered it well, the names of streets, the buildings, the shops and buses. She'd lived in Perth long enough for that city to imbed itself in her pores. Twice she'd lived with Gran and Gramp. Their house had been home, and the old green tent. The places where it had been pegged down had altered, but inside it never altered.

They'd pegged it down in the caravan park the day the truck driver dropped them off at the park gate. They'd lived in it for weeks before her mother could afford to rent a cabin. Had lived in the cabin for almost eighteen months. It had become home.

Then the Clarks' house. The first time Sarah had seen it she'd thought it was a palace. Everything in it had been palatial, the furniture, drapes, the paintings on their walls, the tiling inside, the paving around the swimming pool. She'd walked on tiptoe, afraid to touch.

She could have her own palace now, and as soon as she and Marni moved out, Raymond Vaughn would put his mother into a nursing home even if he had to have her committed to do it – and a few of the neighbours would help him have her committed too. She'd been at war with most of them for years.

Marni was ready to give up on her. She'd phoned her on the second day of their tour, and Mrs Vaughn had told her that the phone was for her convenience, not for ratbag kids to play around with. Marni had refused to disturb her a second time.

They'd lived different lives over here, eaten at night with differ-ent people, and been sought out by one elderly woman who had a fifty-five-year-old deaf daughter. She'd signed, and Sarah, who rarely got the chance to sign, had enjoyed talking to her.

If not for that old bank card, Sarah wouldn't have been on that tour. It was out of date, the account long dead, but the last time she'd withdrawn money from that account there'd been fifteen dollars left in it. Banks might be able to raise old accounts from the dead, and if they could, Sarah had found a way to get rid of some of their winnings anonymously, electronically. She wanted to give some to Jackie and Rena, and Shane, and if it was transferred from that old account, there'd be no way they could trace it back to her.

Almost twelve the day she and her mother had opened that account so Peter Clark could transfer her mother's wages into it. It had been a joint account then. After the funeral, it had become Sarah's own, though had been forgotten by her. Not until she'd withdrawn money to buy her bus ticket to Melbourne had she known that the Clarks received money for fostering her, which they'd paid into that account.

Centrelink had paid into it when she'd lived with Gran and Gramp, after Gran's doctor filled in papers for a carer's allowance. She hadn't spent any of it, not at the farm. After Marni had been born, she'd lived on Centrelink until she'd got the job and cancelled her pension. She remembered putting that card away somewhere safe, in case she'd ever needed those fifteen dollars, then forgotten where she'd put it.

'Are you sure we're on the right road?' Marni asked.

'I know,' Sarah said. She'd driven this way with the Clarks to put flowers on the twins' nana's grave. She'd followed a hearse out this road—

Shook that thought, that day, away, and looked at Marni, who wanted to take a photo of her father's tombstone before they went home. Hadn't told her yet. Almost had at the airport while waiting to board their plane, but told herself that the tour would be enough, that she'd forget about graves.

She looked like him in profile. He'd had a strong face and a stronger will. She'd inherited his will.

And they were here, and Marni determined to be first off the bus, as she'd always been first off on the tour.

'It's a nice place,' she said. 'Nice trees.'

'Yes,' Sarah said and wondered if fate might present her with a John Carter's tombstone.

'Are we going to visit your parents?'

'No.'

'Why not?'

'Because I tell you before.'

'It reminds me of the pinnacles. They looked like a field of ancient tombstones.'

She found the twins' nana's stone. There were two beside it now, identical granite stones, *Sylvia May Clark 1923–1999*, between two *Oliver John*s, one born in 1917, the other in 1980.

'*He fought the long battle bravely,*' Marni read aloud from the young Oliver's stone. 'Do they belong to your foster family?'

Sarah nodded.

'Was he in the army or something?' A shake of her head Sarah's only reply, Marni tried again. 'What battle did he fight bravely?'

'Brain tumour,' Sarah said.

*

Cemeteries aren't silent places. Birds tweet, cars whoosh by on the street, but for a moment there was no noise other than Marni's own heartbeat, rush-rushing every litre of her blood to her eardrums while her lungs sucked in too much air. She opened her mouth to protest, but the words wouldn't come. She swallowed, swallowed nothing. Her mouth was bone dry, and when the words came, they sounded like a five year old's. 'You said John Carter. You said he was a plumber who drove a white kombi van.'

'I say Mrs Carter to Mrs Vaughn. I think I will be there maybe for one week, but I stay and I stay and I can't change it, Marni – so I change us.'

'You can't do this. You can't stand there thinking that it's okay to do this. I don't care if you're deaf or not, you can't do something like this, Mum.'

'I tell you one hundred time, not Perth. You fight me for your father.'

'Why didn't you tell me before?'

'Because . . . because I can't. Take your photo.'

'I don't want a photo of a Clark's tombstone, and if you picked an easy name for Mrs Vaughn, you probably picked a tombstone for me. You probably didn't even know my father's name, or he was married or something.'

'He die very slowly of a brain tumour. You know this forever. You know forever I am meeting him the first time when I am thirteen, that he teach me computer. Everything you know is Oliver. I change his name, not him.'

'Then why not tell Mrs Vaughn you were Mrs Clark? Why pinch some nobody's name to stick on me?'

'Because Peter Clark was his father—'

'You're pure unadulterated stark raving crazy! You said you loved the Clarks. You said you loved your life when you lived with the Clarks.'

'Yes. And I love him too. Always. Forever. Take your photo. I want to go!'

'Stuff your Clarks, and him, and you too. Why would anyone pick this place to tell a person that she wasn't who she thought she was? Why not tell me at home? Why not tell me before we got on the bus?'

Sarah turned her back. Marni turned to the stones, to *Oliver John Clark*'s stone, to stare at his date of birth, his date of death.

He'd been a nineteen-year-old boy when he'd died, not a father, not her father. She'd been looking at white kombi vans since she'd known what a kombi van was. She'd been looking at plumbers' advertisements in the local paper, had stood in the street one day watching two plumbers fix someone's leaking pipe, thinking they might look like her father.

Couldn't believe it. Just couldn't. It was like being punched in the stomach by her own mother, like being punched so hard that everything inside her had fallen out, and if it hadn't already fallen out, she would have vomited it out all over *Oliver John Clark's* rotten tombstone.

She'd asked dozens of times why her mother had no photographs of John Carter. She had a photograph of Oliver Clark. Marni had seen it, or seen a tall boy standing with her mother behind the little Clark girls. She'd held it in her hand, and hadn't even looked at the boy or his sisters, only at her mother.

She looked at her now, watched her wiping her eyes, her nose, on a red serviette she'd picked up from one of the motel dining rooms.

'I hope that dye comes out and your nose turns bright red forever. Why didn't you tell me the night we looked at your old photos?'

'Stop now, Marni.'

'I won't ever stop, and I don't care if you're crying or not, because you're stark raving crazy, and a liar too, and you had no right to take who I was away from me.'

'I take nothing.'

'No? You just set me up with a fake plumber who drove a fake white kombi van, and it's like you wiped out my life before I had one, like you chucked everything I might have been in the green bin with Mrs Vaughn's junk mail.'

'I chuck who I am, not you. I give you his name so I can keep one thing of him.'

She was Marni Olivia. She'd asked once why *Olivia*. Her mother had lied about that too. Olivia was easy to say, like Marni, like Carter.

Her mobile in her hand since they'd entered the cemetery, she was unzipping her handbag to put it away when her mother took it, aimed its lens in the direction of the three stones and probably wasted a dozen shots before Marni snatched it back.

THE CLARKS

*T*hat past week might have been the best of Marni's life. That last night in a Perth hotel was the worst. Sarah turned her hearing aids off, which was her way of making a statement, so to make her own statement, Marni attacked the hotel-supplied chips, Coke and a chocolate bar, then rang down for room service and two steak sandwiches.

They were delivered half-raw. They turned the bread pink, but because it was the bloodiest day of her life and her mother wouldn't eat anything, Marni ate both, then sat googling, which used up more data than their mobile plan gave them and would make the phone bill expensive.

She googled *Peter Clark, Perth*, and when she found too many Peter Clarks, she tried *Peter Clark, solicitor, Perth, Australia*. There was only one of him, and tomorrow morning she was going to get a taxi to his office and tell him who she was – and tell him she wanted to divorce her mother.

They never fought at home. When they were on the tour, sitting side by side all day on the bus, walking, sleeping side by side, they hadn't argued, not once.

But how dare she take her out to that place to tell her something that important, then expect it to be all right? It wasn't all right.

*

She slept. Her mother didn't look as if she had. She was still sitting on the couch, watching television when Marni woke.

One final breakfast in one final dining room, a different breakfast. Marni refused to speak and as soon as they were done, she walked towards the exit.

'We packing up now, Marni.'

Didn't even turn around. Just kept on going.

Her mother came after her. 'Where you going?'

'To visit my grandfather.'

'What?'

'If what you said about Oliver is true, I've got grandparents and I'm going to visit them,' Marni said and turned her back again, like her mother did, except it didn't work for her.

'Why you doing this?' Sarah asked, and Marni had to turn to reply.

'Why did you lie to me for nearly thirteen years?'

'Everything I say about . . . about your father is true. Name don't matter.'

'My name does. I thought I was Marni Carter, and I'm not, and it's like seeing those millions on a bank receipt one day, then going back the next day and the money is all gone. It's like you made me be all gone.'

'I do everything what is best for you. Always, for you.'

'What's best for you, more like it. Meeting my grandparents is best for me,' Marni said.

'Oliver is Peter Clark son. Not Lynette.'

'He had a mother somewhere,' Marni said, and she crossed over a street for no reason other than the lights were green. Her mother didn't. She'd turned the corner to her left, and lost without her in this city, Marni returned to her side.

*

Sarah knew this area well. She'd said goodbye to Lynette and Peter in this same street and was now retracing her footsteps of that final day.

'Keep in touch,' Lynette had said.

For six months Sarah had kept in touch. Ten days after arriving at Gramp's farm, Lynette had written to tell her that Oliver had died peacefully, that he would be buried at his grandmother's side.

Mandy and Miriam had written to her and she'd written special letters to them about stealing honey from Gramp's bees. How many letters? They'd been like a cord, stretching across the vastness, keeping her tied to both ends of Australia.

Then that letter came for Gramp, and the writing on it had made her afraid, and the words she'd read aloud to Gramp she'd had to fight out of her mouth.

Re-hab-il-it-a-shon. It means cured, baby, made better.

Oliver's baby hadn't believed that word, and inside her it had protested and her stomach had cramped and she'd gone outside to walk that cramp away and she'd stayed away for too long. Like a bomb, that letter. It had exploded everything. Gran had got out, and when Sarah had gone back, Gramp was outside calling Gran's name. He couldn't see well enough to know which way she'd gone.

Sarah had got the car out and they'd driven the road searching for her, but another driver had already found Gran. He'd called the police. Gran's doctor had known who she was.

Gramp had argued about moving Gran into a nursing home. Sarah hadn't. She'd given the doctor Uncle John's address in Dubbo.

That was the last time she'd seen Gran. She'd been lying so quiet and still in a hospital bed. The Gran Sarah had known had never been quiet or still, not the younger roly-poly Gran, or the fighting senile Gran.

She'd driven home that night, made up Gran's bed for John and his wife, had cleaned the house, the bathroom, done the washing, then on that morning before they'd arrived, she'd written Gramp a note she'd left on the table with his magnifying glass, a brief note. Had lied to him. Told him she was going home to Perth.

A foggy early morning when she'd crept away with her case. Walked a long way before the white kombi van had pulled up beside her.

Couldn't understand what the driver said but he'd understood her hearing aids, and *Station, train.* He'd understood the bulge of Marni beneath Gran's old blue coat too and he'd got out of his van and taken the case from her hand, and because she couldn't lose that case, she'd let him help her in.

A kind man, John Carter the plumber. He'd carried her case into the station where he'd told her to sit down while he bought her a ticket to the city.

Everything she'd done since, she'd done for Marni. She'd found them a safe place to live, a safe name to wear, had worked for her, cooked for her, so she'd grow strong.

She'd grown too strong, and this morning Sarah felt tired and old and weak and sad.

They walked side by side by a wide-windowed office, then Sarah turned to her right. There was a café around the corner, unchanged in fourteen years. Same door, same small tables and chairs, same cakes and pies set out in the same glass-faced counters.

'We just had breakfast,' Marni said.

Sarah placed a twenty-dollar note on the counter. 'Coffee. In a mug. Very strong,' she said, then, leaving Marni at the counter to order, she walked to a table for two and sat.

Marni came to count the change to the table. She didn't speak, or not until the woman brought two large mugs of cappuccino and one toasted sandwich.

'We paid almost twice as much for two coffees and a toasted sandwich at the airport,' she said.

'Airport know people don't come every day. In this place they come every day.'

'You knew this place was here.'

'Yes.' Sarah sipped her coffee and it was good.

'Peter Clark is my grandfather. I want to see him, Mum.'

'He don't know I have got you.'

'Why?'

'Because . . . because Oliver is like my brother. Because he is dying and everyone is sad . . . because I am too sad . . . and embarrass and scared and stupid. Many, many thing.'

'Can I at least see what Peter Clark looks like?'

'No.'

'Why?'

'You look like Oliver.'

'I look like you and your mother . . . and . . . and I feel as if I'm watching some crazy movie where everyone's lost the plot and it just keeps on getting crazier and more complicated and everyone just wants it to end.'

'What?'

'Nothing, Mum! Tell me about Oliver.'

'He is very beautiful, very clever. He live with us, just weekends and I like weekends very much. He was my friend. After he is getting sick, he is living with us all the time.'

They sat at that table speaking about Oliver until Sarah's watch told them it was time to pack up their room. They spoke of him while they packed, spoke of the Clarks while waiting to check out, and when Sarah took her card from her purse to pay for the Coke and chips and chocolate bar, the steak sandwiches, that old card Marni had found with the photographs came out with it, but disappeared fast back into Sarah's purse.

'Promise you say nothing about Oliver. Promise you will not say how old.'

'I'll be almost twelve. I'll be Marni Carter and my father was a giant . . . and thank you.'

Their backpacks shouldered once more, they walked back to that corner and this time Marni saw the Clarks' names on that glass door.

*

The middle-aged receptionist asked if she could help them, but stared at their faces when Marni asked if they could please see Peter Clark, please.

'Sarah,' the receptionist said. 'Oh my gosh.'

'Pam,' Sarah said, and Pam picked up a phone and before it was down, a slim, middle-aged woman opened a door.

She didn't look the type to squeal, but she squealed and enveloped Sarah and her backpack in a bear hug, then Pam came from behind her desk to hug while Marni stood back, watching a show she'd never expected to see.

A knock on a glass door brought Peter Clark out of his office, and Marni saw the shape of her grandfather, his balding head and dark-rimmed glasses. Watched him with greedy eyes as he took both of Sarah's hands, kissed her cheek then turned to his grand-daughter who he wasn't allowed to know was his granddaughter.

'Three guesses who you are,' he said, and he kissed her and Marni knew she was going to howl in a minute.

But he was with a client and he had go. 'I should be free in fifteen minutes,' he said. 'Don't go away.'

Lynette wasn't with a client. They removed their backpacks in her office and sat on her client chairs, and she asked a hundred questions and Sarah replied, and not as she would to a stranger, but as she would to Marni, and she asked her own questions, about Mandy, who had two children, a tiny boy and a girl, and Miriam, who was working in London and still unmarried.

Then Lynette picked up her phone. 'See if you can delay my eleven thirty, Pam,' she said. 'Then try Mandy's number for me.'

And when the call was put through, Lynette said to the phone, 'Guess who just popped in with her beautiful daughter . . .

Miriam? She'd better not! It's Sarah. Yes . . . Yes . . . Yes . . . Don't you worry about that. She'll be here if we have to tie her to a chair.'

And the phone down, she turned back to her visitors. 'She'll be here in twenty minutes.'

'She will bring her babies.'

'They're at crèche,' Lynette said. 'Mandy is a working mum.'

They waited twenty minutes for Peter Clark to join them, then ten minutes more for Mandy, who came in like a hurricane, howling Sarah's name and hugging her so hard she knocked one of her hearing aids out. They laughed about that.

Marni didn't laugh. She ached at the stupidity of her mother's lie. She ached because these strangers were not her mother's people, only her foster people, but they were Marni's own, or Mandy and Peter were, and she wanted to howl for the loss of not being able to tell them.

And what if Oliver hadn't died? What if he'd fought the long battle bravely and won it and he'd married her mother and Marni had grown up over here with a father and these people?

What if?

Always Marni had known about his brain tumour. She'd been six the first time her mother had explained how her daddy had got a bad infection inside his head that the doctors couldn't make better with medicine. She might have been nine the first time her mother had said brain tumour. She'd always known he'd died in Perth – and hadn't known his name.

Oliver John Clark.

Lynette's appointment moved to one o'clock, she suggested an early lunch, and together they walked to that same café around the corner, Marni at her grandfather's side, her step-grandmother and half-aunt a metre ahead, on either side of Sarah, holding her hands so she couldn't get away. There wasn't a lot that could silence Marni. Being with these people had, and breathing air to talk hurt her lungs anyway.

It was an out-of-body experience walking beside her grandfather, and when he asked what year she was in at school, she said year seven, which she hadn't been when she'd been going on for twelve. Should have said year six.

She sat between her grandfather and aunty at the café, and five people crowded around a little circular table hard pushed to seat four meant they were brushing elbows. She liked it when their elbows brushed, liked it more when her grandfather found space for his arm behind her chair. She took a selfie and got half of him in it, and his arm around her.

Sarah told them about her job, her licence test, her landlady. Mandy said she missed Miriam like crazy.

'She got boyfriend over there?'

'Not that we know of,' Lynette said. 'Peter and I flew over last year. We looked for signs of a male but found none. She rents a one-bedroom unit on the fourth floor of an old building—'

'No lifts,' Peter said, and he spoke about the forty-nine steps he had to climb every time they went out.

His speech might have been difficult to lip-read, but Lynette and Mandy snatched his sentences, trimmed them down to basics, then with word and sign relayed shortened versions. Marni watched enthralled, not by their conversation but by the way they communicated with her mother.

These people worked in a big office. They made enough money to pay a receptionist and a secretary, they had their own daughters and grandchildren, but they loved her mother. It was so obvious. And she'd dumped them. For fourteen years they hadn't heard a word from her – and wouldn't have today if Marni hadn't nagged – and not one word out of them about why she'd disappeared off the face of the planet. They were like the father in that old Bible story about the prodigal son's return. The Clarks didn't kill the fatted calf, but they paid for lunch.

Just wait until Marni told Samantha about today—

Couldn't. Samantha was on Facebook and she put anything on it. She'd put a photo of their granny flat on it and labelled it *Captain Carter's cottage* – because Marni had been made captain of the netball team and Samantha had expected to be made the new captain – which was the only reason Marni had wanted to come to Perth, because Samantha had written worse than *Captain Carter's cottage*. She'd put up lies about Marni having thirty brothers and sisters splattered around the world because her mother had ordered a bottle of sperm from America.

She could have a photograph for herself, and if anyone asked, well they were her mother's foster parents.

'Would anyone mind if I took a few photos?' she asked.

'Go for your life,' her grandfather said.

She got a perfect smiling close-up of him, then two of him, Lynette and Sarah. She took one of Sarah and Mandy, their faces side by side, like foster sisters, then Mandy took the mobile and got a beauty of Marni standing behind her mother and grandfather, her hands on the backs of their chairs.

'I want a copy of that one,' Mandy said, and she wrote her mobile number on a serviette, then Lynette borrowed the pen to add her own. Minutes later, Marni had two more contacts and she'd forwarded that photo to both, and to Maria too – then to Samantha, with a text. *Lunching with the family.*

'How long have you had your mobile?' Mandy asked.

'Since . . . for over here,' Marni said.

'How old are you?'

'Twelve . . . very soon,' – and now she was as big a liar as her mother.

'Your dad must be tall?'

'He had to stoop to get in the door,' Marni lied.

'What's he doing while you're over here?'

'He took off a while back.'

She said no more, but that bit was true. John Carter had taken off since last night. Today he was being replaced by a boy called Oliver.

She sat flicking through her photographs, pleased with most of them until she saw her own angry face looking at her. Her mother had got something when she'd aimed the mobile. It looked like the selfie to end all selfies. She deleted it. She deleted one of her arm and giant hand reaching to reclaim her mobile. She deleted two lopsided tombstones, but studied a semi-decent shot of the three stones. That's what she'd come to Perth to get. She didn't delete it.

Didn't need it either. Her mother had said that morning that she had a photograph of Oliver when he'd been fifteen. And the Clarks would have dozens of them. Once she was home, she'd get them to send some.

Mum was very fond of Oliver. She was wondering if you'd mind sending copies of some of his photographs.

Peter Clark jolted Marni's mind back to the present. He asked Sarah if she'd been contacted about a will.

'Whose will?' Marni asked.

'Your mum was named in her grandfather's will,' Peter said. 'We were contacted in late 2002.' He turned to Sarah. 'Your father—' he began, but Sarah was on her feet and looking at her watch.

'Airport,' she said. 'We flying home today.'

They were flying at four ten. Marni wanted to know more about Gramp's will, and what Peter had been going to say about Sarah's father, but Lynette had her one o'clock appointment and Mandy had to get back to work, so they returned to the office where backpacks were buckled on, where more kisses were exchanged and promises to keep in touch extracted.

Then it was over.

'What did Gramp leave you?' Marni asked when they were walking again.

'I don't know,' Sarah said.

'Why did you get up when he mentioned your father?'

'I said we will see them for five minutes. We see them for more than one hour, Marni.'

'When did your grandfather die?'

'I don't know what day. Mrs Vaughn finding out for me two month after.'

'Did I ever see him?'

'One time. He is in the same nursing home with Gran. He was blind.' She crossed another street, crossed again then stopped outside a National Australia Bank, removed her backpack, placed it against the bank wall and told Marni to wait with it.

'What are you doing?'

'Find out something. Watch my bag.'

It wasn't even their bank. Marni picked up the extra backpack and hauled it in, dumped it on a chair, and joined Sarah as she was called to a teller's window. And she passed that out-of-date bank card to the woman.

'Were you issued with a new card?' the teller asked.

'I change address,' Sarah said, and offered her birth certificate. 'I open my account at this same bank.'

The teller didn't want the card, the birth certificate or the problematic customer, and when she went for reinforcements Marni read what she could of an upside-down birth certificate. The name on it wasn't her mother's, which wasn't a surprise. It was like nothing would surprise her again.

A second woman came to deal with them. She invited them into an office. Marni read the note her mother pushed across the desk.

I did not close the account. When Centrelink stopped making payments, there was fifteen dollars in the account.

'Fifteen dollars!' Marni gasped.

The woman turned to her voice, her expression relieved. 'Accounts, unused after a period of time, are considered to be dead accounts. It is possible, in some cases, to access them.'

'For fifteen dollars! She's a millionaire. She's probably trying to hide some of her money from the tax man,' Marni said, picked up her mother's backpack and got out of that place fast.

ABOVE THE WORLD

*M*arni's mobile beeped while they were waiting to board. Only Bob saying he'd pick them up at the airport.

Our plane gets in late. Mum said we'll get a taxi.

Tell her late is good. Less traffic.

It beeped again minutes later, and it wasn't from Bob but a number Marni's phone didn't recognise.

Mandy just sent me your photo. Hope to be home in September. Don't disappear before I get there. Miriam. xox

Her mother glanced at the message.

'Reply to her,' Marni urged.

'Still night-time over there,' Sarah said.

'She's awake,' Marni said, then she replied and sent her words flying over the ocean to London.

'Have you got any idea how weird it feels? I just messaged my aunty in London. I had no one and suddenly I've got a grand-father, a step-grandmother, two aunties and baby cousins, and I'm changing my name to Clark when I'm eighteen and coming back here to tell them the truth.'

'You not thirteen yet.'

'How do you leave people like them? Will you pack up and leave me one day?'

'I bring you with me when I leave them.'

'You left them because you were having me.' Her mother didn't deny it. 'If you didn't want them to know you were sleeping with Oliver, you could have had an abortion?'

'You talk rubbish.'

'It's not rubbish. Samantha said you walk in pregnant and walk out not pregnant. She said her mother did it while her other kids were at school one day.'

'You learn stupid thing from Samantha.'

'Well, you could have. If you had, you wouldn't have had to leave the Clarks, and if you had, and then gone to live with Gramp, you could have stayed there and looked after him and he might have left you his farm and money and everything—'

'Very good idea,' Sarah said. 'Oliver is dying, so good idea to kill what I got alive of him inside me, eh?'

'You left Gramp because of me.'

'I leave because Gran is . . . is dementia and have to go in a nursing home, and because John and his wife coming.'

'There you go. You just admitted that what I said was true.'

'Poor thing. Everything your fault. Your fault I am Mrs Sarah Carter, payroll/accounts officer. Your fault Maureen Crow giving me fifty-six thousand dollars so I will stay working for her—'

'It's my fault you're a millionaire, poor thing,' Marni said, and she told Sarah what she'd said to the lady at the bank.

'Your fault when the tax man put me in jail,' Sarah said, and they laughed.

*

As on their outward flight, their aisle seat was vacant when the plane launched itself skyward. Today it wasn't the only vacant seat. They had books to read but it's hard to concentrate on printed words when you're above the clouds, when you look down and see the shadows they make on the land, and even more difficult when you're sitting on a wing and can see it vibrating.

Sarah removed her hearing aids. Marni spoke of implants, and Sarah told her about Lynette, who'd also nagged about implants.

'When I am fifteen, she make appointment to talk to implant people. I don't want them. Don't want them to shaving off my hair, make a hole in my head and put wires inside me. One month after, the doctor find Oliver's tumour. They shave all of his hair off, cut his head open, cut off his skull.'

'When he was sixteen?'

'Yes. They taking out like a golf ball tumour, all of it, and everyone said, he is so lucky.'

'How long was he lucky?'

'They find three when he is eighteen. They can't take all of one because of damage. The tumour damage him anyway.'

'You slept with him.'

'He can do that.'

'Why would you, if he was brain damaged?'

'Because . . . because he is Oliver. Because he can. Because it make him feel better.'

'You slept with him to make him feel better!'

'No. Because he is my friend from thirteen, and he is going away. Before, everywhere I live for a while, my father making me to get in the car and I go away and leave my friends. I know Oliver don't want to leave everyone. And I love him very much and I think maybe I can make him stay.'

Marni turned her eyes to the window. The earth so far beneath them now, she could see only cottonwool clouds. The cemetery had been a bad place to find out about Oliver. Riding above the clouds was the exact right place to find out that she'd been made from a love story as sad as *Romeo and Juliet*. There'd been no feuding families to ruin her mother and father's romance. A brain tumour had done that, but it was as sad, and beautiful.

'Oliver and Jillian,' she said. 'Did he call you Jillian?'

'I was Sarah at high school. Sarah Clark.'

'Why?'

Sarah sighed. 'Because . . . because I can't say *Jillian Jones* . . . because I hate that name . . . because everyone knowing *Jillian Jones's* name.'

'Because you were orphaned in a car crash.'

'Because . . . because my father crash his car into one with two boys, eighteen, one girl, sixteen. They are dead. One girl, seventeen, live with a broken spine. And he have got no licence. The judge take it already for being drunk and going fast. He was very drunk. The doctors measure his blood. The newspapers printing everything, funerals, everything.'

'Why would your mother get in the car if he'd been drinking!'

'My mother was . . . she was a very good, very kind stupid lady. He will say, "Get in the car." We get in.'

THE LONG NIGHT

*H*e'd left her tied up for two nights that she could remember. The first night the kitchen had been warm, then it got cold and the floorboards beneath her had felt like ice. The only warmth she could remember was when she'd wet her pants, but once the wet had grown cold, she'd been colder. The second night, she'd been shuddering so hard she couldn't breathe, and her hands were dead. Then nothing. Until a mug of warm sweet milk held to her mouth, and a man holding it and a little yellow light behind him.

Thought she'd been in hospital. She'd been lying on something soft and warm, had a pillow beneath her head and a quilt over her. After she'd woken, that day or the next, she'd found that dog chain in her bed, and it wasn't a bed, only a narrow mattress on the floor in that same kitchen corner.

You won't like my gags, he'd said that first day.

She hadn't liked his gag, but it was off now and her hands were free and she could hear things. She could hear him rattling and banging things. Couldn't see him. Didn't want to see him. Right now she didn't want to know anything other than that she was alive and warm, that she could breathe, and the air she was breathing was warm, and that warmth was beautiful.

It was night-time, but not dark. A light globe swung on a long cord from a high ceiling, but it wasn't making the light. He had one of those old camping lights that sucked kerosene up a wick. It was on a sink.

Closed her eyes when she heard his footsteps approaching and he came close enough for her to hear his breathing, and he must have heard hers, because he stepped back and reached for something on the table.

He had bananas, joined in a bunch. Through slitted eyes she watched him break one off then reach for a knife to cut off its top. She thought he was going to eat it, but he tossed it onto her quilt.

She wanted it, but not enough to reach an arm out from her cocoon of warmth, and it was probably poisoned.

Didn't understand any of it. Didn't care either, or not right now. Knew he was Dr Jekyll and Mr Hyde, that half of him wanted to murder people and the other half gave them warm sweet milk.

She looked at him when he put a small bottle of water near her pillow. Water had meant life in his cage. She'd almost prayed to water bottles. Wanted to get it and put it in the corner, but everything hurt, her face, shoulders, back. She clenched her hands, which had come back to life but still felt like they belonged to someone else.

The bottle had a sucking top. She had to drink water and couldn't remember drinking any since she'd been in the cage – and maybe a bit in the bath.

He stood watching her struggle to lift herself on her elbow, to wriggle herself up high enough to get that bottle, and her hand dropped it and it spurted water on the quilt, but she got both hands on it and, got it to her mouth.

Her mouth was the worst hurting part, and one of her side front teeth felt loose, but she drank as much as she wanted and was placing the bottle down when she noticed her lolly-pink clad arm. He'd put a sweater on her.

Looked at that sleeve, then at the banana. She hadn't tasted banana forever and wanted it, but why give it to her now? He hadn't put her in that bath to clean her. He'd drugged her baked beans and tried to drown her and he'd probably poisoned that banana, and the water she'd just drunk too – except why hadn't he drowned her while she'd been unconscious and frozen half to death? If he'd put her into a warm bath then, she would have curled up in its warmth and gone to sleep forever.

Sleep tight. Don't let the bed bugs bite, he'd said.

She got the banana, got its skin off, and whether her mouth was too sore to eat it or not, she took a bite, then mushed it with her tongue while checking the skin for needle holes. Couldn't see anything, so she bit again, with the less sore side of her mouth, and no banana in this world had ever tasted that good, and how could something that was so good for her dare to taste so good.

He went outside then and cold wind and black night came in before he closed the door. It made the little light flicker, and when he closed the door the room felt safe and cosy and she curled up again beneath the quilt, full of banana and water and closed her eyes.

Woke to an avalanche of light. It wasn't coming from his camping lantern. That was on the sink where it had been before, but wasn't burning now. The light was coming from behind it, through a worn-out blind at a window. Sunlight. She hadn't seen sunlight, not for weeks, and it was too bright.

Saw him then, sitting in an old wicker chair he'd pulled close to the stove, saw his shoes propped on a carton full of wood.

'Are you there?' he asked.

She was here. Couldn't see anyone else. She got herself up, got her back against the wall and he was asleep, his chin on his chest. He was talking in his sleep.

She'd imagined a monster, scarred and ugly. He looked . . . ordinary, was dressed in an ordinary sweater and jeans and sneakers.

And he did it again. 'I can't see you.'

She moved the pillow so it was between her back and the wall and she looked her fill at a man no one could ever imagine would murder four girls.

'Over here,' he said.

Carefully she eased the quilt back until she could look at the chain. Her legs were bare and she was wearing a denim skirt. He'd changed her clothes again, and he'd taken her pants and stretchy shorts this time. She was wearing white cotton briefs, and knowing he'd looked at her naked made her gag.

Wasn't going to. Wasn't going to waste that banana. Closed her eyes, swallowed, closed her mouth and breathed, in and out through her nose, in and out, in and out, refusing to let herself think of what else he'd done.

Knew she'd peed her pants. Maybe she'd done worse than pee, and if he'd done worse than change her pants, she had to be grateful that he hadn't drowned her when he'd had the chance. Didn't know why he hadn't, only that he had to be seriously mad.

The chain was rusty. It had a ring fixed to its end and he'd cut a piece of what looked like ancient dog collar he'd put through the ring, then put a padlock through holes he'd made in both ends of the dog collar, only a small padlock, half as long as her thumb. She'd been like a hamster in the cage. She was tied up like a dog out here.

He had a ton of stuff on the table. The chain wasn't long enough to reach it. He had a long curly metal rod thing leaning against the brick chimney, near where his feet were propped. If she'd seen that the night she'd fought him, she would have got away.

Everything was out of reach of that chain he'd fixed to the bottom of the corner wall with two screws. They were hidden by her mattress now, but before the mattress she'd seen two screws he'd put through two separate links of the chain.

If there was a better and a worse, being chained up and warm and eating a banana was better than being in his cage eating beans, or it was now that the tape was off her mouth and her hands were free. She could see things, hear everything, mainly birds.

She wasn't in the city. Knew that now. There were bird sounds at home, but their calls had always been muffled by the background noise of traffic.

She was so close to him she could see everything, like he needed a shave and a haircut. He had grey hair, mostly grey. He was older than her father, but not old. He wasn't big, wasn't fat, wasn't skinny. He looked normal.

She shouldn't have been able to look at him. Should have been too scared to. She didn't feel scared. She'd thought she was dead when she'd been frozen solid in this corner, but she was alive and warm. Maybe the cold had killed off the part of her brain that produced fear hormones – or it had swapped jobs and started making survival hormones – or she had that syndrome people who were kidnapped developed, a sort of dependence on their kidnappers, an acceptance – Stockholm Syndrome, that's what it was called. He'd given her milk, water, a banana, a warm sweater, a bed . . .

She'd kill him if she got half a chance.

She'd had one chance and blown it. Hadn't expected his house to be empty. Hadn't expected windows that wouldn't open or to find nothing in the house to break them with. In here, there were plenty of weapons. She hadn't seen in here, not when he'd carried her through to the bathroom.

And her head was hurting now. She worked out why. She was sitting on her hair. In the cage she used to be able to comb it with her fingers and plait it, tuck the plait down the neck of her tracksuit. Maybe later. She gathered it into a bunch, twisted it and pushed the twist down the neck of the sweater, then sat, looking at his twitching wrist hanging down at the side of the wicker chair.

Didn't know why she'd grabbed his wrist that night. If she hadn't, she wouldn't have seen where that grey comet of light came from, and if she hadn't seen that it was a hole, she wouldn't have dropped the padlock into it and she'd still be in the cage.

Didn't know how she'd found that lump of something that shouldn't have been in baked beans. Maybe Nan Lane was up there, keeping an eye on things and sending her subliminal messages.

She'd started eating those beans. She must have scooped up two or three mouthfuls before she'd felt a powdery lump in her mouth, and known what he'd been planning. She'd scraped the rest of the beans into her toilet bucket, which he might have found if he'd ever emptied it.

Should have attacked him with that padlock when he'd been lifting her out of the cage. Hadn't found out where he'd put it until he'd tried to push her back in. He'd never get her back in to it. He'd have to take the chain off first, and if he did, she'd get his scissors, or his boiling kettle, or that curly rod thing, or his lantern, anything, everything. Had to get herself strong enough first. Had to crawl to him until she was strong enough.

He had keys on a hook between the window and the door, a whole bunch of them. One would be for the dog chain padlock. If he came close enough when he had those keys in his hand, or in his pocket, if he put his head down low enough, once her bones weren't so stiff and aching, she could use her chained foot to loop the chain around and around his throat. It wasn't long enough to do it with her hands, but if she caught him off guard, her foot might do it.

She was measuring how much chain she had when he moved. Slid down then, pulled the quilt high and watched him through near-closed eyes.

He opened the firebox and packed it in with that curly rod thing. It was long, and looked heavy. Watched him push wood into it then walk to the door and open it.

She saw earth, a tree trunk and green, and glaring sunlight before he dragged the door shut behind him and the outside world was gone.

Heard him out there and not caring whether he could hear her or not, she tugged on the chain, dragged it to the right, jerked it up. The screws didn't move.

Every sound seemed amplified now. She could hear water splashing, hear the creaking of the old joints of his house.

In Sydney, when Grandpa's house had creaked, he used to say, 'The old girl's arthritis is playing up today.' His house had been full of furniture. This one was almost empty. It had the same brown roller blinds as Grandpa's, but his had spent their days rolled up behind curtains. No curtains here, and the blind over the sink was down.

And he was coming.

His door scraped when it opened. He was carrying a bucket she didn't recognise as her cage bucket, but it must have been the same one. It had a lid. He put it beside the table leg, where her chain would probably allow her to reach it at a stretch, then he turned around and went outside again.

That bucket was white and it had three yellow ducks on it. In the dark she hadn't seen its colour or the yellow ducks.

And he was back, and this time he propped the screen door open with a wheelbarrow. She didn't look at him or at what was in his barrow. She looked over him, at the world she couldn't get to.

He carried in a laptop computer and made space for it on the table, carried in two loaded supermarket bags, wood, ice too, then he went outside and came back with an office chair, then a big suitcase that looked heavy.

RENOVATORS
OPPORTUNITY

*T*hey'd crept down the driveway not long before midnight and had been in bed five minutes later, and when Marni's head hit her own pillow, it knew it. That was all she knew about coming home.

Her mother was washing out the inside of the fridge when Marni wandered out at ten, too late to go to school, and because their fridge was empty, they caught a tram to the Kmart Plaza, then paid a taxi to carry their shopping home.

They were unloading supermarket bags onto the nature strip when Marni saw the *For Sale* sign to the left of Mrs Vaughn's letterbox.

It hadn't been there last night, or this morning when they'd walked away, or if it had been, they hadn't seen it. There were photographs of two rooms, and below them it said: *Renovators opportunity, four bedrooms, large lounge/dining room . . .*

'He putting her in a home.'

They hadn't seen her. They'd knocked on her door before they'd gone out. She hadn't opened her door, so they'd decided not to disturb her.

Self-contained bungalow, Marni read. There was no photograph of their granny flat, which wasn't worth photographing, but nor were most of Mrs Vaughn's rooms – though the two they had photographed looked better than they did in reality. Maybe they'd airbrushed them.

Sarah emptied the overflowing letterbox. She found two snail-nibbled bills in with the junk mail, both addressed to Mrs Vaughn. She dropped the phone bill into her handbag, black, small, bought new for their holiday, then picked up four of the heaviest supermarket bags and left the rest for Marni.

No rap on the corner window as the junk mail was redelivered to the green bin. The Hyundai was parked in its usual space.

They packed their poor little fridge, stuffed their cupboards, filled the box where they stored potatoes and onions, fixed the phone bill to the fridge door with two magnets, and with everything in its own space except the cigarettes and Mrs Vaughn's bill, Marni knocked at the old lady's back door, though no longer expecting it to open. It didn't.

Every item of clothing they'd taken with them needed washing. Their *self-contained bungalow* had never stretched to supplying laundry facilities, and the house for sale or not, their rent was paid and they needed the washing machine. Since the week Marni had to climb in through the bathroom window, she'd known where to find an emergency key to the front door, so she ran around and got it and unlocked that door, and if Raymond didn't like it, she didn't care because she didn't like him.

The house looked weird without Mrs Vaughn in it. The chair near that corner window looked lost. And the bedroom was different. Someone had swapped Mrs Vaughn's old blankets and bedcover for a quilt and new pillows.

The laundry was as they'd left it. Marni opened the back door, and Sarah brought in their load of washing.

It was agitating, before Marni placed their landline phone on the charger and noticed a message flashing, only one.

'It's Raymond, Mum. He says the house is being auctioned and we've got thirty days to vacate the premises.'

'What?'

'Wait.' Marni replayed the message, this time listening to every word. He didn't mention his mother. 'It's Raymond Vaughn,' she said. 'He says that we've got thirty days to find another place to live – and he left that message five days ago, so now we've got only twenty-five days.'

'Check email,' Sarah said.

Their new computer, a fast and furious beast, spat out seven messages, two from Raymond Vaughn.

He hadn't put his mother into a nursing home. She'd died in her bed. His second email was a repeat of his phone message. Mrs Carter was required to vacate the premises in thirty days – now twenty-five.

'He probably poisoned her. She was like she always was when we left – and when I phoned her, she was worse than she always was.'

'She taking heart pills a long time,' Sarah said.

'Can we buy a house in twenty-five days?'

Sarah shook her head.

Mrs Vaughn's death cancelled the last of their holiday, and it was impossible to imagine that old lady being gone. They could smell her in the house, and when they emptied their first load of laundry into her tumble dryer, they almost expected her to walk through that door yelling about them wasting electricity. The dryer drank electricity like a camel drank water.

'It smells like she's still here,' Marni said. The walls had absorbed too much nicotine in their fifty years of life. They were stained by it, her ceilings too.

Her ashtray had gone from the coffee table beside her chair. It used to overflow, spill butts and ash. Every door was a dirty brownish beige, as was the carpet.

A renovator's opportunity? There wasn't much else a real estate agent could say about that house.

They locked the front door and hid that key beneath a terra-cotta pot that in Marni's lifetime had never held a living plant, but like the two rusting iron chairs no one sat on, it had retained its space on the old lady's front porch.

*

Marni went back to school. Sarah went back to her driving lessons. She'd paid in advance for ten, and had to get them done before 24 April.

She drove freeways, drove the route she might be asked to drive when she went for her test, then on Friday, she ended her lesson in the Forest Hill car park, aware that she needed to do something about moving some of that money, which couldn't be as embarrassing as attempting to claim Jillian Jones's fifteen dollars.

A woman greeted her at the Commonwealth Bank. Sarah showed her hearing aids and told her that she wanted to get two bank cheques and invest some money. The woman offered her a printout of interest rates, explained that the amount of interest was dependent on the amount invested. She didn't want Sarah's card but told her to take a seat.

Six chairs in a row, three of them in use. Sarah made it four, and there she sat for twenty minutes before an Asian male invited her into a small office. She showed him her hearing aids, then began back at the beginning.

And he couldn't understand a word she said and she couldn't understand him.

She took her notepad and biro from her bag. *I want to invest five hundred thousand for one year. You advertise 4.5 per cent interest.*

He read the note, then spoke as he might to a child attempting to buy a block of chocolate when she had money enough for a musk stick. She'd dressed for her driving lesson, not for a bank, and she needed a haircut. Should have had her hair cut first, should have worn her office clothes, and lipstick. Business people had more respect for well-dressed clients.

She pushed the card across the desk to him, hoping it may buy his respect. He swiped it, and, hot and sweaty from her hand, it worked well enough to raise his eyebrows, for him to stand and excuse himself – then leave her sitting alone for five more minutes.

He wrote his own note when he returned. *I suggest you make an appointment to speak to our financial adviser.*

No thank you. I want to invest five hundred thousand for one year. Also I want two bank cheques for five hundred thousand.

It took many notes, his and hers, but half an hour later she walked away with her investment receipt, two bank cheques, and the promise of a chequebook and second bank card within five business days. Bank cheques cost ten dollars each. In future, she'd write her own.

Still disbelieving that a bank was allowed to charge ten dollars to give her her own money, she walked down to the Bank of Melbourne, where she planned to invest one of the bank cheques in Marni's name, and to open an account with the other one in Jillian Jones's name. It was her maiden name. She had that old card and her birth certificate as identification, and Marni's birth certificate with Jillian's name on it – and her parents' marriage certificate.

The woman wanted her card.

'I want to get one, please,' Sarah said.

'Pardon?'

Again she showed her hearing aids. Again she removed her notebook. *I don't have an account here. I want to open an account here and invest five hundred thousand dollars for twelve months.*

'Do you have a passport?'

Didn't tell her that she wasn't booking an overseas flight. Wanted to, but shook her head.

'A driver's licence?'

Soon she'd have a licence, but not yet, and she sighed, reclaimed her notepad and gave up. She was on her way out when a second woman tapped her on the shoulder.

'Come through,' she said.

Another office, another chair, a better speaker. 'You require identification to open a new account,' she said. 'Do you have a passport?'

'No.'

'A driver's licence?'

'Soon,' she said and giving up on Jillian Jones, she offered Sarah Carter's Commonwealth Bank card, her learner's permit, Medicare card, phone bill, library card, video shop card, then to the pile she added her bank cheques.

Money talks, Gramp used to say, and Sarah Carter had too much of it, which, unless she admitted to having, she couldn't give away. Desperate now to use a toilet, she gave up on the idea of locking money away for Marni. Sarah Carter locked one bank cheque away for twelve months at 4.45 per cent interest, and the other for three years at 4.75 per cent, with accumulative interest – which in three years' time would have made about seventy thousand dollars, and the thought of it made her more desperate to use a toilet.

*

Frederick Adam-Jones had made it to the toilets in the nick of time. He had bowel cancer, self-diagnosed, and his mother's Alzheimer's, self-diagnosed, his heart was on its last legs, and he couldn't go to his GP to get his ills diagnosed because he'd want his blood, and Freddy suffered from DNA paranoia. He didn't count sheep when he couldn't sleep, he listed the places where he'd shed DNA.

He was shedding his wife too – or she was shedding him. She'd taken her pillow and gone to the spare room last night, and when he'd followed her there, afraid of having a heart attack and dying alone, she'd got out of that bed and gone into a second spare room – with twin beds.

'I can't sleep with you tossing around like a fish on a hook, Freddy. I have to get up at five o'clock in the morning,' she'd said.

He'd thought she'd cancel her trip to Greece when they'd found out where their shit of a son had got the merchandise he'd been kicked out of school for selling, when they'd had two uniformed police with guns on their hips knocking on their door at midnight, demanding to speak to Rolland Adam-Jones. Cheryl couldn't stand to sit still, or hadn't since they'd moved to Camberwell. She'd been away more often than she'd been at home.

Thank Christ that boy had been at home, in bed, and the only reason he'd been at home in bed was because his mother had locked every door and window before taking the keys with her to bed.

Two of Rolland's rat pack hadn't been at home. The police caught Steve and Mick red-handed in the backyard of the Vermont house where they'd gone to tend their crop in Cheryl's fernery. That house, vacant since Freddy had moved his family to Camberwell, was no longer vacant. The new owners recognising the greenery as something other than ferns had phoned the police.

At six this morning, when Freddy left to drive Cheryl to the airport, Rolland was sleeping soundly. At seven fifty, when he returned, that shit of a kid's bed was empty – as had been the notes section of Freddy's wallet, which he hadn't discovered until he'd opened it to pay for sixty dollars' worth of petrol. Had to put it on his card, on credit, so he could sign for it, because he had too much on his mind to remember his new PIN.

Should have been at the office by ten. He'd called in sick, and he was. He'd poked his card into an ATM, hoping his fingers would remember his PIN, and when they hadn't, and he'd had to drive to the bank, to queue, and show his licence before they'd give him two lousy thousand, and his bowel was in spasm before the money was in his hand.

His heart missing beats since he'd found his wallet bare, he stood looking at himself in the washroom mirror, looking at a dead man standing – looking at a fat, bullfrog-eyed old bastard, waiting for his heart to give up and stop – until he saw tomorrow's headlines.

BARRISTER DROPS DEAD ON PUBLIC TOILET FLOOR

With what might have been his final breath, he swung that door wide and burst out to the corridor—

And damn near killed another one.

She wasn't wearing yellow and was half his weight. He grasped her upper arm to save her and held on tight because she was alive and he was dead, and he didn't want to be alone.

'Sorry,' she said. Then grasped the hand that held her. 'Uncle Bill?' she said.

He wasn't anyone's uncle. He had two thousand dollars in his wallet and he made a grab for it.

'I am Jillian,' the woman said. 'We live with you. In Brisbane, in your caravan. Long, long time before.'

He didn't know her. He didn't own a caravan, hadn't been to Brisbane in fifteen years, but with his wallet safe in his pocket, he pushed his Alzheimer's aside long enough to remember that Bill lived in Brisbane, that he and his wife had been pulling a caravan down the coast of Western Australia when he'd got the news that their mother was dying. Good old reliable Bill, who'd flown home from Broome to hold his mother's hand – and she wouldn't have known who was holding her hand or if anyone had been holding her hand.

That's what Freddy had told himself. Frog-eyed Freddy who hadn't gone near her, who was a self-serving bastard who deserved to drop dead but wasn't doing it, and his heartbeat had settled back into its rhythm.

'Frederick's the name,' he said. 'You'd be Joe and Stephanie's girl?' Her speech marked her as deaf. He remembered the day Joe and Stephanie's baby had been diagnosed as deaf.

'Sorry,' she said, backing towards the door of the women's toilets. 'You look the same. Like Uncle Bill. I am very sorry.'

Disappeared then, and Freddy walked on, a finger on the pulse in his throat.

Then it hit him. The property. The missing girl. The bastard with a penchant for garbage bags.

That woman could have the information he needed, and he turned on his heel and walked back to watch that door until she came out – and her expression told him she wished he hadn't waited.

*

On a good day, Frederick Adam-Jones could talk a man without legs into buying a pair of shoes, Cheryl had said that a while back. He could sell snow to an Eskimo, pork to a Muslim. She'd said that too.

It took him five or ten minutes to talk a deaf woman into drinking a coffee with him, and she only agreed because he'd told her he'd been at her parents' wedding, that he'd known her as a toddling infant.

'Joe and Steph lived with the family until—' Until Joe had learnt that his perfect female version of baby Jesus was imperfect. *She'll never be any good.*

'I have . . . appointment soon.'

They were seated with their cappuccinos in the food court when he asked if she was living at the farm.

She frowned. 'We live here – not far. I am Sarah Carter now.'

'You have children?'

'My daughter. Marni,' she said, and he told her he had a son, Rolland, and a wife, currently on a plane to Greece, then asked if her daughter was deaf, and when she shook her head, he asked about her husband.

'He die, a long time before.'

'Are you employed – working?'

'I am senior payroll/account officer,' she said, and said it well, and proudly. 'I work for Maureen Crow, in the city.'

Freddy knew all about the Crow mess. Smyth was still totalling up hours in splitting that company down the middle.

'You've done well,' he said. 'Your father became the family gypsy, after he left the farm.'

'Gypsy,' she said. 'Yes.'

Freddy searched his mind for something more to say that might keep her seated. 'Another coffee?'

She shook her head. He spoke of his office, and her eyes spoke of disinterest. She had talking eyes. She sat with him until he emptied his coffee cup, then lifted the strap of her bag over her shoulder and stood.

'Thank you for coffee. I have driving test soon.'

'Can I drive you . . .?'

'My instructor . . . Thank you.'

'What time is your test?'

'My test will be on twenty-fourth. It is coming very fast.'

He handed her his card as she was leaving. She dropped it into her handbag without a glance.

Gone then. He followed her, at a distance. She went up the escalator. He went up. Followed her until she walked across to the bus stop. He walked then to where he'd parked his Ferrari, and when he drove by the bus stop, she was still waiting for her instructor, or the bus. He double-parked where he could keep an eye on her, and he thought of his mother, who'd spent her life worrying about that girl who wasn't being educated. She'd learnt something, somewhere. Crows? The company was worth millions.

There was a man who'd had it all, a decent wife and four kids and he'd gone and buggered up everything with his womanising. Freddy was and would ever be a one-woman man, but he'd buggered up his life anyway.

The bus arrived. He didn't see her board it, but when it moved away, she was no longer waiting, so he tailed it, followed its stops and starts to a roundabout, where she left it to walk.

He drove by her and parked opposite a school entrance. Watched her approach in his rear-view mirror. She glanced at his Ferrari as she passed. Most did. Its windows were darkened. He dropped his chin, turned his face until she walked by.

She turned into a residential street, and he started the motor and followed again, slowly, which was the only way to traverse a narrow street with cars parked on either side. A van approaching from the other direction was prepared to play 'chicken'. Freddy, ever a 'chicken', slid into a driveway and allowed the van through.

She stopped to empty a letterbox. He stopped well back, saw her disappear in behind a neglected garden. There was no mistaking that garden, but he got the number from the letterbox, keyed it into his organiser beside *24 April,* then drove on, and for the first time in weeks he wasn't thinking about faulty heart valves, bowel cancer, DNA or Alzheimer's.

*

The bank receipts safe in the cake tin, Sarah glanced at *Frederick Adam-Jones, Barrister*'s card. She knew that name, hadn't known he was one of her unknown uncles. He was the image of Uncle Bill – or the image of the only photograph she had of Uncle Bill – taken over twenty years ago.

'Stupid,' she said, and thought of Marni, who would have adopted him, would have taken his photograph to add to her gallery of family now decorating the refrigerator door.

She'd wanted to put the print of Oliver and the Clark girls on the fridge door, but had settled for a photograph of the photograph – then taken another of eight-month-old Jillian and her father. Peter Clark and the group photograph were now beneath magnets, decorating that fridge door, which may have been why its freezer had stopped freezing ice-cream.

The business card returned to her handbag, she forced her eyes to her baby self. She'd looked like every other smiling baby. He'd looked happy too. Her mother had told her once that they hadn't found out about her hearing loss until she was fifteen months old. Maybe that's when he'd bought that tent and hit the roads.

The family gypsy . . . Frederick Adam-Jones had said.

They'd been gypsies, always moving on – and of all the people at Forest Hill she could have bumped into, she'd had to bump into someone who'd known her, known him.

That 666 no longer showed up on her bank receipts, but that bulk of money was still there, still pushing her into situations she wasn't ready to handle, like Mrs Vaughn's death was pushing her to buy a house. She wasn't ready for that either.

Bob had suggested they move in with him and his mother. Marni thought it was a good idea.

A life-changing amount, the TattsLotto man had said.

World changing. They'd gone to Perth because they could afford to. If they'd stayed home, Mrs Vaughn might still have been alive. That money had made her go to Forest Hill and bump into an uncle.

She'd seen him on television during the Swan trial. Hadn't looked at him, or not at his face, hadn't wanted to. Never in a million years would she have believed that he was connected to her family.

She knew of a John the Baptist, a minister. She knew his address. She'd known and loved Uncle Bill the electrician, had seen Clarry the truck driver once, or she'd seen his truck driving into the farm. Gone for a long walk that day and hadn't come back until that truck was gone. She didn't know the other brothers' names. Someone must have mentioned them. She knew there were seven of them.

The jug filled and plugged in, she went to the refrigerator for milk – and saw him again before she opened the door, saw his eyes, his smile. She could remember his face when it hadn't been smiling, could remember screaming *thief* at him when she'd been eleven, and screaming worse when she was twelve. He'd had crutches beneath both armpits, policemen at his side that day. Remembered his grimace, his flinching eyes, not because of what she'd screamed but because of how she'd sounded. He might have smiled more often if she'd been a deaf mute.

When she allowed herself, she could remember many things about him. Driving his green station wagon too fast down a dusty road, raising a cloud of dust behind them. She'd believed they'd been chasing a rainbow, that he had to go fast to get there before the rainbow disappeared or he wouldn't find the pot of gold.

He'd had good teeth, had been easy to lip-read.

Shut that bloody whistle up!

She could remember tumbling on soft green grass in a park where they'd stopped one day, halfway between rainbows, and she'd lost the hearing aid that had whistled. Her mother had known they'd find it. They walked backward and forward, searching that soft green grass, looking for its pink.

Get in the car.

He would have liked to lose that aid.

She'd never heard any of her aids whistle. Marni did. She said, 'You're whistling, Mum.' Gran had heard it. *Let me fix your ear, Jilly.*

Remembered running down to Daddy who was digging holes, not for pots of gold but for posts so he could make the fence strong enough so the baby cows couldn't get out on the road and get run over. She'd tried to tell him no more rainbows because Gramp had many pots of gold in his shed.

She'd had a fistful of sticky honeycomb and she'd put her sticky hand on his trousers so he'd look at her.

He'd washed her in the dam, all of her, but he'd got her out, and Gramp had seen what he'd done, and there was roaring, and Gran hadn't cared that he'd got Jillian out, only that he'd put her in.

Get off my land!

It was Gramp's land and his father's. It was Gramp's rifle, but roly-poly Gran had known how to use it.

You leave them where they are, you bastard of a man.

Not the green wagon at the farm, a white sedan with red on the sides and a boot for their tent that wasn't a boot. Boots were for feet, not cars. Seven when they'd left the farm that time, when she'd learned that the same word could mean two things.

Many different roads. Many different cars. A red utility once, then a white sedan. It had almost made it across the Nullarbor before it died.

The kid's deaf and dumb. We've got to get her into school.

Kind truck driver patting her head. He helped load the tent and case and bags into his truck so they could get their deaf and dumb kid to school.

In Perth her father had to work, had to put new tyres on other men's cars, so he could get money to buy a new car. He hadn't liked staying in one place or working. Her mother had. She'd liked cleaning their cabin that had its own bathroom.

Then that final car, the dark blue Ford.

Get in the car.

Jilly needs to go to school, Joey, and I can't up and leave the Clarks without notice. They've been good to me.

Very good. Every week they'd given her a little envelope full of money, until he'd taken it and she couldn't pay the man in the office his rent for their cabin and the next day, her mother couldn't go to work.

Peter and Lynette Clark had understood without words, and when her mother was better, Peter had driven them to his bank to open the account so no one could get money out unless both Jillian and Stephanie Jones signed a piece of paper.

A school day when it happened. She was sitting in the classroom beside her friend when Lynette Clark came in with the principal.

Accident, Lynette's mouth said. *Hospital.*

And Sarah ripped happy him and smiling baby from the refrigerator door and shredded them, pitched the pieces into the rubbish bag, tied that bag tight and ran it out to the green bin. Buried him in the rubbish where he deserved to be.

FOR SALE

*T*hey were celebrating Sarah's new licence with Bob and his mother, and they'd had to unlock Mrs Vaughn's house and borrow two of her chairs for them to sit on. Bob moved the table out from the wall. Marni found enough glasses. Bob and his mother had bought a bottle of wine and one of orange juice, a big bunch of flowers and a cream cake with *Congratulations Sarah* written on the chocolate icing and Bob's mother invited them twice to move into her spare room and Sarah thanked her twice but didn't say she would. They might have to. They'd spent last weekend looking at units, large and small, old and new, for rent or for sale. They toured Danni Lane's house on the internet. It was being auctioned the same day as Mrs Vaughn's. It was empty. Barbara Lane had gone home to Sydney with her father. Martin Lane was living on his brother's yacht, down here somewhere. They'd seen it on television, seen Martin Lane and his brother speaking to a reporter.

Bob was opening his bottle of wine when they heard Mrs Vaughn's doorbell.

'The agent will be showing someone through,' Bob's mother said.

There were no lights on at the house. About to close the door, Marni heard someone at the gates.

'Anyone about?' a male voice called.

'Who's there?' Marni yelled.

'Uncle Fred,' he said.

Bob opened the gate. He brought him inside, and whoever Uncle Fred was, his shape in the doorway looked like Alfred Hitchcock's – and his posh voice in that kitchen made it look more ridiculous than usual, and Marni had to borrow a third chair.

*

He'd bought an expensive box of chocolates, and their table and its assortment of glasses looked ridiculous, and one glass still had part of its cheese spread label stuck to it. She held on to it while Bob poured in half an inch of wine then filled it with orange juice. The others drank pure bubbles.

She saw Bob's second face that night. Her mother always said that he had two faces. He put on his office face and manner for Uncle Fred, who was a barrister, who was the Frederick Adam-Jones who was still trying to get Michael Swan out of jail.

And it was ridiculous that he was her uncle, and Marni kept eyeing her mother, who kept evading her eyes.

They drank the champagne, drank coffee, Sarah cut the cake and Marni found ridiculous plates to put it on and didn't give anyone a fork because they only had three. It was nice cake. Uncle Fred's chocolates were nice, and there were a dozen left when their visitors left, which was when Marni let fly.

'You're still doing it, aren't you?'

'What?'

'Hiding things from me. That's what. How many more relatives are you hiding from me?'

'I talk to him at Forest Hill, only because I think he is Bill, then I say about my driving test, walk away and forget him.'

'You could have told me.'

'I don't want him, Marni. I don't tell him where we live!'

'He probably got a sleazy private investigator to snoop around and find us. Where are his brothers?'

'I know Bill. I thought he was Bill. I don't know, Marni.'

'You said John before. Where's he?'

'In church somewhere. He is Baptist minister, at Dubbo before you were born. I don't know where now. Clarry is driving a big truck somewhere. I don't know where. I don't know their face, Marni.'

'Your family is crazy.'

'Yes,' Sarah said, then went into the bedroom to get the cake tin. The lid off, she tossed a packet of photographs to Marni. 'Find one with seven little boy,' she said, and she started her own search through the second packet.

Marni found the boys, posed for the camera, three small ones seated in a row on a table, four taller ones standing beside and behind them.

'Him,' Sarah said, pointing at the smallest, an infant with over-sized eyes. 'Frederick.' She stabbed the photograph again. 'Bill. See. Already the same eyes.'

One was a fat, wide-eyed cherub, who looked like a perfect model for one of those old religious paintings. Bill may have been ten, a chubby ten.

'Which one is your father?' Sarah pointed to a taller, thinner boy standing beside Bill. 'How come you don't know the other ones' names?'

'I can't hear. I know only thing if people tell me. I don't see them so no one say their name. I know John. He is writing letters to Gramp. I know Clarry. He coming one day in a big truck and Gramp talking about him,' Sarah said, then started packing the photographs away.

'You should buy an album for these.'

'Better in there. I like that lid on tight.'

'Tell me about your father.'

'Go to bed. You got school tomorrow.'

'I haven't. It's Anzac Day. Are car places open tomorrow?'

'Bob will drive us on Saturday.'

'Will we get one like Bob's?'

'I will get a bit old one – so it not hurting too much when someone scratch my paint.'

'Buy Mrs Vaughn's. It's got ready-made scratches.'

'I will very fast if he will sell to me. He won't.'

'Because we stopped him putting his mother in a nursing home.'

'Yes.'

Marni went to bed. Sarah turned on the computer to browse the internet. She didn't find Mrs Vaughn's car advertised on eBay. She found a red Hyundai with fifty-five thousand kilometres on the clock, a used Mazda that looked new. She'd find something on Saturday.

Before closing down, she sent Raymond an email, not about his mother's car, but because the estate agents she and Marni had spoken to about rental properties had asked for rental references. All she had was an old diary listing the dates and amounts of cash she'd handed to Mrs Vaughn. It was a futile exercise asking Raymond for a reference, but she had to try.

A futile exercise to ask about the car too, but she added two lines at the bottom.

If you are selling your mother's car, I would be interested in purchasing it.

She hit *send* then, and it was gone, and second thoughts or not, she couldn't get it back.

It was close to midnight when she returned Mrs Vaughn's chairs, and while the house was unlocked, she did a load of washing. She'd be back at work next Wednesday, and soon after that, they'd be homeless.

They owned no furniture worth moving. If they bought a car, they could load what was worth taking into it and live at a motel.

Bob and his mother wouldn't allow that.

It would be easy to give in, and, as Marni said, just go with the flow. Living with a family changed your relationship to that family. After a time, you became a part of that family.

Used to love being a part of the Clark family, loved watching Oliver's hands pulling apart computers. Had loved his hands before she'd loved him. She didn't love Bob's hands, didn't feel anything when he kissed her.

In some cultures parents arranged their children's marriages and the bride and groom didn't kiss before the wedding. Some of those marriages must have worked. Bob was a good man. He had a good job and was good at it – and maybe he needed two faces to be good at it.

Marni liked him. She liked his mother. Maybe people grow out of that first-love rush of feeling when touching a hand can take your breath away. Maybe it was time to put Oliver away, to grow up and do the sensible thing.

She hadn't kissed a boy before Oliver, and she'd only done it that first time to stop his mouth trying to find words. After that, they'd talked with their bodies and it had been a better way to talk than with words. He'd been so happy, and better too. He'd been better from August to December.

Then he'd got worse.

The day the ambulance came to take him to the hospital, his eyes had known he wouldn't be coming home. He hadn't known what their body talking had done. She'd known. Hadn't told anyone. Hadn't known what she was going to do.

Then Gran and Gramp's Christmas card had arrived. Their usual twenty dollars was inside it but the writing on it wasn't Gran's.

Dear Jilly,
   Gran hasn't been herself for a while now, but we're struggling along and hoping things get better.
   Love, Gramp and Gran

She'd withdrawn money from Jillian's bank account, booked a seat on a bus to Melbourne then bought her own Christmas card, her own stamp.

> *Dear Gran and Gramp,*
> *Thank you for the twenty dollars. I would like to visit you for Christmas. I will be in Melbourne on Thursday 23rd. Can you please pick me up at Eltham Station at two o'clock?*
> *Love from Jilly (Sarah)*

She'd gone to the hospital to see Oliver one last time but he'd already gone to that sleeping place where hurting people go before they die. She'd kissed him, put his hand near the place where his baby was growing, then walked away from him.

Found Gramp old-man thin, toothless and almost blind. He hadn't understood her, and when she'd written him a note, he'd been unable to read it without his magnifying glass.

No dogs to greet her, no Gran, only an angry little lady locked inside, and when they'd unlocked the door, that angry little lady hadn't wanted Sarah in her house – and Sarah hadn't wanted to be in it.

Then Gramp wrote her a note. She still had it in the cake tin.

YOU'RE DEAF, I'M HALF-BLIND, GRAN'S LOST MOST OF HER MARBLES, BUT GIVE US A DAY OR TWO AND I RECKON WE COULD ADD UP TO A PRETTY GOOD WHOLE.

They'd added up well enough from December until June. She'd trimmed Gramp's moustache and he'd started wearing his false teeth, and if she hadn't said too many words, he'd understood.

His sight had deteriorated. Near the end, when they weren't in the house, he'd had to walk with one hand on Sarah's shoulder. Near the end, Gran had become dangerous to Sarah's baby.

Then that letter from Perth. She'd recognised the return address. Hadn't wanted to open it, but Gramp had wanted to know what it said.

Sarah shook that memory away and picked up the flowers Bob and his mother had brought. Pretty things. She owned no vase large enough to hold them so she filled a jug and stood settling the flowers into it and thinking of Mrs Vaughn's garden, a wild pretty place in winter when her camellias and magnolia bloomed.

The new owner would cut those trees down, would probably rip the house down and built a McMansion. The only way to buy a piece of inner city land was to buy an old house and rip it down. A few in this area had been wrecked.

Well after midnight when she unloaded the washing machine, and for the first time looked at its brand name. Whether she bought a house or rented, she'd need a washing machine. She liked this one. It spun her washing near dry.

The house locked, the key beneath its pot, she carried her basket past the Hyundai – and its ready-made scratches. It was three years old, and except for when Raymond had taken it for weekends, it hadn't been driven further than the local shopping centres, doctors and funeral homes. It needed a new battery and its scratches repaired, but she'd buy it tomorrow if Raymond agreed to sell it.

She didn't hang her washing. It would be easier to do in daylight. She checked her emails. Raymond hadn't replied. Too late now for him to reply, so she closed down, turned the power off at the wall and was packing the photographs back into the cake tin when her hands delved deeper, for an old envelope, addressed to *Jillian Jones, c/o Peter Clark.*

She'd kept it, not its contents but the envelope, only because she'd loved looking at the return address. The address was no longer current. Her name was no longer Jillian Jones, so she ripped the envelope in half, in half again and tossed it into the bin.

THE SALE

*H*e'd heard her moving about in the yard. He'd tolerated her for the first year or two, relieved to hand over the responsibility of an impossible parent to paid help – and she had been paid, if not in cash then with free rent and utilities. He hadn't expected her to become a fixture.

For the past ten years she'd been paying his mother a pittance in rent, and she had the nerve to ask for a rental reference. She'd get none from him, or the car. He had to speak to her though. She needed to be told that the agent was holding three open days and two evenings, and he'd said that the unit could be a selling point if the buyer was looking for a rental property.

Raymond was looking at the passenger-side doors of the Hyundai. One of them could need replacing. He wanted to get rid of it, and as it was it had to be worth sixteen thousand.

He unlocked the house and walked through, taking inventory as he went. The piano no one had played in twenty years could have had some value, the glass cabinet, the television was new. He found a notepad and started listing items of possible value, and had worked his way down to the laundry, when he saw her through the window. She was at the clothes line, removing and folding sheets – and she hadn't washed sheets and towels by hand! She'd been in here.

His inventory forgotten, he was out the back door.

She saw him coming and stopped what she was doing. 'I require your key,' he said.

'I paid my rent before we have our holiday,' she said.

'Your key to my mother's house, Mrs Carter.'

'I have got no key for her house.'

His inventory page turned, he wrote, *You have been inside the house. You used the washing machine and I require your key.*

'I have got no key.'

He pointed to the clothes line. 'You deny you used the laundry?'

She snatched his pad and wrote, *If we had a key, Marni would not have to climb through the bathroom window when your mother fell over. Your mother never gave me a key to her house.*

He'd been away at the time of his mother's fall. He'd heard about the eleven-year-old girl who'd climbed through a window and called the ambulance, who'd given the hospital his contact details. And he had better things to do than stand in that yard arguing with pen and paper.

The house will be open for inspection on Saturday morning. I expect your premises to be habitable and accessible at all times.

She scribbled a reply. *We will be looking at cars on Saturday, or I will buy your mother's car. Do you want to sell her car?*

Leave your key beneath the doormat for the agent.

'My rent is paid. The key belong to me,' she said.

'Your rent?' he sneered. 'You paid my mother a pittance.'

'For no stove, no fridge, no nothing. We paid her too much,' the daughter commented as she stepped out to her mother's side.

He turned his back before she mentioned the possible asbestos content of the roof – if she knew about it – which may present problems with the sale, according to the agent.

The land had value. The block was huge by today's standards and its position excellent. The house was a good size. Its brickwork and roof appeared solid. Its interior was a shambles, the bathroom uninhabitable – and whatever he got from the sale, his sister would get half.

*

A windy day, Saturday, which may have kept interested parties away. Raymond sat by his phone, waiting for the agent to ring.

'We had six groups through,' he reported. 'Two expressed some interest in the land.'

Then late on Monday afternoon, Raymond's mobile rang while he was on the road. He put the caller on speaker, and drove on.

'We've had an offer from a Sydney buyer. Five hundred and fifty thousand,' the agent said.

'I'm in heavy traffic and in no mood for hilarity,' Raymond said. 'The land alone is worth more than I'm asking.'

'The old timber homes are easier to demolish,' the agent said. 'She's a cash buyer, and in a hurry to buy close to schools. She may go higher.'

'Six hundred and fifty,' Raymond said. 'I'm not prepared to consider one red cent less before the auction.'

'I'll get back to you.'

He called back at seven. 'The Sydney buyer will go to six.'

'A house in the same street went for seven hundred and eighty thousand—'

'More modern, two renovated bathrooms, two levels . . .'

'Get him up to six forty-five and I'll consider it,' Raymond snarled.

At eight, the agent called again. 'She said she needs a car for her daughter and will go to six thirty-five, if you include the car parked in the drive. She's currently negotiating on two other houses in the area.'

'Six hundred and sixty thousand – with the car,' Raymond snarled.

'She's a cash buyer, Mr Vaughn, eager for a fast settlement—'
Raymond hung up the phone.

At ten that night, Raymond got rid of his mother's house and car for six hundred and fifty thousand, to the Sydney buyer, and he considered it worth the discount to get that place and its possible asbestos off his mind. The details left in the hands of his solicitor, Raymond forgot about it until Wednesday, when he learned that Ainsworth, Adam-Jones and Smyth were handling the sale for the buyer.

They defended murderers. They didn't soil their hands with conveyancing work – unless they'd made the purchase for some Sydney drug lord looking to set up an indoor hydroponic marijuana plantation or ice laboratory. It had the space and the privacy, and was no longer his problem.

The following Friday afternoon he entered his mother's house for the last time and set about emptying drawers, shaking garments, checking pockets before stuffing each item into a garbage bag. During her latter years his mother had developed the habit of hiding money in odd places.

He found four hundred dollars inside the piano, found a hundred and seventy-five tucked between tea towels in a kitchen drawer, two hundred and twenty in a vase on the lounge room mantelpiece, and he wondered how much that bitch had found while she'd been cleaning.

She wasn't about today, nor was she answering her door. The removal van had been ordered for two o'clock. It was now ten after. He walked down to the backyard to knock on the prefab's door. She didn't open it, so he took the opportunity to look at its roof, to peer in through the window, to write her a brief note which he slid beneath her door.

Mrs Carter,
    The property has been sold. Please leave the unit in the condition you found it and the key beneath the doormat.
    Vaughn

*

Marni saw a pile of mattresses and Mrs Vaughn's moth-eaten couch and chair on the nature strip when she came from school. The kitchen table and four chairs were out there too, and there was nothing wrong with them. Those chairs were more comfortable than the ones Marni and Sarah sat on.

The Hyundai wasn't in the drive. She found it parked in the garage. Found the note too and read it.

She'd been shopping for bread and fruit. Her mother was back at work and had used the last of their bread to cut lunches. She'd bought steak too, because a supermarket employee had just marked its price down and Marni loved steak when it was cooked properly. Their magic frying pan cooked it properly.

She stuck the note on the fridge and thought of Uncle Fred, who she'd hated the night he'd gatecrashed her mother's licence party. She called him Hubert now, after a chubby angel she'd read about in a book, who had come into the lives of two elderly sisters as they were about to be murdered by their evil nephew. Hubert had fixed him up fast and sent him down to hell.

Marni's Hubert had fixed up Raymond Vaughn, though only after she and her mother had done the wheeling and dealing on the phone, which had been the most fun they'd ever had in their lives – until the agent said yes, and her mother had stopped laughing and said that Raymond would change his mind about selling her the house as soon as he found out that she was the buyer.

The agent had told Marni that she'd need to get a solicitor to do the legal bits of buying, and barristers were only solicitors with a few more letters after their names, so her mother had found Frederick Adam-Jones's card. Marni phoned him and left a message asking him if he knew a solicitor who did the house-buying stuff.

He hadn't phoned back. He'd called in that night, and Marni had explained about Raymond Vaughn being likely to change his mind when he found out they were the buyers, and that fat old cherub had suggested that they could get around the problem by transferring their money to his office account, and he'd transfer it on, so that's what they did.

But the best part, the absolute best part, was being driven to school one morning in a Ferrari, and Samantha seeing her get out of it, and when she asked who he was, being able to say, he was Frederick Adam-Jones, and her uncle.

*

She stole the four chairs from the nature strip, or swapped them for her mother's old wooden chairs. She took three perfectly good cake tins and a box of assorted mugs, glasses and vases and would have dragged the kitchen table in if she could have, if it hadn't been too big for the space their tiny table fitted into. She took the coffee table that used to live beside Mrs Vaughn's lounge room's corner window with the ashtray ever on it, and it was a nice old table and there wasn't anything wrong with it except for a couple of burn marks where cigarettes had rolled off the ashtray.

Bob's car drove in before six. Marni heard it arrive, heard it leave, and when her mother didn't come in, she knew where she'd find her.

She'd found two Pyrex bowls, a heap of cutlery and a set of better saucepans than they owned.

That night, they borrowed the key again, hoping their house might look better without the furniture. It looked worse. The carpet was piebald, clean and new where the furniture had been but old and filthy where it hadn't.

'We can buy new carpet, and get someone to paint the walls,' Marni said.

'Uncle Fred said guttering first.'

'Have you told Bob yet that we bought it?'

'I will. I have to.'

*

Marni phoned two plumbers to fix the guttering or she left them messages. One called back. She phoned a painter who didn't call back.

Uncle Fred popped in with some papers to sign about the car and Marni found out the names of the seven Jones boys in the old photograph.

'A larger version of that old atrocity hung in our front room until one of the brothers knocked it down and broke the glass. I was unaware a copy had survived,' he said, then he pointed with his stumpy fat finger and listed them. 'Clarry, Joe, Bill, John at the back, Bert, Gordon and myself on the table.'

'Do any of them live in Melbourne?' Marni asked.

'Sadly, our lives went in very diverse directions, Marni.'

He gathered up his signed papers, zipped them into a black leather folder, then stood, looking at Sarah until she looked at him, when he asked if she'd been out to the farm in recent years.

'Before Marni is born,' she said.

'Do you recall the buyer's name?' he asked.

She shook her head. 'Gramp selling one part before . . . before I was there.'

'He retained over thirty acres,' Uncle Fred said. 'You are aware that he altered his will in your favour before he died?'

Sarah didn't catch his words. Marni did. She repeated them, and again Sarah shook her head.

'You would have been contacted.'

'The Clarks said something about your grandfather's will, Mum.'

'That land always go to first son,' Sarah said. 'Always. Gramp is second, but his brother die, in the dam. Bill will know.'

'Bill had no interest in the land,' Uncle Fred said. 'Given the situation when the will was written, our father apparently decided to skip a generation. I am certain that he named you.'

'Because the first son was dead?' Marni said. She was learning stuff, but he was standing, ready to go.

'Perhaps,' he said.

'Too late now,' Sarah said.

'Perhaps not, Sarah. I had occasion recently to drive by the property. It appeared deserted. It may well be worth your while to . . . to look into it. I believe the chap who handled the estate was from Eltham . . . Towers, an elderly chap.'

'Gramp is dead ten year.'

'Is it that long?' He looked at his watch, turned to the door then back. 'Thirty-odd acres of land so close to the city has value, and I've known similar cases where probate has been delayed longer – when there are family disagreements over inheritances.' He looked at his watch again. 'To use our Mr Rudd's expression, I must zip. My wife is flying in from Greece tonight.'

'Thank you very much for everything you doing,' Sarah said.

'It's very little, my dear,' he said.

'We call you our angel,' Marni said.

'Never an angel, Marni,' he said, then he took the hand she offered and like a fat old knight from a movie, he kissed it. 'A few phone calls should put the matter of that land to rest,' and he went on his way.

He may not have had wings or a halo, but he looked like a pink, chubby-cheeked cherub, and as far as Marni and Sarah were concerned, the little hand he raised in salute had performed miracles.

He'd got rid of over a million of their dollars; had paid for the house and car and stamp duty, donated two hundred thousand dollars as a reward for information leading to the arrest of the Freeway Killer, and he'd posted four cheques.

*

Ten seconds after Jackie came into work, everyone in the office knew about her windfall, and when Shane arrived, and they compared amounts, Rena confessed to having received twenty thousand.

Bob had received the same amount. He mentioned it that evening in the car, then he asked if Sarah had received a similar windfall.

'Yes,' she said.

'Who'd be giving away that amount of money?'

'Bonus from David Crow . . .' Sarah said.

'I thought it might have been Maureen, celebrating getting rid of the bastard. You know he's living with Barbara Lane in a posh harbourside unit.'

'When he is bankrupt I have a party.'

'I'll supply the champagne. When are you and Marni moving in?'

'I buying Mrs Vaughn's house, Bob.'

'What?'

Sarah shrugged. 'I buying her house and car.'

'How much was your cheque?'

'Too much,' Sarah said. Almost told him about TattsLotto, but he'd tell his mother and she'd tell her daughters—

'You'll be paying it off when you're sixty!' he said.

'I want something that belong to me, something that don't move so Marni will have one place, her place forever.'

'She could have it with me. I love that kid.'

'She like you too, very, very much. You are a very good, nice man, Bob—'

'But you don't want to move in with me.'

'I don't . . . don't want . . . very close. I am not very true person, Bob.'

'What do you mean, not true?'

'I am not Mrs Carter. I am not marry Marni's father.'

'As if I care—'

A row of cars braked in front, Bob braked, but the car behind him didn't, or not fast enough. It altered the conversation. The damage was minimal, a scratch, a small dent, a bank-up of cars while Bob got the driver's details. They were late home, and there was a stranger leaving the yard when Bob drove in. One of the plumbers or the painter Marni had called – or a robber – or the Freeway Killer. He didn't wait to introduce himself.

Bob got out of the car to walk behind Sarah while she checked the front door and windows. There'd been no break-in.

'You've bought a wreck,' he said.

'Yes,' Sarah admitted, and looked where he was looking, at the guttering. It had grass – or trees – growing in it, and was more rust than metal. The wrought-iron railing around the front porch may not have seen paint since it had been installed in the sixties.

But they didn't have to move in with Bob and his mother; they didn't have to move ever again, and even if they couldn't find workers to make their house beautiful, they could find someone to pull it down and build a new house, because the land it stood on was their own, and to Gramp, holding on to his last few acres had been everything.

'How much did you pay for it?'

'Six hundred and fifty.'

'The land is worth that much,' he admitted.

DAVE AND POP

On Wednesday, Marni found a painter opposite the school gate. He was loading a ladder onto a paint-spattered wagon, and she nicked across the road to ask him if he had time to paint a very messy old house.

'Where do you live?' he asked.

'Not far around the next corner,' she said, and gave him their address. He didn't write it down, but half an hour later his spattered wagon was in their driveway and he was pressing Mrs Vaughn's doorbell.

Marni ran around to the front yard. 'Mum's not home from work yet,' she said. 'I can let you in to have a look.'

'Inherited it, did she?'

'Yeah,' Marni said, because it was easier.

'How bad is she inside?'

'Worse than outside.' Which looked pretty bad today. April was over and the Magic Faraway Tree was losing its leaves and making a mess about doing it, and without its green to hide behind that poor old house looked worse. She retrieved the key from beneath the pot, and, not feeling good with him standing behind her, she handed him the key then stepped back to wait on the porch steps. He was tall as well as heavy, and close up he looked . . . rough . . . and she'd found him on the street, didn't know his name, or phone number, and shouldn't have invited him here.

But she liked the way he'd called that poor old house *she*, like it was a living thing, old and unlived in, unloved and pink with embarrassment because no one had ever loved it enough to give it a bit of care.

Mrs Vaughn's ghost didn't scare him out as fast as it had scared out the last painter they'd got inside. She was beginning to think he'd moved in when she heard him coming back up the passage. She held her ground on the steps and looked at him expectantly. He didn't shake his head. He shook the wrought-iron railing, gave it a kick with his paint-splattered boot where it joined onto the house. He rapped around the corner window frame with huge knuckles, then stepped back, rubbed his chin, and said, 'Your mum's got herself a good solid old house. You don't get rooms that size these days, or those ceilings. She's got big problems, though. That spouting, for one.'

'Spouting?' Marni asked, and he pointed up at the rusted-out guttering. 'Oh, yes. She's waiting on a quote to fix that. Will you be able to do the painting?'

'It's not going to be cheap,' he said.

'She can pay you. She's got a good job . . . in the city.'

He was going. She cleared the steps to let him go. He didn't go far.

'I've got a few small jobs on right now,' he said, and Marni waited for what came next, but he didn't say he was too busy, only asked for Mum's phone number. Marni gave him her own and he said he'd get back to her.

On Saturday morning they drove their car to a place in Vermont to have its scratches checked out, and the man who checked them didn't believe the nearly eight thousand and sixty kilometres on the speedo.

'Only driven to church on Sundays,' he said.

'To doctors and funerals and into a fence,' Marni said, and when he told them how much it would cost, Marni told him they'd get back to him.

The painter didn't get back to them, not that week.

They were sorting through old clothing on Sunday night, deciding what to keep and what to toss, when a current affairs program started and they saw their policeman on it, Ross, from the plane to Perth. He was speaking about their two hundred thousand dollar reward – offered anonymously by a wellwisher.

'Robert De Niro,' Sarah said.

'Robert De Niro is old.'

'I mean before, when he is young,' Sarah said.

'You liked him.'

'You talk rubbish,' Sarah said.

'I meant the actor, Mum.'

'Oh,' Sarah said.

Their policeman spoke about Danni, missing since the fifteenth of March. He spoke of Monica, who had survived for two months and two days. The woman interviewer asked if he had reason to believe that Danni Lane was still alive, and his reply gave Marni goose bumps.

'*She's alive, but time is running out for her,*' he said.

'Do you think she's still alive, Mum?'

'I don't know,' Sarah said.

'*Is it possible that Danni died within days of her abduction, as with Lisa Simms?*' the interviewer said.

The man they knew as Ross didn't reply for a moment. The camera stayed on his face, then he looked right at it and spoke directly to Marni.

'*Other than the mark of bondage on the ankle of Nancy Yang, the killer has not marked his victims. As stated in earlier interviews, Lisa's injuries were consistent with those of a hit-and-run victim.*'

'*Do you have any new leads?*'

'*The short answer is no. An abduction/murder, where there is no relationship between the offender and the victim, is always the most difficult. We have no crime scene, no obvious motive.*'

'*During the early weeks of the investigation into Danni's abduction I believe Crime Stoppers received hundreds of calls. Are all calls followed up?*'

'*We've received thousands of calls. The public is our eyes and our ears, and to answer your question, yes, every call is investigated.*'

'*Is it realistic to believe that Danni is alive?*'

'*The taking of those girls is a game of the killer's own devising. He made the rules with his first abduction and to this point he has not deviated. We believe that he will deliver Danni's body to a place where it will be easily found. She hasn't been found, so she is alive.*'

The woman spoke of the other victims, of Danni's parents. Ross kept his replies brief. She mentioned the FBI profiler then the channel cut to a commercial and Sarah and Marni returned to their sorting until Ross returned and spoke of the killer's cars. They showed pictures, and one of the cars was a metallic dusky blue Hyundai hatchback, and it was Mrs Vaughn's car – their car.

'He's Raymond Vaughn, Mum,' Marni wailed. 'We've bought the murder car!'

'Stop!' Sarah said.

'He used to drive it all the time. He used to take it for whole weekends to charge up its battery. It's him, and I'm going to call Crime Stoppers.'

'You call nobody,' Sarah said. 'They make thousand of the same car, same blue.'

'Ross said we're his eyes and ears, and Raymond's got murderer's eyes and he probably poisoned his mother too, or suffocated her with one of her pillows – which is why he had to buy new pillows and stuff for her bed.'

'Move,' Sarah said. Marni was standing in front of the screen. She moved and turned to look Ross in the eye, and he looked at her eyes, and he spoke to her.

'*We are few. Our resources are stretched to the limit. You are many. Don't forget Danni Lane. Help us find her before her time runs out.*'

Then gone, to be replaced by a smiling man wanting to sell them funeral insurance, no medical test necessary. He got muted.

'How do you know that Raymond Vaughn hasn't got Danni hidden out – out where he lives?'

'Because he married, and you stop now, or you watch no more these things.' She held up a pair of tattered denim shorts. 'You want these?'

'What do you think?'

'I think I fight them off you for washing last summer.'

'I wasn't a millionaire then.'

CHAINS

*H*e seemed to live here now or to be somewhere around here for most of every day. He emptied her bucket every day. She heard water running outside but never heard a toilet flush.

He taped her hands and mouth when he went away for hours at a time, but he never left her taped up at night and his kitchen stove never went out so his kitchen never got freezing cold. He still gave her cold baked beans and spaghetti, which she refused to eat unless she opened the tins, but he also gave her other things, a fried egg sandwich one day, and today he'd come back from wherever he'd been with fish and chips.

She'd smelt them when he'd carried the parcel inside, smelt them more when he'd unwrapped the paper, and had almost choked on saliva behind his grey sticky tape.

He used big scissors to cut that tape from her wrists, then left her to peel off what he'd put over her mouth while he served half of the fish and chips to a party plate then tossed her what was left in the paper. There was a huge slab of fish and a pile of chips in it, and a slice of lemon. She'd eaten the lot, even the slice of lemon.

He always took his laptop computer with him when he went out, probably to charge the battery somewhere. He spent a lot of time on his laptop and drank a lot of red wine from a plastic glass. If he was on the internet, he must have had one of those flash drive wireless things. There were no cords in this room for broadband, no cords at all.

He had an old-fashioned power point near the sink and a light globe, but no power. People had their power cut off if they didn't pay their bills, but he didn't look poverty stricken.

It was like her whole world was this room and she knew it well now. Outside was outer space, and like the scientists, she could only make an educated guess at what was out there. Her father and grandfather would still be out there searching for her.

Animals that got caught in traps gnawed their feet off to get free. A man in America who'd got his arm trapped by a rock had cut it off with a pocketknife. If she'd had a knife, she would have cut her foot off. If she'd had a knife, she wouldn't need to cut her foot off. She'd cut that collar off. If she'd had a screwdriver, she would have unscrewed the chain from the wall. She didn't have anything. He wouldn't even give her a spoon to get the beans out of the can.

She'd tried using the edge of the padlock as a screwdriver. It was too long, too fat, and her foot kept getting in the way of it. She'd tried rubbing the chain against the chimney bricks, which had marked the bricks but not the chain.

She'd felt like his dog, but he knew she wasn't, because all she had to do was point to the bucket, and he'd go outside or up the passage and give her time to use it, which meant that he had to be totally mad. He'd taken her clothes off and put the other ones on her, but he left the room so she could squat on that bucket. Nothing about him made sense.

When she'd been in the cage, he'd never emptied that bucket. Out here, he washed it every morning and poured disinfectant into it. Probably didn't like its stink in his kitchen.

She stank. Her hair stank. She washed her face and hands some nights, with water from her bottle. She'd asked him for paper towels a couple of times but hadn't got any. She'd asked him for something to tie back her hair. Hadn't got that either. It was like he didn't hear her, like she'd stopped hearing that dog barking.

He'd heard the helicopter this morning. It had been flying so low it made the house shake. She'd thought police helicopter and he had too, because he'd come running inside. The dog had barked at it.

In the cage, the only way she could tell night from day had been that grey smudge of comet. Out here there was no total dark. He lit his lantern at night and when he put it out and went to bed she could still see glimmers of light from the stove and sometimes a long wide slit of moonlight that came in through the side of the blind.

She did her exercises when he went to bed. She conjured up Michelle and did squats with her, and jumps on the mattress, push-ups, sit-ups, the splits and leg lifts like she'd had to do when her mother had made her go to ballet, and after that pile of fish and chips she'd have kilojoules to spare tonight.

She added more rules to her cartoon man locked in the castle video game.

Get strong – bold print and underlined.

Keep him calm.

Never take your eyes off him.

Check everything he gives you to eat that doesn't come out of a can. Wished he'd go to bed. Her bones were aching from sitting.

March, the middle of March when the outside world had ended, and with no bars to count, she'd lost track of how many days. She counted bricks now. Knew that April must have been over.

Ecosystem

No one came forward to claim the two hundred thousand dollar reward. On Monday, the plumber sent his quote, via email. It wasn't cheap but they wanted to get something started so they sent a fast email back accepting his price and asking how soon he could do it. He replied and said he'd be unable to start until the trees leaning on the house were cut back.

Then on Tuesday, the painter with the paint-spattered wagon and boots drove in as Marni was leaving for school.

'Mum about?' he asked.

'She goes to work at half past seven,' Marni said. He gave her his handwritten quote. She didn't look at it, just asked him how soon he could start.

'I'd need to speak to your mum,' he said. 'Ask her to give me a tingle, will you?'

'She's deaf, but she said if I ever saw you again to tell you we want it done as soon as possible. Have you got an email address?'

'That's a good place to stay away from,' he said. 'Tell your mum I'd have to fit her in between a few smaller jobs, but if she's happy with the quote, I can make a start on it this arvo.'

'Hold on a tick,' Marni said and she sent his words via text, hoping her mother would feel her mobile's vibration. She did, and her reply came back fast.

Tell him to go ahead. Ask if he can buy the paint and how much deposit he wants.

Marni read the text to him, then offered her mobile so he could read it for himself.

He refused it. 'The wife's got one,' he said. 'Tell your mum, a couple of hundred will do for starters. I'll need to do a lot of cleaning and repairing before she needs to worry about paint.'

He already knew where that key was hidden, and before she left for school, he told her to call him Dave and he gave her his landline number. She keyed it into her mobile as she ran.

His old wagon was parked in the driveway when she returned. Mrs Vaughn's front door was wide open, so she crept in and caught him up a ladder, washing the kitchen ceiling.

'G'day,' he said. 'There's a couple of colour charts on the bench. You might get your mum to have a look over them.'

'White will do.'

'A bit of colour never goes astray—'

'We just want it to look clean.'

'I'll go snow-blind,' he said, and he climbed down from his ladder to talk. 'Tell your mum she's got big problems in her shower. There's an ecosystem of mould growing in there. Painting it will be wasting my time and her money, love.'

'Can we fix it?'

'Anything's fixable. It needs stripping back to basics though, and your pipes need looking at.'

'You can't do it?' she asked, hopefully.

'I took offence at tiling forty years ago and got out of the game. My old man owned his own tiling business for thirty years. Want me to ask him if he'd be interested in taking a look?'

'Yes, please.'

'He's as deaf as a post and no Speedy Gonzales.'

Marni didn't know Speedy Gonzales. 'We don't care. We live out the back,' she said, and back he went up his ladder to wash the build-up of nicotine from the ceiling, and Marni went out the back door, also wide open. Maybe he needed the fresh air.

Sarah wrote him a cheque that night for five hundred dollars. He didn't turn up before Marni left so she took it with her to school. His wagon wasn't in the driveway when she returned, and maybe she knew why. Mrs Vaughn's ghost was doing her block inside, smashing ghostly plates. Her front door was open.

Marni stood listening for a moment, then crept in – and ran into a very old Dave, pushing a wheelbarrow full of broken tiles.

'Hold that screen door for me, darlin',' he said. She held it. He came out, upended his barrow on the porch and went back for more. She followed him.

'I'm Marni,' she said.

'Call me Pop,' he said.

For the next two hours, she became Pop's apprentice. While he did the wrecking, she did the loading and the barrow pushing.

He was almost as deaf as her mother and spoke as if it was the rest of the world that was deaf, but they'd wrecked the shower room and built a small mountain of tiles and rotting masonite on the front porch before Dave arrived at a quarter to six to pick up his father.

They found a gardener that night on the internet. He came when he said he would, but started backing off when Marni told him they wanted to get rid of most of the trees.

'You need a tree lopper, not a gardener,' he said and made his escape.

They found a tree lopper in the local paper, and when he asked what sort of tree, Marni came clean about their forest. 'They're not big trees. There's just a lot of them.'

He must have driven by to have a look, because he phoned the next night to say he could do the job on Saturday morning, for cash in hand, then told them how much cash he expected to receive in his hand.

Marni hired him. On Friday night they tied rags onto the trees they wanted to keep – the two camellias, the fig and the magnolia – and notes that read, *TRIM ONLY PLEASE*, and lucky they had because the tree loppers arrived at seven, three big dark-skinned men who parked a truck with a tree-eating machine attached in the street, and within minutes, their chainsaws were cutting and their machine chewing up Mrs Vaughn's forest. To escape the noise of it, Sarah and Marni went shopping, and when they returned, the spiky plum, the wattle tree and the letterbox had been eaten – and fifty per cent of the camellias, fig and magnolia – and the tree eater was still spitting chips.

Away they drove again, this time to Bunnings, where they bought a new letterbox, numbers to screw onto it and a bag of premixed concrete. An hour later, Sarah counted fifty-dollar notes into a huge brown hand then the men, their truck and machine drove away and Sarah put her aids back on.

They were out the front, digging a hole for their new letterbox, when a neighbour, who'd spent years demanding Mrs Vaughn get her trees cut back, came out and took the shovel from Sarah's hands, then later offered props to hold the letterbox level while the cement set.

It looked good from the far side of the street, and props or not, a junk mail deliverer baptised it.

*

Freddy hadn't been out of the house that day, and nor had Rolland. He ate dinner with them, then went to his room when Cheryl tuned into the football. By ten thirty, Cheryl's team losing and the sitting room not a healthy place to be, Freddy checked on Rolland, and he wasn't in his room. He wasn't smoking weed in the backyard either, so Freddy walked around to the front of the house and out to the street.

He didn't see what else was missing, or not until he was walking back. He ran the last metres to the sitting room to interrupt the final minutes of the football match.

'I'll kill him,' he wailed.

Cheryl was more interested in killing a player. 'He was twenty-five metres out from the goalposts. He could have levelled the score, and he kicked it out of bounds.'

'He's got my Ferrari!' Freddy wailed.

She stopped screaming abuse at the player and turned to Freddy. 'Where did you leave your keys?'

'In the bowl. I'm calling the police.'

'You're not calling anyone.'

'He's got my Ferrari. He's a drug-smoking, ice-sucking, thieving little bastard and someone has to stop him.'

She stopped watching her match to stop Freddy's dialling.

'There's bad blood in him. He has to be stopped.'

'Says the man who wants to put an ice-smoking baby murderer back on the street,' she said, but the siren had gone, and she was gone, with the phone.

He followed her. 'He's killing me, love!'

'The fat around your heart is killing you, and it's a car, Freddy, and you know how he is with that car, and you leave your keys lying around where he can pick them up.'

They had a second phone in the bedroom. She read his mind and beat him to it, and stood across the marital bed, telling him that she'd had her fill of police, and he wasn't calling them on his own son.

When her blood was up, Cheryl Adam-Jones was a fighting woman you didn't want to tangle with, and he could relate to her having had enough of police harassment.

Three times she'd been called into the station to identify items recovered from the Commodore. She'd been unable to identify the remains of a platform-soled shoe. Freddy knew who the shoe had belonged to. The police had nothing on him, other than degraded DNA, and they weren't going to get a non-degraded sample.

He went outside to watch for his pride and joy, his heart lifting each time he sighted a red car, then falling when it was the wrong-shaped red car.

His Ferrari still missing at midnight, Cheryl asleep, Freddy slid carefully in beside her to lay on his back, listening for the song of his motor while going over the last words he'd spoken to Ross Hunter, who'd all but accused him of concocting that carjacking story as a cover-up for his hoon son.

Hunter believed that Cheryl's Commodore had killed that girl. He had no proof and she'd been in Bali. Freddy had no alibi other than the carjacking, and he had to stick to it. Hunter had spoken to Rolland, who couldn't remember what he'd done yesterday, let alone on a Friday two months ago. He'd told Hunter that he wouldn't have been seen dead behind the wheel of an old white Commodore.

Kids used to fear the law, fear their teachers, used to respect their fathers. Not now. The law couldn't touch a minor – nor could a teacher or parent. These days, they feared the kids, or Freddy did.

One o'clock ticked over, and, not game to move from his back and have Cheryl taking her pillow to a spare room, Freddy lay still, thinking of a promise made by a twelve-year-old boy to himself.

He'd found a full-page photograph of a red sports car in one of his brothers' magazines. Maybe he'd heard of *Ferrari* before, but until that day, he'd never seen one. He'd ripped the page out and when they'd driven him back to school, that *Ferrari* had gone with him, in his pocket.

A scholarship boy, little Freddy Jones, a chubby insult to the church-supplied uniform, a homesick, howling little sod until his Ferrari. He'd slept with it under his pillow thereafter, his hand on that folded page.

That was the year the principal had told him and an auditorium full of boys and their parents that no dream was impossible, the second-last year he'd invited his mother to the school. He'd learnt to fit into that uniform and to mimic the way John Swan had spoken. His mother having never learnt to mimic Lady Swan, he'd put an end to his annual torture.

During his final year, he'd got himself a job tutoring a few junior boys which had saved him the agony of weekends at home.

His mother had loved him. He'd loved her but hadn't liked her much. He'd hated his brawling brothers – and John the Baptist, who had managed to separate himself from the family with a priestly dog collar.

The day Freddy had walked into the hallowed halls of Melbourne University, he'd pencilled in that hyphen between Adam and Jones, and it had looked so good, he'd gone over the pencil with a biro, knowing that to have any hope of unshackling himself from his family, he'd needed that hyphen.

Bill had separated himself with distance. Bert had gone further. He'd bought a one-way plane ticket to London twenty years ago. Of the others, Freddy preferred not to know. There was a rotten gene in the Jones family. It surfaced every generation or two. He'd had the snip after Rolland, had quit while he'd been ahead. Should have had it done twelve months sooner.

*

At one thirty-five, a red Ferrari was clocked doing in excess of a hundred and forty in a fifty kilometre zone, through Lilydale. It was now heading towards Healesville, a police car giving chase.

A vehicle guaranteed by its makers to be capable of reaching speeds in excess of three hundred kilometres an hour, in the control of a youth determined to push every boundary, a minor curve in the road—

Two constables saw that vehicle become airborne, watched it attempt to leap over a kombi van travelling in the opposite direction. It failed, but continued its maiden flight until a tree got in the way, a big tree.

The constables were running when the Ferrari exploded. Nothing they could do other than call it in then turn their attention to the kombi, which lay like a bug on its back, wheels still spinning, its lone driver buckled in, upside down, turning the night air blue.

He was taken by ambulance to the Lilydale hospital. The Ferrari driver was incinerated in the inferno.

SUNDAY MORNING

*S*ix o'clock when a phone rang beneath Cheryl's pillow. She'd taken four phones to bed: two landlines, two mobiles. The landline was ringing. She found it, silenced it and eased herself from the bed, speaking in a whisper until the door between her and her sleeping husband was closed, when she told the female on the line that her husband changed his cars like most other people changed their socks, that she'd never had time to memorise the numbers on his registration plates.

She spoke to the woman in Rolland's room, and when she didn't find him in his bed, she ran with the phone out to the garage.

Freddy's Ferrari wasn't there.

*

It took until Wednesday to formally identify Rolland Adam-Jones. It took dental x-rays and a capped front tooth. Steve, his mate, had no recent dental x-rays, but he had ankle and leg x-rays showing two metal plates inserted after a bike accident. The female passenger, seated on Steve's lap at the time of impact, had not been identified when the youths' names were released to the media.

That same Wednesday the plumber and his labourer arrived early to start the ripping down and replacement of guttering and downpipes, while Pop moved out of a shiny blue paradise with shiny new taps and spray rose that was the shower room. He didn't move far. The bathroom was next door.

Mrs Vaughn's ghost had vacated the house. It smelled of paint and tile glue now. Her old curtains had gone out in the green bin, but not her carpet, not yet.

And Pop wouldn't give them a bill for the tiles, only for his labour, and not enough for that. Dave told Marni that when Pop had moved in he'd brought half a tonne of tiles with him.

'Let him be, love,' Dave said. 'I'm getting rid of tiles and he's enjoying himself.'

The plumber gave them a bill and a big one, but it was a big job.

Marni was watching *Deal or No Deal*, and the contestant only had four cases to open and only one was green, and it was the two hundred thousand.

'No deal,' the contestant said, then the channel cut to the news headlines.

'*Dead youth identified as Rolland Adam-Jones, son of well-known barrister . . .*'

He was a cousin. He'd just turned seventeen. Marni hadn't known him but she knew Uncle Fred.

The contestant lost his nerve when he had the two hundred thousand and the fifty dollars left. He took the deal, then found out that he had the green case.

Sarah came in as the news showed what was left of Uncle Fred's incinerated Ferrari, which Marni had ridden to school in, and it felt too personal. They showed photographs of two boys in school uniforms, then the news presenter told Melbourne about the murderer Frederick Adam-Jones was currently defending, and that barrister and Hubert their angel seemed like two different people.

They sent a bunch of flowers to the barrister's office because they didn't know Uncle Fred's address. Marni studied the funeral notices in the newspaper, determined to go to Rolland's because she hadn't gone to Mrs Vaughn's. Her mother said that funerals were dead people in coffins, priests praying and people crying, and that kids shouldn't go to them. There was no Adam-Jones funeral notice in the paper, or not that week.

She found it in Monday's newspaper.

Pop had finished in the bathroom and moved into the kitchen before Rolland Adam-Jones was buried. Dave said he was snow-blind and he tried to talk them into having a feature wall in the lounge/dining room, but they'd ordered their drapes and they didn't want colour on that wall that might clash with what they'd chosen.

Sarah drove to Camberwell for the funeral and she couldn't find a place to park when they got there, and the only one she could find left them a block to walk to the church, and they were late.

And it was packed full of suited men and well-dressed women and boys in school uniform and priests in white nightgowns, and it went on and on forever and every time Marni thought it was over, it started again.

And their policeman was there, outside, probably to protect Uncle Fred from the family of the woman his current client had murdered, according to Marni.

*

Ross was there in a semi-official capacity. Clarence Daniel Jones hadn't yet been located, or John Paul, or Joseph Jacob Jones. It was a big turnout. He'd expected to see a few of Freddy's family there. He'd signed the condolence book so he might take a look at the names of earlier signers. There was no *Jones* in it.

He was thinking of a line from *Macbeth*, thinking that had Rolland Adam-Jones died next week or next month, Lady Cynthia Swan and her neurologist son might not have added their names to that book, or Freddy's partners.

He knew the dead youth had been driving his mother's Commodore when it hit Lisa Simms, knew it in his gut – and in his irritated sinuses. There was the damage to the Commodore's panels, the remains of the windscreen in the boot, the charred platform-soled shoe, which looked like one of Lisa's, or her house-mate had said it did. Ross's gut knew that Freddy's carjacking story was a cover-up, that he'd heard his son's call for help sometime that night and gone running.

He had no proof of it. Nothing, nix, nil, zilch, other than degraded DNA that was a biological match to that of the Jones family. He'd got hold of fat Freddy's phone records, and all they'd proved was that Freddy's mobile and landline had been idle for most of that weekend, that Rolland's had been busy, but only to his friends' numbers. They hadn't found the accident or burial sites, and no more resources were being wasted in looking.

And he saw those girls break away from the crowd.

They weren't wearing jeans and toting backpacks, but their hair, their I'm-on-my-way-to-somewhere walk identified them suffi-ciently for him to drop his butt into his peppermint tin and follow them, at a distance – until they were about to turn down a side street, when he called. 'Marni.'

She stopped, caught her mother's arm, and they turned, waved and walked back to meet him halfway. Marni asked if he'd put a tail on them, and he laughed.

Remembered hearing that same sound in Perth, and on that Camberwell Street the wind playing in the last of the autumn leaves, he felt a few of his years blowing away with them while they spoke of quokkas and tours and Perth hotels and things of little consequence, and the wind grew colder.

A few spits of rain suggested they move on. 'Mum doesn't like driving in the rain. She didn't want to come today,' Marni said.

'He was a relative?' Ross asked.

'Mum's cousin,' Marni said. Ross had already placed Sarah on Freddy's wife's side of the family. She had the dark hair and the looks, but Marni continued. 'Uncle Fred is my grandfather's baby brother. See you around then – on television,' she said.

He followed no further, until the lights of a dusky metallic blue Hyundai blinked.

'How long have you had your car?' he asked.

'The end of April, and Mum needs a bravery award for driving it in here. First we got squashed between two trucks, then we couldn't find a place to park, and when we did, she squeezed it into a space about big enough to park a motorbike.'

'They're a good model,' he said.

'It belonged to our landlady we told you about. She died while we were in Perth.'

'Does she have a husband?'

And Marni pointed a finger at him. 'I know what you're thinking because I thought the same when we saw our car on television. I wanted to ring Crime Stoppers and dob in her son but Mum wouldn't let me. He used to take that car for whole weekends – and he looks like the Freeway Killer too.'

But Sarah was in and eager to go.

'Raymond Vaughn,' Marni said as she got in. 'He lives in Mooroolbark out near Lilydale.'

Gone then. Ross took shelter beneath a leafless tree while he lit a cigarette and watched them – or their car – turn left and disappear into traffic. He'd found another link to the Jones family. Better than that he'd got a name and a general area.

'Raymond Vaughn, Mooroolbark.'

*

He found a phone number and an address in Mooroolbark for a L.R. Vaughn. He called the number but it went through to an answering machine. He gave L.R. Vaughn an hour or two to get home, then drove out to his address, and whoever he was, he was selling up. There was an auction sign on his front lawn.

A MORNING DATE

On Sunday morning, a low dark sky pelted rain down on
Melbourne, and with the bedroom curtains and blind pulled,
the room was dark. Marni might have slept until ten o'clock if
not for the phone, the landline phone. Her mobile lived beside
her bed; she could reply to it from bed. The landline was in the
kitchen, and the floor between her bed and the phone was cold on
bare feet.

'Am I speaking to Mrs Carter?' the caller asked.

She thought it was one of the tradesmen she'd left messages for,
and, wanting to be rid of him fast, said: 'We're right for tradesmen,
thank you.'

'How are you fixed for a bacon and egg McMuffin?' the
caller asked.

'What?' Forgot her freezing feet, told him that they didn't have
one of them, then asked how he'd got their phone number.

'I have my means,' he said.

'Are we on the CIA's hit list because we bought the murder car?'

'Your landlady was the only Vaughn in your general area,'
he said.

'When do you deliver the McMuffins?'
'How does half an hour sound?'
'Mum is still asleep.'
'How late does she sleep?'
'Ten seconds more. Don't hang up.'

*

He didn't arrive for their date in a police car. He drove a white Commodore which he parked behind their car. Marni was telling him about how their landlady who'd been ninety-something had died in her bed when Sarah came out – wearing lipstick and the new black sweater she'd bought to wear to the funeral, and her jeans tucked into her new boots, and they had heels. He looked impressed, and he opened his passenger-side door for her and held it until she got in. Marni got in with the junk in his rear seat then told him where the nearest McDonald's was, and maybe he already knew because he drove straight to it.

They were seated in a cubicle with their bacon and egg McMuffins, hash browns and coffee, when he told them he'd found an address for a L.R.Vaughn in Mooroolbark, and that the house was for sale.

'He's already made his getaway,' Marni said.

'Maybe Singapore,' Sarah said. 'He went there for his business many times.' She told him later that she'd bought her landlady's house as well as her car, only to turn the subject away from her family. He spoke of his unit on the seventh floor, how he could look down on the city and see what the eagle saw when he flew the sky, then he asked again where she'd lived before moving to Melbourne.

'Everywhere,' Sarah said.

'Her parents were gypsies with a tent and she doesn't like talking about them. They got killed in a car crash when she was twelve, which is why she doesn't like talking about them. They were Joe and Stephanie,' Marni said.

*

He drove them home, commented on the size of the block, and when Marni asked him if he'd like to see inside, he turned the motor off and allowed her to give him a guided tour, around paint cans, rollers, cartons of tiles. He commented on the size of their rooms, on their ceilings, how the high ceilings and fancy cornice plaster had gone out of vogue in the sixties.

He stepped around a paint-speckled ladder and on empty tubes of gap filler to praise their kitchen, midway through its transformation. Pop, having finished the bathroom tiling, had got rid of his stockpiled tiny midnight-blue tiles on the worn laminated benches. Dave may have been going snow-blind, but Pop was adding colour, and between them they'd injected hope into that house.

'You've bought yourselves a good old house,' Ross said, and his phone rang.

They locked up and met him in the driveway to thank him for breakfast. He said it was his pleasure and perhaps they'd do it again. Marni told him they were having a combined housewarming and birthday party in July, and when she knew when in July, she'd dial triple zero and ask them to pass on an invitation—

'Or I could add your number to my contacts.'

He laughed and gave her his mobile number. 'Only to be used for invitations and emergencies,' he said, then he left them waving in their driveway.

He'd had a good morning. He liked that kid, and if he'd let himself, he might drown in the liquid chocolate of her mother's eyes. Watchful, honest eyes, except when he'd asked about her family. Their shields had been raised then. She was hiding something, from him or from her daughter, and he had a fair idea of what it was she was hiding.

Joseph Jacob Jones wasn't dead, or he hadn't died in the accident that killed his wife and three teenagers. He'd been sentenced to ten years for manslaughter. He hadn't served those ten years. They'd let him out in late 2001. If he'd died since, Ross had found no record of his death. He'd found no record of his life either, not since 2005, when he'd reapplied for his driver's licence.

*

'He likes you,' Marni said. 'And he's available too.'

'You too cheeky to him . . . about everything. And you tell him everything.'

'You're not cheeky enough. He couldn't take his eyes off you.'

'If I want boyfriend I can have Bob.'

'You said you don't want him.'

LOSS AND GAIN

*A*insworth had ordered him to take some time to mourn his boy. He should have been mourning him. Freddy missed his presence – or lack of it. He missed his Ferrari – he wasn't supposed to miss the courtroom, but he did, or the persona he wore in the courtroom. He was nothing without it.

Cheryl didn't want him underfoot. She told him to see his GP. She'd seen her own before the funeral. He'd tested her for everything except hyperactivity, and maybe he'd tested her for that too. He'd prescribed pills to slow her down. She'd taken one and pitched the rest into the kitchen tidy. Freddy had retrieved them. They slowed him down, damn near stopped him, made him sleep like one of the dead, and when he woke up feeling guilty, he swallowed another one and went back to sleep.

'You make me tired,' he said. 'Sit down and talk to me.'

'I'm better off keeping busy, and so would you be. Go to work, Freddy.'

If she mourned Rolland, she did it in private, and made sure she was never in private to do it. She'd got herself a job, voluntary work, three days a week at the local Liberal Party office where she and her cronies willed Labor to self-destruct. They were pulling it off too, and Freddy no longer cared.

He cared when she left him alone for hours. He looked on the internet for a psych he could spill his guts to, tell about his Technicolor dreams of his mother and Rolland and that girl and Ross Hunter.

An eye for an eye, Freddy.

He dreamt of those girls who'd called him an angel. Dreamt he'd locked them into the boot of the Commodore and torched it and when he had second thoughts and ran back and opened the boot, they were skeletons, and Marni's sat up and said, *We call you our angel.*

He was a heartless bastard. The only reason he'd gone near those girls was to find out who'd bought his father's farm, and when he'd got around to asking them, they'd known nothing about that will.

Every day he told himself to contact them. Every night he told himself he'd drive out to the farm and see for himself who'd dug up that girl, that he'd be Freddy the hero who saved Danni Lane – if she wasn't already dead.

Didn't do it. Didn't do anything. He had no car to do anything in. Didn't want one either, so took a pill, turned on the television and went to sleep until Cheryl came home, when he told her that she was running out of her pills – and she refused to ring up her doctor and get another script.

Left her cooking dinner and walked up at the Catholic church, Cheryl's church – or her parents'. Not Freddy's. Maybe they had the right idea though; sin all week, confess on Sundays and go away sin free. Rolland had been baptised Catholic, only to stop his maternal grandmother's nagging. He'd been buried Catholic to stop her nagging.

And Freddy's mother, a rabid Baptist, would have rolled over in her grave, which was why she was haunting his nights.

Nothing left of Rolland to bury anyway. He should have been cremated and his ashes scattered to the four winds. He should have been a daughter.

We call you our angel.

Freddy might have been sixteen when Jillian Sarah had been born, and his mother besotted by that female infant. She'd been a praying, wailing maniac for a week after they'd found out the baby was deaf. Joe had stayed drunk for a week.

She'd overcome her disability. She'd sent flowers, a beautiful bouquet, to his office, and when a courier delivered them to the house, Freddy had taken them at the door, seen those names on the card and snatched it, pocketed it before Cheryl started questioning him about a Sarah and a Marni Carter.

They hadn't received one of her professionally printed thank you cards, and Freddy felt guilty about that too, guilty about not inviting his mother to his high school presentation nights, guilty about not visiting her when she'd been a mindless dying shell in a nursing home bed.

He'd seen her after she was dead. He'd bought her a new outfit and when the undertaker had made up her face and done her hair, she hadn't looked like herself. She'd looked better.

Spending money on her had been enough to ease his guilt back then. Spending money on Rolland's funeral hadn't.

He had loved that boy. When he'd come out bloody and bleating, he'd held him in his arms and promised him the world – then got so busy working his guts out to give him the world he'd forgotten to watch him grow.

Lost him a long time ago. He'd lose Cheryl too.

'I'd be better off dead,' he said when she served him his meal.

'Keep going the way you're going and I'll assist you, Freddy. Eat.'

'I've killed,' he'd said.

'You bought that fool of a car. You left the keys where he could get them, but you weren't behind the wheel. He was, and he knew he shouldn't have been. He took his own life, Freddy. He didn't want what we gave him, so he threw it in our faces, now for God's sake, let me get over it.'

He couldn't. He couldn't even eat. That was the killer. She'd cooked him a steak, done it the way only Cheryl could, seasoned and fried fast in butter. He tried to eat it. Watched her eat her own. Saw himself digging that grave in the dark, swatting mozzies. Saw himself torching that car and running in his boxer shorts, his toad belly jiggling.

She was in bed at ten, and he was going to do it, send an email to Crime Stoppers, feed them a line about client privilege, blame that phantom client for the information.

It seemed like the answer until Cheryl's iPad woke to his touch, until he googled and typed in *Crime Stoppers*. Then cancelled it fast and got into Cheryl's photographs of Greece.

'Take a holiday,' Ainsworth had advised. 'Take your wife on a cruise, Frederick.'

She'd already been on a cruise and if he'd had an ocean of water around him right now, he'd probably go walking in the night and take the long dive. He killed the photographs, googled again and typed in *tours*.

Found a thirteen-day tour of Western Australia which cost more than a fifteen-day tour of Canada. Found three nights in Sydney that cost more than five nights in Bali, airfares included – and knew why everyone and their dog went to Bali.

He'd never been there. He'd never been to Greece. He'd never been anywhere out of Australia, other than Hawaii. Checked out a tour of China, then one of Ireland. Which offered free flights in and out of Dublin.

It was cheap and half a world away from Melbourne. For minutes he sat staring the iPad in the face. They made whisky in Ireland. He needed a whisky, and the distance, so checked out how to book it – and found out it would cost more to go solo than twin share, so he booked and paid for twin share, online. He hadn't been away with Cheryl in five years.

His passport had probably passed its use-by date. Hadn't used it since Hawaii.

They'd gone there as a family. How long ago? Rolland must have been eight or ten, and the little bugger had whinged for the week they were away, either sick, sunburnt or bored, and Freddy had vowed he wouldn't waste his money again, and hadn't.

Did they let you know when your passport was running out of time? He hadn't fronted up for new photographs. Cheryl used to keep it in the small dressing table drawer – in Vermont.

He'd killed in Vermont. Rolland and his rat pack had grown weed in Vermont, and the iPad and tour forgotten, Freddy ran from Vermont and ended up in Rolland's room.

They had five empty bedrooms. He didn't find the old Vermont dressing table or his passport, and dared not open the master bedroom door.

She'd sleep until seven thirty, rise, walk around the block, come home, shower, make her breakfast then head out the door to give her time to the Liberal Party office.

A cold house when she wasn't in it, colder with the central heating turned off at night. He could have turned it on, but she'd roast in bed and wake, so he walked the house, his dressing-gown trying to trip him. Bought wide enough to go around his gut, it had always been too long, and was longer tonight. A man's guts shrank when he lived on guilt, his pyjama pants slid.

He hitched them high, hitched up the gown, tied its cord tight enough to hold up his pants, then unlocked the back door and walked out to the garage to look at the space where his Ferrari had once lived.

Space to park three cars in the garage, one of his reasons for wanting this place, so they'd have space for a third car when Rolland was old enough to drive. Only one car in residence tonight, her green Honda – and every time Freddy sat in it, he felt like Freddo Frog in green jelly.

He stood in the space where his Ferrari had lived and looked up at an overhead beam, a good place to hang himself. No rope, no chain in his neat garage. The cord of his dressing-gown could have been strong enough, long enough. His pyjama pants would slide down.

DEAD BARRISTER FOUND WITH A BARE ARSE

A cold, lonely, unlucky house, this one. The day it was auctioned, it hadn't looked cold or lonely. He'd paid his deposit then gone home and told Cheryl what he'd done. She'd had plenty to say, but she'd moved.

*

She didn't move from her bed until after a quarter to ten, and when she did, she came out yelling at him for closing her door and not waking her up.

'You told me you'd murder me if I did,' he said.

'I'm supposed to be at the office at ten.'

'They can't dock your pay if they don't pay you,' he said, then he told her he'd put the house on the market.

'Have you gone stark raving mad, Freddy?'

'It's a seller's market.'

'You decide we're moving again without asking me!'

'You're never here to ask.'

'Who are you to talk about never being here? You haven't been around for ten years,' she said, and she stalked off to the bathroom, and when he tried to follow her in, she slammed the door in his face.

Made of tough stuff, that woman. Had the young Freddy recognised her tough stuff when he'd started pursuing her, or had he been blinded by her face? He didn't know and never had. Like with the red Ferrari, he'd seen her and said, she's mine.

She was out in ten minutes, her hair towel-wrapped. She didn't speak to him, but picked up the phone and dialled. 'It's Cheryl,' she said. 'Fred isn't well. I won't be in this morning.'

'You finally noticed,' he said when the phone was down.

'Noticed what, you halfwit?'

'That I'm not well.'

'The only place you're sick is in your head. What made you go and do a thing like that again without discussing it?'

'We don't need the garage space, or five spare bedrooms.'

'Where are you planning to move me to this time? A bloody penthouse at Docklands, you social climbing little shit?' She turned on a fancy hotplate, slammed a pan onto its shiny white and black surface, took an egg from the refrigerator and slammed the fridge door.

'Fry me one,' he said.

'Fry your own. I'm making an omelette.'

'An omelette will do,' he said. 'Do you know where my passport is?'

'With mine,' she said. 'Why?'

'I booked a trip to Dublin.'

'For work?'

'A tour,' he said. 'For two.'

'You're losing your marbles, Freddy? You're seeing a doctor.'

'Ainsworth said I need a holiday. We've got free flights,' he said. 'Eight days on a bus. Two nights in Dublin.'

'I'm not going to Dublin. Cancel it.'

'I tried to. I phoned them an hour ago when I found out we leave on Friday night. We won't get our money back.'

'When!'

'Friday night. I didn't see the departure date when I booked. We got in on cancellations.'

'The only place you're going is to a funny farm,' she said, but she swapped the small pan for one a size larger, then started cracking eggs into a bowl. He watched until she added two dollops of yoghurt.

'I don't eat that stuff.'

'You don't know what you eat,' she said. 'And why in the name of hell, when you've got the whole world to choose from, did you choose Ireland?'

'What's wrong with Ireland?'

'I'm not going there, that's what's wrong with it. I'll go to Italy with you, but not this Friday, you maniac.'

'We'll lose our money.'

'We'll make money on this mausoleum,' she said, feeling the heat of the pan then giving it a spray with canned oil. 'And you can't up and leave. You're defending that wife-murdering mongrel.'

'Ainsworth will do it. He knows more than I do about it.'

Cheryl added salt and pepper to the mess in the bowl, added a dash of milk, a handful of grated cheese, gave the lot a stir then poured it into the pan to sizzle.

'Dublin!' she said.

'It's a bargain. Free cattle class flights.'

'I'll be damned if I'll fly cattle class. If you can upgrade the seats to business class and add a tour of Italy to it, I'll think about it.'

'We flew to Hawaii cattle class.'

'And Rolland vomited all the way.' She placed two slices of bread into the toaster. 'My grandmother Fleming came from Dublin. She had a sister over there who had thirteen kids. We might be able to dig a few of them up. How many days do we get in Dublin?'

THE FARM

A professionally printed card was delivered to their new letterbox on Friday, thanking the receiver for their condolences
on the occasion of our recent bereavement. Uncle Fred had enclosed a
typewritten page with the card.

> *My dear Sarah and Marni,*
>
> *Cheryl and I are leaving for the UK tomorrow evening and
> may be away for six weeks. I have been in touch with my father's
> solicitor, Simon Tower, in Eltham, now semi-retired, but able to
> supply me with a copy of my father's will. The land was willed
> to you. Tower assured me that all reasonable effort was made to
> locate you at the time.*
>
> *The estate has not been settled. Four claims were made on it,
> by John, Clarry, Gordon and your sister.*

'What?' Marni asked. They were standing in the doorway beneath
the light, reading Uncle Fred's letter together.

'I got no sister.'

'It says *your sister*, and down further, *As your next of kin, your
sister . . .* '

'I have got no sister. One deaf one is too many for him.'

'Are they dead? Is that why you didn't want to visit their graves when we were in Perth, because they haven't got graves?'

'I watch my mother die, Marni. All of one day, I am at hospital watching her die. I watch them put her in a hole in the ground.'

I hope I have done the right thing in giving Tower your married name and details. He assured me that he will be in contact with you shortly.

Thank you again for your kind thoughts on the death of our son. Cheryl and I will be in touch when we return.

My fondest regards, Uncle Fred

'We could have owned a farm if you hadn't changed our names,' Marni said.

'They can find me. Government keeping records when people changing names.'

'Then how come they didn't find you?'

'*All reasonable effort* mean solicitor charges money to lick stamps and pick up telephones and if they got no one to pay . . .' She read the page again, folded it and slid it back with the card into the envelope. 'They will look in Perth for me, not here.'

'If you'd kept in touch with the Clarks, you would have known. You could have written to them, Mum. You didn't have to tell them you'd had me.'

Sarah shook her head.

'Did your father have a baby with someone before you were born?'

'I don't know.'

They sat up late that night, studying their new street directory, searching for Gramp's farm that could have been their own, and when Sarah found the general area, Marni plotted a route from their house to that general area, a route crossing many pages.

'Can you drive that far, if it's not raining, this weekend?'

'Too many road, Marni.'

'They're long straight roads, and we know this end of Springvale Road.'

'We looking for carpet this weekend,' Sarah said.

'We can look then go.'

'Maybe,' Sarah said, her finger circling an area of a map where there were no streets but a road that said Yarra Glen. 'I know there. I drive Gramp to Eltham on that road.'

*

At one o'clock on Saturday, the floor coverings chosen, ordered and a deposit paid, the sky still looking clear over Melbourne, they headed off on their longest drive yet, up Springvale Road to its end, where they turned left onto Reynolds Road, also straight. It crossed many maps, but they passed a cemetery, which meant they were coming to their right-hand turn into Fitzsimmons Road.

That's when Marni started wishing she hadn't nagged. It wasn't a straight road, and they got stuck at a huge roundabout, cars going every which way, Sarah propping for so long that the driver behind blasted his horn and scared Marni half to death. They got through it with their lives then came on another one.

'Oh my God, Mum.'

Only God knew how they got through that one, but they did, and as the directory had promised when it had been on their kitchen table, that road led them to Eltham, where they stopped for a coffee.

The last bit was easy, easy for Sarah. She was in home territory now.

'Every week I driving here, for shopping, bank, something.'

She drove that last stretch confidently, and with less traffic pushing her, drove it slowly.

*

Uncle Fred had said that Gramp's land had value. Sarah saw why. People wanted to live out here. Much had altered in the nearly thirteen years since she'd walked away from the farm. Houses had sprung up where there'd been no houses. She drove past the turn-off to Gramp's farm because of a house that shouldn't have been there and a row of trees concealing Gramp's cow paddock fence, but the land ahead didn't look right so she made a careful U-turn and drove back.

'When I am small, Gramp's cows on that land and my father and Gramp make that fence.'

The directory at Marni's feet, the wheels of the car barely creeping, they passed a flat-roofed brown house and a minibus, parked on the side of a too-narrow road. Sarah slowed before the next gate, then nosed the car in close. She knew that gate, but not the padlock and chain locking it.

'Are we lost?'

'We here.'

'It's bush,' Marni said, but Sarah was pointing.

'Honey shed is there,' and she turned off the motor and was out of the car. Marni was slower to get out and join her at the gate.

'I learn to drive in that paddock, around and around. Gramp making me drive up and down, on his drive, reverse all the way down.' Her finger pointing. 'See that big rock, that tree? There. He teach me parking between them. He is a very careful man. I am a good driver before he will let me go out this gate.'

Still Gramp's gate but that chain made it look mean. This land had never been mean.

'Whoever is calling herself your sister doesn't like visitors,' Marni said, giving the gate a shake.

'Uncle Fred say no one is living here.'

'I wouldn't either,' Marni said. 'I thought it would have cows and look like a farm.' It was clay and rock and grey scrubby trees and an ugly in-your-face tin garage, and all she could see of a house looked a hundred times worse than Mrs Vaughn's had ever looked.

'I'm glad you didn't inherit it. What if you'd made me live out here, Mum?'

'Look,' Sarah said, pointing. 'Smoke. Someone here.'

'Want to climb through and walk up?'

'No.'

'That tin shed looks new.'

'Not new. Gramp getting it build for his honey, but inside is too hot. White elephant, he said. Eyesore.' She pointed to the right of the tin garage, to a second, more distant rusty roof lost behind trees. 'He have got his whizzing machine, for spinning honey from honeycomb, in there. When you walk near, you smell honey,' she said, then shook the gate until the chain rattled. 'We don't lock this. We don't close when I am here before you.'

'I was expecting crops and stuff,' Marni said.

'Before, in that bit where we see the new house, is better land. He selling that to get money – before I come here – before you when Gran was very sick and he can't see, can't work. He will never sell the house bit.'

The sky was darkening to the west. Rain had been forecast for this weekend, so they returned to the car.

The minibus was leaving. They gave way to it, and Marni saw a woman removing a bunch of balloons she'd tied to the gatepost. At Forest Hill, a bunch of balloons spelled garage sale, and, wanting some reward for their journey, she wound down her window and called to the woman.

'Are we too late to have a look?'

'Not at all,' the woman replied.

'Rain is coming,' Sarah warned.

'Five minutes. She might have something we need.'

They needed everything. They had a two-door linen press and six towels and a change of sheets each to put in it. They had wardrobes in three bedrooms, cupboards in the laundry and their kitchen was all cupboards and drawers.

The woman, who was clad in a psychedelic poncho, black tights and high-heeled boots, stood waiting to greet them. Her dog didn't wait. He came out to bark at the car.

'Herod,' the woman commanded. He looked at her, didn't want to obey, but did, and Marni got out to eye that monster and wonder if she'd lose a leg to it when it approached to sniff at her jeans.

'He's a big pussycat,' the woman said. 'Offer him your closed fist, dear.'

He was big, and no pussycat, but he had a silly puppy face, and when Marni offered him her fist, he sniffed, licked, but didn't eat it. He turned to Sarah then to check her out before allowing her on his land.

No shed, no evidence of a garage sale, only a small purple/blue car parked beside a semi-enclosed garden. The woman led them through the garden and into a gallery hung with paintings.

'The prices are on them. If you see anything you like, give me a call,' she said, then disappeared through a doorway to their right.

'Let's go,' Marni mouthed.

'Bad manners,' Sarah replied in like manner.

There must have been more than two dozen framed paintings on the walls. Drawn by its heat or its size, Sarah walked towards a bushfire scene where a burning tree in the foreground looked too hot to touch – as was the price sticker on its frame. Marni saw the price, not the painting.

'Let's go, Mum!'

It had eight hundred and seventy-five dollars on it, and even the smaller paintings didn't wear small price tags.

'You want have a look, so look!' Sarah mouthed. 'We say before we want pictures.'

'They're paintings,' Marni mouthed. 'Dimmey's have got framed prints for twenty-five dollars.'

'You make me come in here, so we will buy something.'

'You tell me not to waste money.'

They argued with mouth, not with voice. They didn't need voice, never used it if a listener was close by. They wandered, lip-talking, until the poncho lady returned and told them to help themselves to tea and biscuits, then to hit a light switch which turned on many small spotlights. One lit up over a white tree standing alone against a pink and lilac dawn, and that light made the sky glow as if the sun was about to burst free.

'Who's the artist?' Marni asked.

'My name is on them,' the woman said, and Marni stepped in close enough to read the artist's signature on that lilac dawn, *Sylvia Moon*, and if she wasn't famous, she should have been. There was nothing much in that painting, but what was there was incredible – as was its price.

Sarah had found an old man sitting on a log, an old house behind him, and another incredible tree.

'I want that one,' she mouthed.

'We're going, Mum.'

'That one Gramp and his house.' He had a white beard like Gramp, a cigarette he was about to put into his mouth, a dog at his feet – and the dog and cigarette looked as alive as the man.

'I want that one, please,' Sarah said aloud.

Marni glanced at the artist, busy unplugging an urn. 'It's got six hundred and eighty dollars on it,' Marni mouthed. 'Come on, or you'll have to drive through those roundabouts in the rain.'

Then the woman turned. 'This one,' Sarah said, and the poncho lady smiled and joined them, pleased she'd made a sale. Marni couldn't watch her mother spend so much money, so she went back the way she'd come and the monster dog was out there, waiting to eat – or greet her.

He yipped at her, maybe inviting her to walk with him around to the back of a very strange-looking house, and when she refused his invitation and tried to go back, he nudged her, danced in front of her, blocking her way.

'What do you want?' she asked his silly pup face. His eyes told her he wanted company, so she followed him. She'd never owned a dog, and if she ever did, it wouldn't be man-eater size, but she let him lead her into the bush behind the house where wind was now tossing the high branches.

Herod didn't linger there. He led the way to a fence of posts with strands of wire stretched between them, the top wire barbed. There was no chain or padlock warning them to stay out. Maybe the 'sister' considered barbed wire warning enough. The lower wires weren't barbed. Herod stuck his head between two, then scrabbled the rest of him through to the other side, and was gone, into the scrub.

She yelled his name, looked towards the artist's house, which was well away from the shed. Knew she should go back and tell her where her dog was, but maybe he was allowed, and the artist was busy selling a painting for six hundred and eighty dollars, so probably wouldn't care.

'Herod!' she yelled again, then followed him between the wires.

All of her life she'd heard stories about Gramp's farm and his honey shed. She'd come all the way out to Kangaroo Ground to see Gramp's farm, which wasn't a farm but rugged old Australian bush with barbed-wire fences, but she was out here so may as well have a look at land that might have been her mother's.

Like the dog she made her own path around clumps of scrub towards the roof of a shed that smelled of honey. It was all uphill. The artist had built her house on flat land, close to the road. Gramp, or his father, had built his house halfway up a hill.

And that lunatic dog was barking his brains out at someone, and that someone was yelling at him.

Marni dodged a low branch and ran to the wall of the honey shed, an old grey wall with half of its boards falling off. She sniffed at one gap. It didn't smell of honey, and whoever lived here parked his car in there, a white car.

'Get, you yellow bastard,' a man yelled.

Herod took no notice, so Marni, two fingers in her mouth, let loose a piercing whistle. Herod stopped barking, so she did it again.

And she saw who lived here, just a glimpse of a grey man. He was standing out the front of the metal garage and he had a long-handled rake in his hand and was swinging it at the dog, who must have known how long the rake handle was, because he kept his distance from its sharp end.

'Herod,' she yelled again.

'Get off my land and take your mongrel with you,' the man roared.

Herod wasn't her mongrel. Marni got off his land, making the downhill run faster than she'd made it uphill, and that fool of a dog passed her before she was back at the fence, and he was on the other side before her, and laughing at her mad scramble to get through.

'He'll get the dog catcher next time and put you in doggy jail. You're not allowed to disturb your neighbours' peaceful enjoyment of their properties,' she told him.

Mrs Vaughn had spent a lot of her life yelling that at a neighbour with a barking dog, before she'd started ringing the council and driving them mad. She shut the dog up or the neighbour got rid of it – and Marni had stopped wishing she'd been born deaf. Her mother hadn't heard it – and she was going to be hopping mad about Marni's disappearing trick.

Saw her on the road near the car, and ran down the drive, Herod at her side.

Sylvia Moon was there, probably trying to convince her buyer that her dog hadn't eaten her daughter.

'Sorry,' Marni said, and got into the car. That painting was on the back seat, bubble-wrapped.

Sarah got in. 'Where you been?'

'I had a look at your honey shed. Her dog took off and I had to follow him.'

'I think you get kidnapped.'

'I saw who lives on your farm.'

'Jack James,' Sarah said.

They were moving, the black of the sky following them to Eltham, where they were stopped by traffic lights.

'He writing books. A grumpy old hermit.'

'See, because I wasn't there, you had to talk to her.'

'She talking,' Sarah said. 'She got three daughters and five grand-children. Teach art for school and when she retire last Christmas, her husband die playing golf. Heart attack.'

'Did you tell her you could have owned the land her house is on?'

'No. I ask when she making that painting of Gramp. She said she got photograph before, when she buys Gramp's land,' Sarah said. 'When I want to pay her with my chequebook, she want my licence. The first time, I have got one. She put my number on the receipt.'

Marni told her that the honey shed didn't smell of honey, that there was a car parked in it.

'What he look like?'

'Grey hair, grey beard. Herod didn't like him.'

'What?'

'The artist's dog barked at him and the writer tried to hit him with an old metal rake.'

The lights changed and Sarah drove on. The first roundabout, their bogeyman, was a monster at four fifty, but they got through, and through the next before heavy rain began thrashing their windscreen. It chased them all the way back to Springvale Road, where they weren't keeping up with the speed limit and a big black four-wheel drive sat on their bumper bar, urging them to go faster. It tailgated them to Maroondah Highway, where the driver blasted the horn and sprayed them with so much water they were too busy attempting to see the road between swipes of their wiper blades to worry about why he'd blasted his horn.

They passed him again at Canterbury Road where he was in a long queue, waiting to make a right-hand turn. Marni waved to him, and wondered if the kids in the back of his posh van were his hostages. He and his van looked evil.

They missed the green arrow at Hawthorn Road and Sarah spoke again. 'After her husband die, she is going to sell her house when it is finished, but her daughter buy that dog, and say, "Get on with your dream".'

'I like her daughter,' Marni said, and the lights changed.

They made their turn, and five minutes later were home, still alive, but exhausted by their day. They ate fried cheese sandwiches with a mug of tomato soup, and Marni said, 'If Mrs Vaughn was still alive, we'd be cooking her dinner. If you had a husband, I suppose it would be the same, wouldn't it, like every night, peeling potatoes, heating stew, then washing his clothes on Sunday.'

Their rooms were cold tonight. They had a gas heater in Mrs Vaughn's house – in their house. The utilities had been transferred to Sarah's name. They could have taken their soup and sandwich in there and been warm.

'When are we moving, Mum?'

'After carpet, curtains.'

They had little to move, only the microwave and television, their magic frying pan and clothing. Their laptop couldn't move, or not until they had a new lead for their broadband connection.

'Turn these rooms into our study. Get a desk and chair.'

'Maybe get a man to pull it down then grow things.'

The news was on. Kevin Rudd was on it again. He'd been Australia's Prime Minister until his parliament friends got rid of him – except they hadn't. He was always on the news, and Julia, or Tony.

It was like the television ran the county, not the government, like each channel decided who they wanted to be Prime Minister and pushed their choice every chance they got, so the voters would think it was no use voting any other way.

None of the channels mentioned Danni, or the reward. That was old news. They'd be interested again when they found her.

A football player was having scans on his leg – was that headline news? Maybe to some people. Football was important in Melbourne.

Dave and Pop liked it. Marni would miss coming home to them when they were finished.

The floor-covering people would be here next week to rip up the last of Mrs Vaughn, to roll her up in her old carpet and vinyl and replace it with new. The drapes would be delivered and hung before the school holidays. Sarah was taking the last week of the holidays off to organise Marni's birthday party.

They'd argued about the date. Sarah wanted to have it on Sunday the fourteenth, at lunchtime. Marni wanted it on Saturday night, on the thirteenth, which was a perfect date for a thirteenth birthday party.

'How many you want to invite?'

'Heaps.'

'Not heaps, Marni.'

'We'll get a caterer.'

'What?'

'A caterer, to make and serve the food.'

'No.'

'If we can spend six hundred and eighty dollars on a painting, we can spend the same on a caterer.'

'We got very good oven in there. We will make finger food, like Bob's mother's party,' Sarah said.

'I'm inviting our policeman.'

'You embarrass him.'

'He doesn't have to come. I'm inviting Pop and Dave too, and Dave's wife, and you're inviting Bob and his mother and some of the people from your work.'

'Maybe.'

'If you don't, I'll ask Bob to invite all of them.'

LEMON SEGMENTS

'*The* fish and chip shop must be close,' she said when he tossed her the paper-wrapped parcel. It was conveniently close. He'd be forced further afield tomorrow. His computer needed charging. It took time, but the power adaptor worked. He'd need more duct tape soon, more firewood.

He'd forgotten the constant demand of a wood stove. Each day it forced him into action. Cut a barrow load in the morning and by nightfall that stove had turned it to ash. He had to keep it burning. Without its warmth, the house was uninhabitable.

Two weeks ago, he'd killed two birds with one stone, had hired a trailer, charged up his computer and bought two trailer loads of split firewood – and burnt most of it. Tonight he was considering using the house as firewood. He had twenty litres of petrol in the shed, purchased for the great escape he hadn't made. He had half a dozen bottles of kerosene and the cans of aerosol paint he hadn't used on the Kingswood. He'd got rid of the Hyundai.

Sat watching her pull that slab of battered fish apart with her hands before she bit into it. Watched her stuff chips, two at a time into her mouth. She'd made his eighty-three days and then some, which was all he'd asked of the first of them. He would have released the Chinaman's daughter had she lived for eighty-three days. He couldn't release this one.

The flesh below and above her ankle collar was raw. If he didn't get that collar off soon, her foot would fall off, and he smiled, visualising her escape on the stump. She'd do it.

He'd bought a replacement padlock. In Bunnings it had looked big enough. It wouldn't lock around both bars. He could have crawled beneath the house and located the old padlock. Built on a slope there was a good metre of space beneath the house at the front. Could have. Hadn't. He'd grown accustomed to seeing her sitting there, accustomed to watching her.

Watched her search the paper for one last chip, and when she found no more, she started eating the segment of lemon supplied by the fish and chip shop – and ate the lot, flesh, pith and rind, and when it was gone, for his own amusement, he threw his own squeezed portion of lemon at her. It hit the wall behind her and landed on her bedding. She found it, wiped it on the fish and chip paper, then ate it while he marvelled again at the breed of this fragile being with its steel-reinforced spine.

'What's the date today?' she asked.

He no longer knew Monday from Friday, had stopped counting the days after she'd made her eighty-three. Each day was the same, the stove, the axe, the computer, a meal, and his hard bed and soft bottle.

Watched her fold the fish and chip paper, place it under her mattress.

'Did the police find your other house? Are they watching it?'

He had no other house.

'You used to go home,' she said.

If he ignored her, she shut up.

'How far are we into June?'

June was winter. Winters on this land were cold. He liked the green of springs, the scent of spring. Had chased a blue butterfly one fine spring day, praying to God to make it get tired and settle low so he could get it, and God had answered his prayer. It had settled and he'd captured it in a homemade butterfly net.

The elation, the ecstasy of holding perfection cupped between his sweaty palms. He'd caught a rare and beautiful thing, and all the way home he'd felt the flutter of its wings in the cup of his hands.

Opened them in this kitchen to show off his prize. Found tattered wings, their blue and silver shed to his palms.

'Perfection is only for those free to fly,' he said. It was a mistake to speak to her, but he'd made a lot of mistakes with this one, so what was one more?

He'd made a mistake in taking the second of them. He hadn't meant to. He'd got away with what he'd done to the Chinaman's daughter. Should have quit while he was ahead, but he'd seen her walking in the sun and she'd been Angie, the hair, the legs, even the walk, and because she wasn't Angie, he'd wanted to punish her for being alive to walk in the sun while Angie rotted in her grave.

Hadn't spoken to that one. She hadn't lived long enough.

The last of them had cursed him to the final day. She would have lived longer had he not seen this one, near the carousel. He'd known that day that he'd have her.

Wind howling out there tonight, rattling the sealed windows, lantern flame flickering, playing shadows on the walls. Little of its light reached the corner. If he looked at her through slitted eyes, if he saw only the pink and white of her, she was his Angie.

Her Yankee accent killed the image.

'We had a basement in Kentucky we used to go down to during bad storms. We used to live with my grandparents on a horse ranch. They died when their plane crashed into a mountain.'

'Once upon a time,' he said. 'Once upon a time in this windswept kingdom there lived a holy hog wed to a lapdog. Imagine the progeny of such a union.'

'Pigs don't breed with dogs,' she said.

'They bred mutations. Pigs who yapped like dogs, dogs who squealed like pigs, and one born with the heart of a wolf.'

'What happened to him?'

He stood and opened the door. 'He caught rabies and they shot him,' he said, and stepped out to the howling wind to slip and slide on greasy clay to the shed.

He kept a torch on the bench, and by the light of its beam he found the row of red plastic containers, his great escape petrol, his final solution petrol. Tonight would be a fine night for a fire. It would add its roar to the winds. No need for a grave or the stale words of the resurrection.

WRONG WAY. GO BACK.

If they'd only locked that brainless bastard up.

WRONG WAY. GO BACK.

They'd suspended his licence and sent him home to the loving arms of his wife and daughter.

'You bastard,' he howled to the wind.

He'd driven out here the day he'd buried Angie. Her mother had collapsed and been carted away in an ambulance before the hearse had carried Angie to her grave. He'd followed the hearse, not the ambulance, and after the earth had taken her, he'd driven out here and climbed that hill to howl out his pain where no one would hear him.

Satan had. He'd sent him down that hill with vengeance in his heart, and he'd found relief in vengeance.

It had taken time to find the Chinaman and his daughter, but he'd got her, and for a week, he'd read every newspaper. Then she'd sickened and he'd become afraid of what he'd done. He'd dosed her from a bottle with Angie's name on it, then came out here the next night to dose her again and hadn't been able to rouse her.

Tried to clean her up to take her home and she'd slid down in the bathwater and drowned while he'd been searching for soap.

It had come to him while he'd been dressing her in one of Angie's outfits, how Angie had never got to ride in the Kingswood. The Chinaman's daughter had. He'd tossed her out on the freeway where that brainless bastard had caused the pile-up.

She'd been found at daylight, and all day he'd waited, expecting the police to put two and two together and come knocking on his door. He'd wanted them to come, had wanted his day in court.

They hadn't put two and two together. Given time the media had forgotten little Nancy Yang and the wolf had gone to ground, but as with the swallowing of a handful of pills, once the effect wears off, the pain returns, and is stronger.

HOME BEAUTIFUL

*T*heir painting was titled *Solitude*. Sylvia Moon had written it on her receipt, with the six hundred and eighty dollars. They hadn't seen its title until Sarah found the receipt in her handbag and put it into the cake tin with the others. There was plenty of space in there for receipts. They'd bought an album for the photographs.

They hung *Solitude* over Mrs Vaughn's mantelpiece, and to Marni, it looked better than a few of the paintings she'd seen hanging at the National Gallery. Maybe it would hang there one day when Sylvia Moon was dead. Most artists hadn't been heard of until they'd been dead for a few hundred years and now their paintings were worth millions.

Solitude looked even better once the new carpet was down and their black lounge was delivered. Then they found their dining room suite on eBay. It had a gorgeous timber table they could extend for the party and six tapestry-upholstered chairs. When it was delivered, it didn't fade *Solitude* but did steal the eye's attention away from it.

The curtain man faded it, or the colour they'd chosen for the lounge/dining room drapes did. They were a deep burnt orange, and they'd ordered a fancy pelmet. Mrs Vaughn's corner window looked like a picture from a *Home Beautiful* magazine, and the drapes drew a tiny bit of burnt orange from the chairs' upholstery. They were perfect together. The lounge suite was perfect, but together, they killed *Solitude.*

'We buying her bushfire,' Sarah said.

'We have to,' Marni agreed, and they opened their cake tin and found the receipt and Marni phoned the number on it.

The artist didn't know who Marni Carter was, or not until she mentioned *Solitude.* 'Mum is wondering if you've sold your big bushfire painting yet?'

She hadn't, and would be pleased to hold it for them, however she would be away for most of the weekend.

'I'll be home by two on Sunday,' she said.

They bought sheets, quilts and quilt covers, two big blue/green self-watering pots for their jade trees, and potting mix, and when those trees were in their new pots and on Mrs Vaughn's front porch, they made it look proud enough to be called their patio. Pop called it their patio. He'd spent two days on his knees tiling it after Dave painted their wrought-iron railing.

Those men had done such a brilliant job and were so nice and their bills so cheap that when they were finished, Sarah put an extra five hundred dollars into two envelopes to give them, as a bonus, and when they wouldn't take the money, Marni told them that her mother had won Powerball and that she liked giving money away.

'But don't tell anyone that we won because it's our secret.'

The neighbours probably heard Pop. 'Powerball? Fair dinkum, darlin'?' he'd said. Dave pocketed his envelope then zipped his lips with finger and thumb, while Pop told a long loud story about a cousin who'd won a million a year or two back and went spending mad because she didn't want to lose her pension.

Sunday was cold and windy but not wet, which was lucky, because Sarah had to test the car's brakes at the first big roundabout near Eltham, when a van in front tested its own. They missed it by about two centimetres, but they missed it. They didn't stop for a coffee, and were at the artist's property before two. Her gate was open and her car was there, so they drove in and parked beside it.

She talked while she bubble-wrapped their bushfire, and before Sarah wrote her cheque, Sylvia bubble-wrapped the pink and violet dawn, which would match Marni's bedroom drapes perfectly.

Herod remembered them. Marni couldn't go for a walk with him, but gave him a pat and a scratch, and because they looked so lonely when Sarah started the car, Marni wound her window down and invited them to her party.

'It's a combined housewarming and birthday party on the thirteenth of July at seven o'clock. Herod's invited too. We've got a safe backyard and a lock and a *Beware of the dog* sign on our gate.'

They backed out then, left them standing in the drive, the artist in her psychedelic poncho which must have been warm because she lived in it, and Herod, standing with his head hanging low.

'We buy paintings from her, the same as buying from shops. You don't invite people from shops to your party.'

'I bet that man from Harvey Norman wished I had. He was giving you the eye the whole time we were buying the fridge and stuff there.'

'People stare at deaf people – and he is thinking I am retard who can't pay for anything.'

'You talk rubbish. Anyway, it's different. Shop people don't make what they sell. If I went to the trouble of painting something, I'd want to see where it ended up.'

Sarah didn't turn the car towards home. She drove again past Gramp's land, convinced since their last visit that Sylvia's neighbour was one of Gramp's sons. Whoever he was, he was expecting visitors. He'd left his gate open.

'His name is Jack James, Mum.'

'Writer using different names so they can be . . . anon . . . anonymous,' Sarah said, and she drove onto Gramp's land and up a steep drive that wasn't paved or dry.

*

For one winter, she'd known it well. 'Keep your wheels moving,' Gramp had warned the first day she'd driven it wet. She kept them moving today until the land levelled out in front of the tin shed, where she parked, pulled on her handbrake and wound her window down so she could smell the winter scent of this land.

'Smell is beautiful,' she said. Always the scent of wet eucalyptus, and wood smoke on Gramp's land.

Up here she could see smoke was gusting up from the kitchen chimney. No sign of the writer, but fresh tyre marks led towards – or away from – the old shed. 'Maybe he is go out.'

'He'll come back and block you in and get stuck into you. He told me to get off his land, Mum.'

'He tell the dog, not you. I don't like big dogs,' Sarah said, her feet now on Gramp's land. Marni didn't move, so Sarah walked around and opened her door.

'I'm staying here, Mum, and when he comes out yelling, don't expect me to save you.'

'Invite him to your party. Tell him, bring Sylvia and her dog. Come on. He won't understand me.'

'Write him a note—' Marni started, then she pushed the door wider and undid her seatbelt.

'Thank you.'

'Shush,' she said. 'I can hear someone screaming.'

And she was out and running, down the path that led to the back door, the way Sarah had wanted her to go. She locked the car and took the same path, unconcerned as to why Marni had changed her mind, or unconcerned until she saw the screen door open and Marni hammering on Gramp's old back door.

'Stop that!' Sarah pulled her back by her hoodie.

'Someone is being murdered in there. She's screaming!'

Sarah could hear something. A siren, maybe, or alarm. Something.

The kitchen window was narrow, and well off the ground. There'd always been a gap between the drawn kitchen blind and the window frame – a rarely drawn blind when Sarah had lived here, and never drawn during daylight hours. Gramp's kitchen had needed all the light it could get. Sarah was cupping her hands to that gap, attempting to see in, when Marni swung her out of harm's way, before tossing a lump of firewood at the glass. Two panes cracked.

'You gone mad!'

'We're coming,' Marni yelled. 'Help me, Mum. She knows we're out here. She's yelling to us now.' She bashed out cracked glass with the lump of wood, then reached a hand through to tug at the blind.

It didn't roll up. It fell to the sink.

And Sarah saw what Marni could hear, saw two fighters in the corner where Gramp's radio had lived. A tangled nest of blonde hair and grey, a hand tangled within that tangle of hair; a mouth screaming, 'Help me!'

'Danni?' Marni said. 'Oh my God, Mum! It's Danni!'

Firewood from the barrow their battering rams, they smashed glass, splintering the narrow strips of timber securing those six small panes. Like wreckers, like vandals, they bashed out shards of glass, then, using Sarah's knee as a step, Marni scrambled through, kicked the roller blind out of her way and slid from the sink to the floor. Sarah followed her, Gramp's old wheelbarrow lending her height enough to climb through.

Glass everywhere. A jeans-clad man face down on the floor, a pink-clad rider on his shoulders, one foot at his ear, her two hands gripping a single rein. Not a rein, a dog chain, and her mouth behind that tangle of hair screaming, 'Kill him!'

Marni, armed with Gramp's poker swung it with bloody hands, like a woodsman swinging an axe at a block of wood, but the grey man's head was that block, and it kept moving as he bucked like a crazy horse at a rodeo, attempting to rid himself of his rider.

Some are born pacifists. They lose. Others are born to wage war. They win. Marni waged war with Gramp's poker, and she got his head.

He turned his face then to Sarah and she saw the teeth behind a well-remembered grimace, saw his eyes. And when Marni's weapon connected again, Sarah felt his pain as a spasm in her bowel. It washed the colour from the old brown kitchen, washed it white, like the colours of a spinning top washed white.

Head spinning, making the room spin, she grasped the glass-littered sink to stop her sliding into the spin.

He'd stopped bucking. Marni was on her knees, yelling words as she untangled his hand from Danni's hair. Danni's mouth was making words.

'Keys. Chain.'

'Look for keys, Mum. She's chained up and it's around his throat. Find his keys. There's a padlock on it?'

He kept his keys in his pocket. Always, but Sarah couldn't find the words to say so. Couldn't make herself move. Stood like a rabbit caught in the headlights, unable to look away from him.

'They're hanging up, Mum. Look. Near the window.'

Gramp's keys had always hung on a hook between the window and the door, where she'd hung them the last day she'd driven Gramp to the market. Saw them. Not Gramp's, too many to be Gramp's.

He was dead. Two years after she'd walked away from this place he'd been dead. No one had told her. Hadn't known where she was to tell her. Got rid of her name, her pension, her bank account, hadn't gone to a doctor for five years because she'd been scared to show Jillian Jones's Medicare card number, scared that one day he'd find her.

Re-hab-il-it-a-shon. Always knew that jail couldn't rehabilitate him. Always knew he'd come out angrier than he'd gone in.

Marni got the keys. She'd taken charge.

'My mobile. In the car. Get it, Mum!'

'You bleeding,' Sarah said.

'Get my mobile. Phone triple zero,' Marni demanded and Sarah looked away from him to the old key still in the door latch. Gramp had only ever removed that key when they'd had to lock Gran inside when they went to the market, shops, bank. Couldn't take her out. Like Marni, she'd been born to wage war.

Like him. But today he was the one who was bleeding.

That old door had never wanted to open, not in wintertime. Easier in summer. Sarah's hand remembered that lift, that drag. Her hand got her outside, where there was air, where there was space, where the land smelled of winter's clean.

They'd had a church service for Danni, in Sydney. It had been on the news. Barbara Lane there, clinging to David Crow. Danni was alive and fighting the devil to stay alive, and they'd found her, found her because Uncle Fred had told them about Gramp's will. Marni called him Hubert, their angel. He was Danni's angel too.

That day at Forest Hill when she'd walked into him, today had already been written by the gods. Driving out here, finding Sylvia and her paintings, had been written. Every move she'd made since had been leading Sarah back . . . to the devil.

The mobile was in her hand. She didn't know how to make a voice call. She touched the symbol for phone. It offered choices. She raised a keyboard, touched the zero three times, touched *call*. Didn't know if she'd done it right, if it was ringing, if it wasn't, and today she wanted to hear it. Today she wanted to hear the difference between a siren and Danni's scream. Wanted to hear her voice screaming, 'Kill him.'

The phone vibrating in her hand she ran back to the house to ears that could hear and she had to stand close to him so she could hold the phone to Marni's ear.

He didn't move.

'We need the police. We found Danni Lane,' Marni told the phone.

She should have said the Freeway Killer. Everyone knew about the Freeway Killer. People had forgotten Danni Lane.

He'd gone grey, like Gramp. His hand, palm up on the floor, had never been like Gramp's. Long blonde hairs from Danni's head were entwined between his fingers. He'd liked long hair.

Marni pulled the padlock clasp out of the collar, and when Danni's foot was free, she didn't get off him but snatched the padlock and looped it through a link of the chain she'd twisted around his neck. Fell off him then and crawled away, shaking, shuddering, like she was having a fit.

'We need the police and an ambulance . . . I told you, I don't know the address. It's a farm at Kangaroo Ground. We've got Danni Lane and I'm bleeding everywhere,' Marni yelled at the phone.

Sarah lifted Danni to her feet. She tried to make her sit on Gran's wicker chair. She wouldn't sit, and she said something.

'She's deaf. Talk to her face,' Marni said.

'Tie him up,' Danni said.

'He can't . . . can't hurt no one now.'

The last time Sarah had seen him when he couldn't hurt anyone, she'd screamed 'murderer' in his face. Killed him that day, in her head. She'd made him be more dead then her mother, who had wasted her last breath of life defending him.

Not his fault, baby. He loves . . .

He loves . . . forever more unfinished, because it couldn't be finished, because he'd loved no one. Sarah had worked that out when she was seven, when he'd picked her up and locked her into the boot of the red and white car because her mother wouldn't get in when he'd said *Get in the car*. Remembered nine too, remembered him laughing at a backyard full of tears while little Uncle Bill lay on his back on the lawn, his nose bleeding.

Then eleven, when she'd grown into hating him, it had been a good fit.

'I'm calling Ross,' Marni said.

*

Danni had a roll of pink ribbon, a roll of duct tape, and Ross wasn't picking up.

Then, 'Who?'

'It's Marni. Danni's alive, and we found her.'

'Marni,' he said.

It wasn't what he said, but how he'd said it. 'Say something, Mum. He doesn't believe me.'

'I am Sarah,' she said. 'We find Danni Lane . . . at Kangaroo Ground.'

'It's an old farm,' Marni said. 'Out past Eltham, in the bush. It's got an old house on it and a big tin in-your-face garage, you can't miss—'

'Say 271 . . . in the map book,' Sarah said.

'The farm's on map 271 in our street directory, oh, and there's an artist called Sylvia Moon who lives like half a kilometre away.'

'Moon,' he repeated.

'Moon, as in sky. Tell her we're at the writer's place. She'll know where.'

'You need to get out of there, Marni.'

'He's not going anywhere. Mum's tying him up – and he's probably dead anyway. He hasn't moved.'

'Stay on the line,' Ross said. Marni turned the phone on to speaker and picked up the discarded duct tape and scissors.

The table was a treasure trove. He had food, a laptop that looked brand new, paper towels, tissues.

The side of her wrist was gashed deep and still dripping blood. If it had been at the front, it might have cut a vein. It wasn't hurting, or hadn't been until she helped herself to a bunch of tissues to use as a pad on it then reached for his paper towels to rip off half a metre, she folded it lengthwise to use as a bandage. Couldn't do the duct tape with one hand so waited and watched Danni tie a bow.

At school, she'd envied Danni's hair, and her mobile. She wasn't like the same girl and seeing her like she was made Marni scared. Wanted Ross to come. Wanted an army of policemen.

'Mum.'

Sarah came to use the last of his duct tape, to bind the paper towel bandage tight, and before she was done, Danni was gone up a passage. They went after her.

And Ross was back. 'Are you there, Marni?'

'Yes.'

'Don't hang up on me. We've got Sylvia Moon's number.'

'You're on speaker. Please come fast.'

'We're on our way,' Ross said. 'Stay on the line. What is Danni's condition?'

'She's walking.'

She was running a bath too, in what might have been a bathroom a hundred years ago. It had old metal taps like Mrs Vaughn's garden taps, and a green bathtub with legs – but a modern bathplug, and one of those taps gushed steaming water.

'You should wait,' Marni said. She'd seen enough television police shows to know that investigators didn't want their evidence washed down the drain. Danni didn't hear her, or ignored her. She was stripping, and Sarah helping her to do it. They didn't need words.

Marni kicked what they stripped off out the door, a pink sweater, a denim skirt, a pair of wrecked underpants, and, naked, Marni could see how not-all-right Danni was. She'd been skinny at school. Apart from her face, she was skin and bone and had hip bones that looked sharp enough to cut with, and her ankle where the dog collar had been was red raw and oozing pus.

'Soap,' Sarah said.

There was soap beside a candle on the windowsill and salt on the table, and Dettol. Shampoo too. Sarah used it to wash Danni's matt of hair. She washed her neck, her back with her hands, and maybe her hands or the hot water slowed Danni's shaking. She sat there, being washed like a baby, like she was mesmerised by being cared for.

The back door was open. Marni heard Herod's bark before she heard Sylvia's, 'Oh my God! Oh dear God.'

Herod knew where they were. He was on a lead, but he led the way.

'Oh my God,' Sylvia moaned while Herod tasted the soapy, salty, Dettol-flavoured bathwater, sniffed at Danni's shoulder, licked it a little cleaner, then sat down to laugh about it.

There was a towel hanging behind the door. Danni shrank from it. They dried her with paper towels. She wouldn't look at a man's sweater Sylvia found in a bedroom, but accepted Marni's underpants and t-shirt – and Sylvia's poncho. It came to a long point front and rear so covered the important bits. She accepted Sarah's comb, but couldn't drag it through her hair.

'Cut it off,' she said.

'The police will be here soon, dear,' Sylvia said.

'Cut it,' Danni said. 'All of it.'

She was scary. Her eyes were. Now that it was over, to Marni, this whole place felt unreal, but Sarah, who'd had her scare early, was over it now. She cut Danni's hair, and was combing it when they heard the helicopter, or Herod and Danni heard it. Marni didn't until she went after Herod, who'd let himself out.

He barked at it, and barked more when they heard the distant sirens, when Marni picked up his lead and took him back to the kitchen.

'They're coming.'

'Your mobile?' Danni said, her hand out.

Ross had said to stay on the line, but he hadn't, so she gave it to Danni, thinking that she wanted to phone her mother. She didn't phone anyone. She found the camera and shaking hands attempted to focused it on him.

'You don't want him,' Marni said.

'Take it,' Danni said.

Almost told her he'd give her nightmares, but he'd probably given her enough to last forever, and maybe having a photograph of him tied up like a Christmas present with a big pink bow at his wrists might wash a few nightmares away, so Marni lined up a good full-length shot. Couldn't see his bloody head in it, so she moved around until his head was the main focus, and got a close-up of it and the pink bow – and she hadn't killed him, or not yet. He was breathing.

They came then, like a rowdy television show, uniformed men with guns on their hips and nothing for them to do when they came through that door.

Then he came, their egg and bacon McMuffin policeman, today looking like a worried Robert De Niro playing the role of detective, until he put his arm around Sarah, and when she looked at his face, he said, 'I knew you were my luck. That day on the plane, I knew it.'

A STURDY MODEL

*T*he Freeway Killer didn't look a lot like his enhanced photographs, or not in his current state. The tall, poncho-clad girl with her fringe and pale short bob didn't look like the photographs of the schoolgirl Danni. No rebel left in her eyes, no laughter, plenty of fear and staring distrust.

'She needed a bath. We kept her stuff for you,' Marni said, pointing with a sneaker-clad foot to the pile of rags she'd moved to the hearth, to the nest of tangled hair there.

The paramedics came then, and the girl who was but wasn't Danni, who looked like Barbara Lane, grabbed Marni's duct tape bandaged wrist.

'I want my father?'

Marni removed that gripping hand, and held it. 'I need stitches in that,' she said. 'And you need antibiotics for your ankle. I'll go wherever they take you and stay with you until they get your parents.'

'Where's my father?'

'Nearby. We'll get him to the hospital, Danni,' Ross said. 'I'll bet he's there before us.'

She'd have nothing to do with the stretcher. Marni found a pair of sneakers on the table. Sarah got them onto Danni's feet while Marni held Danni up, then together they walked her out to the ambulance, walked her slow, Danni not looking ahead to where she was going but up and around at the place where she'd been and Ross looking where she looked, at an old house on a hill, a decent old house in its day.

They'd got him. Jack James, the neighbour had called him. They'd got him, or those two girls had got him.

You either know or you don't know when you've met your match. He'd known that day on the plane and denied it. When he'd waved those girls away on their tour bus, he'd wanted to get on it and go with them. Every time he saw them they brightened his day, then he let them get away.

Not this time.

He watched Danni assisted into the ambulance. Marni assisted herself, and Sarah wanted to get in and go with them.

'You have to take our car home, Mum, and our paintings,' Marni said. 'And be careful at those roundabouts.'

You beautiful kid, Ross thought. You give a man hope for the next generation.

He'd given up hope of finding Danni alive. One out of five, he thought. It's poor odds, but better than none out of five.

*

Sarah stood in the biting wind, watching the ambulance reverse down the drive, guided by uniformed men. They were everywhere, swarming like Gramp's bees. She wanted to go from this place, to get into her car and follow that ambulance and Marni. Knew she couldn't. Knew there could be no more running away, and no more need to. This time, they'd lock him up forever.

The police had unlocked the big door of Gramp's eyesore tin shed, and when the ambulance was gone from her view, Sarah turned and walked to the open door.

And there it was, Gramp's old Holden, newspaper stuck over its windscreen, its chrome grille and bumper bar. They'd shown a photograph of a white station wagon on the television, a Kingswood. Should have known it, but it had looked newer, bigger, cleaner than Gramp's and he'd never said Kingswood. Always he'd said the old girl, or the van.

It was parked facing forward. She'd never driven it forward down that drive, always reversed down, her head out the open window, watching the rocks and bushes on the driver's side and letting the other side look after itself.

Ross was beside her. She turned to face him. 'I learn to drive in that. I should know before, from on the television.'

'Do you feel like talking about what happened here today?'

She shook her head, and walked across to the shed, still expecting it to smell of Gramp's honey. Maybe a whiff clung to a shelf or the rafters.

Remembered those shelves, and the day she'd found Daddy's pots of gold, lined up on them. It would have been gold enough for her and for her mother. They could have stopped moving here, lived different lives here. He could have stayed, could have inherited this land.

She'd known him as soon as she'd seen his eyes, his teeth behind that grimace. She'd inherited his teeth. Not his eyes. She had her mother's eyes.

Joseph and Stephanie, hard names to say. J's were the hardest sounds to learn because they were made up of two sounds, a D and a G. He'd had three J's. *Joseph Jacob Jones*. She'd had two. Remembered every year of Jillian Jones, every year of that old green tent, its smell of mould – and the boot's dark spare tyre and grease smell.

Ross was beside her again, and this time she tried to speak of what had happened.

'Danni was fighting him. Marni hit him, with the poker. Like she is chopping wood. Two hands. She hit him maybe three time before he stop fighting Danni.'

'What brought you out here?'

'This,' she said, her hands reaching wide to gather in this land, its mud, its sky, its trees. 'My grandfather own all of this hill. I live with him . . . before . . .'

'You heard Danni – Marni heard her.'

'Yes. I think she is gone mad when she smash the window . . .'

'He's not your grandfather?'

'No!' She shook her head. 'No! No!'

Walked away from him to her car, thinking of Marni, of what she would say when she heard the words Sarah had to say. Maybe she'd understand why Sarah had lied to her, why she'd changed their names, why she hadn't kept in touch with the Clarks. He'd known the Clarks, had known where they'd lived, so they couldn't know where Sarah Carter had lived.

The car unlocked since she'd got the mobile, she locked it, and because Ross was looking up, she raised her eyes to the grey of the sky and to a helicopter hovering overhead. The police? A television newsman aiming his camera at her car? Would it be on the news tonight as the murder car? It was a Hyundai. It was the right colour.

Gramp's land would be in the headlines, and Danni, and Joseph Jacob Jones.

FREEWAY KILLER'S DAUGHTER AND GRAND-DAUGHTER TO RECEIVE TWO HUNDRED THOUSAND DOLLAR REWARD

Like a boomerang, that money. Throw it far away and it came back. They'd spent a fortune on repairs to the house. They'd paid three thousand dollars for their lounge suite, had written a cheque to Harvey Norman for almost ten thousand dollars, but what leaked out of that bucket of money, each month came flooding back. She'd write a bigger cheque soon to give to the taxation department, but that money would come back when her term deposits paid their interest. Maybe the bucket would find its level one day and become stagnant.

But they'd found Danni Lane. Sarah and Marni Carter had found Danni Lane alive when everyone had believed that she was dead. Men had been out searching the sides of freeways for her body in a bag. She wasn't well. Perhaps her father and the doctors could make her well.

That image of that corner, that tangle of pink and grey, the arms, the screaming mouth of a rider on the shoulders of a buck-jumping devil, would stay with Sarah for her lifetime. And Marni's face in profile, Oliver written all over it, his determination to fight to the end.

He lived on in Marni, and she'd fought the devil and won.

Sarah had fought him the day of her mother's funeral. He'd been balancing on crutches, trying to throw a handful of rose petals into the grave. She'd stopped him, or made his petals fall on the ground.

She'd fought him when he'd wanted her to write her name on a withdrawal form so he could get money from Stephanie and Jillian's bank account.

Sign it for him, baby. We're all he's got. He loves us.

Her mother had taught her many things. She'd taught her to read, to write, to speak – and never to be any man's fool.

He was different when I met him, baby.

Perhaps he was or perhaps all men had two faces, the one that said, 'I love you', and the other face.

Bob would book his trip to Peru when he found out who she was. Jackie and Shane wouldn't care. They'd want to know all of the gory details. Maureen Crow would look at her with sympathy and understanding. She knew all about being a man's fool.

Sarah turned to Ross and Sylvia and the dog. They were standing where the garage sheltered them from the wind, Sylvia telling Ross about Jack James. She didn't know much, but was easy to lip-read.

'He kept to himself. I only spoke to him twice, but not for an instant did I suspect . . .'

They caught Sarah eavesdropping, so she walked up behind the old shed and through the scrub to Gramp's flowering gum tree.

It had grown. She put her arms around it, placed her cheek to its pink bark and prayed that there was no heaven, so Gran and Gramp would never know what had happened on the land they'd loved.

And felt Gramp's hand on her shoulder.

Not Gramp. Ross was behind her.

'What hospital where the ambulance is going to?' she asked.

'I'll get Marni home to you,' he said.

'Is he gone now?'

'Not yet,' Ross said.

'He is my father,' she said, and his grip on her shoulder tightened.

Maybe that's what it felt like when people were being arrested – the heavy hand of the law on their shoulder. His hand felt like Gramp's, strong and good and she put her own hand on his so he wouldn't take it away.

'Marni . . . she knowing nothing . . . about him. I will tell her before . . .' She pointed to the sky, to the helicopter, still up there, zooming in on Detective Senior Sergeant Ross Hunter and the Freeway Killer's daughter.

Big headlines for the newspapers tomorrow.

SUCH IS LIFE

*H*e'd thought he was dead when that last blow had rattled his brain. He'd seen heavenly stars – and when he'd seen her standing against the light from the window, he'd thought that dear old God had sent down a welcoming committee.

He wasn't dead and nor was the deaf one. By now, she would have been declared dead, if not for a Chinaman who couldn't read English. Still blamed him for Angie's death. Always had. Always would. The game may have been over but the blame was still alive and well.

He had no one to blame for this. He'd made one mistake after another with the little Yank. That first night when he'd found out who she'd belonged to he should have released her, but the mistakes had started breeding long before that.

He'd made his first in not buying old Nelly a new outfit, a summer frock, a straw hat. It was her unveiling that had led to his downfall. He could have, should have. Should have done a lot of things different.

The day they'd splashed his photograph all over the front page of three newspapers, he should have come out here, painted the Kingswood, dropped off the little Yank and kept on going. It had been *easier to forget to buy newspapers, to control what Joan had watched on television.*

She couldn't walk, had minimal use of her right arm and hand, but insufficient to handle the remote control. She'd had minimal speech and what she'd had had been garbled. There'd been nothing wrong with her sight or her mind. He'd been making her a cup of tea when she'd seen the photographs of the Freeway Killer's cars, his two cars. She'd known that old Kingswood well, had complained about the time he'd spent on attempting to get it going, and she and Angie had chosen the Hyundai together.

A smart woman, Professor Joan Murray, a middle-aged university lecturer, widowed, childless, with more money dripping out of her toffy nose than she'd known what to do with and too much time on her hands.

She'd volunteered at the prison for six months, teaching those who'd wanted to learn. The day he'd walked into her classroom and told her his name was Jones, she'd called him Indiana, and Indiana had played up to her too and she'd liked it. He hadn't been there to learn. He'd been coming up for parole and would have used her, Jesus Christ or the devil to get out of that place.

She'd told him he had a good mind and an interesting way of putting words on paper. She'd told him that he was still young enough to live a useful life. She'd spoken for him at his parole hearing, and when they'd let him out, she'd given him a job, as her gardener, had given him a room behind her garage, fed him at her own table, bought him a suit so she could take her new charity case to church, to theatres. She'd introduced him to another world and he'd been appreciative, so appreciative one night he'd expressed his gratitude in her bed. She'd moved him into her house that night.

A big horse-faced woman, close to fifty, she had never bred and should have been too old to do it. When she'd started doing it, she'd put her symptoms down to menopause and bloat. She was six weeks away from popping that kid before she'd seen her doctor.

He couldn't take off. No car, no licence, no money and if he'd had all three, the cops would have brought him back to serve the rest of his time, and living with her had been better than jail, so he'd stayed, expecting what he'd planted in her to come out dead, with two heads or worse. There was a bad gene in his mother's family. Her infant was three days old before he looked at it. It had one head and two pink feet. He'd known it wouldn't hear when he'd clapped his hands over its crib, but that pale, bald little worm had replied to his clap with that new infant reflex flinch.

Angela, she'd called her, her angel sent from God. She'd taken six months off to nurse her, then gone back to her previous life, and he'd taken over the raising of his perfect creation. Angie had rehabilitated him. She'd been two years old, and already talking the leg off of an iron pot when he'd learnt that his father was dead.

He was the firstborn son. He'd seen his father's will, seen his name written there. My land I leave to my firstborn, Joseph Jacob . . .

Joe Jones had owned nothing. Joan had been his cash cow. She'd paid for the clothes on his back, the food on his plate. He'd wanted that land, had wanted to own something to leave to Angie.

It was Bill who'd told him that the old man had altered his will, that he'd left his all to Jillian. He'd contacted the Clarks. They'd lost touch with her. The solicitor handling the estate told Joan that all reasonable attempts had been made to locate Jillian Sarah Jones, but to that date had failed.

The law is what it is, and those who work within its system are slow devious bastards. Joan hired a solicitor to put in a claim, in Angie's name. The old man's will having made it very clear that Joseph Jacob wouldn't get a red cent. Three of his brothers had made claims but Angie was the missing Jillian's half-sister, and after Joe, Jillian's next of kin.

Before he'd been free to leave Perth, Angie was close to four years old so Joan had taken a twelve-month leave of absence, put renters into her house and bought a caravan and a Ford to pull it. They'd driven across to Victoria and parked the van on this land, had paid the back taxes, put notices in the newspapers of six states, asking for information on Jillian Sarah Jones.

Solicitors cost money. John gave up first, then Clarry. Gordon, more desperate than they for money, had clung in there, as had Joan. She'd wanted to build a retirement cottage out here, had wanted it enough to take work in Melbourne and sell her house in Perth. They'd rented a place in Chadstone, close to Angie's school, and every weekend they'd spent in the caravan, Angie and her yapping little mutt running wild here.

Then Gordon's wife died and left him with six kids and bigger problems to worry about than land. Joan bought him off with a cheque for twenty thousand.

Only a matter of time then before the title was transferred. Only a matter of waiting the necessary amount of years before the missing Jillian could be declared dead.

They were on their way home from the farm that Sunday evening, on the Monash Freeway, a kilometre before their turn-off when along came a Chinaman who couldn't read that WRONG WAY. GO BACK *sign.*

A mash of metal, and they'd been in the middle of it, hit front, side and rear. The Ford had been fitted with airbags to protect the front seat passengers. Angie, strapped into the back seat, no airbags to protect her, had bumped her head, bruised her shoulder.

Newspapers are hard pushed to report a road death. Bumps and bruises and buggered cars barely warrant a mention. They'd been lucky. The car was a write-off, but Joan's insurance company paid up fast and they'd bought the Hyundai, because of its six airbags.

It was six months old the day he was called to the school. Angie had taken a fit in the playground. She was fine by the time he got here.

They'd seen her next fit, and for month they'd sat in doctors' surgeries, telling their tale of the accident, the bump on the head. The doctors weren't interested in old bumps. They diagnosed epilepsy, an inborn fault in the wiring of the brain, a genetic thing.

She'd failed to wake up for school one morning. Seven years old, as beautiful as they came.

Could still hear himself, screaming at the phone for an ambulance.

The doctors failed to wake her. Brain dead, they'd said. He'd made them keep her alive. For eighty-three days they'd given her a semblance of life with their machines, and he'd sat for those eighty-three days listening to their beeping bastard machines.

Joan gave up on her. She told them to pull the plug. He'd sat watching perfection leak away while that charitable bitch had been out there signing papers to donate his Angie's organs.

Then, at the funeral, the parson preaching of that better place, right there, in the front-row pew of God's house, charitable Professor Murray had been reduced to a flung arm, to a twisted mouth fighting for her every garbled word.

She'd never married him. He'd considered hooking up that caravan and going, but the Hyundai wouldn't pull it – and she'd given him power of attorney.

He'd sold the van and zipped the cash into his computer bag.

She'd had a will of iron and top hospital insurance. They'd moved her to a rehabilitation hospital at Forest Hill so he'd rented a house nearby, in her name, bought a wheelchair, and when they'd let her come home for a day, he'd wheeled her home.

The car was registered in her name, so he'd taken her name in Forest Hill, had called himself Jacob Murray – Jake, the caring husband with the crippled wife, who he'd got rid of at weekends to respite care when he'd stockpile more notes in his computer bag and search for Henry Yang, the Chinaman who couldn't read English.

Found him behind a counter, selling milk and bread and newspapers. That's when he'd stopped stockpiling money for his great escape. That's when he'd found a more satisfying escape, when he'd started making his own headlines – which, if not for old Nelly's plaid skirt and wig, he might have continued making.

'You,' her twisted mouth had drooled, while her flung hand pointed at him. 'You,' her eyes had accused. 'You.'

She'd known him young and old, known him as Indiana in his prison uniform, known him in a dark suit and tie, in a sweater. Known him too well.

He'd had no other option than to do what he'd done. He'd done it gently. He'd got her into her nightclothes, got her into bed, given her a sleeping pill, wiped her mouth, kissed her goodbye, then rolled her over so her face was in the pillow. It did the rest while he watched a television show.

And how many times had she begged him to do what he'd done?

H-E-L-P M-E E-N-D I-T, she used to pick out on her alphabet board. D-O-N-T M-A-K-E M-E L-I-V-E L-I-K-E T-H-I-S. L-E-T M-E G-O T-O A-N-G-I-E.

Her doctor had been sympathetic, as had the neighbours. Annie and Luke had offered to look after Snow. Half a dozen of the neighbours had gone to the funeral to support him.

To the end he'd done what Joan would have wanted. He'd collected her ashes and spread them beside Angie's grave, then driven out here expecting to find the little Yank dead.

He'd thought she was dead when the beam of his torch found her curled up in the corner, when he'd smelt her stench. He was cleaning her up for delivery when she'd opened her eyes.

Didn't know why he hadn't finished it that night. Had enough of death, maybe? Felt like Jesus when he'd raised Lazarus? Or was too dog-tired and drunk to get out on those roads again?

Once upon a time, twice, there'd been a man who'd cradled the fruit of his loins in his arms and seen rainbows in his girl child's eyes. Twice he'd lived to see those rainbows turn to dust, and such is life.

Poor old Ned Kelly said that before they hanged him. They didn't hang these days. They caged, but not before they gave their killer his day in court. He wanted his day in court. He wanted to accuse that brainless bastard Chinaman who couldn't read English, to accuse the useless bastards who'd given him a licence to drive and to kill.

Once upon a time there was a big bad wolf, quite charming and disarming.

Born of a dog and a holy hog, he had appetites alarming.

A mutant seed, he feeds his greed.

On pretty toes and button nose and doggies' tails . . .'Knock knock, Daddy.'

'Who's there, Angie?'

'Lettuce.'

'Lettuce who?'

'Let us get some fish and chips for dinner.'

'Daddy, what do you call a deer that's got no eyes?'

'What do you call it, Angie?'

'No idea. Hey, what do you call a deer with no eyes and no legs?'

'You tell me.'

'Still no idea. Knock knock, Daddy.'

'Who's there?'

'Kingswood.'

'Kingswood who?'

'Kings would pay a man to make that old bomb go so we could drive in it.'

She'd been dead before he'd made the old Kingswood go, and because she hadn't got to ride in it, others had. She would have turned twelve this year.

The last time he'd seen the deaf one, she'd been twelve. He'd known who she was when he'd heard her voice – and when he'd seen her. She'd turned out the image of Steph.

If he'd closed that gate, she and her fighting little bitch wouldn't have driven in. If he'd remembered to buy duct tape when he'd gone out to charge his laptop's battery, that gate would have been locked.

Ifs and buts don't count for much.

The house was swarming with cops. They wouldn't find much, other than his fifty-odd thousand dollars of escape money in the laptop's bag. If they didn't divvy it up, he'd get some of it to Annie and Luke. Snow might live for another five years. They'd taken his laptop. Wouldn't find much of interest on it. He'd written no exposé on the life style of the serial killer. They'd find a few grim tales from his child-hood, and photographs, most of them of Angie – and he'd need to tell them his password or they'd bugger it up getting into it.

They might give it back. Crims were allowed to have laptops in their cells — if they behaved themselves. He was too old now to do much else but behave himself, and his hearing was failing. His little Yank had heard that car drive in before he'd heard it, and her scream still rang in his ears.

He'd had to silence it. Fools rush in where wise men never go. He'd never been wise. Had moved too fast and she'd been ready. She'd over-balanced him. He didn't know how, but somehow he'd landed flat out, on his face with that chain wound around his throat.

If not for that car, would she have made her move? Without outside interference, would he have gained the upper hand, or would she have choked the life out of him only to rot with him on that mattress, pad-locked to the chain.

Not that one. She would have smashed her foot to pulp to free it. No fragile butterfly, his little Yank. He'd caught himself a stinging wasp.

His hands were dead. They'd trussed him up like a chicken for the oven. Any attempt to move, tightened the chain around his throat. His head throbbing, his back and shoulders killing him, he was eager for his hunters' handcuffs — and for his day in court.

MORE BESTSELLING TITLES FROM JOY DETTMAN

Pearl in a Cage (Woody Creek 1)

The first novel in Joy Dettman's sensational Woody Creek series.

On a balmy midsummer's evening in 1923, a young woman – foreign, dishevelled and heavily pregnant – is found unconscious just off the railway tracks in the tiny logging community of Woody Creek.

The town midwife, Gertrude Foote, is roused from her bed when the woman is brought to her door. Try as she might, Gertrude is unable to save her – but the baby lives.

When no relatives come forth to claim the infant, Gertrude's daughter Amber – who has recently lost a son in childbirth – and her husband Norman take the child in. In the ensuing weeks, Norman becomes convinced that God has sent the baby to their door, and in an act of reckless compassion he names the baby Jennifer and registers her in place of his son.

Loved by some but scorned by more – including her stepmother and stepsister who resent the interloper – Jenny survives her childhood and grows into an exquisite and talented young woman. But who were her parents? Why does she so strongly resemble an old photograph of Gertrude's philandering husband? And will she one day fulfil her potential?

Spanning two momentous decades and capturing rural Australia's complex and mysterious heart, *Pearl in a Cage* is an unputdownable novel by one of our most talented storytellers.

Thorn on the Rose (Woody Creek 2)

It is 1939 and Jenny Morrison, distraught and just fifteen years of age, has fled the tiny logging community of Woody Creek for a new life in the big smoke.

But four months later she is back – wiser, with an expensive new wardrobe, and bearing another dark secret . . .

She takes refuge with Gertrude, her dependable granny and Woody Creek's indomitable midwife, and settles into a routine in the ever-expanding and chaotic household.

But can she ever put the trauma of her past behind her and realise her dream of becoming a famous singer? Or is she doomed to follow in the footsteps of her tragic and mysterious mother?

Spanning a momentous wartime decade and filled with the joys and heartaches of life in rural Australia, *Thorn on the Rose* is the spellbinding sequel to *Pearl in a Cage*.

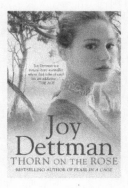